A BLIZZARD OF POLAR BEARS

Also by Alice Henderson

A Solitude of Wolverines

A BLIZZARD OF POLAR BEARS

A NOVEL OF SUSPENSE

ALICE HENDERSON

WILLIAM MORROW
An Imprint of HarperCollins*Publishers*

A BLIZZARD OF POLAR BEARS. Copyright © 2021 by Alice Henderson. All rights reserved. Printed in the United States of America. No part of this book may be used or reproduced in any manner whatsoever without written permission except in the case of brief quotations embodied in critical articles and reviews. For information, address HarperCollins Publishers, 195 Broadway, New York, NY 10007.

HarperCollins books may be purchased for educational, business, or sales promotional use. For information, please email the Special Markets Department at SPsales@harpercollins.com.

FIRST EDITION

Designed by Nancy Singer
Map by Jason C. Patnode

Library of Congress Cataloging-in-Publication Data has been applied for.

ISBN 978-0-06-298210-0

21 22 23 24 25   LSC   10 9 8 7 6 5 4 3 2 1

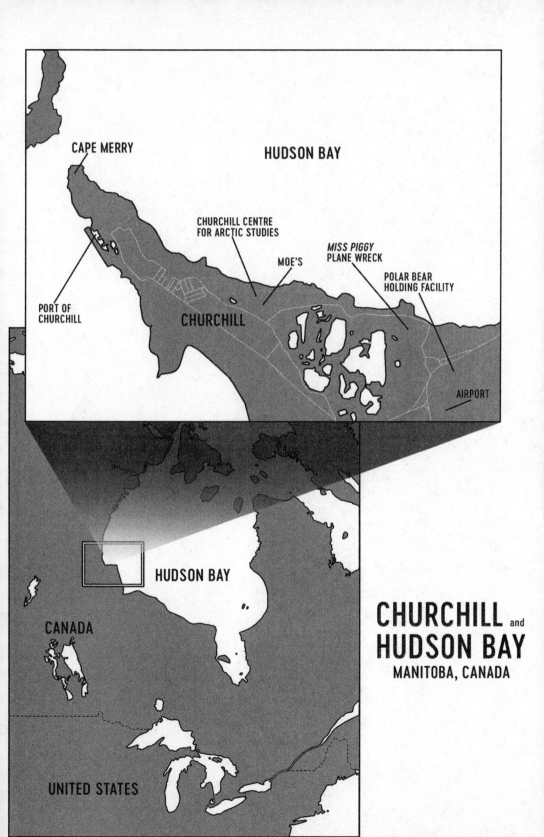

CAPE MERRY

HUDSON BAY

CHURCHILL CENTRE
FOR ARCTIC STUDIES

MOE'S

MISS PIGGY
PLANE WRECK

POLAR BEAR
HOLDING FACILITY

PORT OF
CHURCHILL

CHURCHILL

AIRPORT

HUDSON BAY

CANADA

UNITED STATES

CHURCHILL and
HUDSON BAY
MANITOBA, CANADA

A BLIZZARD OF POLAR BEARS

For Jason, fellow wildlife researcher and activist

For my dad, talented writer and a gentle, warm soul, who instilled
in me a love of wildlife

And for all the activists and organizations out there like Polar
Bears International who are fighting to save endangered species

PROLOGUE

Hudson Bay, Manitoba, Canada

As Rex Tildesen stared in amazement at the sonar image, he had no idea of the danger that surrounded his find. He took in the image, punching a victorious fist in the air. This had to be it. The find of the century. No, scratch that. The find of the last two centuries. The last millennium. When had the Kensington Runestone been found in Minnesota? In 1898? And though it was getting new attention and more analysis lately, it was still not considered genuine evidence of Viking presence in Minnesota. Too far west, the skeptics said. There was no way the Vikings had made it that far.

But Rex, a marine archaeologist, believed they had, and that they'd sailed through Hudson Bay to do it. He studied the sonar image on his monitor, his boat rocking gently beneath him. The shape of the wreck on his screen was the exact dimensions of a Viking longboat, and there were no other historical wrecks in this area. This had to be it. Finally. Proof of his theory! He knew it!

But he had to be cautious. When the farmer Olof Ohman found the Kensington Runestone in 1898, completely enveloped in the roots of an ancient tree, no one believed the stone was genuine. They accused him of creating the stone himself, even though he had no knowledge of how to write runes. Skeptics of the stone had ruined

Olof's life, ridiculed and treated him with suspicion. Rex had to be careful to avoid the same treatment.

The stone told the chilling story of a group of thirty Viking explorers who were on a scouting mission to the west of Vinland. Some of them left camp one day to fish, only to return later and find their fellow men murdered by unknown hands, blood covering the ground. They fled the site of the murders to return to a ship that was waiting for them fourteen days' journey away. A date inscribed on the side of the runestone read 1362, a timing that fit in well with a 1355 mission ordered by King Magnus to contact and re-Christianize the Viking settlements west of Greenland.

But skeptics dismissed the stone as a hoax. They pointed to rare runes and claimed they hadn't been in use in the 1360s, even though documents had now surfaced that clearly showed they had been. Current dating methods confirmed that the granite crystals inside the etched runes had been weathering for hundreds of years, a far longer period of time than if Ohman had created the stone.

Still, even now, most Viking scholars clung to the old, dismissive views on the stone, not looking into the new findings. Over the years, Viking swords, adzes, and axes had been found scattered throughout eastern North America. If Rex could prove that Vikings had sailed through Hudson Bay, he could make a case for how they reached Minnesota.

So Rex had to be careful. His reputation was already in tatters for his vehement belief that the Vikings had made it this far to the west of Labrador and Newfoundland.

He had to dive now, see if he could find any artifacts. Anxiously he geared up, checking over his scuba equipment, excitement coursing through him. He knew he shouldn't dive alone, but his partner was laid up onshore with a bad case of the bends, the result of a previous dive in which she'd surfaced too fast.

Sasha. His partner. He'd been so excited he'd nearly forgotten to radio his location. It was a lame backup system, but there was no way he was going to wait on this dive. Not after chasing this all these years.

He got on the radio and heard his partner's familiar warm voice as she answered. "Enjoying the weather out there?" Sasha asked him.

"Just like Malibu."

Ice was difficult to navigate. He'd had to stick to a narrow band of water between the land and the pack ice.

He could have waited a couple more months, but he'd gotten cabin fever, impatiently waiting for the hunt to resume. He scanned the sky, seeing a gray storm on the horizon. Nearby, the white mass of pack ice glittered in a patch of sunlight streaming through a break in the clouds.

"You find another mess of shipping containers?" she asked.

A shipping route, Hudson Bay had its share of sunken cargo.

"I really got something this time. It's just the right dimensions. And it's in only forty feet of water. I have to check it out."

"Hey," she said. "This was supposed to be recon only. Keep cataloging wreck locations. Don't you go down there without me."

"If you weren't laid up, I wouldn't have to." He knew it was killing her to stay behind and recuperate. "I'll only be down for a few minutes. Just want to get a closer look."

"If it's what we think it is, it can wait another few days."

"Maybe it can," Rex said, "but I can't. I'll radio you as soon as I'm topside again." He read his coordinates to her, then signed off before she could object further.

As he fell backward off the side of the boat, he could feel the cold water pressing against his dry suit. He descended slowly, turning on his powerful dive light, which pierced through the murky gloom.

Soon the wreck came into view, the decrepit seventy-two-foot-long remains of a ship. A lot of it had rotted away, but he could still make out some detail, including several long, slender, silt-covered shapes that might have been oars and a mast. Disappointment sank into him as he realized it had decayed too much to discern if it was a Viking longboat. But it didn't mean it wasn't, either.

Lumps lay scattered around it, and he waved the debris off the shapes. Most were objects so corroded he'd have to clean them before he could really tell what he had. He picked half a dozen pieces off the seafloor, placing them carefully inside his dive bag.

He checked his time. Still twenty minutes before he had to surface. Swimming the length of the ship, he took in the sight with wonder. He'd have to dive again with a camera. See if he could find any distinctly Viking features.

He found a few more objects scattered near the wreck and placed these in his dive bag, too.

Then he started the long ascent, doing a safety stop along the way. He nearly burst with impatience. He wanted to examine the objects in the light. Start to clean them. See if any of them were cloak pins or the arched blades of adzes or spinning whorls . . . One piece was even large enough to be part of a broken sword.

Light crept into his world as he neared the surface. His head broke through to the air and he flipped his dive mask up to the top of his head. Swimming the last few feet to his boat, he noticed that the storm was moving his way.

He hauled himself out, carefully placing the dive bag on the floor of his boat.

He was just stripping off his dry suit when the sound of another boat's engine drew his attention. He turned around, seeing a beat-up fishing trawler approaching quickly. He froze in mid-strip-down, the top half of his dry suit folded down, the towel in his hand forgotten as he paused from drying his face.

For a second he thought the boat was going to hit him, but it pulled up short, its wake rocking his boat so violently he had to grab on to the railing to keep from losing his balance.

The boat slid up alongside his, and two men and a woman jumped aboard.

"What's going on?" Rex demanded.

"Heard you over the radio," one said. He seemed to be in charge, standing in front of the other two. He was portly, with a beige, weatherworn face, longish black hair, and a goatee. A scar ran across the bridge of his nose. Another man stood tall and threatening, jet-black hair shorn close to his scalp, menacing brown eyes staring out from a shrewd sienna face. He crossed his arms, a tower of muscle, staring down at Rex. The woman was the scariest of them all. She looked like she would kill puppies before breakfast and then make her way to blow up a nursing home, just for the fun of it. She wore her long brown hair in a tight ponytail, and the dead look in her piercing blue eyes gave Rex the chills. Her unmoving face was carved out of ivory.

"What did you find down there?" the leader demanded.

"Down there?" Rex asked lamely.

The leader stepped forward, and the woman cracked her knuckles, stretched, and then adjusted her neck, as if she were warming up for a round in a cage fight.

"Am I not speaking clearly?"

Rex took a step back. "Um . . ."

"You have a problem answering simple questions?" the man asked. The others remained silent.

"No, I . . . uh . . ."

"Then what did you find?"

"A wreck," Rex said. "Just an old wreck."

"What kind of old wreck?"

What was this? Archaeology pirates? "I don't know how old."

"You said on the radio you'd been logging a lot of wreck sites."

"Yeah. I'm a marine archaeologist."

"We're looking for a specific wreck. You got a list of the ones you found? Their locations?"

Anger flashed inside Rex and his ears burned. If these were some kind of looters or pirates, there was no way he was going to give away the locations of his explorations. Not if one of them *was* a Viking wreck. He had worked too hard for this. He wanted official recognition from academia about his find. He wanted it to be validated just as Anne and Helge Ingstad's find was at L'Anse aux Meadows.

"I don't see why I should show you anything. Who the hell are you?" Rex demanded.

The leader pulled out a gun and aimed it at Rex's head. "We're the people you're going to spill your guts to. And these guys?" he added, hooking his thumb back at his silent compadres. "Love to make people talk. It's a skill."

The woman pulled out a pair of pliers from her leather jacket and Rex felt his knees start to shake. He was freezing. Standing out here with his chest exposed. Needed a shirt.

She advanced on him, shoved him backward into a seat, and reached toward him with the pliers. The pain burst white hot in his head. He tried to resist, tried to fight them off, then couldn't bear the pain anymore. He struggled to speak, but they didn't like any of his answers. The last thing he noticed before he blacked out was his blood spraying over the pristine white of the deck.

ONE

Snowline Resort Wildlife Sanctuary, Montana

The wolverine had gone straight down the cliff. Alex Carter teetered on the edge of the precipitous slope, staring down in disbelief at the wolverine tracks that veered down the nearly vertical face of the mountain, moving deftly from ledge to ledge. There was no way she could follow that. She pulled out her binoculars and focused them at the bottom of the cliff. In the far distance, she saw a ragged line of disrupted snow where the wolverine had disappeared into a copse of subalpine fir.

After discovering the tracks in the midafternoon, she'd followed them all the way up here, hoping to see more signs of the wolverine's activities along the way. But it had marched straight up the side of a mountain and straight back down the other side, without stopping to eat anything. Alex had to blaze a freshly switchbacked trail on her skis, climbing slowly, astounded at the animal's energy and vitality.

For the last few feet she'd taken off her skis and climbed in her boots. These giant members of the weasel family didn't let anything stop them. They treated terrain as if it were flat, no matter how many vertical feet lay between points of wolverine interest.

She stood up on an icy rock to get a higher vantage point, studying the landscape below with her binoculars, and caught a moving dark dot as it emerged from the fir trees and crossed a patch of snow. It marched in a straight line, never pausing, until it reached another dense copse of trees at the edge of a rise. Alex lost sight of it.

Turning on the rock, she almost lost her footing on the icy surface, and her heart hammered suddenly in her chest as she caught her balance again. She stepped down, retrieving her skis. She'd backtrack now, following the wolverine tracks to see where it had come from.

She skied downward to where the wolverine's path leveled out, following a ridgeline across the face of a mountain. Her skis slid through the powdery snow, her breath frosting in the cold air. As she worked her legs and arms, navigating up a steep embankment and down the other side, she noticed other tracks joining those of the wolverine. An ermine's delicate little paw prints pounced along beside the deeper wolverine ones, and a coyote's prints joined them a few feet later.

During her time out here in the field, she'd noticed that other carnivores often followed wolverines, hoping to locate any food the scavengers had discovered. A half mile later, Alex arrived at the edge of an avalanche chute, a steep section on the side of a mountain where, over time, avalanches had stripped away all the trees. The wolverine had marched straight across it.

About twenty feet away, the snow lay disturbed, dug up, some brown peeking through. She peered up at the snowy slope above her, looking for dangerous overhanging cornices of snow that could come down. She didn't see any, and after a moment's hesitation decided to ski out the twenty feet to see what lay in the snow. All the carnivore tracks she'd been following converged at this point, along with some grizzly tracks and those of a fox. Wolverine prints circled the excavated area.

She leaned over, brushing some snow away from the brown shape with a mitten. Beneath the white surface lay the frozen carcass of an elk. Alex stared up again, searching the steep slope. An avalanche had careened down in this section, probably only a few days ago, judging from the still-rough pattern of the surface snow. It likely caught the elk unaware.

Wolverines were experts at digging up frozen creatures from the snow, and usually had a network of food sources that they tapped over the winter, roaming tirelessly from one to the next.

She bent down, pulling out her camera, and snapped a few photos of the wolverine tracks. She could see slight differences in the forepaws and suspected it was actually two wolverines that had met up at this spot, likely a parent and a juvenile that was spending its first full winter out and about, learning the best foraging spots from its parents.

Her photos taken, Alex retreated to the safety of the tree line and continued higher. She picked up the tracks again on the far side of the avalanche chute, but they climbed up and over another cliff where she couldn't follow.

She'd spent the last few months doing this almost daily, recording the location and number of wolverines living on this newly designated wildlife preserve in northwestern Montana. She'd loved the solitude, the silent hush of the snow-laden forests, the magic tinkling of snow on her parka hood. A network of remote cameras she'd installed around the sanctuary were ready to snap photos of any wolverines that crossed their infrared beams.

She climbed higher, making her rounds, swapping out the memory cards and batteries on one of her cameras. She didn't see any more wolverine tracks, so she returned to the warmth of the old ski lodge as darkness crept over the sky and the temperature dropped.

The sanctuary had originally been the site of a popular ski resort that had declined in the latter part of the twentieth century. The owner had donated the property to the Land Trust for Wildlife Conservation. She'd landed the amazing gig to come up here and do a wolverine study, the only resident now of the abandoned resort, and the experience had been exactly what she needed to move forward with her life. But now she looked ahead at the unknown. The study ended in just a couple weeks and she hadn't lined up her next gig yet.

As Alex leaned her skis against the exterior wall and stamped her boots on the front stoop, she heard the phone ringing inside. She closed the door and hurried to the old rotary phone sitting on the reception desk. It was a landline; there was no cell reception out here.

"Hello?"

"Alex, it's Sonia Bergstrom."

Alex smiled at hearing the voice of her old grad school friend. They'd met in Berkeley while earning their PhDs in wildlife biology and had spent a season together tracking and tagging polar bears in Svalbard, Norway. Sonia had gone on to dedicate her career to polar bear research and had worked at a number of study locations throughout the Arctic. She now worked with a nonprofit organization called the International Institute for Polar Bear Research.

"Hey, Sonia! How are things?"

"Good. Really good. In fact, I've just had a bit of a break."

Alex sat down on one of the stools behind the desk. "With your research?"

"Yes. You know how I've been waiting forever on permits to come through to study the Western Hudson Bay polar bear population?"

Alex did. The permits kept getting held up, and Sonia had been waiting several years to get in. Other researchers' permits had also been stymied. "They finally came through?"

"Yes! I can't believe it. A set of happy coincidences finally made it happen. The new Minister of Environment and Climate Change has a special interest in polar bears. He came out to the Northern Beaufort Sea and volunteered for a week, helping with our study up there. I mentioned my struggles with getting a permit for the Western Hudson Bay, and lo and behold, a few weeks later, they've finally come through."

"That's great!" Alex knew polar bear populations were in trouble, and the more data they could gather on the reasons and rate of decline, the more they could inform policy makers of ways to help.

"But there's a hang-up. I'm in the Chukchi Sea and I'm waist deep in the study up here. Our NGO didn't have anyone lined up for this Hudson Bay study because we didn't think it was going to go through anytime soon."

A surge of anticipation suddenly welled up inside Alex. Did her friend need . . .

"When does your wolverine study end?"

"In two weeks," Alex told her, almost holding her breath.

"Want to take this one?"

Alex grinned. "Absolutely."

She heard Sonia breathe a sigh of relief. "Oh, I can't tell you how much this means to me. This whole thing has been strange. For years I've been able to get in there and do multiyear studies. I'm not sure what's changed, but I don't like it. Listen, I've got a grad student lined up who can assist you. His name's Neil Trevors and I've worked with him before in Greenland. He can fly out to Churchill in the next week and get the ball rolling, line up a helicopter pilot and get all the gear and equipment in order. Can you come out after that?"

"Yes. This is amazing. And perfect timing. I didn't have anything lined up yet." Alex's face lit up. Manitoba. The Canadian Arctic. Polar bears. And she knew it also meant tracking them by helicopter, which made a thrill pass through her. She loved being up in the air, loved the season she'd spent in Svalbard. "Thank you for thinking of me."

"Of course! I'll call you later with the flight details. What's the nearest airport?"

"Missoula," she told her friend.

"Okay. Thanks again, Alex."

They hung up, and Alex remained on the stool, motionless for a moment, taking it in. Flying out of Missoula. She thought of how she'd flown into that airport last fall, making a major change in her life as she left for this remote place. Now a new opportunity awaited her, and she was more certain than ever that she'd made the right choice all those months ago when she'd left behind an unhappy relationship and the noise, pollution, and clamor of Boston.

She stood up. A sense of pure happiness infused her and she punched a joyous fist in the air.

Alex drove to the box at the bottom of the lodge's long drive to retrieve her mail and returned to the warmth of the lodge. She spread it out on a table and sat down to go through it. She delighted to find a care package from her father in Berkeley. He'd sent along some homemade cinnamon cookies and several articles he'd cut from the *New York Times*. One was about wolverines and the other about a new sauropod that had been discovered in Mongolia.

A letter from the Center for Biological Diversity asked for a donation. On the bottom of the stack lay a postcard. She rose, staring at it. It showed the historic downtown of the closest city to her, Bitterroot, with its elevated wooden sidewalks and marble post office built in the late 1800s.

JUST CHECKING ON YOU, read the postcard. KNOW I'M NEVER FAR IF YOU NEED ME. It was unsigned.

Moving over to one of the writing desks in the resort's lobby, she gripped the postcard. At the desk, she opened the drawer, pulling out other postcards that had arrived in that same block handwriting.

She laid them all out, back sides up, so she could read them. She'd started to receive these mysterious messages when she arrived in Montana. Originally they'd been sent to her old address in Boston and forwarded out here by the postal service. She'd paid a moving company to pack up her few possessions earlier in the winter and move them to a storage facility when she'd ended the lease on her apartment there. They'd shipped a few essentials out to her in Montana: her backup laptop, some hard drives, her favorite pair of bird-watching binoculars. The movers had found a postcard pushed under the door of her flat, not postmarked but hand delivered, and they'd added it to the shipped box.

She arranged them all in order now. All were unsigned, and she didn't recognize the handwriting. She had no idea who they were from. The first one seemed to be the one that had been hand delivered in Boston. It featured an image of Paul Revere's house and read, HOPE YOU WERE UNHARMED. It must have arrived shortly after she'd attended a wetlands dedication ceremony where a gunman had turned up. Intent on killing as many people as he could, he was stopped only when an unknown person had shot and killed him. That person had never been caught and remained a mystery.

The second postcard had been sent to her old Boston address and forwarded to her in Montana just after she got this job studying wolverines. The card depicted the famous clock tower at the University of California, Berkeley, where she'd earned her doctorate.

On the back was a simple message: HOPE YOU ENJOY YOUR NEW POST.

The third had also been forwarded from her Boston address. It showed a mountainous vista dotted with the iconic shapes of tall cacti from Saguaro National Park in Arizona. She'd spent time there tracking Sonoran pronghorns.

The card read, I CAN SEE WHY YOU LOVE THIS PLACE.

Then her father in Berkeley had received a mysterious package containing a GPS unit she'd lost in New Mexico while surveying for spotted owls. He'd forwarded her the package, and now she held up the handwritten note that had accompanied it. In the same block lettering, it read, THIS CAME IN HANDY. The package had been mailed from Cheyenne, the exact area she'd gone to after New Mexico to do a black-footed ferret study.

So this mysterious person had found her GPS unit in New Mexico and brought it to Wyoming, right in her tracks. Had he followed her? Or was it just coincidence? Maybe he lived in Cheyenne and just mailed it back at the first opportunity he had, using the address registered with the device, which was her father's.

Then a padded envelope had arrived here in Montana, not forwarded, but showing her current address at the old resort. In it was a DVD containing footage from a body camera worn by an unknown person. The video jostled as the wearer ran, holding out a gun in front of a decidedly masculine arm. Then he fired two rounds, killing the vengeful shooter at the wetlands dedication ceremony. The body cam wearer had saved her life. She could still remember the chill she felt as words scrolled across the footage: *Alex, you had my back, and now I have yours.*

She still had no idea what he meant by that, how she had his back, nor any idea who he could be. After the arrival of the DVD, he'd gone quiet for a while. But a month later, in the dead of winter, she received a postcard of the snowy landscape of nearby Glacier National Park that read, *It's beautiful country up here. Quiet. A person could get used to living in the mountains.*

A few weeks later, one had arrived showing nearby Flathead Lake. The familiar block print read: *Things have been quiet. It's nice for a change.*

And now this latest postcard, written in that same unmistakable block print. She read it again. *Just checking on you. Know I'm never far if you need me.*

Staring at the card, she shook her head silently in confusion. *Need him?* She didn't even know who he was. What had she done to draw his attention? The earliest reference to her past was the card depicting UC Berkeley. Had he known her back then? She stared at his block print. And the first evidence of him having some kind of *physical* contact with her was when she'd lost her GPS unit in New Mexico. He'd either found it or taken it from her without her knowing. And the unit had stored all the places she'd been before, including Berkeley.

The New Mexico spotted owl study had been after the Sonoran pronghorns, so he might have backtracked to that location using her saved GPS waypoints. She thought back to the people she'd met on that New Mexico trip. Some friendly land trust folks, but she was still in communication with them. She couldn't picture any of them sending strange, anonymous postcards. Why would they? She'd also encountered a few angry developers who wanted to turn the spotted owl habitat into a luxury golf resort. Their designs had been thwarted, so they certainly wouldn't "have her back."

She thought of evenings she'd eaten out, other researchers she'd talked to. No one stood out in her mind.

She turned the new postcard over in her hand. What was his interest in her? Did he mean her harm? And if so, why this game of sending her postcards?

She returned all the cards to the drawer, her mind still churning over who they could be from. Finally she made some dinner and turned in for the night.

OVER THE NEXT TWO WEEKS, Alex made her final journeys out into the field, retrieving all of her remote cameras and dismantling the bait stations she'd used to attract the wolverines to be photographed.

She felt bittersweet about leaving the preserve. She'd come to think of these steep mountain trails as her new home.

The last few days she spent gathering up all the remaining equipment around the resort and leaving it for the next researcher who would call the preserve home for a few months. She stowed her clothes in her backcountry pack, knowing she could secure any additional gear in Churchill, Manitoba.

She said a silent goodbye to the place. It had been a welcome refuge, a place where she could start the next chapter in her life, and she'd miss it. Then she stepped outside and locked the lodge door for the last time.

She was ready for the Arctic.

The familiar sound of Jolene Baker's ancient truck rumbled up the long drive to the resort. Jolene lived on an adjacent property on the east side of the preserve and did volunteer tasks for the land trust when no researchers were living at the resort.

After parking, Jolene jumped out enthusiastically, helping Alex toss her pack into the bed of her truck. They embraced, then started the trip to the Missoula airport.

"Thanks again for driving me," Alex told her. "You didn't have to do this."

"Glad to," Jolene said. "I'll give Ben the keys next time he's up."

Alex handed over the keys to the resort, melancholy washing over her. Ben Hathaway was the regional coordinator for the land trust, and they'd met a couple times during her stay. She enjoyed his company, a kindred spirit and fellow lover of wildlife.

The farther they got from the preserve, the sadder Alex felt, even though she was excited about the polar bear study. She'd gotten close to Jolene and some of the locals during the winter. Jolene chatted amiably, talking about her latest artistic projects and her husband. Alex didn't have to talk much when Jolene was around, and she welcomed the friendly outpouring of information. It made it easy just to listen and be still with her bittersweet feelings of leaving.

At the airport, they hugged each other again and Jolene took a selfie of the two of them standing in front of the terminal. "We'll miss you, kid," Jolene said. "You take care of yourself."

"I will. You too." And she left Jolene, passing through into the terminal and giving a final wave.

As the plane took off, she watched the snow-covered mountains of Missoula fall away beneath her. "Goodbye," she whispered to the wolverines. "Good luck." She hoped finding their presence on the land meant more land trust donors would chip in to improve the wolverine habitat on the sanctuary.

She settled back in her seat, reading a variety of recent papers on the Western Hudson Bay polar bear population. They were one of nineteen populations that spanned the globe and were one of the groups that was in decline because of reduced sea ice, environmental pollutants, and a number of other factors.

A man behind her kept coughing. When the flight attendant came by with drinks and pretzels, Alex dared a look at the passenger between the seats. He coughed again, not bothering to cover his mouth. *Oh boy.* The last thing she needed was to get sick after they set down. She hoped he wouldn't be on the next leg of the journey.

There was no direct flight into Churchill, which had a tiny airport, so in Saskatoon, Saskatchewan, she transferred to a smaller airliner, and in Gillam, Manitoba, she transferred to a much smaller prop plane. Turbulence on the approach to Churchill made more than a few people sick, and she was glad for her strong stomach as she jostled in her seat, the plane sometimes making alarming dips before recovering. They passed through a dense layer of clouds and then Churchill appeared beneath her, a sweeping white and gray landscape. Tiny spruce trees dotted the ground, part of the circumpolar taiga forest that covered the landmasses of the Arctic. She could see the ice-covered expanse of Hudson Bay to the north and a surge of excitement buzzed through her. And then they were touching down on the tarmac, bouncing to a rough stop.

She was here. Churchill, Manitoba, the Polar Bear Capital of the World.

TWO

Churchill, Manitoba, Canada

Alex climbed down the plane's stairs onto the tarmac and entered the airport's small terminal. It had only one luggage carousel operating, and she waited with the rest of the passengers for her backpack to appear.

She spotted it, hefted it up over her shoulder, then exited into the gray and white world. The cold instantly robbed her lungs of air and she coughed involuntarily. Even though it was overcast, the glare was bright. She donned her sunglasses. Fog rolled over the landscape, limiting visibility to only a quarter mile or so.

She stood only for a few minutes before a blue SUV pulled up. A thin man in his twenties stepped out, the frigid wind tossing longish brown hair around his pale, sunburned face. He brushed it back from his eyes and approached her. "Dr. Carter?"

She smiled. "Yes."

"I'm Neil Trevors. I'll be your research assistant."

They shook hands. He gripped only her fingers in a weak shake, and she tried not to immediately dislike him for it. She had an unproven theory that how a man shook a woman's hand said a lot about how he viewed her. A strong, confident handshake let her know that he viewed her as an equal.

He opened the back door while she shrugged off her pack and set it inside, then set her laptop case next to it.

As they pulled away from the airport, he said, "The Churchill Centre for Arctic Studies is where most researchers bunk when they come here. But the CCAS is fully booked right now on this short of notice, so I found you a room at the Borealis Motel. It's not exactly the Waldorf Astoria, but you have your own bedroom and bathroom, which is something you wouldn't have at the Centre. It's four to a room there."

"The motel sounds perfect." Alex didn't know if she would have been ready for communal living anyway, not after so many months on her own. She had to slowly dip into it.

"You'll probably want a car while you're here. Windows to fly are rare, and if we get a clear day we'll have to leave immediately. The helicopter will be waiting at the Centre, so you'll want to drive there. There's a car rental place about a block south of your motel."

As they drove, she took in the town. They passed the blue and white building for the Itsanitaq Museum and the Churchill Town Centre Complex, a large brown and gray heated indoor structure where residents could work out, go to the library, get health care, and socialize during the long winters.

"When do we start? Have you found a pilot?" she asked.

Neil nodded. "Ilsa Angstrom. Some of the other researchers have used her before in previous seasons. She's good."

He leaned forward over the steering wheel and stared up. "If this fog lifts, we should be able to go out tomorrow." He drummed his fingers on the wheel.

"Great!" Alex wanted to dive in.

"You want to go by the CCAS first?" He pronounced it "see-sass."

Alex was tired from the long flights, but really wanted to see the Centre. When she wasn't out in a helicopter or sleeping in her hotel room, the Centre was where she'd be doing her work. She'd read that they even had a lab there.

"Yes, thanks."

He flipped around on La Vérendrye Avenue and turned down a long paved road until they arrived at a squat gray one-story structure. A colorful mural decorated one side, featuring a polar bear and her cub beneath a stunning black sky filled with green and red auroras.

Several large picture windows gazed out over a small cluster of spruce trees in an expanse of snow. Two roll-up docking doors stood on one side where vehicles could be stored or worked on.

A helicopter waited in front of the Centre, powered down in the inclement weather. She took in its streamlined body—a Bell, similar to the one she'd flown in at Svalbard.

"Our equipment's already loaded and ready to go at a moment's notice," Neil told her. "The spreadsheet, field equipment, survival gear."

The spreadsheet, Alex knew, was a record of every bear captured. It recorded age, weight, sex, date of last capture, ID number, location, physical condition, and body measurements. It helped researchers keep track of the population and avoid recapturing a bear that had recently been caught. Each bear was assigned its own unique number during its first capture, and a small white plastic disk with that number was attached to the bear's ear.

They climbed out of the SUV and entered the warmth of the Centre. Alex immediately felt the buzz of research activity, the energy of learning, crackling through the place. A young woman with tumbling red hair passed them, sipping from a coffee cup and reading something off her tablet.

Neil stopped her. "Dawn, this is Alex Carter. She's here for Sonia." Turning to Alex, he added, "Dawn's an atmospheric scientist."

Instantly Dawn lit up. "So nice to meet you. I've met Sonia before. Really admire her. Welcome!" She pressed on through to a cafeteria.

Alex followed Neil as he made a round of introductions to a number of biologists and climatologists who were sitting around a table eating dinner. She tried to make a note of each of their names and their study focus, but knew she'd have to be reminded later. One did stand out to her, though, because she'd just been reading one of her research papers on the plane.

"This is Mirabel Esperanza," Neil said, gesturing to the woman. "She studies sea ice extent."

Alex reached out a hand. "Wonderful to meet you. I've been following your research."

Mirabel beamed, shaking Alex's hand. *"¡Mucho gusto!"*

"I'd love to talk to you about it while I'm here."

"I'd be delighted," Mirabel told her.

Alex instantly took a liking to the woman.

Neil toured Alex around the facility, showing her the outdoor gear room, a communal area for reading and socializing, and the lab, which sported state-of-the-art equipment: a centrifuge for spinning samples of polar bear and seal blood, microscopes, a gas analyzer, and more.

Housing was comprised of rooms with two bunk beds. The Centre even housed people who were there on educational vacations— people who wanted to learn about the aurora borealis, belugas, wildflowers, or birds.

A small library offered comfortable chairs to sit in and a plethora of books on arctic research. Wi-Fi was available here, and a few researchers were taking advantage, glued to their phones and computer screens.

When the tour was done, they passed again through the cafeteria. "Nice to meet everyone," Alex said.

Mirabel gave her a wave, and Dawn, the atmospheric scientist, looked up from her coffee and said, "Looking forward to having you here!"

It felt good to be around fellow researchers, people who were dedicating their lives to better understand the planet and the myriad creatures they shared it with.

She braced herself for the cold as Neil opened the main doors and they returned to his car.

They continued their trek through the town, passing motels, a grocery store, the Royal Canadian Mounted Police station, and a post office.

He pulled up in front of a small motel of painted blue wood. Twelve rooms ran its length, with a metal chair and a small table outside each door.

"I've already checked you in." He handed her the key to room 6. It hung off an old-fashioned plastic motel keychain that listed the motel's name and address with the request *Please drop this in any mailbox if you forget to return your key.*

Alex retrieved her laptop and backpack from the back seat. "Thanks for picking me up."

"No problem. I'll send you a text tomorrow morning when I learn what the weather's going to be."

"Sounds good." She shut the door and he pulled away.

She juggled the key and her gear and entered room 6.

Inside she found a clean and simple space. A queen bed, a desk and chair, and a coffeemaker, microwave, and small refrigerator. Compared to some of her field assignments over the years that had involved simply her backcountry tent and a water bottle with a filter, it was all quite luxurious.

Sitting down on the edge of the bed, she turned her phone back on. Several missed calls flashed on the screen: her closest friend, Zoe Lindquist; her dad; and Sonia. She called Sonia first, letting her know she'd arrived and met Neil. Sonia was excited for Alex to get started, and Alex promised she'd report back after her first day in the field.

Then she called Zoe. Zoe was a successful actor who lived in Laurel Canyon in L.A. But right now she was on set in North Carolina. Of a six-week shooting schedule, Zoe had only another couple weeks or so to go.

"Hey," her friend said when she picked up. "How is the snowy north?" She'd sent Zoe a text from the Missoula airport, letting her know she'd taken a new assignment in the Arctic.

"Snowy."

"Seen any polar bears yet?"

"Not yet, but we should be going out on the ice sometime in the next few days. We have to wait for a window in the weather."

"I know how you feel," Zoe declared mournfully. "It's been pouring rain here for the last three days and we haven't been able to shoot anything."

"What's the film like?"

"It's a period piece. Set in the 1700s. Revolutionary War. I'm wearing the most ridiculous bonnet right now, and this corset is killing me. But we think we might have a couple hours of shooting time coming up. There is a tiny patch of blue sky on the horizon." Alex could hear her shifting around, the phone muffled, then clear. "How did women function in these things?"

"I think the idea was to prevent them from functioning."

"Well, job well done. I can barely breathe and have to sit ramrod straight all the time. It's exhausting."

"How are the rest of the cast and crew?"

She let out a disgusted exhalation. "Nick Buchanan is in this one. But everyone else is great."

Nick had been a Hollywood staple for decades yet had never learned to be humble about his successes.

"You've never heard such ridiculous demands," Zoe went on. "He'll only take one specific kind of bottled water that has to be flown in from Thailand. He has his own craft services table that no one else is even allowed to look at. Sautéed broccolini, a specific kind of French Brie with a specific kind of Italian crostini, his own barista, and his own sommelier at night. He has a curated wine collection on set, Alex. Curated. I swear, there's a guy here who pours each glass and explains how it has hints of citrus or leather. Leather. I'm not kidding you. Apparently it was stored in a barrel with leather straps, and that's a good thing.

"And he only has about five scenes in the whole movie. He's playing a hoity-toity British general. At least that part will come naturally to him."

Alex laughed. Zoe always complained about being on set, but Alex knew she absolutely loved it.

"So what is it like there?" she asked Alex.

"Small town. Very flat. Covered in snow and these amazing little spruce trees. I'm so far north that I'm in the taiga."

"The what?"

"This circumpolar boreal forest that wraps all the way around the northern stretches of the globe. It's responsible for a lot of the natural carbon sink of the planet, drawing down CO_2 from the atmosphere."

"Well, at least that's good. I bet it still can't make up for the carbon footprint of Nick's demands for thinly sliced dragon fruit flown in specially from Uruguay every day."

Alex chuckled. "Probably not. I'm looking forward to exploring, though. If the weather doesn't clear enough for the helicopter, I might take a drive around Churchill tomorrow, orient myself."

"Don't get your face eaten off by bears. When you were in Svalbard, my heart was in my mouth."

"Getting my face eaten off is definitely not on my agenda."

"Any word from that cute guy who works with the land trust?"

Alex thought about Ben. "We've only talked a few times. He mentioned some opportunities they might have coming up when I finish here."

"You sound happy."

"I am happy."

"Moving out of Boston was the right thing to do. This kind of thing is where you belong," Zoe told her.

Alex smiled.

Zoe went on. "Though I'd still like a best friend I could shop with on Rodeo Drive. I mean, you can't believe anything sales help tells you over there. 'Oh, yes, Miss Lindquist. That orange bag of a dress looks fabulous on you. Especially with those neon-pink pouf sleeves and the six-inch powder-blue stilettos.' I need a reliable opinion. When a famous dress designer makes a gown for me for the Oscars, I want to know if it makes me look like a languishing orange walrus. They can't all be Chanel."

"Who's Chanel?" Alex teased. "Oh, wait. That's a perfume, right?"

"Oh, stop it. No, my best friend has to be up in the Arctic watching polar bears crunch on cute baby seals. I have all the luck."

"Life is hard. So what's your next scene?"

"I'm supposed to pour ale for a bunch of drunken British redcoats, but I'm secretly listening in because I'm a spy. Then in a later scene, I encrypt the troop movements and have to sneak through the town at night to deliver the intel to the Continental Army. There's going to be a shootout. I get to use a black powder pistol and everything."

"That sounds cool."

"I think it will be if we ever get back to shooting outdoors. That patch of blue sky I mentioned earlier? It's already gone. And the humidity here! It's like *rain already*. I mean, we're practically breathing water anyway as it is. Might as well pour down from the sky and just make us drenched all over." Zoe chuckled. "I have such a hard life. You have no idea." She paused, briefly muffling the phone to speak to someone else. "Looks like we're jumping ahead to film an indoor scene."

Alex heard a man shouting through a bullhorn. "Okay, people. Places! Places!"

"That's my cue," Zoe said.

"Good luck with the shoot."

"Good luck with your study. And remember—no getting your face eaten off!"

Alex laughed. "I'll do my best."

They hung up and Alex dug through her bag for her charger and phoned her dad. She lit up when she heard his voice.

"Hey, pumpkin. How was your flight?"

"Uneventful," she told him. "No kid kicking the back of my seat. But a coughing guy saw fit to hack continuously without covering his mouth. Mostly I just read and stared out of the window. I just arrived in Churchill."

"Sounds like a peaceful trip. Except for the hacking."

"How are things with you?"

"Good. My barbershop quartet has a gig this Saturday at an open-air market."

"Wonderful! You nervous?"

He laughed. "Of course! But it'll be fun. You all settled in there?"

She stared around at the motel room. "They didn't have room at the Centre, but they booked me into a nice little motel in the middle of town. I can walk to the grocery store."

"That sounds like a bit of all right."

"So far, so good."

"When do you go out on the ice? That's going to be exciting. In a helicopter like you did in Svalbard?"

"Yes. And soon, hopefully. Keep your fingers crossed that we get some good weather. I'll send pics when I'm out there."

"Please do. So what's on your agenda in the meantime?"

"Nothing too exciting. If it's still foggy tomorrow, I'll get some food for my room. Put in a change of address at the post office." She paused. "Have any more strange packages arrived there?"

"Like the one your GPS unit came in?"

"Yeah."

"Nope. Not a one. You figure out who that was from?"

"No. But I got more postcards with that same handwriting."

"Sounds a little creepy," her dad said, concerned.

"To me, too."

"You be careful, pumpkin."

"I will."

Their conversation turned to the books they were currently reading, and they gave each other suggestions. He described some interesting articles he'd read in the *New York Times* about climate change and carbon taxes. She told him interesting polar bear facts she'd read about on the plane.

"I'd better get some sleep before tomorrow," she told him. "Good luck with your gig on Saturday. I love you."

"Thanks. I love you, too, kid."

They hung up, and she turned to her backpack to retrieve her clothes and toiletries. She thought of the coughing man on the plane and fished out some vitamin C, then stripped out of her clothes and took a short, hot shower. She was so tired her back muscles were starting to ache, so she put on her pj's, retrieved the polar bear research papers, and lay down in bed.

When the plane landed, she'd been in the middle of a fascinating yet disturbing study about the loss of sea ice in the Arctic. She made a mental note to talk to Mirabel, the researcher at the Centre who was studying it.

She finished the paper and picked up the novel she'd been reading on the plane, a thriller about an archaeologist who discovered a lost civilization. She jerked awake as the book thumped down against her chest. Putting it aside, she turned off the light and drifted to sleep, dreaming of the adventure ahead.

THREE

Alex woke to a layer of fog so dense the world outside looked like something out of a fantasy movie, an ethereal realm of mist. She showered and dressed, then walked over to the car rental place. Her boots crunched on the snow as she navigated through the fog that swirled with her movements. Snow came down, adding a fresh white layer to the already ivory landscape.

The rental place had two cars left, a Ford Explorer and a Jeep Wrangler, both four-wheel drive to accommodate for the snow. She opted for the Jeep and filled out endless paperwork while the clerk dealt with a computer issue. Finally he handed over the keys and she was set.

She stopped by the post office and filled out a mail-forwarding form, changing her address to the Centre. That way if a room opened up at the Centre later, she wouldn't have to change it again.

With an unsettling feeling, she wondered if the strange, unsigned postcards would start arriving again.

Shrugging off the feeling, she took La Vérendrye Avenue and then the smaller road out to the Centre, enjoying the gray and white vista. Churchill was very flat, with willows and small green spruce trees peeking out from the snow. The Centre lay on the outskirts of town. Flurries continued to fall, dusting the windshield. On the road's surface, small ground blizzards blew by, white snow snakes writhing across the black asphalt.

When she got to the Centre, she stood outside for a few minutes, lifting her face to the sky. The cold sprinkle of snow felt good on her skin. She breathed in the crisp arctic air and reveled in this change of scenery.

Inside, the Centre was abuzz with activity. The cafeteria was empty except for two researchers eating breakfast, chatting about diminishing sea ice extent. She recognized Mirabel from the day before but hadn't met her colleague. In his early thirties, he had unkempt brown hair and a beige, weathered face that reflected years out in harsh elements.

Alex bought a breakfast burrito with black beans, rice, and avocado and approached them. "It's Mirabel Esperanza, isn't it? We briefly met yesterday," Alex greeted her.

Mirabel looked up, smiling. "Yes, Dr. Carter, right?"

Alex reached her hand out to the sea ice expert. "Alex, please."

Mirabel shook Alex's proffered hand and gestured toward her colleague. "This is Kyle Zander."

He took Alex's hand. "Great to meet you."

"Likewise." She turned to Mirabel. "On the plane here, I read your fascinating paper on predicting sea ice extent."

At this, Mirabel broke into a bigger smile. "Thank you very much."

"Of course!"

"Won't you join us?" Mirabel asked. "You don't mind, do you, Kyle?"

"Not at all, but I think my results are almost ready in the lab. I'd better get back to it." He turned to Alex. "Nice to meet you."

"You too," she said as he gathered up his things and moved to the bussing station. She pulled out a chair opposite Mirabel.

The researcher grinned at Alex. "So what do you think of the Centre so far?"

"I love it. So much wonderful energy here. How long have you been here?"

"Two months. I love the lab. And being able to see the aurora, of course." She leaned forward conspiratorially. "My three bunkmates all snore like lumberjacks taking down sequoia, but I'll live."

Alex laughed. "Sounds restful."

"Where are you from?" Mirabel asked.

Alex smiled ruefully and gave a small laugh. "I guess nowhere in particular," she mused. When Mirabel lifted a puzzled eyebrow, Alex added, "I move around a lot for my job. But I guess if I'd call one place home, it would be in Berkeley, California, with my dad. It's where I got my degrees."

Mirabel beamed. "I love the Bay Area! So much culture, and you've got the ocean right there, plus the mountains just a few hours away. I grew up in L.A." Then her face fell. "But California is scary now."

"What do you mean?"

"The fires," she said, her eyes wide. "They actually tie into my research in a tangential way."

"How so?"

"With my sea ice extent research, I've been studying the Ridiculously Resilient Ridge and trying to predict when it could happen again."

Alex was intrigued. "I'm not familiar with that."

Mirabel's eyes lit up. She clearly loved her research. "See, the reduction in sea ice has an atmospheric effect. As sea ice decreases, it creates a high-pressure system off the Pacific coast. It's called an atmospheric ridge. When coupled with warming sea surface temperatures, these ridges cause havoc, deflecting storms away, causing weather to be incredibly dry. The Ridiculously Resilient Ridge formed in 2013 and lasted until 2017. It was a huge factor in a bad five-year drought in California."

Alex leaned back in her chair. "Wow. And are these ridges getting worse? I know California's drought certainly is."

She nodded. "It's led not just to less rain, but reduced snowpack in the winter. Snow drought is becoming more and more common."

"Snow drought?"

"It's when winter precipitation falls in the form of rain instead of snow. Unusually warm winter temperatures cause it. They also prematurely melt the snow that does manage to fall. Then the snow-pack is melting off throughout the winter instead of providing runoff into the spring."

"That's terrible." Alex knew from her own research in the Rockies that summers were arriving earlier and lasting longer. Yellowstone National Park alone experienced an extra month of summer now. Species that relied on seasonal plants suffered as growing seasons went off-kilter. Pollinators arrived in areas only to find flowers already bloomed and gone.

"It's fascinating work, but alarming all the same. So what's your specialty?"

"On this trip, polar bears."

"Exciting! You get to use the helicopter?"

"Yep!"

Mirabel turned as Kyle called her name from the lab doorway. "Can you help me with something?" The woman looked back at Alex and winked. "Oh boy. No rest for the wicked. Not even at night, when the lumberjacks are in full swing."

Alex chuckled. Saying goodbye to Mirabel, she watched the researcher make her way to the lab.

Alone now at the table, Alex checked the weather forecast on her laptop. It was a graphical forecast of the area, or GFA, something she'd learned to read during her season in Svalbard. It was comprised of the most likely weather conditions to occur below twenty-four thousand feet over a given area, which aided in planning flights. It would allow her to figure out if a flight window would open soon. GFAs were released four times a day. Each GFA provided charts offering a variety of information: near-term, six-hour, and twelve-hour forecasts, all displaying the clouds (CLDS), weather (WX), icing (ICG), wind turbulence (TURBC), and freezing levels (FRLVL).

Alex studied the latest GFA and perked up when she noticed a possible window might open up later that day.

As the fog lifted, she finished her burrito. Eyeing the hot beverage choices, she opted for tea, which she sipped while staring out at the world of white. Then she made her way to the lab and explored it more thoroughly.

When she returned to the cafeteria, Neil was just entering, stamping snow off his boots. "The weather's lifting. I've texted the pilot."

Grinning, Alex slipped on an extra fleece layer and her parka, followed by waterproof pants. Eager to get out there, she threw on a fleece hat and donned her soft purple Turtle Fur neck warmer, which would also protect her face once she was out in the helicopter.

Two minutes later a tall Viking of a woman strode in, cold air swirling in her wake. Her straight blond hair was pulled back into a loose ponytail, and her reddened face was windburned, with deep crags and chapped lips. She carried a shotgun. Being out on the ice in polar bear territory meant someone in their party was required to carry a firearm. Polar bears were curious. If you were out on the ice, milling around a tranquilized polar bear while wearing bright, interesting clothing, other polar bears would sometimes come by and check you out. Thankfully, researchers almost never had to use a gun, and when they did, the blast of a shot fired into the air was generally enough to scare off curious bears.

"You ready?" the woman asked Neil.

Alex joined them.

"Yep. This is Alex Carter."

The pilot nodded, crushing Alex's hand in a fierce handshake.

"Ilsa Angstrom." She turned on her heel and passed through the door. Alex followed her out as the pilot strode toward the helicopter. Alex emerged into an entirely different scene. The sun streamed down, creating a dazzling white world that blinded her. She donned her sunglasses but still had to squint in the shimmering brilliance.

While Ilsa fired up the engine, Alex double-checked their supplies: the spreadsheet, survival gear, emergency food and water rations, medical kit with signal flares, tranquilizer gun with its case of preloaded darts, all the equipment they'd need to sedate and tag a bear. The gear took up most of the space in the helicopter, with two seats in the back. Since she was the one who'd be firing the tranquilizer gun out of the helicopter, she took the seat next to the sliding door. Neil took the seat up front beside the pilot.

Alex pulled on a headset as Ilsa did the last of her preflight check. The rotors beat above them and a rush of excitement coursed through Alex. Then they were airborne, tiny spruce trees below the only hint of color, snow blown off their green branches.

The helicopter tilted its nose down, heading for Hudson Bay.

Alex thrilled to the sensation. She stared out the window, watching the snow-covered banks give way to a small section of open water. Gray waves, tossed in the wind, chopped at the rocks there. Next to Ilsa, Neil clutched his stomach and looked a little green. Turning away from the window, he stared at a fixed spot on the horizon.

"Airsick?" Alex asked him over the headset.

He looked back at her with wormy eyes, then returned to staring, giving a nod.

"Don't puke in my bird," the pilot barked sharply over the comm. "There are airsick bags under your seat."

"I won't," he croaked, swallowing hard. "Just give my stomach a minute to settle."

Alex stared out her own window, watching as the open water gave way to a vast expanse of snow-covered ice. As they cruised over the pack ice, she searched for a lead where seals could emerge to breathe. That's where the polar bears would be. But it had to be a very narrow lead, just a seam along the ice. It was too dangerous to tranquilize a bear near open water. The bear could jump in and drown as the sedative kicked in. So they searched for leads with small sections of broken ice, just tiny open places where a seal could stick its head through.

They passed an area of rough ice, sections with large open leads and gigantic jumbled masses of enormous floes pressed against one another, creating pressure ridges and whimsical, towering shapes. One looked like an elephant to her. Another, a leaning bowling pin.

Leaving the rough patches behind them, they flew over a vast stable section. She spotted numerous seams and started scanning for tracks. Pulling out her binoculars, she searched the dazzling landscape. She watched for the color difference of a polar bear on the ice. Though they looked white against land, on the ice they exhibited a yellowish hue that was easier to spot. Polar bear researchers called it a *freebie* when a polar bear was spotted without having to follow tracks. But she didn't see any.

She searched, too, for scavengers like glaucous and ivory gulls, and for Arctic foxes. They often gathered in an area of a recent polar bear kill, devouring the leftovers.

As they banked to the northeast, keeping above the good stretch of ice, Alex spotted a line of tracks trending in a north-south direction.

"There," she said, pointing.

Ilsa followed her gaze. "I see them. Taking us lower."

When they got low enough, Alex determined the tracks were heading north. Ilsa took them along the line, moving to the left of the tracks so Alex could continue to follow them with her binoculars.

They flew on, Neil not looking any less sick, despite his assurance he just had to get used to it. But he hadn't thrown up, and that was something.

And then, after several miles, she spotted the bear, strolling purposefully north. Normally to determine gender from the air, she'd have to spy the broad width of a male bear's neck or the telltale yellow of urine beneath a female's tail. But knowing this one was female was easy. Alex lit up as she saw two little cubs following along behind it.

Biologists indicated bears with a black marking crayon after they'd been tagged each season. No such mark was present on the female, so Alex directed Ilsa to get lower.

As they neared, the bear family spooked, breaking into a run. Through the binocs, she could see that the bear wore a GPS collar, so it had been tranquilized and studied in a previous season. Alex felt bad for scaring them. But if these magnificent creatures were going to survive, researchers needed data on how well they were doing under current laws, to determine if those laws needed to be strengthened. And Alex knew they had to be.

Leaning over in her seat, she flipped open the case for the tranquilizer gun and picked up the weapon. The tranquilizer darts were already preloaded by a biologist at the Centre who specialized in the process. From three ranges of size, she chose the best one for the bear's estimated weight.

She slid the dart into the gun and moved the case away from her feet. She wouldn't dart the two youngsters. Cubs tended to hover around their mothers when researchers tranquilized them.

With the safety line clipped onto her harness, she spoke through the headset. "Opening the door." Gripping the handle, she slid the door open, the sudden blast of freezing air hitting her like a visceral force. For a second the breath was robbed from her chest. Then she swung her legs toward the outside of the chopper and lifted the barrel.

The bear, bolting now, glanced over her shoulder at the helicopter. The little cubs struggled to keep up.

They had to get within fifteen feet to make the difficult shot. She aimed the barrel at the bear's rump, struggling to compensate for the movement of the helicopter. A gust of wind hit the chopper, thrusting it to the port and blasting her with arctic air. Alex lost the bead on the bear. She relaxed her shoulders, lowering the gun as Ilsa brought the helicopter back into alignment with the tracks, moving a little lower. The bear raced forward full tilt, powdery snow kicking up behind her.

Alex raised the rifle again, bracing a foot against the landing skid of the helicopter, and leaned forward, letting the harness take her weight as she stabilized herself. She narrowed in again on the bear's rump and fired. Quickly lowering the rifle, she saw the telltale red feathering bouncing along against the white of the bear's fur. She'd made the shot.

But the cubs had now bolted in the opposite direction.

Ilsa drew back so as not to scare them. The mother continued in the direction she'd been running, starting to slow down as the tranquilizer took effect. But the cubs weren't stopping for anything. They raced away, gaining more and more distance.

Alex leaned back inside the helicopter. "We'll have to land and scoop them up if they keep heading in that direction," she told Ilsa.

As the mother slowed, shifting from a run to a walk, Ilsa followed the cubs as they loped north. She flew past them and gently set the helicopter down at enough of a distance not to spook them further. It wasn't unusual for biologists to have to wrangle cubs in situations like this, and it didn't hurt the young bears to be bundled up and returned to their mother.

Alex unhooked herself from the harness and stepped out, ducking down as she moved away from the helicopter. The rotor wash pushed at her parka hood.

Neil hopped out after her, and they raced after the cubs.

FOUR

The two cubs stopped abruptly and stood staring. As the biologists approached, one of the cubs moved toward them, curious. The cubs were tiny and probably fresh out of their den, putting them at a little over three months old.

A female polar bear reached sexual maturity when she turned five. She could have cubs from then until she was twenty. The cubs stayed with her for two to two and a half years, so females tended to have a litter of only one to three cubs every three years. Over a lifetime, a mother bear typically had ten cubs. However, cub mortality was so high, with only a 40 to 60 percent survival rate, that polar bear populations grew very slowly.

Alex hoped these little guys would make it.

She knelt down and held out her hands, and the cub moved forward, sniffing her. Then she scooped it up, holding it against her chest. It lifted its muzzle, sniffing her face. She felt the wet cold of its nose against her cheek and couldn't help but break into a grin. She felt bad she'd scared this family and was eager to reunite them.

She turned, seeing Neil chasing after the other cub. It loped along, peering over its shoulder as Neil slid on the snowy ice and cursed.

Finally he caught up with it and pounced, scooping up the cub.

She headed back toward the helicopter, the cub nestled against her. She wanted to be sure it stayed warm during all of this surprise and temporary separation from its mother.

At the helicopter door, she paused and let Neil climb in first, his cub struggling in his arms.

"Feisty little devil," Neil murmured, finally managing to get inside the helo. The cub stared around, a bundle of energy, wanting to play and explore. Neil got into his seat and buckled up while the cub planted its paws on his knees and leaned forward to sniff at Ilsa.

Alex's cub was just as squirmy, and she stepped up into the chopper and buckled in, struggling to maintain a grip on it. It stared up at her, bleating out plaintive baby bear noises.

Leaning over, she hefted the door closed and Ilsa powered up the helicopter again. They banked south, finding the mother just plopping down into the snow, the drug taking effect.

Ilsa deftly set the bird down and Alex slid open the door. Holding on to the cub, she walked over to the sleeping mother and knelt down. The little bear immediately jumped down and climbed up onto its mother.

Neil appeared, the squirming white bundle in his arms, and set his cub down when he couldn't hold it any longer. It raced over to its sibling and mother, then stood, its forepaws resting on its mother's side.

They grabbed gear from the helicopter and immediately went to work. They had to move quickly before the sedative wore off. On the spectrum of too much sedative to not enough, biologists always erred on the latter side. If it wore off before they were finished, Alex had a syringe with additional sedative. But hopefully they wouldn't need it.

While Neil monitored the bear's heart rate, temperature, and breathing, Alex knelt down by the massive white form. She took the bear's ear in her gloved hands and examined the small white plastic disk with the bear's ID number. She peeled down the bear's lower lip to reveal the matching lip tattoo. Examining the spreadsheet, she learned the bear was nine years old and that these two cubs were her second litter.

According to the database, the bear had last been collared four years ago. Because that was the upper limit of how long a collar could last, Alex removed it. They had less invasive technology now. 3M had developed the Burr on Fur, a small GPS tracking device that adhered to a bear's coat. She recorded the device's ID number on the spreadsheet and then worked it into the bear's hair.

Next she broke out the measuring tape and they took morphometric measurements of the mother, recording her length and girth. Alex calculated her weight using these readings. The bear was decidedly underweight, but not dangerously so. She and her cubs had a fairly good chance of surviving the year if they were able to catch some seals. She measured the head width and length, and then checked the condition of the bear's teeth.

Her teeth looked healthy.

Alex took a number of other samples, including swabbing between the mother's massive toes for bacteria. She took a photograph of the bear's facial profile for the Whiskerprint Project. Each bear had a unique pattern on its face, places where black spots on their muzzles were visible, where whiskers grew. Photographing in this way was a noninvasive means to ID a specific individual from a distance, and Alex wanted to contribute to the growing database of the project.

Finally, opening up a small vial, she took a sample of the bear's milk. From the milk, she'd be able to learn how many environmental pollutants the mother was passing on to her cubs.

They flipped the bear back over onto her stomach. Alex marked her back with a black animal-marking crayon so they wouldn't capture her a second time this season.

The bear lifted her head groggily, staring around. Time to get back to the helicopter. Alex and Neil packed up their supplies while Ilsa stood watch with the shotgun. They didn't want any other bears to approach while the female was still groggy and her cubs vulnerable. Male polar bears were known to kill and eat cubs.

But the ice was clear as they made their way back to the helo. The mother got up on her front legs, her cubs jumping on her back and nuzzling under her nose.

They loaded all the gear into the chopper and Ilsa fired it up. They hovered for a few minutes while the mother stood up and sniffed over her cubs. Ilsa lifted off, gaining enough altitude to watch the mother bear from a distance that wouldn't spook her. She continued on her way with her two cubs. After searching for other bears for a while, they'd fly back by this way again, just to make sure all was well and the family was safe.

Alex grinned. "Well done, everyone."

They flew around, searching for more tracks, with no luck. They doubled back to check on the mother and cubs. They were making steady progress along a seam. Relief washed over Alex. It always made her nervous to sedate an animal. And she didn't like the invasive nature of capturing and tagging.

For the rest of their time in the air, they didn't spot any more trackways. Another weather system threatened to close in, so they headed back to Churchill. Alex felt a little disappointment they hadn't seen more, but the family they had found, with the mother in relatively good shape, made her feel better.

By the time they landed in Churchill, Alex's stomach was rumbling. She longed to eat some dinner and go over the notes from the day. Wanting to see a bit of the town, she turned to Ilsa and Neil. "What's the best place to eat around here?"

"Moe's," Ilsa told her. "It looks a little dicey from the outside, but they've got great food."

They entered the Centre, Alex's spirits high. It had been a great day out. She switched from her heavy parka and outer snow gear to her lightweight fleece jacket.

Ilsa left as soon as they got back. "I'm going to Moe's to drink," she told them, and walked the half block down to where the orange neon sign declared MOE'S outside a wooden roadhouse-looking establishment with a steeply sloped snow roof.

Alex thought about joining her, but the camaraderie of the Centre's cafeteria pulled her in. The cafeteria was doing brisk business, all the researchers collected for the dinner hour.

She chose a hot dish of mac 'n' cheese, then a chocolate brownie for dessert.

As she ate, she listened to the conversations at the next table. Neil was trying unsuccessfully to hit on a woman. Unfortunately, he was pulling the "let me talk at you so you can see how fascinating I am" approach without ever expressing any curiosity about her. The woman's eyes were glazing over, and soon she just began talking to the others at the table. Neil didn't seem to notice that he'd struck out. He just kept talking to whoever looked his way. Alex felt a little sorry for him.

Two researchers approached her table, including Dawn, whom she'd met yesterday. "May we join you?" Dawn asked. Her colleague looked to be in his thirties, with a friendly windburned face.

"Of course!"

"This is Malcolm," Dawn said by way of introduction.

As they settled in, Alex asked them, "What have you been working on?"

"STEVE," Malcolm said enthusiastically.

"The atmospheric phenomenon?" Alex asked.

Dawn lit up. "That's it!"

Alex had read about the Strong Thermal Emission Velocity Enhancement, or STEVE, a phenomenon that researchers had only begun delving into as recently as 2016. No one knew quite what to make of it. At first observers thought that the light display, a single shimmering purplish white strand that manifested nearly perpendicular to the ground, was another type of aurora. But then researchers discovered that STEVE didn't contain the charged particles that auroras did.

Fascinated, Alex had followed news stories about it and hoped one day to see it. She knew that STEVE could span more than six hundred miles across the night sky.

It had just been recorded again earlier that year in northern Canada, and the two researchers talked excitedly about what it could be.

"It's got to be some kind of ionospheric process," Malcolm surmised.

"We just need more data," remarked Dawn.

Alex finished a bite of her mac 'n' cheese. "I read that a European Space Agency satellite passed directly through it."

Dawn pointed her fork at Alex. "That's right! It recorded temperatures fifty-five hundred degrees Fahrenheit hotter and air five hundred times faster than the surrounding night sky!"

"Incredible," Alex breathed. "Must be exciting to be at the forefront of the research."

"It really is," Malcolm agreed.

They continued to talk about atmospheric phenomena and Alex's bear study as they finished dinner. She got a cup of coffee as Dawn and Malcolm headed off to the common room to check their emails.

As researchers began to retire to bed, Alex still felt wide awake. She decided to do a little lab work before returning to her motel.

The coffee and long day out had made her teeth feel fuzzy, so she stopped by the Centre's little gift shop just before it closed and bought a small toothbrush and toothpaste to keep at the building. She brushed her teeth in the restroom and then started organizing the samples they'd collected in the field that day. Grateful for her fleece jacket, she shivered a little in the nighttime chill of the lab. She checked on the refrigerated blood and milk samples and prepared the hair sample for examination. She looked forward to discovering what she could from everything they collected.

The Centre felt quiet and dark as the researchers all retired, and Alex worked a little longer in the silence of the lab. As much as she loved this research project, it was nice to have a little time to herself. She wasn't adjusted yet to being around a lot of people.

The lab prep work done, she glanced at her watch. It was eleven P.M. Time to go back to her motel and get some sleep.

She swapped out her lightweight fleece jacket for her heavier coat, leaving the toothpaste and toothbrush in the fleece pocket. She hung her fleece on a hook in the gear room for future use in the chilly lab.

Then she braved the cold out to the parking lot and made her way back to the motel. Clouds had moved in, the waxing gibbous moon illuminating them from above, lending a silvery glow to the snowy landscape around her. She smiled all the way back to the motel, eager for her next chance out in the field.

THE NEXT DAY, ANOTHER GLORIOUS window of clear weather opened up. As Alex flew over the ice with Ilsa and Neil, her heart felt light. With the new green-minded Minister of Environment and Climate Change in place, their submitted research could do some real good.

Alex spotted a long line of tracks and pointed them out to Ilsa. They followed, Alex enjoying the hum of the helicopter's engine through the back of her seat. Soon she spotted a bear out on the ice and was delighted to see three little cubs bounding along behind her.

Ilsa brought the chopper in closer and Alex took the shot, landing the dart in the mother's rump. They pulled away to let the sedative take effect. This time the cubs stayed with their mother. As the mother lay down in the snow, Ilsa landed and they filed out.

Alex examined the small white plastic disk in the bear's ear. She checked the spreadsheet. This was the mother's second set of cubs.

She'd had two in a previous season, who were tagged when older, and both had survived into adulthood. Alex sat back on her heels, hoping that all three of these cubs would survive, too.

They took measurements and samples, moving around the curious cubs, who climbed all over the mother's back as they worked. The mother was a healthy weight, and the cubs all looked vibrant and alert. She'd know for sure when she got back to the lab, but given the mother's weight, she'd had some success catching seals over the winter.

Alex clipped some fur from the back of the polar bear. A polar bear's fur was actually transparent, not white. Pockets of air formed beneath the thick hair, trapping in heat. And beneath that fur, their skin was completely black, allowing them to absorb the sun's warmth. A thick layer of fat just under the skin further aided heat retention, and their short ears and tails kept body warmth from escaping.

She moved along the length of the bear, taking a small six-millimeter fat sample from her rump. This she could examine for the presence of organic pollutants like polychlorinated biphenyls, or PCBs; heavy metals like mercury; and levels of the stress hormone cortisol.

With Neil and Ilsa's help, she flipped the bear over onto her back. The cubs immediately climbed up onto their mother's stomach. They kept nudging Alex with their noses as she tried to work. She took a blood sample from under the mother's foreleg and rear leg, then a sample of her milk.

She recorded the bear's information on the spreadsheet, glancing over the stats for other bears that had been tagged in different areas so far that season.

Many bears were dangerously underweight, including sixteen mothers with cubs. With arctic ice growing smaller and smaller each year, it was harder for polar bears to catch seals, because they needed to use ice as a hunting platform. Ice became rotten and unstable, and it was missing altogether in huge areas that formerly had provided excellent feeding grounds.

They finished the rest of the samples and recorded measurements.

As the mother began to stir, they returned to the helicopter and took off. They set out in search of another bear, intending to double back later to check on the mother and the three cubs.

They spotted a gigantic male meandering along a seam in the ice and darted him. He'd also been tagged in a previous season. He was the biggest polar bear Alex had ever seen. Like the mother with her three cubs, this bear had undoubtedly had some success hunting for seals. Alex took measurements and samples, marveling at the monstrous size of the bear's paws as she swabbed them.

They broke out the measuring tape and took morphometric measurements, recording his length and girth. Alex calculated his weight at a staggering fifteen hundred pounds using these readings. He had a good chance of surviving the year if he could continue to catch seals. And polar bears had adapted over millennia for just this task, with their long necks for plunging their heads into seal holes and their elevated eyes that allowed them to peer above the water while swimming. This gave them the ability to use the aquatic stalk method, in which they pursued seals from underwater.

Polar bears could swim for astounding lengths of time and distance. A watery trek of thirty miles was nothing to them, with their huge paddle-like paws. In fact, Alex knew a female polar bear held the record for swimming four hundred and twenty-six miles over nine days. But she'd lost 22 percent of her body weight in doing so, and such epic swims were unfortunately becoming more and more necessary as sea ice diminished.

Alex measured the bear's massive head width and length, and then checked his tooth condition.

Normally they would extract a tiny little tooth that was evolutionarily on its way out and no longer needed. From the tooth, biologists could take a thin slice and look at the growth layers, much like how dendrochronologists looked at the growth rings of a tree. They'd be able to tell the age of the bear and which years had been lean ones. But because this bear had been tagged in the past, the tooth had already been removed. She swabbed inside the bear's mouth, placing the swab into a vial. The saliva would tell Alex which bacteria were present.

His teeth looked healthy.

She jotted down his information on the spreadsheet, realizing how lucky he was.

Anthropogenic climate change, caused by human greenhouse gas emissions, deforestation, and poor agricultural practices, had resulted in the hottest decade on record, and sea ice had diminished to alarming levels. The Arctic was warming far faster than lower latitudes. Some polar bears starved. Multiyear ice, ice that stayed around all year long and was added to annually, was now vanishing from Hudson Bay, and many bears had formerly used this ice as their summer home. More and more bears were having to come to land when the ice vanished completely in the summer, trolling beaches for any food they could find, some even entering towns. The food they found to eat there didn't provide the right nutrients, and so bears lacked the much-needed fat to survive the summers, when seals were unavailable.

So this bear was quite lucky to have had success hunting seals and fattening up.

As they finished, the bear groggily lifted his head. They retreated to the helicopter, waiting until he stood up and began meandering away.

They'd had a successful day. They checked on the mother and three cubs, finding them happily continuing their journey across the ice. As the sun inched toward the western horizon, the helicopter headed back into town.

After dropping off her samples in the lab, Alex realized she was starving. One peek revealed that the cafeteria was crowded. Glancing through the windows of the common room, she saw the inviting glow of Moe's sign down the street. Donning her fleece coat, she headed out.

She huddled down into the warm jacket during the brisk walk to the restaurant. But when she opened the door and saw how crowded it was, she almost left. There wasn't a single empty seat in the place.

She stood just inside the doorway, casting her eye around. Neil was in the far corner, playing a game of darts with two other researchers she recognized from the Centre. She was about to turn and leave when a couple got up from the bar and put on their coats. She made her way over to one of the now-empty stools and sat down.

The bartender, a burly man with a bushy brown beard that hung down to his sternum, threw a towel over his shoulder and approached her. His long brown hair framed a friendly tawny face. "You need a menu?"

"Yes, please."

He pulled one out from behind the bar. "Be back in a minute."

She perused the offerings the way most vegetarians did, quickly scanning along the last word in each menu item, searching for a dish that didn't contain meat. She passed up blackened Caesar chicken, slow-roasted pork, tri-tip steak. Most places didn't offer a lot of vegetarian choices, usually just a veggie burger and a few salads. But as she got to the bottom of the menu, she did a double take. This place surprised her by offering a delicious-sounding dish of crispy tofu with a miso ginger glaze.

When the bartender came back, she ordered the tofu and a small side salad. "It's a popular dish," he told her. "What can I get you to drink?"

She eyed the tap handles behind him, spotting a kind of dark beer she'd never tried. "I'll take a pint of the Aurora Porter."

"You got it."

As he poured, she leaned back and took in the crowd. Neil high-fived his companions, and it looked like he was winning at darts. A couple sat in a corner booth, talking quietly.

The bartender placed the porter down in front of her. "I'm Dave if you need anything else."

"Thanks." She sipped it, finding it chocolatey with hints of coffee.

The door opened, inviting in a draft of cold air, and Alex turned to look at the new patron. She was tall, in her late fifties, Alex guessed, with long, braided black hair framing a kindly sepia face. The woman shook snow off her coat and spotted the only empty seat in the place, next to Alex.

She walked over and claimed the barstool, hanging her coat on the hook on the underside of the bar. Around them swelled the sound of conversations, and music emanated from a jukebox in the corner.

Alex took another sip of the porter and her food arrived. It smelled amazing, and the tofu was crispy and glazed in a sauce that was one of the best she'd ever tasted.

"That looks good," the woman beside her said.

"It's great."

"I might get the same thing."

When Dave returned, the woman did indeed order the crispy tofu and a tangerine wheat beer. While Dave poured it, the woman extended a hand to Alex. "I'm Sasha."

Alex clasped it. "Alex. It's nice to meet you. Are you a local?"

Sasha shook her head. "No. I'm from Halifax. I came up here for work."

"What is it you do?"

"Marine archaeology."

Alex wiped her mouth with a napkin. "That sounds fascinating!"

"It is, normally."

Dave placed the beer in front of the woman, and a darkness passed over her eyes as she gazed down into it. She rotated the glass with her fingertips, her brow furrowed. Alex could sense sadness wafting off her.

"Is everything okay?" Alex asked.

The woman came back to the present. "Oh yes. Sorry. Just have a lot on my mind."

"So are you working any wrecks here?"

Sasha bit her lip. "Not at present. But hopefully soon." She took a few bites of her tofu. Then she turned to Alex. "What brings you up here? Or are you a local?"

"No. I'm just visiting. I'm working on a polar bear study."

"Now *that* sounds fascinating."

"It really has been."

"What are you hoping to learn?" Sasha asked, sipping her beer.

"We're looking at a number of things. How much the early breakup and late onset of ice is affecting their ability to hunt seals. How underweight they are. If pollutants have worked their way into their bodies."

"Sounds like interesting work."

"It is. I'm lucky to be able to do it."

They talked for a little longer. Sasha told her about growing up in Halifax, diving wrecks with her father. How they loved poring over historical documents and then making guesses as to where they could find sunken treasure. Sasha was warm and funny, and Alex took an immediate liking to her.

But she noticed that the woman had barely touched her meal. Finally Sasha signaled Dave, the bartender. "Can I get a take-out box?" She looked at Alex, and again Alex noticed that the archaeologist seemed deeply troubled. "Guess I don't have much of an appetite tonight. But it's been great talking to you. It's lifted my spirits."

Alex felt the urge to ask again if she was okay but didn't want to invade Sasha's privacy. The archaeologist paid and stood up. "Hopefully we'll run into each other again."

"I hope so, too."

Sasha pulled on her coat and left, her exit ushering in another swirl of cold air.

Alex finished her own food, then paid and headed back to the Centre. She couldn't wait to get back out onto the ice again, feeling the tug of adventure.

FIVE

When Alex awoke the next day, no bright light streamed through her curtains. She peered outside, seeing only socked-in gray. She dressed and showered, then headed out to the Centre in a dense fog with falling snow. At the Centre, she checked the GFA, delighted to see that a window of clear weather would open up in the late morning. She took advantage of the downtime to run tests on her bear samples in the lab.

First she ran a test for persistent organic pollutants containing chlorine, fluorine, and bromine. Then she examined the samples for the presence of industrial compounds like PCBs. These could compromise a body's ability to produce antibodies, making humans and wildlife more susceptible to infection.

Both mothers with cubs and the big male she'd tagged did not have dangerous levels of PCBs, but they did have some. Alex saved her data, backing it up, then took a break and drank a cup of tea. She munched thoughtfully on a granola bar, hopeful about the bears she'd tagged thus far.

Ilsa showed up just as the weather cleared, and soon Alex and Neil were bundled in their warmest clothes and speeding with her out across the ice.

They spotted a bear soon into their flight, a rangy female. She had never been tagged before, so Alex affixed the small white disk to her ear. Alex guessed her age at around six years old. If she found a mate this spring and fertilized an egg, then like all female polar bears, she'd have delayed implantation and actually get pregnant in the fall.

Alex picked up one of the massive paws, as big as a dinner plate. Using a little potato peeler, she took a very thin sliver of one of her claws. Whatever was circulating in the bear's blood would accumulate in her claws. Examining the claw was another way to detect the presence of poisonous heavy metals like mercury.

Still holding the enormous paw, she swabbed between the bear's toes. Grizzly bears rubbed trees not only to scratch their backs, but also to leave behind their scents. Polar bears didn't have any trees to rub against out here, so they left their scents behind on the ice each time they stepped down. These chemical trails allowed bears to mark their often vast territories, which spanned barren landscapes. Because a bear could roam over 4,500 miles in a single season on the ice, and their home ranges could encompass more than 200,000 square miles, it could be hard for bears to find each other. The scent trails enabled a bear to sniff out one individual's tracks over another's, allowing it to follow or avoid the bear of its choosing. A female with cubs might want to avoid a dangerous male, and a male might want to follow a female in estrus.

Their gigantic feet also served as nonslip pads. Covered with tiny protuberances called papillae, their special pads allowed them to easily grip the ice.

The female bear wasn't as fat as Alex would have liked, but she wasn't malnourished, either. But underweight bears affected cub and subadult survival. The ice that did form now was thinner, and if it was too thin for females to den on, they were forced ashore, where they had to fast for longer, resulting in fewer cubs. A female would also stop nursing sooner if her body had lost too much fat, causing a longer fasting time for the cubs and significantly reducing their survival rates.

As Alex worked the Burr on Fur into her hair, she hoped that this bear would have continued success with seals and would give birth to a healthy litter next season.

After the bear was up on her feet again, they took off, scanning the ice. They lucked out that afternoon, finding more bears, but unfortunately, these bears weren't faring quite as well. A male bear was underweight, and a mother with two cubs weighed in on the thin side, too.

As Alex worked, measuring their girth and swabbing between their toes, she sent out a constant stream of positive thoughts. *Let this bear make it,* she wished silently with each magnificent creature. *Let this bear make it.* She hoped that all the samples she'd collected would reveal low levels of pollutants.

Then she sent positive thoughts out to the Minister of Environment and Climate Change, feeling excited that between her research and that of scientists like Mirabel, who studied sea ice extent, the Canadian government would take even more action to slow climate change, inspiring other countries to take similar or even greater steps.

They flew back to Churchill in high spirits, pleased at the successful day out and the state of the bears.

Back at the lab, Alex ran tests and frowned to see that the male bear from today wasn't doing so well; he'd definitely been consuming seals, but it had led to a higher concentration of PCBs in his fat layer. Still, it wasn't an alarming number, and a glimmer of hope sparked in Alex.

If more measures to limit global warming could be put into place, then polar bear decline could be slowed enough to help their population start to recover.

Next she ran tests on the male bear for the presence of heavy metals. These pollutants, such as lead, mercury, selenium, and cadmium, were released into the environment through a variety of human activities, ranging from fossil fuel burning to the production of cement to the process of metal smelting.

She found high levels of both mercury and cadmium in the male, unfortunately. The six-year-old, though, had far lower levels of heavy metals, which was an excellent sign. Alex hoped this trend would continue for her.

She ate dinner in the cafeteria again, talking with Mirabel about her latest findings, and enjoying the buzz of activity around the Centre. Deciding to turn in early, she headed back to her motel and fell asleep reading a novel.

THE NEXT DAY ALEX AWOKE to a thick fog hovering outside her window. She logged on to her computer and checked the GFA. Conditions didn't bode well for the day. There was no way they'd be able to go out.

Alex showered and dressed, deciding to spend her time in the lab going into more detail with the samples they'd collected thus far.

At the Centre, she found the lab busy but not crowded. First she fired up the mass spectrometer and ran a stable isotope diet analysis on the bears' hair, claws, and blood.

She analyzed the carbon and nitrogen isotopes. The higher a species was in the food chain, the higher its level of heavier isotopes. So a whale would have more than a fish. Each species had its own unique isotope pattern, so Alex could determine what the bears had been eating by examining their isotopic signatures.

The hair and claws recorded a bear's diet as they grew out. Blood revealed what a bear had eaten in the last month. If she'd had a portable gas analyzer in the field, she would have been able to test the bears' breath and find out what they were currently digesting.

She learned that the bears had been eating ringed and bearded seals, glaucous gulls, kelp, horseflies, sedges, and willows.

She next ran additional tests on the fat samples and pored over the results with concern. The mother with the two cubs she'd tagged yesterday showed high levels of pollutants.

A huge concern with PCBs was biomagnification. As they worked their way up the food chain, PCB concentrations became higher and higher. Contaminated algae might consume a particle, and then a small crustacean might eat several pieces of algae, gaining a higher concentration. Then a fish might eat a quantity of crustaceans and a seal a number of fish, and by the time a polar bear ate a few seals, the concentration of PCBs had become all the more dangerous.

These pollutants were lipophilic and collected in the fat. But as fat was lost, the pollutants became more concentrated and levels in the blood rose.

Next she tested the milk samples.

Polar bear milk contained more fat than the milk of any other bears. When cubs were first born, the milk of a healthy mother contained 40 percent fat, and by the time they were weaned, it dropped to between 5 and 20 percent. During the ice-free periods in their first year, when bears couldn't access seals, cubs drank sixteen ounces of milk a day, and four and a half ounces a day once they reached a year old.

Because of the high fat content they gave to their cubs, mothers who were able to bulk up on seal blubber during the icy period of the winter had a higher survival rate than those who weren't able to catch enough seals.

Alex ran a test to determine the level of pollutants in the milk from the mother she'd tagged the day before. She found high levels of PCBs and mercury. These were getting passed on to the female's cubs, and the more fat she lost, the more highly concentrated the pollutants would become.

She frowned, then backed up the test results onto a flash drive. So far her data had shown a mix: some bears were managing, but others were definitely struggling.

She'd been so focused on her lab results that she hadn't noticed that it had grown dark outside. She was now alone in the lab and could hear the buzz of activity coming from the dinner rush in the cafeteria.

It was almost eight, and every table was full in the dining area.

She thought of the delicious vegetarian offerings at Moe's and decided to walk over there.

Donning her coat, she left the Centre. The cold hit her like a visceral force. She hurried, shivering, over to the restaurant. Inside, it was going full force: hockey fans watching TV, people playing pool and darts, friends gathering for lively conversation. She was amazed to see three free stools at the bar.

She hurried to one, hanging her fleece jacket on the hook beneath the bar.

"Hey there," Dave said, recognizing her and smiling. "You want the porter again?"

"Sure."

He slid a menu over to her and she perused it while he poured. "The Impossible Burger sounds good," she told him when he returned with her pint. "And a side of french fries, please." She hadn't yet tried the Impossible Burger, a plant-based meat.

"Comin' right up," Dave told her, retrieving the menu.

As she sipped her porter, the door opened, a chill wind sweeping around the place. Alex smiled to see Sasha's familiar face. The marine archaeologist spotted Alex at the bar and walked over.

"Good to see you again," she told Sasha as the woman took the stool next to her.

"You too." She nodded at Alex's drink. "What's on tap for tonight?"

"The porter. It's really good."

When Dave returned to take Sasha's order, she got the porter, too, and ordered the veggie risotto. Sasha asked how Alex's research was going, and Alex regaled her with tales of their successful days out on the ice. Their food arrived, but once again Sasha didn't seem to have much of an appetite. She moved the risotto around on her plate.

Alex couldn't help but notice once again that the woman seemed deeply troubled. Alex turned to face her. "Hey, I hate to pry, but you seem really sad."

Sasha let out a long exhale. "I am upset."

"Do you want to talk about it?"

She gave Alex a sad smile.

"What is it?"

Sasha stared down into the porter as if the answer might be floating in it. She took a deep breath. "It's my dive partner, Rex. We were up here scouting possible sites. We don't usually dive in such cold waters. We took a short preliminary dive, and I ended up getting the bends. The next day he went out on his own. He did a dive, and now he's completely disappeared."

Alex pivoted on her barstool toward her. "That's terrible."

"I've called the Canadian Coast Guard and the Mounties, but so far there's been no trace of him. I'm not sure what to do next. They found our boat off the coast of Churchill, but it was empty, just floating there, anchored." She paused, biting her lip. "And they found blood on the deck."

"Oh no. Do they suspect he was attacked?"

"They're not sure. There was no sign of a struggle. He might have just hurt himself. Maybe fallen overboard."

"What are you going to do?"

Sasha stared back at her glass and began rotating it. "I'm not sure. Stay here to see what the authorities turn up." She gazed up at the colorful bottles above the bar. "At some point I'll have to return to work. I've started to dip into my savings to stay here." She gave a little smile. "Though one guy did ask to rent my boat. But he wanted to take it out alone, and he seemed a little shifty." She gestured around Moe's. "Apparently this is the choice hangout for off-duty fishermen, and some of them rent their boats out. But he'd struck out with the others. Felt kind of bad for turning him down." She pushed up her sleeves and took a sip of her beer, revealing a yin and yang–style tattoo of two koi fish on the inside of her forearm. When she noticed Alex admiring it, she added, "My partner has a tattoo of koi, too."

"It's beautiful," Alex told her.

"The guy that wanted to rent my boat had some ink, too," she said absently. "A pair of cards. An ace and a king: 21 in blackjack." Sasha went silent then.

Alex studied the sad lines of her face. "Do you think there's any chance they'll find your partner?"

Sasha pursed her lips. "I told him not to dive alone. I don't see how he could have survived out there if he had a diving accident. I think at this point, we're just looking for a body."

"That's awful. I'm so sorry. Were you partners for a long time?"

Sasha nodded. "Since grad school. And that was, gosh . . ." She lifted her head, gazing up at the ceiling. "Thirty-four years ago." She smiled shyly. "Anyway, sorry to unload on a total stranger! Feels good to talk to someone."

"No need to apologize. I can't imagine how hard it must be, to be up here alone, not knowing what's happened to him."

"Yes."

They ordered dessert, but in the end Sasha couldn't eat all of hers. She just picked at it, struggling with her appetite. She pushed the plate away. "I guess I'd better get back to my motel. See if there's any news tomorrow. Normally I'd sleep on my boat, but I just can't face it yet."

"I really hope you find your partner," Alex told her. "Maybe someone found him in distress and picked him up in their boat. He could be in a hospital right now, recovering, and just hasn't reached you yet."

"Maybe," Sasha said.

Alex pulled out her phone. "Why don't we exchange numbers? Call me anytime you want to grab a bite to eat or talk."

Sasha managed a smile. "Thanks. I'd like that."

They typed their numbers into each other's phones. After paying, they pulled on their coats and walked out together. Sasha climbed into a Ford Explorer and pulled out of the parking lot, giving Alex a wave as Alex walked back toward the Centre.

Alex didn't feel tired at all. She considered going back to the motel to read. Usually delving into the adventures of characters in exotic locations made her mind stop churning over the day's events, but she was too excited about the polar bear study. She looked at her watch. It was only ten-thirty. She could return to the lab and work a little longer.

This late at night, with the lab likely empty, she could use all of the equipment without having to wait or disturb anyone else's work. She'd always been something of a night owl—a blessing when she'd done bat and owl studies.

She let herself into the Centre and was almost to the lab door when she saw a beam of muted light flash inside the lab. The walls were glass, and she could see a dark figure inside, moving around, shielding a flashlight with his hand.

Had the lab blown a fuse? No. She could see the small LEDs glowing on the switched-off monitors. The power was definitely on.

Alex froze. Someone had broken into the lab.

SIX

Alex watched the person. He was shoving things into a backpack, going through papers. He leaned over a computer and pulled a flash drive from its CPU, then stuffed more items into his pack. He wore a thick, black parka with the hood up and a ski mask covered his face.

She stepped to the door. Suddenly he looked up, flashing the light in Alex's direction, momentarily blinding her. She threw her hand up in front of her face and was struck by the glass door as it flew open.

She stumbled backward, catching herself on a desk. The man bolted for the front door, the backpack slung over his shoulder.

Her breath caught as she realized he'd been at *her* workstation.

"Hey!" she shouted.

She flipped the light on in the lab, instantly seeing that her un-refrigerated samples had been taken.

"Stop!" she shouted, running after the man.

She reached him before he made it to the door and grabbed his pack, pulling him backward. He spun, striking out at her face with a meaty fist. She ducked under his swing, her Jeet Kune Do train-ing kicking in. He swung past her and she grabbed his arm, using his momentum to propel him farther in that direction. He went off-balance, crashing into a table. He turned, lashing out again. She dipped low, kicking out at one of his knees. He crumpled, sprawling on the floor.

"Someone call the police!" she yelled to the darkened Centre, not sure if anyone was even awake to hear her. But there must be someone still up, going over research, running simulations on their laptop.

The man struggled on the floor, managing to get to his feet. He squared off against Alex, gripping the strap of the backpack and swinging it at her. She deflected the blow with her arm and he took the momentary distraction to move past her again, heading for the door. She kicked her leg out, tripping him, sending him careening across the floor. He slid to a halt. Turning on his side as she approached, he kicked out. The blow landed painfully on her shin. She leapt back as he kicked again.

He scrambled to his feet, making it to the door. He threw it open and ran into the parking lot, then yanked on the driver's door to a black SUV.

She ran after him, almost slipping on the icy asphalt.

He started up his engine and peeled out of the parking lot. Alex raced to her Jeep and jumped in, taking off after him. He drove dangerously in front of her, taking the curves so fast she could feel her own car momentarily leaving the pavement as she went up on two wheels. No other cars were out on the road.

He rounded a corner, pulling way ahead of her, sliding precariously on the icy roads. She followed, but he was so far ahead, she couldn't get the plates or even the make of the car. If she drove much faster, she'd go off the road. Her Jeep hit a patch of ice and spun out, sending her careening to the side of the road. Her heart hammering, she turned into the spin, coming to a halt beside a small group of spruce trees. The SUV's taillights disappeared into the night.

She got her car back on the road and followed for a time, but she'd lost him. He must have turned off somewhere. She flipped around, going down a few side streets, searching, but came up empty.

Finally, reluctantly, she drove back to the Centre.

As she pulled into the parking lot, she saw that lights now

gleamed from the Centre's windows. She came through the front
door to find a few researchers up, milling about the toppled table.
"What happened?" one of them asked Dawn, the atmospheric scientist she'd talked to earlier.

"I have no idea," answered Dawn.

"It was a thief," Alex told them, crossing to the lab. "I caught
him in here, pocketing samples and messing with the computers."

She hurried to her workstation, finding that the computer had
been turned on. Her folder with the lab test results was deleted. The
hard drive and flash drive she'd kept next to the CPU were gone, as
were the hair and claw samples.

She moved to the lab refrigerator. Rooting through it, she found
that her blood and tissue samples had been taken.

But other researchers' samples were still there. One was studying bearded seals, and her samples still stood on the shelves, along
with another researcher's ringed-seal samples.

"I don't understand," she said, turning to Dawn, who stood in
the doorway. "He only took my samples. Why would someone want
polar bear blood?"

Dawn's brow furrowed. "This is too weird. I have no idea."

Alex shifted back to the computer, double-checking the contents. "He even erased my test results." She checked the computer's
recycle bin, finding it empty. He'd hard-deleted everything.

The sea ice extent researcher Alex had met earlier, Kyle, appeared in the doorway. "I've called the Mounties. What all did he
take?"

Alex stepped aside. "You two are more familiar with the lab's
contents. Let's make a list."

They woke up a few more researchers, who checked their hard
drives and samples. Only Alex's research had been taken.

Headlights flashed through the windows, and Alex stared out
to see an RCMP cruiser pull up. A young constable stepped out.
Alex opened the door as he approached. He looked to be in his

early twenties, tall, with a long black braid hanging down his back. As he approached, he was just finishing a phone conversation in a fascinating-sounding language she didn't recognize. She wondered if he was part of the Cree First Nation.

He held out his hand as he entered the Centre, giving her a warm smile. "Police Constable First Class Bighetty."

She shook his hand. "Alex Carter."

He took her statement and examined the lab, his kind manner reassuring. "There's not a lot of crime in Churchill, but we do occasionally have petty theft and drug charges," he told her. "We'll keep an eye out for the black SUV, but without a license plate, or even a make or model . . . this will be challenging."

"If it helps," she told him, "I don't think this was a simple theft. If they were looking for money, they could have stolen valuable lab equipment." She gestured to the stereoscopic microscope and the centrifuge. "Or raided the cash register in the cafeteria or gift shop. But they only took samples and deleted files."

PC Bighetty closed his little black notebook. "It's a mystery, for sure," he told her. "But we'll keep our eye out for the items you listed."

Alex didn't feel very hopeful. And even if she did get them back, she couldn't trust that the samples wouldn't be contaminated. She'd have to start over. She hoped she could at least recover her deleted test results.

After the constable left, she sat by herself in the lab, running a data recovery program to no avail. Discouragement took root inside her. The others had long since gone to bed. Feeling disgusted with the events of the evening, she finally drove back to her motel, her mind poring over who would want to sabotage her study.

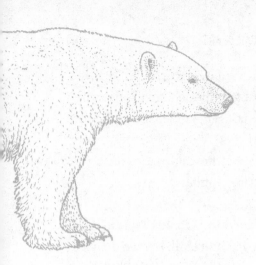

SEVEN

Alex stirred from her sleep, feeling low and discouraged. But as she rolled onto her side, she saw sunlight streaming in through the edges of the curtain. She glanced at the clock, seeing that the sun had been up for an hour. She sat up, still a bit hazy, then moved to the window. Pushing aside the curtains, she squinted at an absolutely dazzling day without a cloud in the sky. It had been light for at least an hour and a half. This was a perfect day for flying. Why hadn't Neil called her? He must be at the Centre with the helicopter, waiting for just this opportunity. She checked her phone. He hadn't texted.

She called him, and it rang through to voicemail.

Sitting back on the bed, she flipped open her laptop and checked the GFA. It was going to be clear for hours. She hurriedly showered and dressed, then drove to the Centre, half expecting to see the helicopter gone. But it still stood in front of the Centre, ready to go.

She headed through the main doors, hearing the usual buzz of activity around her. She cast around unsuccessfully for Neil, asking a few people in the lab if they'd seen him. Dawn walked by. "I'm surprised you're not out there today. It's brilliant."

"I know. Have you seen Neil or Ilsa?"

The researcher shook her head. "Haven't seen Ilsa since the last sunny day." She glanced around. "Or Neil."

Alex thanked her and moved to the cafeteria, where she ordered a cup of tea. She bought a granola bar and stuffed it in her pocket.

Then she sat down and called Neil again. No answer. She regretted that she'd left the planning details to him. She didn't have Ilsa's phone number. Moving off to a quiet table, she checked the forecast again, feeling the time slipping by, wasted.

Then the door swung open and Neil walked in on a swirl of frigid air, his face downcast.

He stomped his boots on the mat. Spotting her, he headed over, frowning. He plunked down in the chair opposite her and leaned forward, concerned. "I heard about the break-in last night. Are you okay?"

She lifted her eyebrows. "Yeah, it was pretty intense."

"And the guy got away with all our samples?"

"And the test results from my lab work."

"That's crazy!" He shrugged out of his coat.

"I know. The cops don't think we'll have much luck recovering anything."

"Damn." Neil shook his head. "Who the hell could it have been?"

"I have no idea. Someone really wanted that data."

He bit his lip. "Well, I've got some more bad news. We lost our pilot."

Alex's mouth fell open. "What?"

"I've been at the airport all morning, trying to find a replacement. Called all the charters. No one's available."

"What happened?"

He shrugged. "She just quit. Sent me a text last night."

"I thought we'd secured her for the duration of the field season. Did she give a reason?"

"She just said she got a better offer and had to take it."

"Unbelievable."

"It happens sometimes. Tour companies can pay more than we

can. And oil and natural gas extraction companies will pay pilots to take them out to remote places to scout."

"She was good," Alex said, lamenting. "Can't believe she just quit like that." She gestured at the windows. "And we're losing an amazing day."

He leaned back in his chair, exhaling. "I know. I'll keep calling around. Guy out at Arctic Tours told me he might have a lead."

The researcher with long blond hair that Neil had tried to talk to the other day walked by their table to get food. Neil watched her. "Guess we'll have to spend the day here." Alex followed his gaze, noticing the intrigued expression on his face. "I'm going to get some coffee." He got in line conveniently behind the woman, and Alex leaned back in her chair, crossing her arms as she gazed out at the perfect weather.

What a day to waste! She opened her laptop and checked over the spreadsheet. She looked at the data that had streamed in from researchers in other polar bear population areas, like Greenland and Svalbard, so far this season.

Alex felt deflated. Their first days out had been so successful, and she'd hoped they'd have many more like them.

At the cafeteria counter, Neil struggled to ingratiate himself with the blond-haired researcher. She gave him a polite hello. Alex couldn't help overhearing him as he talked about his background, his current research, and then how he'd gotten a great deal on the jacket he was wearing. The woman just nodded politely, a gesture she'd seen on so many women's faces over the years. Once again, he didn't ask about her own interests or research at all, just continued to drone on about himself and his accomplishments. Classic mistake. She'd seen too many men do this—thinking that they could impress a woman by bloviating on, without realizing that the way to go would be treating her as an actual person and inquiring about her interests as well. Too often women were expected to be polite and congenial, even when they were being talked at by a one-sided conversationalist. She felt the woman's pain. *Smile and nod. Smile and nod. Hope you can extract yourself from the "conversation."* She herself had done it far too many times in her life and had been trying to break herself of it.

Neil continued to talk at the woman, following her over to a table. The researcher glanced around, probably for someone else she knew, but didn't spot anyone. She sat down and Neil hovered, still talking. Had the woman said anything at all beyond hello? Neil shifted nervously from foot to foot, still chattering away. A weary expression chiseled away at the fading smile on the woman's face. She ate a few bites of her salad, then gestured toward the bunkrooms. "I have a Skype call coming in in a few minutes. I better finish eating in there," Alex heard her say.

"Well, I'll catch you around," Neil told her.

The woman scooped up her salad and walked away, giving a slightly nervous glance over her shoulder to see if Neil was following. He wasn't. He was still standing at her now-empty table, his head bent.

Then he spun on his heel, facing Alex. "Well, I'm going to go make some calls. See if I can scare up a pilot."

"Okay. Thanks. Let me know."

"I will."

He disappeared into the communal reading room and Alex finished her tea. She had the day to herself. She hadn't investigated Churchill yet, so she decided to spend her time exploring.

She returned to her Jeep and drove through the center of town. She stopped first at the Churchill Town Centre Complex. With heated interior walkways, the Complex offered everything for the mind and body during the long winters. It housed a library, a health center, a hockey arena, a gymnasium, and more. Alex marveled at the incredible Inuit wall hangings and art in the hallways. She found a pamphlet on the town's sights and read through it.

She knew she wanted to see the Polar Bear Holding Facility

and Cape Merry, the spit of land that extended out into Hudson Bay to the northwest of town. An old plane crash also intrigued her. Dubbed the *Miss Piggy* Wreck, it was a Curtiss C-46 "Commando" cargo plane that had crash-landed in 1979.

She returned to her Jeep and first checked out Aurora Domes to the south of town, a travel destination that offered glass domes where you could sit and watch the aurora borealis in heated comfort. It sounded amazing.

Next she headed down Kelsey Boulevard, passing an area of large lakes to the north. She stopped to look at the live polar bear traps set out for display at the Manitoba Polar Bear Alert. The system worked to keep humans safe from bears and bears safe from humans by staving off bear-human conflicts. Manitoba Conservation kept track of the bear situation in town. A department of the Manitoba government, Manitoba Conservation oversaw a number of biodiversity aspects of the province, including forestry, endangered species, environmental stewardship, and more. If bears approached town, conservation officers drove them off.

She continued on through town, taking the little turnaround on Button Street, and pulled up in front of the Polar Bear Holding Facility. A unique building comprised of three large connected domes, it had been painted to look like a sleeping polar bear. In the front waited a huge red and white tubular bear trap for catching bears.

During the fall, when the ice formed again on Hudson Bay, polar bears congregated in Churchill to await the freeze. If conservation officers were unable to drive off a bear that had wandered into town, the bears were tranquilized and held here at the Polar Bear Holding Facility. Five air-conditioned cells held bears until the ice returned to Hudson Bay, when they were released. They even had a heated holding cell for orphaned bear cubs.

With ice forming later each year due to global warming, more bears congregated close to town for longer, extending the time when potential bear-human conflicts could occur.

Wanting to next check out the *Miss Piggy* crash, Alex headed back toward Amundsen Road. She spotted a huge mansion on her left, ridiculously gigantic compared to the other houses in the area. Its size made her marvel. It was built in a faux Georgian style, obviously quite new, and she guessed it must have been at least nine thousand square feet. A four-car garage nestled against one side of it, and no lights were on. Undisturbed snow in the long driveway told her that no one had been home in quite a while. She wondered if it was a rich tourist's vacation home that they visited only once every few years.

Alex continued north, making a left off Amundsen to reach the *Miss Piggy* Wreck.

Unrelated to the Muppet of the same name, the C-46 was dubbed *Miss Piggy* in the 1940s because of the large loads it transported throughout the north. One November day in 1979, the C-46 had just departed the Churchill airport when engine oil problems prompted the crew to return to town. But it couldn't maintain its altitude and made a rough impromptu landing on rocky terrain just short of the airport. To this day, Alex had read, the craft sat on the edge of a cliff and was visited by tourists to Churchill.

Alex parked in the small circular drive at the end of the road and climbed out of the Jeep. She could see the gray lapping waters of the bay to the north, and beyond it a stretch of ice. Only one other car occupied the parking area, a beat-up truck covered with a beige tarp.

She left her Jeep, not seeing the owner of the truck or anyone else at the site. Small clusters of spruce grew around the plane, interspersed with massive gray boulders covered in a dusting of snow. She weaved between the boulders until she got close to the plane.

She took in its silver gleaming sides with its faint circular white logo on the tail. On the far side, she could still make out the white lettering LAMBAIR CARGO above a faded red stripe. Decades of graffiti covered it. Someone had painted black teeth along the nose cone.

Another artist had decorated the tail section with skeletal hands holding a cluster of pink and white flowers.

She peeked inside one of the broken windows, finding a long, empty silver fuselage. Graffiti artists had been at work inside the plane, too, red lettering sprayed on the floor. The wind whistled through the openings and mist curled around the wreckage.

Alex pulled her head out of the window. She was just rounding the side of the plane when she heard a man's angry voice.

"We had a deal," he hissed. "Where are you? I can't just haul this stuff around town."

Alex stopped where she was, out of sight, listening.

"We already agreed on a price." She dared a look around the edge of the plane's nose cone. A few dozen feet away, a man stood near a cluster of trees, talking angrily into a black satellite phone. He jabbed his finger at the air. "We agreed on fifteen thousand dollars each. You can't back out now. I've come to town with them."

She took in his features. His skin was so leathery and sun damaged she couldn't decide how old he was. He could have been in his forties or seventies. His greasy brown hair was plastered to a sunburned scalp, and she could see bits of pink skin peeking through where he was going bald. He wore what she guessed was a sealskin coat, which hung down to his knees. On his legs he wore matching sealskin pants that were so worn the fur had rubbed off the knees. Sealskin boots completed his rugged outfit.

"Where are you? Because I'm coming to see you, that's why. Don't you dare hang up on me!" he roared. He jabbed a finger at the air again and then held the phone out at arm's length, staring as if it had offended him. "Goddamnit!" he cursed. He was trying to keep his voice down, but sounds carried so easily outdoors and he was so angry that Alex had heard every word. For a second, she thought he was going to fling the sat phone into the trees, but he decided against that and stormed back toward the parking area.

Alex had a bad feeling about him. What was he trying to sell?

He was almost to his beat-up white pickup truck when the sat phone rang. He stabbed an angry finger to answer it.

He listened intently for a moment, then his voice went a little quieter. "Thought you'd see reason. What's your offer?"

Whatever he was trying to sell, he'd come into town with it. Alex stared around the side of the plane, staying out of sight. The man had his back to the wreck, gesticulating angrily again. The wind kicked up and she could catch only snatches of conversation now, but she thought she heard the word *pelts*.

She hurried to the edge of the trees and passed in between the trunks. Moving swiftly forward, she angled her way back toward the parking area. She spotted his truck and paused, taking stock of where the man stood. He was still closer to the wreck, arguing.

A beige canvas tarp had been tied down over the bed of his truck. She spotted the tarp company's logo, TOUGH TARP, above a black design of a bear paw trying unsuccessfully to rake through the material. Alex ran to the far side of the vehicle and crept along to the back. She dared a look at the man again. He was turned away, so furious he was spitting into the phone. She quickly picked up one corner of the tarp and peered inside. She spotted two hunting rifles, a cooler, boxes of ammo. There was something else closer to the cab of the truck that lay in darkness. She lowered the corner of the tarp and glanced back at the man. He was still arguing, not seeing her by the truck.

She crept toward the cab and lifted the corner of the tarp on that side. White fluff met her eyes. She reached inside to feel it. Fur met her bare hand. Polar bear fur. She lifted the tarp a little higher, and enough light spilled in to reveal two full polar bear pelts.

It was illegal for anyone to hunt polar bears in Manitoba.

He was obviously a poacher, trying to unload his illegal kills.

EIGHT

She got into her car and pulled out her phone. No service.

The man hung up and stormed toward his truck. Alex quickly pulled her copy of *The Arctic Field Guide* out of the back seat of the car, pretending she was just another tourist with no interest in the man. Then she thought better of it and grabbed the town map that came with her rental car, opening it over the steering wheel and poring over it intently. She heard him slam his truck door and fire up his engine. He roared out of the parking area, sending up a rain of little rocks at her Jeep. When he'd gone a few hundred yards, she swung out after him, following at a distance. If she could learn who he was planning to sell to, she could report him when she got to an area with cell service.

He pulled out onto Amundsen Road, and she followed, keeping back. Other cars were out and about, so she felt like she was blending in.

The man drove fast, furiously swerving to pass other, slower cars. Alex was reluctant to do the same, but she didn't want to lose him. She sped up. A slow car in front of her turned off, and she drew closer to the poacher's vehicle. For a moment, she thought he might cut through town. She'd get a signal then. But he didn't. He took outer roads, skirting around the main area of Churchill. Then he took a road headed west and turned off on another road. She could see the expanse of the Churchill River before them as he pulled into the port.

A few small fishing vessels were tied to slips, and a huge, expensive-looking sailing yacht called the *Great White* had its own dock with a locked gate blocking public access. She wondered if it belonged to the same person who owned the gigantic mansion out on Amundsen Road. Nearby, the Port of Churchill building towered on the river shore, a gigantic white square with a taller section in the middle.

Enraged, the man swerved into a parking space. A few other cars were out in the lot, and Alex parked a short distance away. She checked her phone. Still no signal. But maybe the boatyard had a pay phone.

She drove through the lot, searching, but didn't see one.

The man climbed out of his truck and untied one corner of the tarp. He retrieved two huge beat-up duffel bags from the cab. Then he leaned over the edge of the truck, infuriated, stuffing things into the bags. Alex saw a glimpse of white fur go in. He grabbed his two rifles, slammed the truck door, and then beelined for a boat docked in one of the slips. It was an older boat called the *Fortune and Glory,* with peeling paint and a few messy patch-repair jobs. In the back she spotted a snowmobile and a makeshift wooden ramp that he could use to unload the machine onto the ice.

He stormed down into the cabin of the boat, struggling under the weight of the two duffel bags, then emerged a few minutes later without them. He cast off the lines, started up the engine, and roared away onto the river, angling toward the narrow strip of ice-free water on the edges of Hudson Bay.

Alex drove her Jeep next to the man's truck and peered inside. He'd unloaded everything from the back, including the pelts. She wrote down his license plate and the name of the boat as it motored away out of sight.

She heard a door shut behind her and watched a port employee walking out to his car.

She hurried to him. "Do you have a phone?"

"It's not for public use," he said, watching her with a slight frown.

"This is important. I want to report a poacher."

The man raised his eyebrows. "Old Sam?" he asked, gesturing in the direction the boat had gone.

"You know him?"

"Everyone knows him."

"And he's a poacher?"

"Not so as anyone's been able to prove."

"But he had two polar bear pelts."

The man shrugged. "Okay. But if he did have pelts, he'd sooner dump them than get caught."

The man ushered Alex inside to a small room that smelled of cigarette smoke. He looked up the number for Manitoba Conservation for her. The person who answered took her report efficiently and quickly. Alex gave her the man's boat name and license plate and described what she'd seen.

Alex could hear her typing in the information. "What can be done?" Alex asked.

"We're aware of him," the woman answered.

"He's been investigated?"

"I'm not at liberty to say. But we'll look into it."

Alex thanked her and hung up, feeling let down. That was it? He could have killed two of the Hudson Bay population.

The man could see her disappointment. "They'll look into it," he assured her. "They take poaching very seriously."

"Okay," she said. "Thanks for letting me use your phone."

He nodded and came out from behind the counter. He walked her out, then locked up his office again. He was knocking off for the day.

She returned to her Jeep, feeling sad. She hated just passing information along and hoping agencies did the right thing. Many times they were overworked and understaffed and things fell through the cracks.

Other times, she'd passed along information about the population decline of a species only to have it ignored by the government. In the western United States, she'd experienced this with the information she'd reported on the wolverine and the American pika. Images of her time in Montana flashed through her mind, long stretches of wolverine tracks, and pikas bounding from boulder to boulder.

She loved little pikas and smiled at the thought of them. Cold-loving relatives of the rabbit, pikas lived in alpine terrain and had to move farther and farther upslope as the earth warmed. They couldn't disperse to other mountains because they couldn't survive the hot journey from one range to another. Soon there was nowhere higher to go, and populations had died off. And so their overall population was declining. The U.S. Fish and Wildlife Service had been presented with this evidence many times by her and other researchers, and each time the agency didn't extend protections to the species. Because pika populations in the Rockies were faring a little better than their comrades in other ranges, some government officials decided it was okay to let them die out in the Sierra Nevada and throughout the Great Basin.

She hoped Manitoba Conservation would pursue the poacher information. It sounded like they'd already checked on this guy more than once. Maybe this time it would stick.

She sat in her car for a moment, staring out at the river, her mind going to the bears out there right now, vulnerable on the ice. She felt disenchanted and decided not to go back to town just yet. She'd wanted to check out Cape Merry anyway.

Reluctantly, she started up her Jeep and continued on her outing, taking Cape Merry Road to where it dead-ended. There she pulled into an empty parking lot. The gray and white landscape around her was dusted with fresh snow. Large, smooth gray rocks dotted the distance between the parking area and the bay.

She parked next to a small brown Parks Canada building. The Canadian flag flapped in the wind above it. A picnic table stood beneath a lone spruce tree. She climbed out, huddling down into her coat to brace against the wind.

A boardwalk led out to binoculars mounted on a stand. She hurried along the wooden planks, her eyes tearing in the wind. Beyond, gray waves tossed on the bay, mist obscuring the far distance. She listened to the roar of the gale and the lapping waves. It was peaceful out here.

As she stared out, three cars pulled up, a big group of people evidently traveling together. They all had similar features, and Alex guessed they were an extended family. They talked loudly and excitedly, calling to one another. The kids horsed around the boardwalk's railings, climbing and shouting. They all crammed onto the walkway.

Alex decided she'd have to find another place for a little solace, so she returned to the warmth of the Jeep. She'd spotted some nice quiet pull-outs along Cape Merry Road before it dead-ended, and she headed there.

No one else was on the road when she reached the first pull-out. She angled to the side of the road and got out, stretching and breathing in the quiet atmosphere.

The white expanse of snow-covered terrain stretched out before her. Dense willows grew along a line before giving way to a rocky landscape. Wind buffeted her parka hood and fog had descended, bringing with it snow. It dusted the delicate willow branches and covered the rocks. She walked farther, enjoying the solitude, breathing in lungfuls of fresh, cold air.

The snow created a pristine blanket on everything and the flakes tinkled musically on her parka hood. The gray boulders now all looked white. As she gazed out at the line of dense willows, she jumped with surprise when one of the rocks moved. It stood and shook itself off—a polar bear, taking a nap in the lee side of the willows. She pulled out her binoculars and watched with fascination as it stretched. While all polar bears had guard hairs, coarse hair that protected their softer underfur, only the males grew excessively long guard hairs on their forelegs. This was definitely a male. But he wasn't a healthy one. Ribs stuck out from his sides and he looked dangerously malnourished. Obviously he hadn't found much success hunting seals this season.

She could see the tiny white disk on his ear that showed he'd been captured in the past, but she was way too far away to determine the ID number. He moved slowly and painfully, obviously starving. The number of scars on his muzzle let her know he was likely elderly. Male bears fought fiercely for the right to mate, biting and scratching one another's faces. This bear had so many scars that he had likely been a formidable force in his heyday.

As he passed another large clump of willows, he suddenly turned and started sniffing the ground with interest. He followed a scent to the base of the plants and began rooting around with massive paws like shovels. Pulling up dirt and roots, he dug eagerly. She adjusted the focus, trying to hold the binoculars steady against the buffeting wind.

The thin bear tore something long and gray from the ground. He ripped at it, shredding it in half, then turned and walked away with a piece of it hanging from his jaws. For a moment she thought it might be a seal, dangling limply from the bear's muzzle. But as she tracked the movement, she froze.

It was no seal. It was a human leg, encased in a torn dry suit.

NINE

The bear moved off, and when it became a dot in the distance, Alex cautiously approached where it had exhumed the leg.

She swallowed hard, horrified by what lay before her. It was a man in his late fifties or early sixties, wearing a dry suit. The bear had unearthed the head and part of the chest, then dug up the legs.

Any thought she'd had that the bear might have killed him evaporated when she saw the two bullet holes—one in the man's bruised and battered head, and one in his chest. Years of watching crime films made the phrase *execution-style* leap into her head. Looked like he'd been beaten beforehand, too, so severely that his face would be unrecognizable. She stared down at him, wondering how he'd come to be buried in this shallow grave in such a lonely place. Not wanting to contaminate the scene, she backed away slightly, also wondering if the RCMP would be able to find boot prints from whoever had buried him here.

She scanned the horizon for the bear. He had been so malnourished that he might come back to eat more of the body. She pulled her GPS unit out of her pocket and took a quick recording of the location. Then she hurried back to her Jeep and grabbed her phone. No signal. She climbed in and started back down the road, grateful for the warmth pumped out by the heater.

Periodically she checked for bars, and when she got closer to

Churchill, one popped up. She pulled over and dialed 911. The operator didn't disguise her shock when Alex reported a homicide victim. Alex read off the coordinates to her.

"Stay where you are," the dispatcher told her. "I'm sending police to your location. They may need you to find the site again, and they'll want a statement."

"Of course." Alex gave the operator her name and then switched off the motor, settling in to wait for the police. She stared out as the fog swirled around the car, visibility down to just twenty feet or so. Snow dusted the windshield.

Just as Alex's car began to grow cold again, she saw an RCMP car on the road up ahead. The cruiser pulled up next to her and she recognized PC Bighetty, who'd helped her after the lab break-in.

"Dr. Carter? Are you okay?"

"For the most part."

"You say you found a body?"

"That's right. He was shot. Twice." She shivered, feeling colder than she thought she should with all the layers she wore.

He glanced at a laptop mounted on his dash. "I've got the coordinates here, but if you wouldn't mind riding with me to the site, I'd appreciate it. Then you can give me your statement."

"Of course." She climbed out of her Jeep.

He stepped out of the cruiser and opened the back door for her, and she couldn't shake the feeling that he was treating her cautiously. Once again she flashed back to crime films she'd watched over the years. Didn't they say that the person who reported a crime was often the one who had committed it?

But he was pleasant enough as he shut the door and climbed back in the driver's seat.

And she guessed polar bear biologists didn't routinely go around shooting people execution-style.

She directed him to where she'd parked and pointed toward the location of the body. From this distance, with such dense fog, the area wasn't obvious, so he put the coordinates into his phone and stepped out.

"I'll be right back," he said amiably, and set off, wending his way through the rocks and willows. He went a little too far to the left, and she watched him scan the area, then fix suddenly on the location of the body. He approached, grimacing. He talked into the radio on his shoulder, then leaned over the body, examining it visually, never touching it. He talked more into the radio, then backed away from the scene using the same route he'd taken to it.

When he got back to the car, he looked a little sick. Alex wondered if it was his first murder victim.

"You were right. Shot at least twice." He turned to face her. "What brought you out here?"

"My team couldn't go out on the ice today because our pilot quit, so I just decided to explore Churchill and the surrounding areas. I came up here to get out of town and walk for a while."

"There are some polar bear tracks up there."

She told him about the bear, and how it had discovered the body. She pointed in the direction the bear had headed. "That's where the leg went."

He swallowed and said simply, "I see." Pulling out a small notebook, he took down a more detailed statement. "As soon as another constable comes up here to secure the scene, I can get you back to your car."

Alex thought back on Sasha and their conversation at Moe's. She leaned forward in the seat. "I don't know if it's related, but I met a marine archaeologist the other night at Moe's. She mentioned that her partner had disappeared while out on a dive. She reported it to you guys, so you probably already know. I wonder if it might be him."

"Okay. We'll look into it. Thank you."

She waited in the back seat while radio chatter streamed into the cruiser. Seemed like the whole force was weighing in, organizing units and relaying updates. Another RCMP cruiser pulled up, and PC Bighetty got out to speak to the other cop. She was just as young as Bighetty, her brown hair cut short, her freckled pink face an expression of surprise at the homicide call. She nodded to Bighetty and he climbed back into his own cruiser.

"I'll take you back to your car now."

"Thank you."

"We'll need you to come down to the station to make a formal statement when you can."

"Of course."

They rode back down the road in silence. He pulled up next to her Jeep and climbed out, then opened the door for her. Alex felt numb and a little shaky, and she nodded at him as she moved to her car. As soon as she climbed in, he was back in his cruiser heading toward the crime scene.

Alex shivered and turned up the heat full blast. Slowly she made her way back to Churchill, her hands trembling on the steering wheel. It wasn't the first time she'd seen a dead body, not even the first time she'd seen a gunshot victim, but the image of the man's face was seared in her memory. Who had he been?

When she reached town and got a signal again, she lifted her phone, staring at Sasha's name in her contacts. Should she call her? Finally she decided she would. Sasha answered on the second ring.

"Hello?"

"Sasha, it's Alex Carter."

"Hey! I was thinking of going down to Moe's again tonight. You going?"

"Are you at your motel right now?"

"Yes. I'm still waiting for the RCMP to release Rex's boat. So I'm here for now."

Alex paused, struggling for words.

"Is everything okay? You sound stressed."

"Can I swing by in a minute?"

"Sure." Sasha sounded worried. "It's the Polaris Motel, room nine."

"Okay. I'm on my way."

At the motel, Alex parked next to Sasha's car. Her room door opened as Alex switched off the engine. Worry creased her new friend's face. "What is it?" she asked before Alex had even shut her Jeep's door.

"Let's go inside."

In the room, Sasha perched on the end of the bed after offering Alex the lone chair.

"Sasha," Alex started, then stumbled. It might not be Rex. But her gut told her it was.

"Yes?" Sasha pressed.

"I'm not sure how to tell you this. I . . . just found a body out by Cape Merry. It was a man about your age, dressed in a dry suit. The RCMP are out there now."

Sasha stood up rigidly. "And they think it's Rex?"

Alex craned her neck to look up. "It might be. No one knows yet. But I thought you might like to go down to the station."

Sasha's eyes glazed over. "Yes," she said distantly. "Yes."

"Do you want me to drive you?"

For a long moment Sasha just stood there, immobile, lost in shock. "I . . . I can drive there. Who knows how long I'll be there."

"I can go with you."

Again Sasha took a long time to answer. Absently she walked to the dresser and took her keys, then just held them, frozen. "No . . . I can go. I think . . ." Alex stood up and gently touched her friend's arm. The contact brought Sasha to life. "Maybe it's not him. I should ask to identify the body. I'll bet it's not him. I mean, why would he still be in a dive suit if he was on land?"

Alex decided to let the police mention the gunshot wounds. If it did turn out to be Rex, hopefully they had a counselor or someone there who could handle the situation better than Alex could.

Sasha walked glass-eyed to the door, and Alex spotted the

woman's coat hanging in the closet. She grabbed it for her and caught up. Sasha moved to her car like an automaton, not bothering to close the room door. Alex made sure it was locked and stopped Sasha before she climbed into the driver's seat.

"Here," she said, helping Sasha don her coat. "Let me drive."

They were only about half a mile from the police station. Alex knew it would be cold walking back to her own car, but this way Sasha would get there safely.

"Okay," Sasha said, distractedly handing Alex the keys.

They drove the distance in silence. Alex reached over and squeezed Sasha's hand in support. At the station, Alex walked her inside. "Call me if you need anything," Alex told her. A constable took Sasha into a back room and Alex left.

The walk back to Sasha's motel helped Alex clear her head. Snow swirled around her face, catching in her eyelashes. She felt so sorry for her new friend. Maybe it wouldn't be Rex. But that just meant some other person would be grieving. Alex shivered inside her parka.

Returning to her car, she started up the engine, letting the warm air of the heater wash over her. She considered just eating a small dinner in her motel room, but as she drove through the streets of Churchill, she decided having some lively people around her might dispel the gloom that had settled over her. She wondered if that poacher was out there even now, readying to take another bear. And the murdered man—just then the police were probably photographing the scene, preparing to remove him to the morgue.

She drove across town and pulled into Moe's parking lot, finding only one space left. As she stepped out, the smell of french fries wafted on the air.

Inside the place was jumping. Every table was filled, so she sat again at the bar.

The bartender, Dave, greeted her warmly. "Hello again! What can I get you?"

This time Alex ordered a chocolate stout and sat sipping it while she looked around. Neil sat at a corner table with a handful of researchers she recognized from the Centre. They were shooting a game of pool. When he saw the grim expression on her face, he walked over.

"Is everything okay?"

She sipped her stout. "I saw a polar bear just outside of town. On Cape Merry. It was starving."

His brow creased. "What did you do?"

"It's even worse than that. He was rooting around in the willows and he dug up a body."

"What? Like a human body?"

"Yeah. He tore off the leg and made off with it."

"You're kidding me."

"No. The Mounties are out there now."

"Who was it?"

She took another sip of her beer. "I have no idea."

"And the bear?"

"He dragged the leg off. He was long gone before the police arrived."

Neil rocked back on his heels. "Whoa."

"The body was in a dry suit."

Neil raised his eyebrows. "Like, he drowned diving and washed ashore?"

"No. He'd been shot and buried."

"Jesus. Sounds like you've had an intense day."

"Definitely. And that's not all. I overheard a poacher trying to sell polar bear pelts. Followed him out to the boatyard, where he took off. So we should be careful out there. He might return to the ice and try to kill more."

Neil rubbed his head. "Damn. You know, when most people take the day off, they go see a movie or have drinks with friends."

She managed a small smile.

"Yo! Neil!" one of his friends called. He was a burly man wearing a Winnipeg Jets hockey jersey. She didn't recognize him and thought he might be one of the locals. "It's your turn."

Neil hooked a thumb in that direction. "Better get back. Let's hope we find a new pilot and don't run across that poacher."

"Definitely. Have a good game." She swiveled back around to the bar and drank more of her stout. Dave came by and took her order for a simple grilled cheese sandwich.

It arrived, but as she chewed it, it turned to dust in her mouth. The clamoring voices around her, which she thought might pull her out of her gloom, only made her feel more alone. She wondered how Sasha was faring. She finished the sandwich, paid her bill, and headed back to the motel, giving Neil a wave as she left.

Back at the room, she called Zoe.

"This a good time?" she asked when her friend picked up.

"Perfect. I'm waiting for my makeup artist Marigold to come pick me up. How are things going there?"

"Remember when you told me not to get my face eaten off?"

"Don't tell me . . . a bear ate your face off?"

"No, but there's been other trouble."

"A bear tore someone else's face off?"

"No, it tore his leg off."

"What?"

"I was out by the shore and spotted a bear, not too far away from town. It had dug up a murder victim."

"Are you kidding me?"

"No, it tore off the guy's leg and carried it away."

"Jesus, Alex."

She told Zoe about the poacher. Hearing her old friend's voice was comforting. "It just feels so insurmountable sometimes, you know?"

Zoe remained silent, listening.

"Here we are, trying to save this iconic species, and other people just want to kill it to make a quick buck. I don't get people, Zoe."

"I don't, either. But there are more and more people like you, Alex, who care and are helping, like you did with the wolverines."

Alex smiled. "Thanks, Zoe."

Her friend was silent for a few moments. Then she shifted gears. "Hey, speaking of wolverines, I remember you saying that they were so solitary, there was no group name for them, so you decided to call them 'a solitude of wolverines.' What's the group name for polar bears?"

Alex laughed and could tell her friend was trying to lift her spirits. "Well, like wolverines, they're pretty solitary, too, unless it's a mother with her cubs. There's a group name for bears in general, but not specifically for polar bears."

"So what are you going to call this group of bears you're studying?"

Alex smiled, thinking of the snowfall and fog, the whiteout conditions. "How about 'a blizzard of polar bears'?"

"I like it!"

"So how are things there?" Alex asked her.

"Right now I'm gazing out of my hotel window at another rainstorm."

"So not a lot of filming's been done."

"Hardly any. I've just been sitting around. But I might go out later for fun. There's this little jazz club. They have a band that plays there. The pianist is quite talented."

Alex saw right through her friend, who'd never mentioned being into jazz in the past. "The pianist, huh?"

"He's just slightly cute. We may have shared a glass of wine or two last night."

"Think you might have a North Carolina fling?"

"It does sound rather nice, doesn't it? Strolling through meadows with fireflies. Cozying up during a thunderstorm. Taking in the waterfalls and mountains. It's actually really gorgeous here. I can sort of see why you're into stuff like that. This is where they filmed *The Last of the Mohicans,* you know. The '92 Michael Mann version."

"Sounds divine."

"Especially if you have a cute pianist to experience it all with."

Alex chuckled. Zoe changed whom she dated as often as Alex changed her toothbrush. She had been dating someone named Rob until recently, but that had ended when he insisted she run a 10K with him and she had to admit that she hated running, and always had.

"How is the filming going?"

Zoe sighed. "It's ridiculous, Alex. So it's been pouring rain constantly, right? And we have this big rainstorm scene coming up. So how about this for Hollywood efficiency—we've been waiting for the rain to stop so we can break out the rain machines and shoot the rain scene."

Alex cracked up.

"Everything's wet and muddy. But they rented those rain machines, and by god, we're going to use them. And don't even get me started on the cow-in-a-box."

"Excuse me?"

"The cow-in-a-box. So there's this scene where some jerky British soldiers kill this farmer's cow, his only source of income. Of course they can't shoot a real cow, so they arranged to have this puppet cow."

"A puppet cow."

"Exactly. So the SFX crew orders this thing. We're all ready to shoot during a rare break in the rain. They bust this thing out of its packing box and, Alex . . . it looks like a deranged llama."

"What?"

"Yeah. A deranged llama that had way too much to drink the night before. The neck is just . . . way too long. And its eyes, Alex, one's all droopy and the other one is narrowed like it's giving you the stink eye. I mean, this thing is freaky."

"What did you do?"

"Well, the director starts barking questions to the assistant director and producer. 'Can we write a llama into this thing? Did they even have llamas in colonial America?' and so on. Then to the DP, 'Can we shoot it from the back with its head lowered and out of sight?' 'We'll see what we can do,' they tell him. So we start shooting anyway. Halfway through the scene, the deranged cow-llama's head falls off."

Alex couldn't stop laughing.

"'Fix it in post!' the director shouts, causing groans from the VFX crew, who are supervising the shot. They try to stick the cow-llama's head back on, and it starts pouring rain again. Now it's a soggy cow-llama that's looking more and more possessed with its askew head and those creepy eyes. You just know that thing's going to come to life at night and haunt the set."

Alex wiped a tear from her eye. "You have such a challenging job!"

"Tell me about it. And a gross job. I have this kissing scene tomorrow with Nick Buchanan. You remember, Mr. Prima Donna Actor?"

"That bad?"

"He's notorious for never brushing his teeth. I'm going to have to slip some mints into these special watercress sandwiches he's now demanding." Zoe sighed. "You have no idea the stress this job involves."

Alex chuckled. "I'm sorry I can't be there for you to help you through this hard time."

"Yeah, as usual, my best friend has chosen smelly old bears over me."

"Well, just try to survive."

Alex heard a knock on Zoe's door. "Just a sec. Oh, it's Marigold. We're going over to that little jazz club together."

"Have fun! And call me later if you want to fill me in on any developments involving cute pianists."

"Thanks, Alex. You be careful up there."

"I will."

Tired, Alex put on her pj's and crawled into bed. But the warmth from talking to Zoe slowly leached out of her. She shivered, her mind flashing on the gruesome sight in the willows, wondering who had killed the man.

TEN

Alex awoke to her phone buzzing. She hadn't slept well. Each time she dozed off, she startled awake, the image shuddering through her of the severed leg encased in the dry suit. Before she could grab her phone, it stopped buzzing. A text.

She closed her eyes again, dispelling the image of the leg. Then she reached for the phone on the bedside table. Neil.

Got a new pilot. He can get here at 10 a.m. Meet then at the Centre?

She looked at the time, 7:16 A.M., and felt some relief wash over her. She could still catch a couple more hours of sleep.

She texted back, *OK,* then rolled over on her side.

Closing her eyes, she drifted into a fitful sleep.

AT TEN, SHE WALKED INTO the Centre, finding Neil talking with a tall, lithe man who looked to be in his mid- to late thirties. His black hair was longish and styled, and his blue eyes peered out from a beige face with a slight growth of whiskers. Neil noticed her and waved her over.

"This is Dr. Carter," he told the man. To Alex, he said, "This is our new pilot, Casey MacCrae."

Casey extended his hand. He shook hers in a firm grip, warm and dry, web to web, the way she liked. "A pleasure to meet you," he said in a Scottish accent that surprised her.

"Thanks for stepping in on such short notice," she said, smiling.

"No trouble at all. I was just telling Neil that I came out here with the promise of a job with a touring company. I guess they weren't doing too well, because they just folded. And here I was without a job."

"Serendipity," Alex said.

"Just going to check on our gear," Neil said and stepped outside.

Casey gave a rueful smile. "I've already checked and double-checked the gear and weighed it. Guess he wants to be sure I put everything back." He smiled at Alex. "I appreciate this opportunity. And to make you feel better, I've flown for polar bear researchers before, in Greenland. So I know my way around the ice. I'm licensed and have firearm training, too, so I can be the shotgun bearer out there."

"We're glad to have you. We've only been grounded for two days, so we haven't lost a lot of time." Her mind flashed to yesterday afternoon at Cape Merry, and the image of the leg came back, dangling from the bear's mouth.

"Let's check the weather again," Casey suggested. They moved to the small library and Alex pulled out her laptop, connecting with the Centre's Wi-Fi. The weather looked like it would hold until at least midafternoon, giving them a few hours out on the ice.

Not wanting to waste another minute, Alex hurried to the gear room and donned her hat, balaclava, parka, Turtle Fur, and thick gloves. She pulled on her waterproof pants and winter boots. Two minutes later, she met Casey by the door and they walked out to the helicopter. Neil waited out there, staring down at his phone. He typed a hurried text message and then they piled into the chopper.

Casey started up the bird and soon they were airborne, passing out over the spit at Cape Merry.

They flew over a narrow stretch of open gray water, and soon the brilliant white expanse of ice filled her view below. She scanned with her binoculars, looking for tracks. They searched in a new area from the previous outings, giving special attention to seams in the ice that would attract seals.

Twenty-five minutes into their flight, Neil spotted tracks off the portside of the helicopter. Casey veered the bird to follow them. His motions were even smoother than Ilsa's had been, and Neil didn't look nearly as green as he had on their previous outings.

Soon a lone polar bear came into view. Alex was hit with a sense of awe for the animals. A cub could be raised out on a section of ice, and later in its life have cubs in the same area. Alex was astounded that, without landmarks like trees or mountains to orient itself, and with the wind and drift of the ice constantly keeping it on the move, a polar bear could still return to the same area. Biologists still weren't sure how polar bears managed to pull this off, but somehow they had the ability to move in a certain direction without fixed reference points. Perhaps they used the stars during the long winters. It was even possible they used the earth's geomagnetic field to navigate, just as whales and homing pigeons did.

The thundering of the rotors spooked the bear and it began to run. Alex studied it with her binoculars. From the thick neck, which was as wide as its broad head, she could tell that he was a male. He didn't have too many scars on his muzzle, which meant he was a younger bear.

Estimating his weight, she selected one of the preloaded tranquilizer darts and strapped into the harness. Casey swung the helicopter around so her side faced the sprinting bear.

She slid open the door, the blast of freezing cold stealing the air from her lungs. She leaned out, feeling the reassuring cinch of the harness, and aimed for the bear's rump. Casey held the helicopter steady, and she landed the dart on her first try.

"Got him," she said over the comm.

Casey took the helicopter up and away, giving the bear some room. They followed him at a distance as he slowed, the sedative taking effect. When the bear stopped and slouched down on his rear end, Casey gently touched down about fifty feet away.

The polar bear slumped completely down to the ice, and she and Neil quickly went to work while Casey kept watch with the shotgun.

The bear had been tagged before, three seasons ago. Alex was grateful it had been, too, because when she unpacked their equipment, she noticed that the tattoo clamp was missing, along with their supply of white ID ear disks. He didn't have a GPS collar because male bears' necks were so thick the collars just slipped right off their heads.

"Where's the rest of the stuff?" she asked.

Neil shrugged.

She rooted around in the kit, finding the handheld sedation syringe missing, too. If the bear started to wake up before they were finished, they wouldn't be able to inject any more. They'd have to take off, even if they weren't done yet.

"Is it in the helicopter?"

"I don't think so," Neil said. "I pulled everything out. I know I packed it all. I went over it twice last night, and again this morning."

"Maybe we forgot a bag back at the Centre."

"Maybe," Neil said noncommittally.

They took measurements and samples of the bear's claw, fur, blood, and fatty tissue, swabbed between the toes and in his mouth, and attached a Burr on Fur. Some of their swabs were missing. They had enough for only this one bear. They'd have to head back early today.

Searching for the missing equipment had taken them a little longer than expected, and the bear began to move his head, lifting his muzzle groggily. They gathered up their equipment as the bear moved his front paws, ready to drag himself up.

They hurried back to the helicopter, Casey starting up the motor and hovering as the bear fully regained consciousness and got to his feet. As he moved off away from them, Casey deftly resumed their journey.

"I may have some bad news," he told them over the comm. "I've been keeping my eye on the weather, and it's not looking good. A low-pressure system is moving in, and we may have to set down before we make it back to Churchill."

The arctic day was already dwindling, and a bank of clouds had moved in on the horizon. Weather changed quickly out here, and researchers always carried emergency gear, including tents, sleeping bags, and extra cold-weather clothing.

"If it's as bad as it looks, we may have to spend the night out on the ice."

ELEVEN

Neil groaned, and Alex looked back to the camping gear they'd stowed. It would be a cold night, but with their subzero-rated mummy bags, winter-rated tents with stormflies, and sleeping pads that would keep them elevated off the ice, they could make it through.

Already feeling cold, she zipped up her parka, pulling the hood on over her wool cap.

They flew in silence for the next twenty minutes, Casey checking the barometer. "Yep. Sorry. We're going to have to set down."

"You really think we'll have to spend the night?" Neil said, looking a little wide-eyed.

"Not sure. It's coming in fast and might leave just as quickly. We'll set down for a bit and see what happens. If we do, we've got plenty of gear. We'll be snug as a bug." Casey's voice, calm and reassuring over the comm, seemed to settle Neil down a bit, but the grad student still frowned, staring out the window.

"I was hoping to get a beer tonight," Neil complained. "There's this cute intern at the Centre, and she asked if some of us wanted to meet for drinks and darts . . ."

Alex was sure it couldn't have been the disinterested researcher with the blond hair. Obviously someone else had already caught his eye.

"I'm sure the lass will forgive you for being stuck due to weather," Casey told him.

"I guess," Neil grumbled, staring out at the approaching clouds.

Casey set down the helicopter, and they prepared to wait out the storm.

During grad school, when she and Sonia had spent the spring tagging polar bears in Svalbard, another grad student on their project never shut up. When they had to set down to wait out weather, he would talk and talk until Alex felt like she would wilt away inside her cold-weather gear and sink down into her boots. He'd had an uncanny ability to choose topics that held zero interest for other people and then go into extraordinary detail. *I had this cousin who built decks for a living,* she could remember him saying. *Some of them were sixteen feet long. Or were they fifteen? I think they might have been fifteen. No, wait, I remember now. They were seventeen feet long,* he'd go on, and before you knew it you were in for an hour's worth of detail about tenpenny nails, spacing between boards, and whether the wood had been *cedar—no, wait, it was oak. I'm pretty sure it was oak. No, now that I think about it, it definitely was cedar. Though it could have been redwood, I guess . . .*

But now it was the opposite. Everyone fell quiet. Neil gazed impatiently out the window. Casey looked over his instruments, continually checking the barometer. The low-pressure system hit them, bringing with it dense fog and flurries. Alex watched the snow fall, hoping for a "freebie" in the little she could see of the misty terrain, but no polar bears came ambling by the helicopter.

The cold set in. Without the distraction of flying and searching, she realized how cold it really was. She crossed her arms and bounced her legs up and down, hoping to spark up some heat.

Soon she couldn't see anything outside the helicopter. She picked up the spreadsheet and went through all the bears in the area that had been recorded in previous years. It was interesting to read about how the ice compared from earlier field seasons, how many seals had been spotted. Once she gathered more data, she'd be able to compare a previously tagged bear's body fat, stress hormone levels, and pollutant concentration with its current status.

Neil impatiently checked his watch.

Alex wondered what the police had told Sasha.

Casey took off his headset and turned around in his seat. He lifted a thermos. "You two want some coffee?"

"That sounds amazing," Alex said, leaning forward with her insulated cup. He poured in some of the steaming concoction, and the inviting smell filled the chopper.

"Neil?" he asked.

Neil waved him off. "No thanks. I can't drink it this late in the day. I get the jitters." He jiggled one leg, checking his watch again.

"Seems like you already have the jitters," Casey observed.

"Just . . . just wanted to get to Moe's tonight."

Casey turned back to Alex. "I've got a question for you, Dr. Carter."

She smiled. "You can call me Alex."

"Okay, Alex. I keep hearing about polar bear/grizzly bear hybrids. Aren't they two different species? How can they mate?"

She sipped the coffee and settled back in her seat. "They are. But they're able to interbreed because polar bears evolved from grizzlies. Researchers aren't quite sure when they branched off, but it was somewhere around seventy thousand to a million years ago. It's hard to say because polar bears live and die on the ice, so not many fossils have been found.

"During the last ice age, there was this really warm period starting about one hundred and twenty-seven thousand years ago called the Eemian interglacial, and it's possible polar bears split north to stay where it was cold, separating themselves even more from grizzlies.

"But even after they split off, they probably continued to mate with grizzlies occasionally over the millennia, allowing the two species to stay somewhat genetically similar. If they hadn't done this, by now the two species wouldn't be able to have offspring."

Casey sipped his coffee. "Pizzlies, right? Half polar bear, half grizzly?"

Neil laughed. "Or grolar bears."

"There's also the Siglit Inuvialuit term *nanulak*," Alex added. "It mixes together *nanuq* for polar bear and *aklaq* for grizzly."

Casey grinned. "Those are much better names. *Pizzly* isn't exactly majestic. Are the offspring fertile?"

Alex nodded. "They are. So the two species are still pretty close genetically."

Casey turned more in his seat to face them. "How do they even run across each other to mate? Don't they live in totally different terrain?"

Neil shivered, rubbing his arms. "Grizzlies have been seen way up north." He turned to Alex. "Didn't they spot one on Melville Island?"

"Amazing, right? That's at seventy-four degrees north. Way up in the Canadian Arctic."

Casey smiled. "Incredible."

They sat for a while longer, relapsing into silence. The fog began to clear, lifting slowly. Soon Alex could see the ice around them. On the horizon, the sun broke through a thick bank of clouds, sending down golden rays of light.

Casey checked the barometer. "It's rising. We should be on our way soon."

Alex drank the sweet coffee. Casey had made it just how she liked it, and the warm liquid spread through her core.

After a few more minutes, Casey started up the engine. "Okay! Back to Churchill!"

They rose through the air, Alex scanning the ice as they returned, searching for bears.

But she didn't spot any, and soon they hit the small patch of gray open water just off the coast, and then the land sped by beneath them.

They set down in front of the Centre and filed inside, stamping snow off their boots. Neil immediately made for Moe's. Casey took off for his motel.

After storing their new samples, Alex pulled out her phone and called Sasha.

The marine archaeologist sounded anxious when she answered. "Hello?"

"Sasha, it's Alex."

"Did you learn something new?"

"No, sorry. I was just calling to see how you were doing."

"They haven't identified the body yet. They want me to come down tomorrow to look at it."

"I really hope it's not your partner."

"Me too. But I have a bad feeling."

"How are you holding up?"

"Feeling useless and nervous. Just waiting around to learn more. How is your research going?"

"Pretty good. We have a new pilot. Our last one quit. But I like this new guy."

"Did you tag more bears?"

"We did indeed," Alex told her. Sasha grew quiet on the other end, so Alex added, "Anything I can do to help?"

"You're so nice. No, I don't think so. But thank you for calling."

"Okay. Well, don't hesitate if you need anything."

"Will do."

They hung up, and Alex sent a good thought out into the universe for her new friend. Returning to the lab, she checked again on her new samples and replacement backup drive, making sure nothing had been tampered with.

Alex's stomach started to growl. Once again, the Centre's cafeteria was filled to capacity. She spotted a lot of new faces and suspected a fresh influx of ecotourists had taken residence. She looked out the window, where the wind drifted snow against the glass. Moe's neon sign glowed just down the block. A fair number of cars in the parking lot told her they were going strong for dinner. Rather than don her bulky parka, she slipped on her fleece jacket for the short walk and headed out.

At Moe's, Alex took a stool at the bar again. She shrugged off her jacket and hung it on the convenient hook under the bar. The place was crowded again tonight. Groups of friends and couples occupied most of the tables, and the music from the jukebox was barely audible over the din of conversation. All she could hear were the drums and bass line, but she couldn't make out the tune.

In one corner of the bar, Neil laughed and drank beer with his fellow grad students in front of a dartboard. He kept grinning shyly at one woman—likely the intern he'd been so eager to get back to. Alex briefly thought of joining them, but still felt like an outsider in this new place. And after her winter alone studying wolverines, she still wasn't used to the idea of hanging out with other people.

The burly bartender, Dave, approached her with a friendly smile. "Hello. Want the porter again?"

"Sure. That sounds good." She checked over the menu. "And the veggie risotto?"

"Coming right up."

Alex glanced around the place once more. A couple in a corner booth were talking intently, holding hands across the top of the table. Three men dressed in hockey jerseys sat in another booth, sharing a pitcher of beer and laughing. Along with other patrons, they were fixed on a hockey game being played on a variety of TVs around the bar: the Winnipeg Jets versus the Tampa Bay Lightning.

The Jets scored and patrons cheered. People talked around her, enjoying the company of their friends and loved ones. Alex felt a wave of gratitude for her father and Zoe.

She may not have a lot of friends, but the ones she had were lifelong and solid, and she counted her dad among them. And she'd known Zoe since her undergrad days.

Her mind drifted to Brad, a lawyer she'd had a serious years-long relationship with until last fall. It had ended, and not well. Though she hoped one day they could talk again as friends, Brad wasn't ready for that yet.

She thought, too, of Ben Hathaway, the regional director for the Land Trust for Wildlife Conservation. It had felt good to spend some time with him in Montana, a kindred spirit who loved wildlife and the wilderness. She hoped to see him again.

And on an unsettling note, she couldn't forget the mysterious person who sent her those creepy postcards. So far she hadn't received any forwarded mail from Montana, but she wondered if a new postcard would be in the stack when she did. She'd brought them all with her, still puzzling over the man's intentions.

Her risotto arrived and was soft and cheesy with slim pieces of sautéed asparagus. It was delicious. As she chewed, half paying attention to the hockey game and half listening to the conversations around her, that feeling of isolation crept up on her again. She carried out her work largely alone in the field. This assignment was definitely an exception. The bears were too big to handle solo, and she needed a pilot to track them by air. But she welcomed this degree of human contact, even if it was only work related. If she could strike some balance between helping wildlife and having a bit of a social life, she thought she might be happier.

One of the men wearing a hockey jersey accidentally bumped into her while getting another pitcher of beer at the bar. He didn't even notice, and her awkwardness intensified. She wished she'd at least brought a book to read. Then against a far wall she noticed a bookcase with the sign TAKE ONE, LEAVE ONE. Maybe she'd go over there when she finished her meal and read while she drank her beer.

She was just chiding herself for feeling lonely and sorry for herself when the stool next to her scooted out and a man sat down.

"Hiya," he said to her, nodding.

"Hello," she greeted back.

He stripped off his parka and hung it on the hook next to him beneath the bar. He was thin and a little unhealthy looking, with gray circles under his red-rimmed eyes and his skin so pale it almost glowed. She could smell that he was a smoker. He ran a hand through greasy long brown hair. "Dave!" he called to the bartender. "Whiskey."

The huge man turned. "Steve! Where you been keeping yourself?"

"Here and there."

Dave reached out and they clasped hands over the bar, doing a one-armed hug. "I wondered where you'd gotten to. I was worried about you, man! You sure you should be around here?"

Steve smiled. "Thanks, but I'm doin' okay. Still have some things I need to take care of."

Dave clapped him again on the shoulder. "Okay, man, if you're sure." He brought him a tumbler with several fingers of whiskey.

"That good?" Steve asked Alex, eyeing the last of her risotto.

"Very good."

"I'll have to try it sometime. Hey, Dave!" he called. "Can I get a basket of fries?"

"Sure thing."

He turned back to her. "I'm Steve."

"Alex."

"You staying up at the Churchill Centre for Arctic Studies?"

"What gave me away?"

"I just didn't recognize you. New faces in here are usually from the Centre. This is the closest place to get a drink."

He shifted on his stool nervously and kept turning around to glance at the other patrons. Downing his whiskey in one gulp, he turned the glass tumbler anxiously in his hand, rotating it around and around. "I don't suppose the Centre has a boat for hire, does it?" he asked.

As he rested his arm on the bar, his sleeve came up a little, revealing a tattoo of a pair of cards, an ace and a king: 21 in blackjack. This was the same guy who had been looking to hire Sasha's boat.

"Sorry. We do our research by helicopter."

He frowned, disappointed, and turned around on his stool to survey the other patrons. Then grimacing, he turned back to her. "You got a pen?"

"I think so." Alex rummaged in her jacket pocket under the bar and brought out a ballpoint.

"Thanks." He grabbed a cocktail napkin and started to scribble something on it, then scratched it out, bouncing one leg nervously on the stool's footrest. He scratched over the words more thoroughly, then, shaking his head, tore off the top of the napkin and tossed the crossed-out portion into the trash behind the bar.

He stared around the restaurant, bumping Alex with an elbow. "Oh, sorry."

She finished the last of her risotto as he suddenly sprang off the stool and made a beeline for the Take One, Leave One shelf. He grabbed a book seemingly at random, not even bothering to look at any of the titles, and returned to his seat.

Alex pushed her empty dish away and took a sip of her porter, glancing inadvertently at the title of the book. It was *Daisy Mouse and the Mystery of the Haunted Dollhouse.*

Not the choice she would have pegged for him.

He flipped through the pages as if searching for something. His fries arrived and he dumped so much ketchup on them that she didn't see how he could taste the potatoes at all.

By the dartboard, it was Neil's turn to throw. He got two bull's-eyes in a row, which elicited a roar from the opposing team.

The man next to her was now engrossed in *Daisy Mouse*. He alternated between shoving french fries in his mouth and scribbling on the torn cocktail napkin.

She took a few more sips of her beer, feeling awkward and wondering if she should have just eaten takeout in her motel room.

Steve suddenly lost interest in the book, closing it and jumping off his stool. He returned it to the shelf, and Alex wondered if he would pick something else, but he didn't. He pulled out a small piece of paper from his pocket, about the size of a receipt, and tore it up. After tossing it in the trash, he came back to the stool and handed her the pen. "Thanks."

"Of course." She slid the pen back into her jacket pocket under the bar.

A freezing draft wafted into the bar as the front door opened. Two men and a woman entered, scanning the place. They locked eyes on Steve and he turned around abruptly, facing the bartender, his leg now going like a jackhammer. He craned his neck around to see where they were, jostling her again. "Sorry," he mumbled.

One of the men crossed his arms, glaring at Steve. He had longish black hair and a goatee, his skin weathered and beige. A deep scar ran across the bridge of his nose. A beer belly spilled over his belt. An empty table stood next to the bar and the group took it, sitting right behind Alex. But they didn't sit around the table in a circle. They pulled their chairs together so they'd all be facing the bar. A server came to the table and the other man, an edifice of muscle with closely shorn black hair and a sienna complexion, ordered a beer. The woman then waved the server off with irritation, her brown hair tightly pulled back into a ponytail, framing narrowed, cruel blue eyes in a pale, stony face.

They stared at Steve. Alex could feel their eyes boring into her neighbor and grew all the more uncomfortable.

She finished her beer and paid the check. Retrieving her own jacket from its hook, she pulled it on. "Nice talking to you."

Steve nodded nervously back but didn't say anything.

She zipped up her fleece and crossed to the door. Opening it, she braced herself for the blast of cold. The temperature difference made her cough. She was only a few steps into the parking lot when the bar door swung open again. Steve jogged down the stairs and ran to a car in the lot. He wrenched open the door just as the group barged out of the bar in pursuit. Steve turned the ignition and swung out into the lot, roaring away. Tires crunched on packed snow.

The threesome ran to another car, piling in. "Go!" she heard one man shout. They took off after Steve, barely missing Alex in the parking lot. She jumped to one side to avoid them as they tore after him.

As she watched their taillights disappear down the road, her breath frosting in the cold air, Alex wondered if Steve, whoever he was, was going to be okay.

TWELVE

An hour later, Alex sat in the back of the grounded helicopter at the Centre, going through their gear. She checked off a list of their supplies: emergency camping gear, food, water, survival suits in case they had to ditch in the sea. Then she went over the needed supplies for the study: lip tattoo clamp, the spreadsheet, spare white ID disks in case they tagged any new bears, the new, smaller ear satellite trackers, the Burrs on Fur.

She replaced all the missing supplies and refilled the tranquilizer dart case with new syringes in different sizes. When she finished checking everything over, she double-checked it all.

Finally she climbed out of the helicopter, then slid the door shut. If they had clear weather tomorrow, they'd be ready to go.

Bracing herself for the blast of cold, she jogged across the parking lot, returning to the warmth of the Centre. She wanted to get to work on the new samples they'd collected today before returning to her motel.

In the lab, she ran a few preliminary tests, then backed up her findings and raw data onto a portable hard drive. She secured the blood and tissue samples back in the lab refrigerator.

Feeling tired, she swapped out her lightweight fleece for her heavier coat. It was late now, the Centre completely quiet. As she stepped outside into the numbing cold, she decided to make sure she'd locked the helicopter door. She knew she had, but given everything going wrong with the study, with the lab break-in and missing supplies, she wanted to be certain. She angled around to the passenger side of the helicopter, finding the door still shut. But when she moved to test the lock, she saw faint scratches by the handle. Someone had been trying to force their way in. She tested the handle. It remained closed.

Immediately she backed away from the helicopter, scanning the parking lot and the sides of the Centre. She took off at a jog, skirting the back of the building, then around to the other side. She didn't see anyone and hadn't heard a car pull up. But she hadn't exactly been listening for cars, and someone could have come and gone and escaped her notice. She unlocked the chopper and stepped inside it, finding things exactly as she had left them. She double-checked all the gear and supplies to be certain, but nothing seemed to be missing.

Then she locked the sliding door again and stood staring at the bird. The neon light of Moe's sign cast a diffused orange glow. It was possible someone had walked from there. Had she interrupted them when she came out, and they'd fled on foot, giving up on trying to break into the helicopter?

They could return as soon as she left for her motel.

She ran down the street toward Moe's, curious to see if anyone was walking back that way in the fog. But she didn't see anyone, and Moe's had shut down for the evening. No cars waited in the parking lot. It was possible the person had parked at Moe's and then sprinted back to their car when she emerged from the Centre.

Or had the scratches been there before and she just hadn't noticed them?

Returning to the helicopter, she considered unloading all the gear and putting it back in the Centre. But it was too much to load quickly and be sure they had everything, especially the way things had been going missing. The clear-weather windows to leave were so tiny that she didn't want to waste time reloading the helicopter and double-checking all the supplies. They had to be ready to go on a dime.

Not sure what to do, or how to prevent more thefts, Alex returned to her car. Then she moved it so it was parked right next to the helicopter. She put her hood up and leaned the car seat back. She'd just spend the night here and hope her presence would dissuade any further thefts.

But it was too cold. Her breath frosted in the frigid air of the car. She shivered, unable to get comfortable. Finally she jogged back into the Centre and donned all her cold-weather gear. Hurrying back outside, she returned to the slightly less freezing interior of her car and tried to get comfortable. It was going to be a long night.

ALEX AWOKE TO A CLEAR day and Casey rapping softly on the window. She stirred, groggy, and unfolded her arms. They felt frozen in place, her body stiff and sore. She straightened up in the seat as Casey smiled through the glass. She turned the key in the ignition to lower the window. It crackled with ice as it descended.

"What are you doing out here?" he asked.

"See those scratches on the door of the helicopter?" She pointed them out. "Were they there before? I thought someone was trying to break in, steal our supplies."

Casey walked to the helicopter and scrutinized it. "It does look like someone was trying to pry open the door. But they didn't get very far."

"I think I interrupted them."

"Did you see anyone?"

She shook her head.

"This is too weird. Neil told me about the lab break-in the other night, too. Is this stuff worth a lot of money?"

"Some of it is, but not the data and blood and tissue samples they took."

Moving closer to the chopper, he ran his hand along the scratches.

"They're definitely fresh. But I don't remember if they were here before or not. I'm going to check the bird over. But we're ready to go. The weather's perfect."

Alex looked down at her phone, expecting to see that she'd missed a call or text from Neil. But he hadn't reached out to her. She called him as Casey vanished around the other side of the helicopter.

Neil answered on the fourth ring. "Dr. Carter?"

"We've got great weather. We can leave. Where are you?"

"In the Centre. I texted you."

She frowned, looking down at her phone. No messages had come through. She checked her signal. It alternated between one bar and no bars. "It must not have come through," she told him. "You ready?"

"Sure thing."

"Can you grab me a couple granola bars on your way out?" she asked. "I've got to come inside and brush my teeth."

"No problem."

She used the Centre's bathroom to freshen up, splash water on her face. She moved her car back to her former spot in the parking lot, and a few minutes later Neil emerged.

She saw with gratitude that he also carried her insulated cup she'd left in the common room.

He reached her just as she stepped out of the car. "Rinsed this out for you and brought you some tea, too." He handed her the cup, a couple granola bars, and a foil-wrapped burrito. "Thought you might want something a little more substantial than granola bars, so I grabbed you a breakfast burrito, too."

"Thanks!" The burrito felt warm in her gloved hand.

They piled into the helicopter. Alex devoured the breakfast burrito, which was a delicious steaming concoction of brown rice, black beans, and avocado. She took sips of the hot tea as Casey finished his preflight check.

"Ready?" he said over the headset.

Alex balled up the aluminum foil the burrito had come in. "Let's go." She took a final sip of her tea and then they were lifting off, speeding across the snowy landscape below, heading out to the ice of the Hudson Bay.

In the distance, Alex spotted the telltale sign of several ringed-seal breathing holes, running a crooked line to the east. Polar bear tracks connected them, with the snow around each hole disturbed by a bear alternately circling and lying down to wait.

"Tracks!" Alex said excitedly.

"I see them," Casey said, bringing them lower. She scanned the horizon for the yellow dot of a polar bear but saw only the tracks vanishing into the bright sunlit terrain. Casey followed them, and after they passed a third breathing hole, the tracks continued in a straight line to the east.

She spotted a black dot on the horizon, standing out vividly against the otherwise unbroken white landscape.

"What's that?" she asked, leaning forward and pointing so Casey could see.

"I'll check it out."

Neil zeroed in on it with his binoculars. "What *is* that?" He echoed her thoughts.

When they got closer, she could make out that it was a black box on a tripod. Then the breath caught in her throat. Crimson blood spattered the snow all around it. And she could make out a large yellow-white mound lying on the ground next to it.

THIRTEEN

"Oh no," Alex breathed.

Casey set the chopper down thirty feet away, and they all climbed out.

He took the shotgun with him, holding it at his side.

The gigantic bloodstained mound lay immobile, a dead polar bear with a bullet through its head. A chunk of frozen meat with smooth, mottled gray skin lay next to it. The meat was attached to a cable that led to the two-foot-wide-by-one-foot-high black box on top of the tripod.

Inside, she could see the barrel of a rifle pointing out.

"It's a set gun," she murmured.

She knelt down beside the bear. It had encountered the trap, pulled on the meat, and triggered a powerful blast from the rifle. The bear looked to be an older male. A white disk hung in his ear where it had been previously tagged. Alex read the number.

Set guns were not just illegal, but were indiscriminate. If this bear had been a female with cubs, the cubs would have starved. Poachers didn't care who they killed—a male, a pregnant female, an older one like this. They cared only about the pelt and making a few bucks.

Casey knelt down beside the set gun. "What kind of meat is this?"

Neil frowned at it. "Looks like part of a narwhal."

Alex shook her head in disgust. "So this poacher killed one imperiled animal in order to kill another?" She thought of "Old Sam" and scanned the horizon for any sign of his snowmobile. Suddenly a sinking feeling washed over her. "Who knew we were going to take this route today?" Alex asked.

Neil shrugged. "Anyone who looked at our itinerary or schedule."

"So anyone in the Centre?" Because polar bear researchers were so highly coordinated and their itineraries and schedules would be on the distributed spreadsheet, she knew that Neil was right. Anyone could have looked at it, even a member of the public who came in to visit the Centre.

Missing supplies would delay them. If the person had been successful in breaking into the helicopter and taking things, they might not have left today, might not have flown over this particular stretch of ice.

She scanned their surroundings. On the lee side of a towering jumble of ice, she could make out the vague impression of snowmobile tracks where the newly fallen snow hadn't yet covered them.

Alex looked down at the bear and her body temperature shot up in fury; she unzipped her coat partway. "Polar bears are struggling enough without some asshole out here trophy hunting them." She told Casey about "Old Sam" and the polar bear pelts he was trying to sell.

Casey shook his head, then moved to examine the set gun.

"Have you seen something like this before?" she asked him.

He nodded grimly.

So had Alex, on Svalbard. Set guns had been used for years, killing thousands of polar bears until the guns were finally banned everywhere. But poachers still used them.

"Alex?" She felt the weight of Casey's hand on her shoulder and realized he'd been talking to her.

She met his eyes, her own simmering suns of fury.

"You okay?"

"No," she said, staring down at the fallen bear. "I'm not okay at all."

He crossed his arms. "Me either."

She glanced over at Neil, who was documenting the scene with his camera. He took a GPS reading of the location.

Her heart hammering angrily in her chest, Alex bent down to examine the bear's ear tag in detail.

With shaking hands she flipped through the spreadsheet until she found him. He'd been tagged for the first time twelve years ago. He was seventeen years old this year. He looked relatively healthy. But he'd been taken out of the population because of someone's greedy ambitions.

Grinding her teeth, she stepped away, blinking back angry tears. She unzipped her coat the rest of the way, letting the arctic air cool her outrage. But it only replaced it with a sickened sense of grief.

Neil joined her. "This is unbelievable." He flipped through the photos on his camera. "We'll report this to Manitoba Conservation. They'll catch the guy."

Neil photographed the gun in detail. Then Casey began to dismantle it. Alex walked slowly to the helicopter, trying to slow her breathing. She found a box in the back full of emergency camping gear and dumped it loosely onto the floor of the helicopter. She carried the box over and she and Casey piled the evidence into it.

While Casey carried the box to the helicopter and Neil climbed into the copilot seat, Alex stood out on the ice next to the polar bear. She knelt down and touched the fur of his head. "I'm so sorry," she whispered to him. How many times had she uttered similar words over the bodies of wildlife?

She distinctly remembered the first time. She had been only four. Her father would always pull over and move box turtles to the side of the highway if he found them crossing a dangerous stretch of road. Alex loved it, loved helping him with the turtles, loved seeing them happily saunter away into the bushes on the far side of the road, safe and continuing their journeys. She could still vividly re-member the feeling of the sun-warmed skin on their powerful legs as she carried them to safety.

He did this with opossums, too, stopping his car so that they could cross safely. Sometimes he scooped them up and moved them off the road if they were frozen in fright.

Then one day as they journeyed down a rural road, a beat-up pickup truck was driving in front of them. They reached a straight-away, and she spotted an opossum crossing the road. It was still in the empty oncoming lane, moving slowly, and she pointed it out to her dad. No one was coming from the other direction, so she knew they'd be able to pull over and save it if it froze in place. Then sud-denly the truck in front of them swerved purposefully into the on-coming lane and hit it. She could see the men inside laughing and high-fiving each other. They roared on down the highway.

Her father pulled over and they climbed out. The men's aim had been bad, and they'd only clipped it. The opossum stood stunned in the road. Alex's dad bent down and examined it. "We need to get him to the wildlife rescue center," he told Alex. He took off his jacket and gently bundled the opossum inside.

As they made their way back to the car, Alex asked, "Why . . . why did they do that?"

He tucked the opossum into the back seat. "Some people enjoy killing."

Alex stared up at him, not understanding. "Why?"

He put a hand on her shoulder. "I don't know, pumpkin."

They rushed the opossum to the rescue center, where it was ex-amined. They set its broken forelimb while Alex and her dad waited, then said that it should recover, and they'd release it back into the wild. Alex wondered how many opossums hadn't been so lucky.

"I'm so sorry," she'd whispered to it when they left.

Until that moment, she'd thought that all of humanity were good, that they were all like her father. It was incomprehensible that some could be the antithesis of him, that for every turtle or opossum he saved, others were crushed on the road as some form of perverse entertainment. It staggered her, and she had ridden in silence all the way home.

That was the day Alex dedicated her life to helping wildlife.

They returned to the helicopter and continued to search for tracks, but now a somber mood pervaded the helicopter. The elation Alex felt earlier had evaporated, and a sick feeling crept into her gut.

"I see another breathing hole," Neil said. He pointed it out to Alex. No trackways yet around it, and a small jumbled circle of ice a few hundred feet from it signaled the existence of a second hole. "There!" Neil said.

Casey dropped down and they hovered over the second hole. Tracks approached from the north and circled it, then moved off to the east. Casey followed them. As Alex's gaze swept over the terrain, following the tracks and looking ahead for the bear, her heart sank as another black spot on the horizon appeared.

"Oh no," she said, her heart plunging down into her stomach. A sick, shaky feeling pressed down on her chest. "I think it's another set gun."

FOURTEEN

The polar bear tracks headed straight for the set gun. Maybe they could intercept the bear before it reached the weapon.

But as they approached, Alex could already make out red splattered around the snow in front of the gun.

Casey set down the chopper and Alex jumped out. She didn't see a bear, just a streak of blood where one had been shot. Briefly she wondered if the poacher had already removed the body, but there wasn't enough blood on the ice if a bear had been fatally shot.

Casey went to work dismantling the set gun and placing its parts in another box, while she and Neil scanned the horizon for the bear. A blood trail left a weaving crimson line running roughly to the southeast. Alex thought she could make out some movement in the distance.

Quickly they piled back into the helicopter and Casey took off, following the blood trail.

Soon the bear came into view, loping across the ice. It was a large male, his coat almost yellow against the brilliant white of the snow. Even from up here, Alex could see a red smear on the bear's left shoulder where the set gun bullet had struck him. She loaded the tranquilizer gun and leaned out of the helicopter. Bracing herself as the helicopter banked, one foot planted firmly on the landing skid, she felt the reassuring grip of the harness and took aim.

The polar bear glanced over his shoulder, looking nervous as the helicopter descended. Casey banked around him. Alex saw an opening and fired the dart into the bear's rump. The bright red feathering flashed against the white of his fur. He picked up his pace, running now.

Casey pulled back, giving the bear room as the tranquilizer kicked in.

The helicopter circled and Alex waited. In front of her, Neil leaned forward in his seat, looking a little green as the helicopter banked.

The bear started to slow down, his long back legs wobbling as the drug kicked in.

When he slumped down onto the ice, Alex went to work. She cleaned the wound, finding it to be a graze and thankfully nothing life-threatening.

Then they took measurements of the bear's girth and length, swabbed between his toes, and recorded the number on the small white disk in his ear on the spreadsheet. They took blood and fat samples and swabbed the inside of his mouth. He was a healthy weight, and Alex had high hopes for his future if the poacher could be caught.

Finally she attached a Burr on Fur so they could track his movements by satellite.

Casey stood guard with his shotgun, scanning for the poacher and other bears. The bear began to stir and they packed up their equipment, heading back to the helicopter. This time they hovered, keeping the bear in sight, until he was well on his way.

She still didn't see any sign of the poacher. "Should we scan for other set guns in the area?" she asked Casey.

"Definitely."

They moved in widening circles, scanning the horizon for the telltale black boxes, but didn't see others. Nor did they see any more snowmobile tracks or blood trails.

The smooth white landscape gave way to a section of rough ice.

Blue water snaked through open leads, small icebergs floating between patches of ice. She spotted tracks in the fresh snow, but this
was a bad place to tag a bear. If you hit it with a dart and it dove into
open water, it could drown.

"Let's see where these tracks go, Casey," she said over the headset. Maybe the bear was past this section of rough ice and they could
tag it some miles away.

Casey veered in that direction. Alex stared intently out the
window, squinting in the bright light. She was so focused on trying
to spot the bear in the distance that when a loud boom suddenly
sounded above her, she jostled out of her seat so hard she banged
her elbow on the chopper's fuselage.

"What was that?" Neil shouted over the headset.

The rotors made a terrible grinding noise, and the helicopter
pitched violently to starboard. Neil almost flew out of his seat, his
legs dangling momentarily in midair as they went sideways, only
the safety belt keeping him in place. All of Alex's weight fell against
the door.

Another boom shook the helicopter and Alex felt a blast of
heat erupt from the tail section. She craned her neck around, fighting against the motion of the wheeling helicopter, and saw flames
shooting out from the tail section. Bright orange and yellow glowed
outward, quickly obscured by thick, acrid black smoke.

"We're on fire!" she yelled over the headset. The heat blasting
from the rear hit her with an intense wave. The stench of burning
plastic and electronics filled the cabin and Alex gasped for a decent
breath. Black smoke poured thickly into the cabin.

Another violent explosion wracked the chopper. The nose
dipped down and Alex braced her feet against the floor in front of
her as the ice came rushing up beneath them.

She saw open water and jagged pieces of ice within feet of the
chopper's nose when Casey managed to pull it out of the dive at
the last second. The tail spun around suddenly and Alex's head

slammed into the wall. She brought a hand up as Casey gained a little bit of altitude, barely bringing them above the level of water.

Jagged towers of ice and pressure ridges swam up before Alex's vision as he veered the helicopter hard to port, narrowly missing the terrain. He gained a little more altitude. Alex coughed as black smoke continued to pour into the cabin. She pulled her Turtle Fur up over her nose and mouth.

"What is happening?" Neil screamed. She could see him flailing in his seat, the smoke searing her eyes.

Alex gripped her seat as Casey managed to wrest control of the helicopter. He pulled the nose up, barely clearing a serrated pressure ridge that threatened to smash them to pieces.

"We're going to have to set down. Trying to find a place," he said over the headset. She could see him fighting with the stick, his feet working the anti-torque foot pedals.

He pulled the nose up again and they rose, sailing over another pressure ridge. Up ahead Alex spotted a relatively flat piece of ice. Casey headed for it, but another loud explosion wracked the helo. The tail started spinning out of control. Alex held on to her seat and braced one arm against the wall as the chopper spun erratically. She felt the burrito come up into her throat and swallowed hard, forcing it back down.

"Oh god!" she heard Neil wail. The world swiveled around so fast Alex lost track of which direction they were heading.

Acrid smoke enveloped her and she began coughing uncontrollably. She couldn't see anything but black and could hear only the whine of the tortured engine as it shook itself apart. She squeezed her eyes shut, baring her teeth, and then the chopper slammed down hard. Alex jolted forward in her seat as the helicopter screamed across the ice, its sickening spin finally stopping as they slid violently forward.

Flames from the rear leapt forward as Alex tore off her seat belt and threw open the door. Smoke poured out, filling the cold arctic air. She stumbled out of the helicopter, going down on her hands and knees on the ice. She coughed, retching, gasping for a breath of clean air. Then Casey was beside her, lifting her up.

She got her bearings, seeing the helicopter on fire. "We've got to salvage as much gear as possible!" she shouted. Neil piled out, running some twenty feet away, gagging and coughing. He bent over, hands on his knees, retching onto the ice.

Casey dove back into the helicopter, throwing out supplies. Their tents, sleeping bags, a cookstove. Emergency rations of food, the med kit. His shotgun. Alex joined him, tossing objects out onto the ice.

She threw out the samples they'd taken that day and the printed spreadsheet for the polar bear study. She followed with their survival suits—lightweight gear that would allow a person to survive for a short time in frigid water. Neil joined her, tossing out their water supply, backpacks, flashlights, a survival kit with a flare gun, and emergency blankets. Then Casey moved to the front of the helicopter and grabbed the satellite phone. Alex grabbed the tranquilizer gun and the case of darts, wincing at the hot handles. The fire crept farther into the helicopter cabin. Her face felt blasted with heat, her hands raw from the nearness of the flames. She tried to grab the boxes with the set gun evidence but felt strands of her hair catch fire. Frantically she slapped at the flames around her face, extinguishing them.

"That's it! Get back!" Casey shouted. She had to abandon the boxes. They dragged supplies away across the ice, trying to move upwind from the caustic plume of black smoke that billowed outward. The flames caught the rest of the helicopter, and Alex collapsed in the snow next to their camping gear and food, still hacking, her lungs rebelling from all the smoke intake. Casey slumped down beside her, gasping for breath.

Neil continued to drag equipment away from the helicopter. He looked panicked and pale, soot covering his face and the white trim around his parka hood. When he looked like he was going to drag a tent right over a pressure ridge, she called out to him. "Neil! You can stop now. It's okay."

He stood still, blinking in the bright sun, staring at the helicopter, his chest heaving. A cloud of breath hung around his face. He was hyperventilating. She struggled to her feet and hurried to him. "Hey, it's okay. We're all okay." She put a hand on his shoulder. He leaned over, hands on his knees, and retched again into the snow. Alex looked away. Watching someone vomit was often contagious. She felt bile rise in her throat, her mouth starting to water, and fought the urge to follow suit.

Neil recovered, straightening, and for several long moments, they just stood and watched the helicopter burn, all of them too surprised and stunned to do much more than stare.

Slowly the reality of their situation sank into Alex. They were way out on the ice, supposed to be on their way home. On the horizon she saw a storm moving in.

"What's your pressure at?" she called to Casey, still standing with a comforting hand on Neil's back.

"Twenty-nine point seventy-nine and falling," he called back. "If this hadn't happened, we would have headed back soon."

"So, rescue chopper?" asked Neil.

Casey glanced again at his barometer. "They'd have to wait before they could get us. I'll call in." He stood up and grabbed the sat phone.

Alex made soothing circles on Neil's back. He bent over again, hands on his knees, spitting into the snow.

"You doing okay?" she asked.

Neil stuffed some snow into his mouth. "Yeah. I think I'm done throwing up. Don't think I've got anything left."

She patted his back again. "That was a hell of a ride."

"That's one way to put it." He straightened up, staring at the burning helo. "What do you think went wrong with it?"

She put her hands on her hips, watching the flames snake between the black tendrils of smoke. "I have no idea. C'mon. Let's see what Rescue says." She started off toward Casey with Neil following behind, a little wobbly on his feet.

Alex was just glad they all were unharmed, save for lungfuls of smoke, and that they'd managed to get their emergency supplies safely offloaded. She even still had the samples they'd collected that day. They'd just have to wait a few hours, maybe spend the night, and she would be back at the lab, analyzing their findings.

Casey was just wrapping up the phone conversation when they reached him. "Understood. We'll keep our eye on the weather from here, too." He signed off.

"What's the scoop?" Alex asked.

"Looks like the weather won't break until after dark. They're going to come out tomorrow if the weather clears."

Neil's jaw fell open.

"Okay," Alex said, then turned to the grad student. "We'll be fine. We've got all the supplies we need."

They watched the wind carry away the plume of smoke. She turned to Casey. "What went wrong?"

Casey shook his head, taking a deep breath. "I have no idea. I checked and double-checked it before we went up. I don't understand it."

She bit her lip. "The lab break-in. The missing equipment. Someone is trying to sabotage our study." She turned to Neil. "How far do you think they'd go?"

Neil's wide eyes stared back at her. "You think someone did this to us *on purpose*?"

Alex regarded Casey. "What could have caused the chopper to crash like that? Could it have just been mechanical failure?"

"I can't imagine how. It was in great shape. The maintenance records were all up to date."

"Could it have been an explosive?"

Casey's eyes met hers, grim and foreboding. "Yes."

"Shit!" Neil yelled, throwing his arms up. "Holy fucking shit! Who the hell would *do* that? I mean, grounding us is one thing. Deliberately ensuring we'd crash? Who the hell would do that? And why?"

It was exactly what Alex was wondering. They all could have died if it weren't for Casey's quick thinking and flying abilities.

Someone wanted to end their study and was willing to kill them to do it.

Casey lifted up one of the tent bags. "Let's start pitching." He pointed to a pressure ridge some hundred feet away. "We should have a break from the wind if we pitch on the far side of that. It's going to be a long, dark, freezing-cold night." He threw another bag to Neil.

Neil blanched, missing the tent as it arced to him. It landed on the ice with a puff of snow. He stared down at it, not moving. Alex started to worry he might be in shock.

"I'll help you," she offered. She grabbed the third tent and her backpack and they set off for the shelter of the ice formation. Casey brought his shotgun with him.

Once in the shelter of the ridge, Neil came mechanically to life, emptying the sack and helping Alex with his tent. Designed to be deployed in a hurry, it was self-erecting. She pulled the strap and watched the spring-loaded poles leap into action, instantly pitching the tent. A soft breeze began to pick up into gusts that buffeted the tent material, and they struggled to peg it in place.

"That weather's arriving," Casey said, glancing down at his wristwatch with its built-in barometer.

Alex pulled out her portable Kestrel weather unit and held it up. The barometer was 29.78 and dropping. Clouds gathered on the northwestern horizon, charcoal tones in their undersides.

The wind gusted and howled, tearing the rainfly from Neil's grip. He caught it before it went hurtling away across the ice. Grumbling under his breath, he clipped it in place. Soon his small yellow tent was pitched, and she turned to her own.

When they finished, the bright yellow tents stood out on the monochromatic landscape, patches of vivid color stark against the white. Hot food and drinks usually cheered people up, Alex thought. The rest of their gear was still over by the helicopter, and she remembered some freeze-dried mac 'n' cheese and coffee making it into one of the packs.

A low thrumming brought her attention to the west. Below the gray nimbostratus clouds there, moving on the ice, approached two small black dots. They murmured and hummed.

Neil pulled binoculars from his jacket pocket. "Snowmobiles?" he asked.

Alex dug her binoculars out, too, and adjusted the focus wheel. The two dots drew closer. "Looks like it." Though some areas of ice had already broken up enough for a boat to navigate carefully through narrow channels, she knew there were still quite a few places where the ice hugged the land, and wondered if they'd launched from there.

"Hunting party?" Neil asked. "Or poachers?"

Casey borrowed Alex's binocs and stared out to the west.

The thought of encountering poachers out here on the ice, when they'd dismantled two of their set guns, sent a wave of fear through Alex. Mentally she went over their weapons: Casey's shotgun and the tranquilizer gun. The poachers would likely be armed far more heavily.

Neil's tone perked up. "Or they've sent mechanics on snowmobiles to get us in the air tonight?"

Casey shook his head, handing the glasses back to Alex. "They wouldn't send anyone out on snowmobiles to repair it. They knew the chopper had burned. And they're here way too fast to have responded to our Mayday."

He exchanged a concerned glance with Alex.

"I don't like the timing," she murmured. "Someone may have

sabotaged the helicopter and then a few minutes later people show up?"

"Maybe they saw us crash. Decided to come help us," Neil said hopefully.

Casey grimaced. "I don't know. I'm going for the sat phone."

As they moved back toward their gear, Neil hurried to keep up. He tugged on Casey's sleeve. "You're saying this could be whoever grounded us?"

"That's what I'm worried about." Casey's eyes fixed on the approaching snowmobiles. The roar of their engines grew louder. "It might be nothing, but I don't like it."

Neil turned to him, still looking hopeful. "I think it's just a hunting party and they're coming to help."

"Maybe," Casey said noncommittally.

Alex didn't like it, either. If someone had intentionally brought down the chopper, and she had no reason to doubt Casey had checked everything over carefully, then they could be out to salvage their gear or, worst-case scenario, finish the job the helicopter crash had failed to bring about.

"But who would want to hurt us? We're just bear biologists, for chrissakes. Who cares?" Neil asked.

Alex set her mouth in a thin slash. "Fossil fuel executives who don't like us pointing out that polar bears are quickly losing habitat. Poachers who don't want us to tag bears and keep track of them."

Now the snowmobiles were drawing so close that Alex could make out three individual riders, two of them riding together. She saw the barrels of rifles sticking up from their backs. Though a person had to be armed out here, they didn't strike her as a maintenance crew. And Alex and the others were still more than seventy-five feet away from their gear and the sat phone.

Neil noticed the rifles, too. "Well, that's great and all, but I'm still betting it's people who saw the crash and want to check on us. Maybe they can give us a lift back to Churchill. The rescue crew can fly our stuff back tomorrow."

Just as the wind carried away the hopeful tones of his voice, the first shot rang out.

FIFTEEN

The crack of the shot faded away. Alex couldn't see where it had hit.

Neil instinctively crouched down. "Are they firing at us?"

Alex saw the rider on the back of the lead snowmobile lower a rifle in their direction.

"Oh my god, they're firing at us!" Neil yelled, his voice pitching high. He wrenched the shotgun from Casey's grip and took off across the ice, heading back toward their tents and the protection of the pressure ridge there.

Alex dove down just before the rifle went off again. A patch of ice kicked up ten feet to her left. Then she scrambled to her feet. They couldn't make it to the sat phone, which sat out in the open, too far away. Neil had already taken shelter behind the high ice ridge. Alex didn't think she could make it there in time. Another ridge stood closer, but it was shorter and offered less shelter. It was only seven feet tall or so, but it would work in the short term. She headed for that one, glancing around for Casey. She spotted him on the ice just a few feet to her right. He'd flung himself down, too, and was just now getting to his feet.

She headed for the smaller ice ridge, Casey just behind her as the rifle rent the quiet air for a third time.

The ice cracked and gave slightly as she reached a softer patch of thinner ice. A bolt of fear shot through her as it dipped down several inches beneath her boot. She was going to break through. Water sloshed up over her toe.

She jumped for a thicker section just as a lead widened a few yards away. She veered from it, crossing behind Casey and pointing it out to him.

As she ran, another shot rang out. She glanced back to see the ice kick up twenty feet behind them. Another crack split the air over the droning sound of the snowmobiles, this time impacting the ice some forty feet behind, even though now the snowmobilers were even closer and their aim should be better. Granted, it was hard to fire from a moving snowmobile, but she began to doubt they were actually trying to hit them.

She met Casey's eyes as they ran, seeing the same question there.

They reached the shorter pressure ridge, and from this angle, she could see Neil taking refuge behind the larger one, the shotgun gripped in his hands. He'd slumped down with his back to the ice and was squeezing his eyes shut.

"They weren't trying to hit us," Casey said, catching his breath.

"I thought the same thing."

The snowmobile engines grew closer, then slowed and cut out entirely.

Alex placed her back flat against the welcoming ice, gauging the terrain around them. Another pressure ridge, one even taller, stood two hundred feet to the north, beyond where Neil sat by the tents.

"I'm going to see where they are," she whispered, and crept to the edge of the ice barrier. Peeking around, she saw them dismounting next to the biologists' gear. There were three of them. She couldn't make out their faces. Their snowmobile suits, balaclavas, and goggles completely covered their features, but she could tell that one of them was a woman. Another one was portly, the third one muscular and tall. The heavyset one pointed to various gear and ordered the others around. He seemed to be in charge.

They started picking through their belongings. They shook out their sleeping bags, overturned their boxes of gear.

With regret she spotted the tranquilizer gun case. If only she'd grabbed it! They opened it, dumping out the rifle, then opened the small case containing the darts and dumped those out, too.

"What are they doing?" Casey asked.

"Searching our gear." She eyed the next ridge. "Should we run for better cover?"

"Getting some distance wouldn't be a bad idea," Casey agreed.

Then Alex noticed with a sickening feeling that their tracks in the snow led straight here. A slight wind blew, but it wasn't enough to wipe out the trail.

"Our tracks would lead them straight to us," she said.

"Maybe they're just thieves," Casey said hopefully. "Maybe they'll go away after taking our stuff."

Beyond them, Neil raced from the ridge where their tents were to an even taller formation. He disappeared behind it.

Angry arguing brought her attention back to their gear. The search had gotten more desperate. Now they tore things apart, smashed boxes.

"It's not here," the woman announced.

"They must have it on them," the leader responded.

"Maybe it was inside the helicopter," the other man suggested, watching it burn.

"What do you want to do?" Casey whispered.

"Let's go for it," Alex said.

Together they made their way to the next large ridge. She knew that to be caught out on the ice with no gear could mean death. So as they sped by their tents, she grabbed their prepared survival kit out of her backpack and slung it over one shoulder. To grab the whole heavy pack would have slowed her down too much.

They tore on, passing the jumble of ice where Neil had now taken refuge, and she waved for him to follow. He shook his head adamantly, gripping the shotgun, his knuckles white. *I can't!* he mouthed to her.

She thought of doubling back for him, but then saw the gunmen had spotted their tracks and were following them. *Come on!* she urged him silently with a wave of her arm.

As they pressed on, Alex noticed that the lead in the ice had gotten wider, a dark blue line snaking through the white terrain, smaller chunks of ice bobbing along the edges.

She and Casey reached the next ridge, taking a moment to catch their breath. Alex dared a peek at the snowmobilers. The woman remained behind by the helicopter, still going through their belongings. The other two moved boldly to the tents. They tore through them, slashing the tent walls and shaking out the stuff sacks. Then they moved to where Casey and Alex had first hidden, splitting up to flank them on either side of the ridge.

Their leader called out, "Come on out! You can't hide out here. We just want to talk to you."

She could see Neil still pressed against the other ridge, rocking back and forth, gripping the shotgun.

"You have something of ours. That's all we want," the leader shouted. "We won't harm you."

"What are they talking about?" Casey asked. "What do we have?"

"I have no idea," Alex told him. "The samples? Those are still by the helicopter. They could just take them."

"Do you have any idea who they are?" he asked her.

"None."

"We know you have it," the leader shouted.

Casey peeked out. "Can we somehow double back? Steal their snowmobiles?"

The woman pilfering through their gear was only feet away from the machines, a rifle strapped to her back.

Their only other option would be to wait here or cross to another large ridge, and the next one was at least two hundred feet away. If the attackers caught up with them, they'd be at their mercy, having to trust their word that they meant no harm. And though their shots had fallen short before, now they were more desperate. She didn't like the idea of counting on their goodwill.

The two men reached the pressure ridge where she and Casey had first hid and sprang around it, one of them firing several shots that would have cut right through them if they'd remained. So much for goodwill.

"Okay," Alex said. "We need a plan."

The two gunmen split up again. The leader moved toward Neil's hiding place. The second man followed Alex's and Casey's tracks. They had to make a stand now. Alex knelt down and flipped open the survival kit. The upper tray contained bandages, painkillers, antiseptic cream, small silver rectangles that would unfold into emergency blankets, a whistle, a compass, waterproof matches, a magnesium fire starter, and a signaling mirror. She lifted off the top tray. Beneath lay a flare gun with a single flare.

Casey picked it up and loaded it. Then he moved to the edge of the ridge where he could sneak glimpses at the approaching man.

He narrowed his eyes, taking a deep, steadying breath. Soon Alex could hear the crunch of the man's feet on the snow. He was only meters away. Casey sprang around the edge of the ice formation, pointed the flare gun at him, and fired.

Hot crimson streaked through the air, impacting his chest. Instantly the man's clothes caught on fire. He screamed as his synthetic jacket flamed and melted. Shrieking, he struggled to shuck off his jacket, getting tangled in his rifle strap. The woman heard the screaming and came running.

She reached her burning comrade and fought to free him from the rifle strap. But she was rewarded with an accidental blow to the face from his panicked movements. She fell backward, sprawling across the ice, cursing. As the man's jacket went up in flames, igniting his waterproof pants, he wheeled backward, screaming. The woman got to her feet and managed to unclip the rifle strap. Instantly her comrade shucked off his jacket, then his melted thermal shirt beneath. He tore off his boots and pants, leaving only his boxers, socks, and balaclava intact. Burns marked his bare sienna skin.

His companion stripped off her own jacket and draped it around her whimpering cohort.

She knelt in front of the wounded man, assessing the situation. "Goddamnit! We got to go!" she yelled toward the leader.

"Give him your jacket!" he shouted back to her.

"I already did!" She started helping the burned man back toward the snowmobiles. "If we don't leave now, he's not going to make it!"

But the leader didn't listen. He steadily approached Neil's hiding place, gun at the ready. There was no way Neil could run for a different spot of cover now. Not when the man had a rifle. And Alex didn't know how familiar Neil was with the shotgun.

"You got any more flares?" Casey whispered.

She shook her head.

She motioned wildly for Neil to stand up, pointing at the approaching gunman. Finally the grad student got to his feet. He braced the shotgun against his shoulder and peered out. As the attacker grew closer, still ignoring the cries of his cohorts, Neil gripped the shotgun with trembling hands. Then he sprang out, barrel waving wildly, and fired. The blast hit the man in the inner thigh and he cried out in surprise.

With blood streaming out onto the ice, he clutched at the wound and tried desperately to stanch the flow. Neil used the precious seconds to tear over to where Casey and Alex hid. The man spotted them and raised his rifle, giving up trying to compress the wound. "I'll kill you!" he shouted, advancing once more.

Alex watched viscous red pool beneath the man's boot.

"Are you crazy?" shouted the woman. She'd loaded her burned friend onto a snowmobile. He shuddered and groaned. "We have to go back!"

The man's leg continued to bleed at an alarming rate onto the white ice.

The woman tried to reason with him. "You could bleed out! Neither of you is going to make it if we don't leave right now!"

Gritting his teeth, the leader unzipped his snowsuit, tugging a belt from around his waist. "Goddamnit!" he cursed. He cinched the belt around his upper thigh. "This is not over!" he shouted, and started limping back toward the snowmobiles.

Alex watched them go, daring a look from behind the ice. They climbed aboard their snowmobiles and took off toward the west just as snow began to fall. Alex and the others stayed put until the sound of the engines had faded into the distance.

"What are we going to do now?" Neil asked.

Alex emerged from behind the ridge. "We assess the damage," she said, walking toward their gear.

"And then get the hell out of here," Casey added. "They'll be back."

SIXTEEN

Returning to their gear, they laid out their remaining supplies: three slashed all-weather tents, two undamaged sleeping bags and one slashed one, one intact sleeping pad and two that had been gouged with a knife. At least they hadn't been able to destroy the metal pegs they needed to stake the tents into the ice. Deep knife slashes had eviscerated the two tent bags, their contents thrown out and scattered.

The sat phone had been smashed, parts strewn over the ice. Casey stared down at it. "This is an unfortunate turn of events."

The blood, hair, and other samples were still there.

Alex stared out at the open landscape. "We have to move. Rescuers at least know where the helicopter went down. They can sweep the area and find us."

"Won't those gunmen do the same thing?" Neil asked, his forehead so creased with concern that dark red lines marked his skin.

Casey checked his watch barometer and examined the sky. "This storm will dump more snow. It'll cover our tracks. And they'll have to go back, seek medical attention. We can look for a place to hole up for the night."

Grabbing her backpack, Alex started stuffing additional gear into it. She rolled up a torn sleeping bag, a pad, and a tent and strapped them to the pack. She grabbed food, water, and an ice ax. Neil and Casey grabbed food and water bottles as well, then strapped sleeping bags and tents to the outside of their packs. Soon they stood facing each other, ready to set off. Alex stowed the samples and grabbed the tranquilizer gun. Already the arctic sun was setting, and for a moment it burst through a hole in the thick layer of clouds, casting a golden glow over the ice.

"Let's go," Alex said, her breath frosting in the frigid air.

They set off across the ice.

As they walked, the sky turned gold and then red and then a deep purple faded to gray.

"Who do you think they were?" Alex asked them. "The poachers who had placed out the set guns? Is that what they were looking for? Given their appearances and builds, none of them was Old Sam."

Neil trudged along in silence, shell-shocked.

"I have no idea," Casey answered. "And were they the ones who sabotaged the helicopter?"

"And how did they know where we went down?" she wondered. "A tracker? Or did they just see the smoke?"

Casey adjusted his balaclava as the wind picked up. "Maybe the poachers have been the ones doing the sabotage. If they did put a tracker in the helo, it would let them know if we got close to the set guns."

"Or maybe it's someone intent on sabotaging this study. Wanted to know where to find the wrecked helicopter to ensure the samples were destroyed," Alex wondered.

"One thing for certain," Neil said, speaking for the first time. "They were looking for something specific, and it wasn't the samples. They didn't take them."

Alex watched her boots crunch through the snow. "So what, then? Those snowmobilers were unrelated to whoever is trying to sabotage the study?"

"They could have been after the set gun evidence. They didn't know it had burned in the crash," Casey suggested.

Alex furrowed her brow. They *could* have just come from

checking the guns and discovered they'd been removed. But how did they find Alex's team when they'd been moving by air? Maybe they'd seen the helicopter go down? Or seen the plume of black smoke? But then they'd have to be in the area already. "Do you think they *could* have placed a tracker on the helicopter?"

Casey crossed his arms against the cold. "They may have figured we were the ones who had removed the guns."

They walked on in silence, covering miles of icy terrain. Night set in, and with the vanishing of the sun, the temperature plummeted. They pulled out headlamps and trod on. The snow began to fall, covering their tracks. A few times they stumbled in the darkness, tripping over jagged, uneven ice. Dangerous leads snaked through the white expanse, unstable sections where they could fall through. More than once they stepped on seemingly solid sections that tipped up dangerously, sloshing water over their boots. Alex was grateful for the waterproof material.

When they'd covered miles from the helicopter, they reached a section of somewhat stable ice that was surrounded by large pressure ridges. It offered good cover. Neil shivered in his parka and Casey had gone silent.

Alex stopped, examining the area with her headlamp. "This looks like a good spot."

The others shrugged off their packs, emptying the contents.

Alex stretched out the tents, assessing the damage. All three had large rents along the sides. She rummaged through the tent bags and came up with a repair kit. Giving a silent thanks for the kit, she went to work with Casey, cutting the tent repair tape to the right lengths to fix the rips. Neil moved around the scattered equipment, gauging the state of the sleeping bags and pads.

With the repairs finished, they put up the self-erecting tents, examining their handiwork.

"Not bad," Casey said.

Alex took in the tents as they fluttered in the wind, the bright red and blue strips of repair tape vivid against the yellow tent material. On the horizon, the sky looked even darker, thick clouds obscuring any stars. The wind had turned decidedly chillier.

Casey followed her gaze. "Going to be a cold one tonight."

She met his blue eyes, grateful he was with them. She felt strangely comforted by his presence. He was capable and kept a cool head in spite of the hell they'd been through.

"You doing okay?" he asked her.

She managed a smile. "Yes. I'm just glad the tents are intact."

He took in their handiwork. "For the most part."

She examined the slashed sleeping bag and used the remaining tent repair tape on the gashes.

"I'll take that one," Casey said. "I'm used to the cold."

They each ate an MRE, a Meal, Ready-to-Eat, in haste, eager to slide into the relative warmth of their sleeping bags. Then they retired. Alex shivered in the tent, her hands shaking so much with the cold that she struggled to unzip the mummy bag. She managed to untie her boots and pull them off. Crawling inside the bag, she draped her parka over her chest and zipped up the final few inches of the bag.

True night had descended over the ice. The wind buffeted the side of her tent, forcing freezing air through the zipper.

More than ten hours of darkness stretched ahead of them. She pulled the hood part of the bag up over her hat and couldn't stop shivering. She rubbed her legs together, rubbed her arms, and tried to stop her teeth from chattering. She could hear Neil shifting around in his tent to the right of her, zipping and unzipping his bag, moving gear around. On her left, she'd heard Casey zip up his bag and fall silent.

She switched off her headlamp, letting the darkness enfold her. She crossed her legs inside the sleeping bag and rubbed her feet together, then rubbed her hands over her arms, her shivering violent. Her eyes watered in the cold and instantly she could feel ice forming on her eyelashes. Neil stopped zipping things, and she could hear him doing the same thing, rubbing his arms vigorously.

Slowly the mummy bag started to do its job and her body heat became trapped inside. Her shivering eased as warmth spread over her, and finally her shoulders and the rest of her body relaxed. She wasn't tired. Not after the insanity of the day. And how could she sleep knowing those three could find them again, despite the miles they'd covered? She could hear the patter of snow against the stormfly and hoped their tracks would be covered quickly. The snowmobilers would likely approach from the west again, nearest to land, and the crushed-up tower of ice Alex's team had pitched their tents behind offered cover if anyone scanned from that direction.

Casey had the shotgun now and, with his training, would be a better shot than Neil. Alex had the tranquilizer gun.

She closed her eyes, but sleep wouldn't come. So she lay there, staring up at the seams in the tent ceiling, alert to any sound outside. Finally she closed her eyes, willing her body to rest. She dozed fitfully.

She wasn't sure how much time had passed, hours at least, she thought, when she heard Casey moving around. She heard his bag unzip, then his tent door, and his boots crunching on the snow.

She opened her eyes, noticing that the dark gloom of the tent ceiling she'd stared at for so long was now suffused with a strange green glow.

She heard Casey give a soft gasp. "Alex," he whispered. "Are you awake?"

"Yes," she whispered back.

"You should come out here."

Alex unzipped her bag, instantly feeling the cold seep in. She zipped it back up so it would retain some heat, pulled on her boots and parka, and stepped outside. The storm had moved off, and magnificent green and purple light danced in the sky. Alex stood mesmerized, staring up, as green curtains waved and raced across the sky. On the northern horizon, more curtains dropped, fading down into red, moving so quickly and sinuously she was struck silent by the beauty and magic.

The light intensified, and a curtain dropped down right over their heads, opening up into a rare, dazzling corona display. An emerald and white window unfurled above them, and she could see the stars through it. She stared up in awe, feeling like she was gazing into the heart of the cosmos itself.

"Neil!" she whispered. "You've got to see this."

She heard him grumble, undoing zippers, pulling on his boots, and he staggered outside. "What is—" His words cut off as he stared up in wonder.

The three of them stood out on the ice in silence and amazement, watching the celestial display. Pure joy infused Alex. Despite everything they'd been through and their current predicament, in this moment, she was utterly enchanted by the magnificence of the sweeping and dancing lights.

The cold forgotten, they stayed out until the last of the lights shimmered away. Then, as the others climbed back into their tents, Alex stayed out a few more minutes, gazing up in astonishment at the number of stars. The Milky Way swept across the entire arc of the sky. She could easily see the Andromeda Galaxy with her naked eye. The nebula in Orion's Belt glowed with a soft white luminescence. The familiar W shape of the Cassiopeia constellation was so filled with visible stars that it was almost difficult to pick out. Bright bands of nebulosity wove through the Milky Way next to dark dust trails. She'd never seen such a brilliant sky.

Finally, reluctantly, she started back to her tent, casting around in the starlight for any signs of attackers or curious polar bears. She saw only the shadowed shapes of the ice.

She crawled back into her bag and started the shivering all over again. But finally warmth found her and she managed to doze off.

IN THE MORNING, ALEX WOKE to muted white light spilling into her tent. She pulled on her parka and stepped outside, disappointed to see a thick layer of cloud cover above them and dense fog that limited visibility to just ten feet.

Casey was already up, and he'd prepared some freeze-dried meals and made coffee. He offered her a cup as she approached the little Sterno stove. Neil was still in his tent, but she could hear he was awake, shifting around.

"Don't think there's much chance of a rescue this morning," Casey said as he handed her the cup.

She took a sip of the bitter brew, welcoming its warmth. She glanced around at their camp. "It might not be a bad idea to have our stuff packed up and ready to go. If those snowmobilers attack us again, we don't want to lose what we have left. They could destroy the rest of our gear."

Casey nodded. "That's a good point."

When she finished eating, Alex returned to her tent and let the air out of the bedroll, then stuffed the sleeping bag inside its sack. When she climbed out, Neil was up, yawning and gazing around bleary-eyed.

"Are we moving?" he asked, watching her begin to take down her tent.

She straightened up. "I think we should just pack up, in case we need to move in a hurry."

He stared back at his tent. "Good idea."

After wolfing down his meal, Neil returned to his tent and started packing his own gear. Casey turned off the Sterno, waiting for it to cool. Alex attached her tent, sleeping bag, and pad to the exterior of her backpack and brought it over by Casey.

He stood up, scanning the landscape. "I think I saw a flat patch of ice to the north of us yesterday," he said. "It was next to some pretty steep pressure ridges. We could scrape out a big SOS in the snow there and take refuge on the lee side of a ridge. The snowmobilers wouldn't be able to see the SOS from the ground, so we'd still be hidden."

"That's a really good idea."

When they'd finished packing up their gear, they hefted on their backpacks and started again across the ice. The wind blew, buffeting Alex's hood, ice crystals stinging her face in the small gap between her balaclava and her sunglasses. Neil trudged along at the rear in silence.

They crossed a section of rough ice and had to be careful not to move too quickly. They could see only a few feet in front of them, and open leads here loomed suddenly out of the fog, forcing them to walk parallel until they found a place to cross.

The weather started to improve and the fog lifted a little, revealing more of the landscape around them. Ahead Alex saw the flat, unbroken stretch of ice that Casey had mentioned. Closer to them towered ridges and whimsical sculptures of jumbled ice, good places for cover.

They walked alongside a lead, the blue water sloshing quietly at the edges of the ice. A bearded seal surfaced and snorted out air, followed by two others. Their mottled tan and brown fur wet and dark, they stared at Alex with curious black eyes, then disappeared again. She scanned the area. Where there were seals, there were polar bears.

A wind picked up, so strong that it actually knocked Alex forward when it caught her back. They cast around and found a dense jumble of ice formations, all clustered together. They slung their packs down on the east side of it, away from the wind and out of sight of any snowmobilers who might be approaching from the west again.

She gazed skyward. A low level of clouds still hovered above them, but if it cleared, search and rescue would hopefully make a flight over the area and spot them.

All three walked out onto a flat stretch of ice to create a letter. Shuffling along the ice, kicking up the snow with her boots, Alex started on the first *S*. Neil made the *O* in the middle, with Casey scraping out the final *S*. The wind burst in gusts across the ice, and Alex wondered how long it would be before all their work was obliterated.

They'd been at work for only ten minutes when they heard snowmobiles roaring toward their location.

SEVENTEEN

"Get to cover!" Alex shouted, and they raced for the pressure ridge. Not wanting their gear to be all in one place, they quickly stashed their packs in different locations.

Alex's tranquilizer gun was loaded, and Casey checked the chamber on his shotgun. Neil held the flare gun. They'd found two more flares in their supplies, and Neil had reloaded it.

The snowmobiles drew closer, and Alex hoped vainly that the riders wouldn't spot their tracks in the snow. Maybe they'd just speed by.

She scanned the ice to spot them, eyes tearing in the gale, and saw a single polar bear making its way toward them. It lifted its nose, sniffing the air, catching their scent. They were upwind of it. Intrigued, it moved closer.

She pressed her back against the ridge of ice, moving out of sight. The snowmobile engines slowed as they came across their trail, then she heard shouts. The engines cut out. She couldn't see them, and she crept along the ridge to risk a peek.

Alex was glad they'd walked all over the area, searching for the best spot to lay their gear, because the myriad trails didn't lead directly to them. The three assailants dismounted from two snowmobiles. Balaclavas completely covered their features. One began barking orders in a familiar gruff voice, and when he dismounted from his snowmobile, his limp revealed he was the one Neil had shot in the leg.

Their pursuers split up, unslinging their rifles from their shoulders and following Alex's team's tracks. They were so intent on staring down that none of them noticed the approaching polar bear.

The woman walked along the open lead, her rifle at the ready, studying their trackways and glancing around her every few seconds.

A ringed seal surfaced next to her, letting out a great snort of air, and she whirled, taking aim at it. It dipped back below the surface, giving a mottled-gray flipper splash as it swam away.

Alex, Casey, and Neil's location amid the maze of jumbled ice formations created an ideal cover, with myriad ways of ingress and egress and windows to defend against their attackers.

Casey pointed to himself and to one of the men who was approaching their location, then gripped his shotgun. He patted Neil on the shoulder and pointed to the leader, who was skirting around an ice formation to their left. He pointed to Neil's flare gun and Neil vigorously shook his head.

"I can't!" he whispered. "The others'll spot me!"

"I'll take care of the others," Casey whispered back. "Just get that guy."

Neil shuddered and pressed against the ice. "I can't. It's too loud. Too bright. And not exactly deadly. Give me the shotgun, or at least the damn tranq gun."

Alex dared a glance at the polar bear. It was almost at the edge of the SOS sign, curious and heading straight for them.

She handed the tranquilizer gun to Neil. "Here. Take it." He grabbed it. His attention was already directed toward the leader.

And then all hell broke loose.

Neil jumped out from behind a formation to take aim at the leader. But before he could fire, she heard the crack of a rifle and it echoed off the ice walls around them. Neil slumped down, red smearing the ice wall behind him, the tranquilizer gun tumbling to the ground.

Alex ran to his side and grabbed the tranq gun, raising it up just as the leader readied to take a second shot. She fired, the dart hitting him in the soft tissue of his neck. He grabbed at the dart, tugging it out, and slipped backward on the ice, landing hard on his back. She shoved another dart into the chamber, watching as the leader staggered away.

Then she knelt beside Neil, blood seeping through a hole in his parka. Synthetic down puffed out, stained red.

Casey set down the shotgun and tore off his hat and thick balaclava. He pressed them to the wound. Neil's breathing came ragged and wet.

"It's punctured his lung," Casey breathed.

In their moment of distraction, they didn't realize the second man had zeroed in on their position until it was too late. He swung around from behind an ice tower, just feet away from them, the barrel of his gun pointed at Alex.

Casey moved so suddenly that Alex jumped back. He didn't have time to grab his shotgun. Instead he leapt forward, driving the man's rifle barrel skyward, then grabbed it and twisted the weapon around, spinning the man with it, and began to strangle him with the rifle strap. The man's foot hit Casey's shotgun, sending it skittering away across the ice, out of reach.

On the far side of the fight, the sedated leader groggily stumbled back toward the machines.

The man Casey fought with got his fingers between his own neck and the strap and twisted violently, kicking backward into Casey's knee.

Alex whirled. Where was the woman? Then she spotted her, jogging toward their location. Soon she'd come around the side of the ridge and spot them, and Neil was in no condition to be moved. Alex eyed Casey's shotgun, but it was so far away and out in the open that the woman could easily pick her off if she went for it. Alex had to somehow lead her away. The bear drew ever nearer, too, curious at the commotion. As the wind screamed around her, Alex got an idea.

She crouched over Neil. "I'm going to try to lure them away. Maybe we can circle back and get one of the snowmobiles. Get you to safety."

He gritted his teeth and nodded, his face slick with sweat despite the cold. Alex bit her lip. Even if she did manage to get Neil away, could they get to shore, get him medical attention before it was too late?

Casey still fought furiously against his attacker, and Alex was running out of time.

Her backpack lay the closest, and she raced to it. Returning with it to Neil's location, Alex pulled out the ice ax and tent. She stuffed the tent inside her parka. Grabbing a coiled section of rope, she draped it over her shoulder. Then she pulled out a small tin of bandages and dumped the contents into her pack, pocketing the tin. Alex pressed the flare gun into Neil's hand, then set off toward the nearest tall pressure ridge.

Behind them, the woman was skirting around the ice formations. Every now and then, Alex caught a glimpse of her black snowsuit through the breaks, but the woman hadn't zeroed in on Neil's location yet.

Alex raced to a tall pressure ridge a hundred feet away. She needed to be visible, but still have cover. At the jumbled base of the ridge, she swung the ice ax and it caught hold. She raised her body up, then kicked footholds to move upward. Again she swung the ax and pulled herself up, chipping away at footholds, finding narrow crevasses for the fingers of her left hand. It was difficult and slow-going in her gloves. But she started to gain height. The pressure ridge was about twenty feet high, offering plenty of cover once she was on the lee side. The wind tore at her parka hood, pushing it farther down, sometimes covering her face and blocking her vision. Finally she tugged it back. Soon she'd be high enough that the woman would spot her, offering the attacker a clear shot. Alex had to move more quickly. She dared a glance back but, to her dismay, didn't see where the woman was. The leader was still staggering back toward the snowmobiles. She couldn't see Casey or his attacker at all.

Alex chipped away with her toes and swung the ax again. She was almost at the top of the ridge. Suddenly her feet slipped and all her weight came down on the ax. Her gloved hand gripped it tightly, the fingertips of her left hand desperately clinging to a tiny crevasse in the ice. Her arms trembled. She was about to crash back down. She brought her legs in forcefully, arcing toward the ice with as much force as she could muster. One toe found a tiny ledge to put her weight on. Her fingers got a better grip. She dug in her other foot and slid upward. And then she was at the top, pulling out the tent and unwrapping the cord.

Quickly she made a large slipknot with one end of the cord, tying the other end to the deployment strap on the self-erecting tent.

Now exposed on the ridge, she braced herself against the unbearable wind. It gusted at her back, threatening to knock her off. She turned to see where the woman was, her eyes instantly tearing in the bitter gale. She spotted her, moving between the formations, getting dangerously close to Neil. Soon the woman would find him.

Alex arranged the tent down in the snow, making sure the door was open and unzipped, then covered up the tent as best she could. Then she tossed the middle part of the rope down the leeward side of the ridge.

"Hey!" Alex called, waving her arms. "We give up!" She held up the small tin. She figured whatever they were looking for, it must be something fairly small, since they had dug through their packs and even opened small containers in their search. "Here's what you want! Just take it and leave! We don't want any trouble!" She placed the empty bandage tin in the center of the cord loop, making sure snow covered the rope.

The woman stormed in her direction, lifting the rifle to her shoulder, readying to fire.

Just then a powerful gust of wind hit Alex with visceral force. She struggled to keep her balance, arms windmilling. She couldn't stay upright. Then she was free-falling headfirst off the top of the ridge, away from the woman. The ice formation slanted outward and her back struck it hard, her body tumbling violently all the way down. She hit the bottom with such force that a plume of snow erupted around her and the air exploded from her lungs in a sudden gush that left her reeling.

She tried to get a breath. Couldn't. She stared up at the gray sky, mouth gaping, the swirls of snow now collecting on her face, in her eyelashes, in her open mouth. She struggled to sit up, feeling like a turtle on its back, and finally the air rushed back into her lungs just as explosively as it had left. She could breathe.

Alex wondered how much progress the woman had made. It would take her longer to climb to the top without an ice ax. Alex fought in the snow to get to her feet, finding the center of the cord and gripping it. Then she pressed close to the lee side of the ridge, staring upward. As soon as the woman bent to take the tin . . .

Alex waited, not hearing any gunfire, wondering how Casey and Neil fared. She could hear a little better above the wind on this side, and she welcomed the warmth of being out of the chilling tempest. An open lead of water snaked just to the east, about two hundred feet away, and she watched as whitecaps kicked up on its surface.

A curious seal popped up its head, gazing in her direction. It was followed by a second, then a third. She'd completely lost sight of the polar bear and hoped it had moved off in another direction.

This was taking too long. Her stomach clenched at the thought of Neil. Was he still applying pressure to the wound? Was he bleeding out, even now?

A black shape appeared at the top of the ridge. Alex braced herself, gripping the cord. The woman bent to pick up the tin. As soon as her hand met the snow, Alex yanked on one side of the cord. The loop at the top cinched around the woman's wrist. Alex pulled the other end, deploying the tent. It instantly sprang to its full dimensions, the wind gusting into the open door.

"What the—" the woman managed to say before the tent rocketed up into the air, caught in the gale. Alex released the cord and it pulled tight as the tent sailed away. The rope yanked on the woman's arm, sending her off-balance and careening down the lee side of the ridge. Alex leapt out of the way as the woman crashed down, crying out in surprise. The tent soared away, dragging her across the ice.

The woman flailed, managing to hold on to her rifle while trying in vain to dig her feet into the snow to stop her sliding. But the wind was too strong. The tent flew along just above the ice like a windsail, pulling her behind, straight toward the open lead. A plume of snow arced up around her, and Alex watched as she was dragged all the way to the water. Airborne, the tent crossed the lead and kept going, still caught on the powerful gust. Then the woman hit the open water and wasn't so lucky. She plunged into the icy slush, letting out a terrified shriek of surprise as the frigid water enveloped her. Splashing in the water, she struggled to untie her wrist from the cord.

Not wanting to lose another second, Alex raced around the ridge, back to where Neil sat. He still pressed Casey's balaclava and hat to the wound, but so much blood had spread out on the ice that Alex swallowed hard.

Casey and his attacker were still locked in combat, but had moved a dozen feet away into the open. The man's rifle had skittered away onto the ice. Casey stood in front of the man and landed a brutal roundhouse kick to the attacker's face. The man flew backward onto the ice, cracking his head.

Alex grabbed the flare gun and came around the side of the formation, taking aim at the man on the snow, but Casey dashed in to kick him, blocking her shot. The man on the ice struggled to a sitting position. Casey came at him. Grabbing him by the hood, Casey swung his body down onto the ice behind him. He gripped the man's neck, squeezing, and then with a brutal twist snapped his neck. The man slumped lifeless onto the ice.

Movement to her left drew Alex's attention. The polar bear was now just twenty feet away, sniffing the air, winding through the ice formations toward them. She heard labored breathing and snapped her gaze to the far side of one of the ice towers, seeing the shivering, drenched female attacker lurching toward the snowmobiles. The bear stood in her path, but the tower blocked her view of it.

She was going to pass right by Neil. The woman came around the formation and spotted him and the tranq gun, snatching up the weapon. Her whole body shook violently. Anger glittering in her eyes, she raised the gun at Neil. But just then the bear meandered around the tower and she spun wildly, spotting it, fear sweeping over her face.

The bear towered up on its hind legs, facing off against the woman. The shivering snowmobiler struggled to raise the tranq gun. The bear sniffed the air in front of her and the woman screamed, firing the tranq rifle into the bear's neck. Startled at the sudden sting, it took a swipe at her and she ducked, sprinting away. She passed her comrade's discarded rifle and snatched it up.

In the distance, the leader had finally reached his snowmobile. Groggily, he swung his leg over it and started it up. He turned it in an arc, bringing up a spray of snow. The woman staggered to the second machine and whipped it around, taking off right after him.

But the leader had motored only a few feet before Alex saw he was heading straight for an open lead. He slumped in his seat, the engine roar dwindling as he slackened off the controls. Then he slid entirely off the moving snowmobile, unconscious. It continued forward for a few feet, plunging into the crack in the ice. She watched its paddle tracks sink below the dark water.

Behind him, the woman stopped and dismounted. She ran to him, then dragged him back to her machine.

Casey raced for the shotgun, whipped it up, and fired off a blast, but they were out of range.

With some effort the woman lifted the prostrate man's dead-weight onto the back of her snowmobile. Then she took off, snow flying up behind them.

At the roar of the engines, the drugged bear spooked, trying to lope away across the ice, but moving too slowly to get very far.

The lone snowmobile raced away into the distance.

Alex and Casey hurried back to Neil. He had slumped down completely onto the ice, sprawled on his back.

Casey pressed the makeshift compress to his chest while Alex dug out the medical kit.

Neil reached a bloody hand toward her. "I'm sorry," he breathed.

"None of this is your fault," she told him.

She could barely hear him. "They paid me to mislay equipment. Sabotage the study. I didn't think they'd resort to this." Tears streamed down his temples and he squeezed his eyes shut against the pain. "I didn't . . . I didn't mess with the helicopter."

"Don't try to talk," she told him. "Hold on."

Alex pulled out gauze and Casey pressed it to the wound.

"It's so cold." Neil's body shuddered, blood already soaking through the new compress. Neil opened his eyes and said in a suddenly calm voice, "That girl. The intern? I think she really likes me. I should ask her out." Then his eyes went glassy and his jaw slack. A long exhale escaped his body and the shuddering stopped.

Casey pressed two fingers against his wrist. Waited. Then tried Neil's carotid. Finally he took out a signaling mirror and held it to Neil's mouth. Nothing. "He's gone."

Alex rocked back on her heels. Crimson blood streamed over the ice beneath her. She shook her head. "I can't believe it." She stared down at his body, blinking back tears of shock. "This can't be happening." He was so young. Just starting out in his career. And that fast, he was gone. In the distance, she could still hear the whine of the snowmobile engine as it faded away. "Who the hell are these people?"

Casey knelt in the snow, gazing down at Neil's body. A great sadness had swept over him, a deep dejection. She sensed it was far more than the loss of Neil, but a deeper grief he carried around with him, that Neil was just the latest in a long string of sadness. "I couldn't save him."

She reached across and squeezed his arm. "You were amazing. I've never seen someone fight like that."

"It wasn't enough. He was just a kid. He didn't know how to fight."

"It's not something you expect to have to do when taking a job doing polar bear research."

She looked back at Neil's slack face. His eyes were starting to film over. "What should we do?"

Casey wiped at his nose and stared up. Thick gray clouds still blanketed the sky above them. They showed no signs of lifting. A thin snow continued to fall. A search party would be a long time coming.

"They came back once," she said. "They could come back again."

"We'll have to move again. Hope that the snow will cover our tracks."

She stared down with regret. "We'll have to leave Neil's body, won't we? The RCMP will want to examine the scene." She pulled her GPS unit out of her jacket and took a reading of their location. The pack ice drifted, but hopefully it wouldn't have moved too far before they could find help.

Casey strode over to the man he'd killed and tore off his balaclava. "Do you recognize him?" he asked Alex.

She joined him, staring down at the man's face, his neck marked with burns. He was obviously the attacker Casey had shot with the flare gun. He looked familiar. Then it hit her. This was one of the men who'd been in Moe's, coming after the nervous little guy Steve.

"I do," she said. "I saw him once at Moe's. But I have no idea who he is. He was with a man and a woman. It's got to be the same people."

She thought back to the portly man from the pub. He must be the leader of the snowmobilers. She wondered what they'd done to Steve. Maybe killed him? How was it all connected?

They'd been after Steve. Pursuing him. He must have had something they wanted. Information? Something more physical, like an object of some kind? And she'd talked to him that night. They'd seen her. Did they think he'd given her something? Told her something? She frowned. It couldn't be something he'd mentioned. Not with the way they were searching through their belongings. No, it was something physical. And given how they'd torn apart even their smaller supply boxes, it wasn't very big. But he hadn't given her anything. Hadn't even told her anything.

But they were desperate. And where was Steve? Had he, out of desperation to save his own life, told them he'd passed whatever it was on to her?

Casey threw the balaclava onto the man's chest. "No one knows what trouble we're in," he said quietly. "As far as the rescue team is concerned, we're waiting comfortably in our tents until they can reach us."

They moved to where Casey and Neil had flung their gear, and Alex's breath froze. Both packs were gone. In the chaos, the attackers must have grabbed them, or even gone through them and tossed what they didn't want into the open water, where they'd sunk out of sight. Only Alex's pack remained.

"Oh no," she breathed. "Our supplies . . ." They'd be dangerously low now. No tent, one sleeping bag, little food.

A loud splash made her jump. She snapped her gaze to the direction of the lead. The sedated polar bear had fallen into the water and was trying to swim away. But the drug had fully kicked in, making him struggle.

He was drowning.

EIGHTEEN

Hastily Alex tore through the remaining pack, pulling out the survival suit inside. She stripped off her parka and slipped on the suit, cinching the neck closure tightly so her clothes wouldn't get wet. Then she ran across the ice. Ahead of her, the bear chuffed and struggled in the water, trying to keep his head above the surface.

Steadying herself on the edge of the ice, Alex lowered herself into the freezing water. She felt the pressure close around her arms and legs. Feeling a wave of fear, she pushed off the ice's edge and swam toward the bear.

He was already ten feet out, realizing his predicament. Now he clambered toward the opposite edge, anxious to pull himself out. His limbs hung limply, the tranquilizer taking disastrous effect. His head went under.

Alex kicked powerfully, swimming up beside him, realizing how massive the bear was next to her small frame. She thrust her hand up under his chin, keeping his muzzle above the water.

The bear coughed and sputtered, limbs failing him. Alex swam flush against him, keeping his head up. *Please. Don't let him drown.*

She struggled to keep her own head above the freezing water, fought to keep her hand on his muzzle. Frigid droplets splashed in her face. They had seven feet to go. She kicked and the bear flailed. His head went under again as he fought to paddle to shore, and a powerful swipe of his front paw sent her reeling under, too. She surfaced, gasping, the shocking cold of the water burning her face. Once more she resumed her position beside the bear, holding his muzzle aloft. Five feet to go.

He churned in the water. Alex almost lost contact. She swallowed frigid seawater. Three more feet. Two.

Then the bear seized the edge of the ice with his gigantic paws and began to heave up onto the cold surface. Alex kicked away from him, giving him room. She watched with a powerful sigh of relief as he pulled himself up onto the ice and slumped down in a dripping pile. He lowered his head. Already he was falling asleep.

Moving a few feet away, she hooked her elbows around the ice's edge and kicked her feet to rise to the surface. She found a narrow crack in the ice and wedged her fingers inside, then pulled herself out.

Soon she and the bear both lay on the ice, Alex gasping for breath and the bear fast asleep.

Casey had run along the lead, finding a narrow place to cross, and leapt over to her side. He knelt down beside her, placing a hand on her back. "That was amazing!"

Alex gasped for breath, already violently shivering.

He helped her up. "Let's get your hair dried off and get you out of that thing. Back into your warm parka."

"Yes," she managed to say, struggling to stand. Beside them the bear breathed evenly.

With Casey's help, she walked on wobbling legs back to where Neil lay, the adrenaline flooding out of her system and leaving her shaky. She shucked out of the survival suit and donned her warm parka. For several long minutes, she sat next to Neil's body, trying to still her breathing. With the fight over, she now felt sick and unsteady. Casey knelt beside her and they said their silent goodbyes to Neil, her mind still reeling about his admission that he'd sabotaged the study. Who was behind all this?

She didn't want to leave until the bear had woken up, so they remained like that, silently breathing in the foggy afternoon, watching the faint shadows shift around the ice formations as the filtered sunlight came and went.

Finally the bear stirred and stood up, blinking. It glanced their way but was no longer curious. It moved off, snow pluming behind its gigantic paws. When it had walked a mile on the ice, becoming a mere yellowish dot moving into the distance, Alex realized it was time to move on, too.

At first she didn't think she'd be able to get up. Casey hooked a hand under her arm and helped her. She stood on trembling legs as Casey donned the backpack. At least they still had a compass and her GPS unit.

In silence, they set off across the ice. A few minutes later, bright yellow movement attracted Alex's gaze. It was her tent, hung up on an ice formation. Her spirits lifted at the sight of it. They hurried to the tent and reattached it to the pack.

They walked for several long miles. Casey bled from a cut above his eye, and he stopped for a moment to break into the survival kit to stop the bleeding. Alex felt numb, cold leaching into her bones, watching him as he worked. The cut cleaned, they moved on, neither talking.

They passed over sections of rough ice, stepping over narrow leads and working around areas that felt spongy beneath their boots. Alex trudged on, not even really feeling her legs, her mind blank as she squinted into the overcast afternoon. Her breath had caused ice to form on her balaclava, and before she realized it, a thick rime had formed on the material, the weight pulling it down. She trundled on, scraping at the ice absently with her glove.

Next to her, Casey struggled with some inner turmoil he didn't share. In the moments when Alex drifted into a better awareness of her surroundings and him, she sensed he was far away, preoccupied with grave thoughts of some kind. He clenched his jaw and walked with his fists balled at his sides.

Snow drifted down, muffling the world around them. The quiet solitude of it matched the stillness that had crept into her heart and mind. She felt cocooned in cotton, like the world was turning in slow motion.

The afternoon wore on, and still they walked, pausing only to drink from their remaining water bottle. To refill it, they stuffed it with snow, then tucked it inside one of their parkas to melt. Casey came more and more back to the present, glancing over at Alex on occasion, checking on her.

On the far side of a section of rough ice, they discovered a wide, flat stable area on the lee side of a pressure ridge.

"I think this might be a good spot to camp," he said, his voice quiet in the still of the snowfall.

"Okay." Exhaustion suddenly overcame Alex, as if upon finding the place, she'd given her body permission to feel how tired she actually was. He slung the pack off his back. Together they pitched the tent and unfolded the remaining sleeping bag and pad. They each ate one MRE, chewing in silence. The wind picked up, flapping the stormfly.

He glanced at the barometer on his wrist. "Storm's getting worse. Maybe the snow will collect on the tent. Give us a little insulation."

As they sat facing each other in the tent, Alex began to feel a little better. She drank some of the melted snow and the food made her feel less shaky.

Casey looked at the sleeping bag. "We'll have to share. Is that okay with you?"

"I don't think we have a choice. We'll freeze if we don't."

He nodded.

Once again she was struck by the feeling of comfort she got from his presence. He was a good ally. Someone she felt she could count on. They stripped off their bulky parkas so they could lay them over their chests. Alex untied her boots and left them by the tent door, then she crawled into the bag.

Casey shucked off his boots and climbed in next to her, pulling the parkas over them. Without her coat, she started shivering. They couldn't zip up the top of the bag with both of them inside it. He tucked her coat in around her shoulders, then lay down on his back.

She rested next to him, their shared body heat beginning to warm the space inside the sleeping bag. Where their shoulders made contact she felt a slight zing of electricity. In the close interior of the tent, she caught his scent for the first time, alluring, almost spicy. The wind howled and buffeted the sides of the tent.

She shivered on her back and rubbed her arms, her teeth chattering. Next to her, she could feel Casey shaking, too. She moved a little closer to him, their feet touching at the bottom of the bag. She thought of Neil, of his body, of his admitting that he'd sabotaged the study. She couldn't stop shivering.

"I can't believe Neil is gone."

Casey was silent.

"And that he'd sabotaged the study. He must have been the one to remove our gear from the helicopter—the missing equipment we needed that day, the lip tattoo clamp, the extra syringe. Who do you think paid him to do it?"

Casey exhaled. "I have no idea. But I don't think he realized they would resort to lethal measures."

"You think whoever paid him also sabotaged the helicopter?"

"It makes sense. We could have been killed. The study would be over." He shifted. "You said you recognized one of the men."

Alex told him more about Steve, how the group had chased him out of Moe's. "But I don't know what they were after. All I know is that Steve was looking for a boat to rent." She told Casey about Sasha and her missing partner, and the body Alex had found. "I wonder if it's all connected. I don't think those snowmobilers have found what they're looking for."

Casey rubbed his arms for warmth. His expression became grim. "Well, they have one less person now." His shoulders shook. "I wonder if that will slow them down. They're definitely determined."

She watched his sad face. "Are you okay? I mean, after what happened out there?"

He pursed his lips. "I didn't want to take a life. But we didn't have much choice."

She shook her head in disbelief. "Part of me can't believe we're stuck out here like this. That Neil is gone."

"Me either."

She continued to shiver. Instead of getting warmer, she felt herself growing colder, as if the events of the day hovered in the air around her, pressing cold hands against her.

"Here," Casey said, turning on his side to face her. He lifted his arm, exposing the space against his chest. She turned on her side, away from him, and moved backward into the warm space. He wrapped his arm around her, pulling her into him. Now she could really smell him and was all too aware of their proximity. Her shivering slowed, then stopped. Her jaw ached from her teeth chattering, and finally it relaxed.

"Thank you," she said.

They lay together in the dark, her wide eyes staring at the shuddering tent wall as the wind howled around them.

"How long do you think the storm will last?" she asked.

He lifted his arm to look at the barometer on his watch. "It's still dropping."

Even that small removal of contact made her cold again. He replaced his arm, warmth returning to her shoulder. The electric zing she'd felt at the touch of their shoulders came back.

"I'll bet you're so glad you took this job," she said, smiling a little.

"Thrilled," he said with a small chuckle.

"Easy money."

He broke into a genuine laugh that was infectious and she laughed, too. It felt good after the ordeal they'd been through. *An ordeal we're still going through,* she thought.

She listened to the sound of his breathing, the scraping of wind-blown snow against the tent. Finally she asked, "How did you learn to fly a helicopter?"

"My dad. He ran a search and rescue operation in Scotland. Taught me how to fly as a teenager, though I'd been up and down in helicopters my whole life."

She flashed to the image of him fighting on the ice. "Where did you learn to fight like that?"

He was quiet for so long, she thought he might have fallen asleep, but his breathing hadn't changed. "I trained with the UN Peacekeeping Forces. Learned how to fight. I joined because I wanted to help people, but ultimately, the thought of being in a situation where I'd have to actually kill someone gave me serious pause. In the end, I trained as a combat medic."

"Where did they send you?"

"A few places in Africa. We mostly dealt with places where war-lords were in power and the areas were in turmoil. The worst was Darfur. A warlord there had seized a large piece of territory, hold-ing villages in a constant state of terror. We tried to protect people, but the warlord was powerful. He was so rich he always greased the right hands and was able to bring in more and more guns." He swallowed, going quiet again. Then, more softly, he said, "I've never seen such brutality. Women raped and murdered, children killed. Old men and women savagely beaten to death by men who grinned while they did it. The warlord gave his soldiers carte blanche to steal, terrorize, and burn down any villages they pleased."

She could feel his sadness, the catch in his throat. She reached up and touched his hand where it rested on her arm. "I'm so sorry," she whispered.

"To stand by, feeling so helpless, watching while innocent people were butchered, was too much. The system just wasn't working. Two times we closed in on his location and he came out, unarmed, to surrender. But both times when he was taken into custody, he bribed his way to being released."

"What happened to him?"

"Someone killed him. One of his own men, they think."

"And his followers?"

"Without his money and influence, they dispersed."

"How long were you with the peacekeeping forces?"

"Eight years. When I got out, I traveled for a while. Flew helicopters for tourists in Bali, Thailand, Hawaii, the Grand Canyon. Then I started taking on jobs flying scientists. Some glaciologists in Wrangell–St. Elias in Alaska, and then with a polar bear project and the Greenland Ice Sheet Project."

"Sounds really cool."

They fell into silence as the wind tore at the sides of the tent. She could see that the windward side sagged, covered in snow. At least they'd be a little warmer now.

"And you?" he asked. "How did you come to be a wildlife biologist?"

She smiled. "I've always been fascinated with wildlife. My dad really got me interested when I was little. My mom was a fighter pilot with the air force, so we lived in a lot of different places. My dad is a successful landscape painter, so he could work from anywhere. Whenever we moved, he would dive into learning all the local fauna. He had this uncanny ability to spot wildlife, too. It was like creatures just came out to look at him. On Saturday mornings, he'd get up before me and my mom, and sit outside drinking his cup of coffee. By the time I got up to join him, he would point out at least a dozen little snakes or turtles or birds who had gathered near him. I swear he was like Snow White or something. He'd sing or whistle, and all these creatures would appear—garter snakes slithering in the grass, box turtles tromping through the leaves.

"My mom told me that on their first date, they decided to go for a hike, and as they crossed this glade, he said, 'There should be a salamander under this rock,' and when he flipped it over, sure enough, there was a salamander beneath it."

"Whoa."

Alex laughed. "My mom was pretty impressed. Over the years, he taught me all about reptiles and amphibians. He loved all animals. In the evenings, we'd sit out on the porch and gaze at fireflies or watch raccoons rooting around in the yard. He had a whole stack of field guides, and whenever we moved, we'd learn the local birdsongs together."

She felt a little warmer thinking about her dad. She imagined him at his house in Berkeley, reading an Ellery Queen novel by the fire or sitting at his easel, gazing dreamily at a new landscape painting. "As I grew older, I read more and more books about wildlife." She stared at the tent wall. "I remember how devastated I was when I first learned about extinction. I didn't understand how an animal could just vanish off the face of the earth. And I was horrified to learn that humans were responsible for so many. It's one of the reasons I dedicated my life to doing all I could to help."

She laughed. "In elementary school, my friends thought I was a little crazy. I used to do chores for my neighbors so I could earn money to send off to Greenpeace and Defenders of Wildlife. That's how I wanted to spend my weekends, and I roped a few of them into helping sometimes. Other days I'd ride my bike down to the local wildlife rescue center and muck out cages."

"So you always wanted to study wildlife?" Casey asked her.

"There was a brief time when I wanted to be a private investigator," she confessed, "and solve mysteries like on reruns of eighties shows like *Simon & Simon* or *Magnum, P.I.* You know, high-speed chases, wearing disguises and infiltrating the bad guys' lairs. And when I was four, I was pretty sure I wanted to be a rabbit when I grew up."

Casey laughed.

"But yeah. Protecting wildlife has been my dream for a very long time. In high school I volunteered with just about every organization I could find as we moved around. I did tons of citizen science projects: mist-netting birds and bats, wolf tracking, American pika monitoring, monarch butterfly winter counts."

She exhaled, feeling both there with him in the tent and also a million miles away with all the challenges that faced struggling species. "There are so many battles to fight, Casey. I wrestle sometimes with how insurmountable it feels. Monarch butterflies are vanishing. American pikas are disappearing as the earth warms. Wolves and grizzlies are being killed in staggering numbers, gunned down by trophy hunters and governments; vast tracts of habitat are being destroyed; acidification of the ocean; the vanishing of polar sea ice . . . I never feel like I'm doing enough."

She shifted, rubbing her feet together in an attempt to warm them. "When I was a kid, I thought one person could make a difference, that I could take my sheer power of will and go out into the world and make people listen, make governments create protective legislation.

"But the battle is so much harder than I ever could have imagined, and while some people are out there fighting the good fight, many others who *do* care feel paralyzed by a lack of hope and don't do anything. And that just makes me feel like I have to work ten times harder to make up for the people who are depressed into inaction. Not to mention the people who simply don't care at all, and there are a hell of a lot of those."

She shook her head, suddenly feeling self-conscious. "I'm sorry, that's probably way longer of an answer than you wanted."

"No," he told her, his voice intense and genuine. "No, that's a perfect answer."

Something about the darkness and his warmth and proximity lent a feeling of intimacy, of hushed confidentiality. She hadn't felt close to someone like this in a long time, and she grew all the more curious about him. "Do you still spend a lot of time with your dad?"

Casey shifted his position slightly. "Not as much as I'd like to. I don't get home too often."

"And your mom?"

She felt Casey's warm breath on the back of her neck. "She passed away when I was twelve. There was a bombing in London. Three people died."

"That's terrible. Did they catch who did it?"

"No. And no one ever claimed responsibility."

Alex rolled over and faced him. "I'm so sorry."

"Thanks. It was rough. My dad was really lost after that. Started drinking a lot by himself." He stared up at the tent ceiling. "Not that he was a mean drunk or anything. He just wanted to be numb. He didn't really know how to talk to me about her loss. He'd get upset if I ever mentioned her name. And I looked a lot like her and had similar interests, so I think I was a constant reminder.

"She was really into astronomy. We had this telescope, and we'd spend hours up on our roof, watching the stars. She had a special little platform built for it." Casey's eyes met hers in the dark. "After she was gone, that platform felt like the emptiest place in the world. I lost all heart for looking at stars.

"My dad and I started spending evenings apart. We used to all eat dinner together. But after she was gone, we spent more and more time by ourselves. He got really quiet. He never really recovered. When I left to join the UN Peacekeeping Forces, he drove me to the airport. We hugged and he teared up. I'm not sure, but I got the feeling that he regretted wasting those years we could have spent time together. But he still wasn't recovered from her loss." He looked back at the ceiling. "I don't think we ever really recover from loss like that."

He sighed. "Some days you're okay, and other days you see something that reminds you of the person, and it's like a punch to the gut.

A couple years after she passed away, when I was fourteen, I was going through her things, looking for a memento of some kind, and came across a brand-new case with telescope eyepieces. She must have bought it just before she died. She'd never had the chance to try them." He swallowed. "I just burst into tears and couldn't stop keening for two days. My dad didn't know what to do. He brought me water and tried to get me to eat, but he was just as lost as I was."

Alex squeezed his arm. "I'm so sorry."

Casey wiped self-consciously at his eyes. "How about you? Do you have a big family?"

Alex shook her head. "It's just me and my dad. I lost my mom, too, at the same age."

He turned his head to her. "You're kidding me."

"So I understand how painful it is. When you're a kid, you think your parents are immortal, infallible. They'll go on forever, and you'll always have a home with them. You'll always be loved by somebody, and no matter what happens, there's a place you can go where you'll be safe."

He pursed his lips. "Yes."

"My mom died suddenly, too. She flew a lot of missions in places she wasn't allowed to really talk about. So whenever she left, it was always a bit of a mystery, not quite knowing where she was or when she'd come home. My dad liked to entertain me with stories about all the crazy adventures she was up to. My favorite was that she'd discovered a surviving herd of sauropods in the Congo that she had sworn to protect."

Casey smiled. "Ooh, I like that one."

"So did I. He had other stories, too. One about how she'd discovered a family of sasquatch and they'd taught her their secret language, and another where she'd found a mysterious cavern that allowed her to travel back in time and befriend woolly mammoths.

"When I was really little, before I realized he was making these up, I'd ask her about her missions when she came home. 'How are the dinosaurs?' I asked her one night at dinner. 'What do you feed them?' She looked confused and my dad burst out laughing. He had to explain to her that he revealed some of her 'top secret' missions to me. Then she started laughing, too, and began making up her own stories. She was stern, but she could be really playful, too.

"We played a lot of games together as a family—board games, charades. There was a lot of laughter in the house. But the craziest thing was my mom's survival games." Alex laughed. "She'd make up these situations and tell me I had to figure out how to get out of them or I'd die."

"What?" Casey's eyebrows went up.

"Yeah. I had to think of escape plans with whatever objects were at hand."

"Wow. Sounds like a crazy thing to do to a kid."

"My dad didn't approve, that's for sure. He thought it gave me nightmares." She shook her head, smiling at the memory. "She also taught me how to handle just about every kind of gun you can think of. And she was always really supportive of my fascination with martial arts."

"You know martial arts?"

"Jeet Kune Do. You know the style that Bruce Lee invented? He took all the strengths from different martial arts and mixed them together. So, like, grappling, kicking, and the close-quarters combat of kung fu."

"Sounds like you had a unique childhood."

"I did. Even though my dad was right. I did get nightmares sometimes. I'd hear a sound in the house and think it was intruders."

"Did anyone ever break in?"

She laughed. "No. It was always just a window rattling in the wind or the house settling. But I was ready for anything." Her throat went tight at the thought of losing her mom. "Or I thought I was ready, anyway."

"What happened?"

"One night, while my mom was away on a mission, my dad and I were eating dinner together. The doorbell rang. It was two airmen in uniform. They asked if they could come in. This numb feeling stole over me. I just knew it was about my mom. I couldn't breathe. My dad invited them in. They made us sit down and my heart started hammering. Everything moved in slow motion. My throat was so dry I couldn't swallow." She shook her head. "I remember thinking, 'Say it! Just say it! She's gone!' I wanted to scream at them.

"They told us that her plane had been shot down in enemy territory. It had . . . burned. They couldn't say where. Just that it was classified. They didn't know why she hadn't ejected and parachuted out. They suspected she might have been shot and unconscious."

"They said all this? In front of a kid?"

She nodded. "I insisted I wanted to know. I wouldn't leave my dad's side. They didn't want me to hear the details, but I had to. They said they were shipping her remains back to us, and how sorry they were, but that she had saved many lives on that final mission, including those of her wing mates.

"They shook our hands and left. My dad and I just sat there in the living room. He held my hand. I never remember him looking so gray. He wept. But I couldn't. I just couldn't believe it. I sat there, feeling numb, like I was suddenly living in a world of murky gauze and cardboard. A fake stage with fake airmen actors who delivered fake lines.

"We forgot about our dinner and went upstairs. But when he went into their bedroom, he started sobbing, so I pulled him over to mine. I only had a little twin bed, but I got him to lie down on it. I sat in my chair by my desk while he cried. On my desk were maps she'd drawn of our last survival game. I stared at them, at her handwriting, and just couldn't comprehend what had happened."

"Alex, I'm so sorry," Casey breathed.

"Thank you. I was numb for a long time. Just walking around in shock. I didn't cry. I felt like an automaton. My dad took care of me, made sure I ate and got to school, but he'd been dealt such a deep wound, he was a shadow of himself.

"We moved off the air base into a little house. We'd moved before, just the two of us, when she was away on missions and we had to transfer to different air bases. We were used to getting new houses ready for her return. So the rhythm of it felt normal. But I was unpacking boxes and came across one of her coats. I was about to go hang it up where she could use it when she got home, and even got all the way to the hook. Then it hit me. She was never going to wear that coat again. Never going to come home again, or sit with us at the dinner table, or make up crazy stories about where she'd been on her latest mission. Her missions hadn't been protecting dinosaurs in the jungle, but had been real, dangerous missions that got her killed. I gripped that coat and cried and cried and cried. My dad came in from outside and found me on the floor. I wouldn't let go of the coat. He carried me over to our couch and just held me and we both cried in silence."

She felt tears sliding down her face and wiped them away. Casey was right. Loss like that didn't go away.

They lay together quietly then, their stories told to each other and the darkness and the storm. Alex closed her eyes, feeling the tears seep down into her hair. She listened to Casey breathing next to her. She thought of Neil's body, out there on the ice, and how his family would now be dealt a blow just as Alex's and Casey's families had suffered. They'd know this pain now.

Finally she caught herself jerking awake and realized she'd dozed off. She pressed into the warmth of Casey's body and let herself fall into a deep sleep, wondering what awaited them out on the ice.

NINETEEN

The next morning they donned their boots and parkas and crawled out of the tent, blinking in the overcast day. The cloud ceiling was low, covering the ice in a dense layer of fog. There was no way a search and rescue helicopter would be out that morning.

"What do you think?" Casey asked as mist swirled around him.

"What's your watch say?"

He looked at the barometer. "No signs of letting up. Should we continue to make our way west? We don't have a lot of food. We'd be closer to rescue if we headed that way."

"We also might be closer to our two attackers."

Casey pursed his lips. "True. But SAR will be searching the area nearer the downed helicopter first, and that's west. It might be our best bet. They might not sweep this far east. They might even think we've fallen in and drowned."

Alex bit her lip. He had a point. "Okay. West it is. We'll just keep an eye out."

They packed up the tent and supplies. Alex took the first turn with the backpack.

As they worked their way west, trudging along the ice, the cloud ceiling began to lower. Casey checked his barometer. "We're in for another storm."

Bundled in her parka and multitude of layers, Alex was warm now, carrying the pack. But she knew when they stopped to rest, the cold would seep in. The mist descended, swirling around them. The wind picked up, pressing against her clothes. Her hood flapped against her ears.

The wind droned, a low, mournful sound, and she perked up, stopping.

Casey fell in beside her. "What is it?"

"I heard something . . ."

She put her hood down, tensed. The low groan wasn't the wind. It sounded like an engine, somewhere far off. "Do you hear that?"

He frowned, trying to pinpoint the direction. "Yeah."

They stood together, listening, as the sound faded away.

"Snowmobile?" she asked.

"I think so."

"Maybe just one, though."

"That's what I was thinking."

They stood motionless a few more minutes, listening, but the sound didn't come again.

Finally she lifted her hood, grateful for the warmth. Her eardrums ached from the cold wind.

"I'll take that for a while," Casey offered, gesturing to the pack. They traded. The cold moved into the middle of her back where the pack had been.

They continued west, and soon a dark smudge in the distance attracted her gaze. She pointed it out. The fog was so thick she couldn't make out what it was, but it was immobile. They made their way toward it, and she saw with a sinking feeling that it was another set gun. As they drew closer, she saw with relief that no polar bear lay sprawled at its base. Another large chunk of narwhal meat was attached to the wire leading to the trigger.

"Goddamnit," she cursed, staring down at the frozen whale meat. "How many of these things are out here?" Carefully, she de-

tached the wire, bracing herself at the thought of accidentally setting off the gun.

They had nowhere to keep the evidence this time. She removed
the gun from the box, then unstaked the entire contraption from
the ice. Glancing around, she spotted a towering edifice of ice in the
distance. Snow had drifted at its base. "Let's drag the meat over
there. Cover it up. When the poacher comes back, it'll make it
harder to set up another trap if there's no bait."

Casey stared down at the butchered remains. "Good idea."

He picked up the meat and she followed him with the gun as he
dragged it to the formation. At the base, they laid down the narwhal
piece and covered it with snow. They did the same with the dismantled wooden box.

"What about that?" he asked, gesturing to the set gun.

"I'll take it with us. It only has one round, but even that is better
than just your one shotgun."

"Let's get some distance between us and that trap."

She nodded, and they set off again. The ice became rougher and
their progress slowed. Jumbled and cracked, with strange, whimsical shapes rising up on all sides of them, the ice became a mysterious
and dreamy landscape in the fog. They weaved between formations,
climbed up and down jagged ridges, and skirted around others.
Open leads snaked through the area, smaller chunks of white ice
bobbing in the gray water.

The wind blew dry snow into her face, tiny ice crystals stinging her skin. They walked on in silence, Alex feeling sick at the
thought of the set guns, of losing Neil, of her samples being stolen
from the Centre. Sonia had been so excited when her permits had
finally come through, but the entire study had been a disaster. Neil
had been paid by someone to mislay equipment, and Alex didn't
know by whom. She walked with her face down, trying to let the
brunt of the wind hit the top of her hood instead of her skin.

She felt Casey's hand on her shoulder. "Alex, look."

She peered up into the wind, her eyes streaming, seeing another shape looming up in the fog. This one was big and rectangular, taller than her. They stopped, staring at it.

"It's a base tent, I think," Casey said. Once again Alex thought she caught the distant hum of a snowmobile, but it faded away. She stared at the tent, not seeing any movement. Finally they approached it.

It was an old army-green canvas tent, its front door tied shut. They listened, not hearing anything, and Alex gently lifted up a corner of the tent door, peering inside.

"Empty," she said. She untied it and entered.

Alex sucked in a breath. A folding table sat in the center of the room. On it lay a polar bear hide.

She felt her jaw clench and she stared down at it, a sudden tight feeling constricting her throat. A crumpled tarp lay jumbled under the table, beige with a Tough Tarp logo. Anger flashed inside her. "I recognize this tarp. This is the same guy I saw in town," she told Casey. "He was trying to sell polar bear pelts. I followed him out to the boatyard, but he left. He had a snowmobile in the back of his boat."

She came around the side of the table, finding a folding chair with a lantern sitting next to it. A thermos sat in the cupholder on the chair's arm. She touched it, finding it still warm. "He's nearby," she whispered. When she turned to look at Casey, she saw the horror that lay under the table.

A magnificent narwhal tusk. Anger washed over her. Suddenly she wasn't cold. Her hand tightened around the set gun rifle and she clenched her teeth till they ached.

Casey knelt down beside the tusk, elbows resting on his knees, staring in silence. She wondered where Old Sam had come across the narwhal. At this time of year, it would have been killed to the north of here. She wondered how far this poacher ranged. She knew the tusk could fetch him up to $15,000 and felt a hotter flush of rage race through her, at these two magnificent creatures dead because of a man's greed.

Casey stood up. The tusk still had a small section of meat attached. "He must have been using this kill to bait the set guns. Let's hide it. I don't see any other meat here he could use."

"Unless he retrieves that first bear carcass we saw." But that was miles away now, and he might not pass by that area again for days. He might not even know yet that his set gun there was successful.

Casey hefted up the narwhal remains and they exited the tent. She paused on the outside, listening for the sound of the poacher's snowmobile, but didn't hear it. She thought about taking the polar bear pelt and burying it, too, but worried its absence might inspire him to go out and kill another bear, so she left it. Besides, having this pelt might tempt Old Sam to try to sell it in town, and this time Manitoba Conservation could nail him.

She stepped back into the tent to take one more look around, hoping to find more ammo for the set gun, but the poacher must have had the additional ammo with him.

They walked in silence, and again she could feel darkness wafting off Casey, a deep sadness. The towering formations of ice around them took on whimsical shapes. One looked like a swan with a gracefully curved neck, another like the back of an orca, its tall dorsal fin stretching up into the sky.

"How about at the base of that one?" she asked, gesturing at the orca.

Casey nodded and carried the tusk over. They covered it with drifted snow, packing it down tight. Then they stood over the remains silently for a few moments.

Finally they turned west again. They came across a wide lead and had to skirt south until it grew narrow enough that they could step across it. They trudged into the wind. It kicked up into powerful gusts, snow swirling around them. Soon Alex couldn't feel her nose or lips, even with her balaclava on. The fog intensified, lowering visibility. She kept thinking it was getting dark, but it was only the thick layer of clouds blocking out the sun. They'd have to make camp if the storm got worse.

Snow began to cake the front of their parkas. She looked over at Casey, who walked in silence, the muscle in his jaw clenching and unclenching. "You want me to take the pack for a while?" she asked.

"No, thanks. Besides," he said with a smile, "it's keeping my back warm." They passed a few more whimsical shapes: a lounging ice bison and one that looked like a man pointing north. She shivered, thinking of Arctic explorers like John Franklin who had come before them and never returned.

They still had plenty of light left, but the storm was worsening, ruining visibility. They crossed another lead, the ice cracking and shifting, strange noises emanating up from the deep: thrumming, twanging, snapping.

Casey turned to her, the wind catching his hood and ripping it down off his head. He yelled over the howling of the wind. "Let's start looking for a place to set up camp!"

She nodded, squinting into the blinding snow, searching for a section of stable ice.

They'd walked only a few steps more when a gunshot rang out.

TWENTY

Alex spun, ducking down, and Casey did the same. She pivoted, trying to figure out where the shot came from. Moving at a crouch toward the nearest ice formation, she stared into the snowstorm. Another crack of the rifle sent a chunk of the ice splintering in front of her, spraying shards outward. A sharp sliver struck her in the face. Casey shrugged off the pack and swung his shotgun around to the front. They took cover behind the ice formation. Alex peered out into the fog, seeing a sudden muzzle flash pulse in the whiteout like a muted sparkle of light.

The bullet hit the ice inches above her head. She flinched, hunkering down. "There!" she said, pointing out the shooter's location. Fog swirled around them. The attacker, dressed completely in white, was only a smudge of movement against the whiteout. "We have to move!"

She took off for the next formation, weaving, Casey close behind her.

The white smudge was on the move now, circling around them. She gripped the rifle from the set gun, knowing she had only one round. She couldn't waste it.

Casey hunched over, slinking to one formation and then the next. She could see the efficient, alert way he changed positions, his military training kicking in. Now she didn't see the distant smudge of the shooter, didn't know where he'd moved to. She felt exposed and vulnerable against the ice formation. He might have flanked them. Might have a clear shot even now. She stared around desperately in the fog. In this gale, she couldn't hear the crunch of snow under the man's boots.

Casey moved farther away, flanking the man's last known location. He disappeared into the mist.

She heard another shot go off, somewhere to her left. She spun. It sounded too distant to have been from Casey. She wheeled farther in that direction, taking cover behind the opposite side of the ice.

Then suddenly a shape loomed up in front of her, only twenty feet away. A man stood there, gun pointed at her, his solid-white snowsuit blending in with the ice, his dark goggles shielding his eyes. But she recognized his face. It was Old Sam.

He lifted his gun. "You fucked with the wrong person!"

She snapped her rifle up and fired. But the gun, designed to kill animals at very close range, didn't have much accuracy. The shot went wide. Old Sam dropped and rolled, moving away into the fog. A boom echoed from Casey's gun some distance away, and the poacher ran for cover in the opposite direction.

She moved farther away to a different formation and kept going, wanting to put as much distance between her and the poacher as possible. She glanced back to where Casey's shot had come from. Searching around for his dark parka in the fog, she didn't see him.

Another shot rang out. She couldn't pinpoint the location. Then she heard a loud splash.

"Alex!" she heard Casey call out. "Alex!" She heard someone thrashing in the water.

She set off in that direction, weaving between formations, looking for a hint of movement, for the man dressed in white. She paused to listen but didn't hear Casey again. She ran in the direction she'd thought she'd heard the splash. Maybe he'd fallen in. Or pushed the poacher in. Moving cautiously, she gripped the now empty rifle. If she found more ammo, it could come in handy, so she held on to it for now. At the very least she could use it as a club.

She stopped, listening. Nothing.

She backtracked, finding their pack. They couldn't risk losing it, so she strapped it on. Then she moved steadily eastward, looking for fresh tracks, expecting any minute for another shot to ring out. She reached the wide lead they'd encountered and made her way south again, finding the narrower spot where they were able to cross it. Their tracks were already fading, filling with windblown snow.

She passed the orca-shaped tower where they'd buried the narwhal tusk.

No one had come back this way, so she returned from where she'd come, trying to get close to where she last saw Casey. The snow fell harder, blowing sideways, pattering on her parka hood. The air became a fury of flakes, obscuring her view. Now she followed the faint traces of Casey's tracks as they wound around several large formations. But the snow and wind did their work to cover his trail and she kept losing it. She tried to follow it as best she could, but soon it was completely obliterated.

She stooped, resting a moment, staring around her for any sign of movement or sound. But none came to her.

She was alone.

She moved in widening circles, trying to pick up Casey's trail. She found isolated footprints here and there, tracks protected in the lee of ridges. The rough ice got worse, growing rotten. She found a disturbed place in the snow where tracks came from another direction and spotted Casey's boot prints and a set of prints she didn't recognize—the poacher's. They were beside a section of mushy ice, and her arms windmilled as she stepped down on a piece that gave way beneath her boot. Stepping back to safety, she prodded the section with the butt of her rifle, finding the ice there loose and bobbing. The snow was disturbed here, as if someone had fallen in and then scrabbled for a handhold to get out. She'd nearly fallen in herself—would have if she hadn't been walking slowly and cautiously.

Leading away from the loose patch of ice, she spotted drag marks. The poacher's boot prints continued. She could guess what had happened—the poacher had surprised Casey, gotten the better of him. Casey had fallen in the water. But it looked like the poacher had then pulled him out, dragged him off somewhere.

Why wouldn't he just have let Casey drown?

She followed the drag marks, moving quietly, crouched low, weaving between the prominences of ice. In the distance now, a boxy form came into view. She swallowed. Another set gun. She could free it from the ice, and then she'd have one more shot. Cautiously she approached. She didn't see any movement, but now that she knew the poacher was dressed entirely in white, she kept an especially sharp eye out for him. A small upwelling of ice lay about twenty-five feet from the gun and she crept to it, then lay down on her belly, watching. No movement. She drew closer. The bait attached to this gun was a lump of something black. She couldn't make it out in the fog. She drew closer, and with a start realized what it was.

Casey lay sprawled on the ice, unconscious or worse. The poacher was using him for bait. And Alex was sure he was still out there, planning to do the same to her.

TWENTY-ONE

Fearing the worst, Alex hid the pack behind the ice mound and hurried at a crouch to Casey's side. She knelt down beside him. He wasn't moving, and she could barely detect a breath from him. His clothes were soaking wet. When she touched his face, it felt ice cold. She placed a hand on his back, glancing around her to see if the poacher was there.

"Casey." She jostled him gently. "Casey." He didn't stir.

A flash of movement in the fog caught her eye. The poacher was coming back. But he was moving laterally, away from the set gun, and she didn't think he'd seen her. Casey's shotgun was gone. She could guess either the poacher had it now or it had sunk down into the bay when he fell through the ice.

Then the poacher turned, heading back. She had only seconds. She could grab the set gun now, fire at him, but with its inaccuracy, she couldn't be sure to hit him. And since he had more than one shot, she didn't like her chances.

Gently she detached the wire from Casey's clothing and held the end in her hand. Then she lay down next to him, moving flush against his body, then scrunched in under him. Their parkas and snow pants were both black. She hoped she'd blend in with the fog, make it look like it was still just Casey lying there.

With her face pressed against Casey's side, she heard the poacher approaching, his feet crunching on the snow. He muttered under his breath as he messed with his rifle, probably opening the bolt to reload. "Goddamn greenies. Stealin' my meat. Didn't think about the fact that *you* was made of meat, did you, you piece of shit?" He kicked snow onto Casey's body. She heard the flakes hit her parka and knew he was standing right over them. She yanked on the wire and the set gun went off with a deafening crack.

Above her the man cried out in pain. She jumped up, closing the distance to him. The bullet had ripped through his right shoulder, tearing a hole in his snowsuit. He cursed and gripped the dripping wound with his left hand, his rifle dangling, a look of utter shock on his face.

She moved quickly inside his space, using a sweep of her arm to send his rifle sprawling.

He backed away in surprise and she came after him with a straight blast, a furious rain of blows to the center of his chest. She struck his solar plexus and heard the wind gush out of him.

He raised his left hand, trying to fend her off. She brought an elbow up into his throat, staying inside his space. It hit him hard in the Adam's apple and he floundered backward, losing his footing. He slammed down on a sharp edge of ice and struck his head. When he struggled up, she saw blood on the ice there. She advanced and he turned and ran into the swirling fog. She gave chase, but with him dressed in white, weaving between the ridges, she struggled to keep an eye on him. Not wanting him to double back and get his rifle, she hurriedly returned to where Casey lay and picked it up. She checked the chamber. It was empty. He must have the extra ammo in his jacket. Damn.

She knelt beside Casey, worried the poacher might have another rifle somewhere. He would be back.

Hurrying to where she left the pack, she scanned for the poacher. Nothing but snow and fog met her eyes, so she slung on the pack and returned at a low run to Casey. Gently shaking him, she hoped he would wake. But he didn't stir. Ripping off her glove, she reached a hand down to his cold, blue mouth, but if a warm breath met her hand, she couldn't feel it in the gale. She bit her lip, pulling on her glove again.

Grabbing him under the arms, she dragged him away from the set gun, pulling him up behind an ice mound.

With that little bit of cover, she pressed her face against his lips, and this time she did feel a small breath. She felt his carotid and to her relief found a pulse, but it was weak and barely discernible. He was obviously freezing, hypothermic. She had to get him to warmth and fast.

She gripped him under the arms again and started dragging him away. The snow fell harder, and though it made the going tougher, she was grateful for the cover it gave them, and it began to bury the new drag marks.

She lugged him until her shoulders and back screamed in protest, and then she hauled him farther. Her boots slid on the ice and she headed for an area with a complicated jumble of ice formations. Her hands and arms now feeling numb, she pulled him into the maze of ice, twisting and turning through narrow corridors and up and over small rises.

At last she felt they were far enough away, and the tall ice formations offered some degree of shelter from the wind. She quickly pitched the tent, threw in the sleeping bag and pad. She managed to stuff Casey inside the tent, part pushing, part pulling. She peeled off his wet jacket, then his wet fleece, sweater, and polypropylene shirt. The freezing wind had left them stiff and hard to maneuver. Undressing an unconscious person was more difficult than she imagined, and her back was throbbing from the effort of dragging him and trying to lift him up to get his frozen shirt off. She yanked off his boots and wet socks, then pulled off his pants. With it this cold, it was going to take a long time for his clothes to dry. If they ever even unfroze.

Kneeling down next to him, she managed to roll him into the

sleeping bag. Then she zipped him up. She stripped out of her own clothes. Shared body heat was the only way he was going to survive out here.

She crawled into the bag next to him and pulled her parka over them. The icy feel of his skin against hers robbed the breath from her chest. She wrapped her arms around him, draped her legs on his, and vigorously rubbed his arms and chest and legs.

At first it only seemed that the freezing cold of his body was spreading into hers instead of her heat warming him. But then he started to feel warmer. His skin wasn't quite as cold to the touch. He stirred slightly, murmuring.

Outside the wind pushed against the tent material, bowing the tent poles above them. She hoped they wouldn't snap.

She pressed against Casey, making a silent wish to the universe that he would make it through this. Her heart hammered as she imagined that even now the poacher was out there, trying to track them through the storm to finish the job.

She kept her hands moving over his arms, back, and legs until her limbs were so tired they felt like rubber.

Casey murmured but wasn't making any sense. "I can't have the pecans. Not with that many equations."

As the sun began to set, darkness crept into the tent. In the lingering light of the gloaming, Casey finally opened his eyes.

"Alex?" he asked groggily.

"I'm here."

"What happened? I remember falling in. Then . . . I don't remember getting here."

"The poacher's still out there. Do you know where your shotgun went?"

"I had it on me when I went in."

Then he drifted off. His breathing was even, and Alex hoped he'd just passed out from exhaustion and wasn't slipping back into unconsciousness. She herself was so tired she fought to keep her eyes open. Part of her brain told her they should stay awake, but it grew harder and harder to resist dropping off.

ALEX AWOKE WITH A START. She hadn't realized she'd fallen asleep. Beside her, Casey breathed slowly and evenly, his body finally warm. She wasn't sure what had woken her, but an almost preternatural sensation was prickling at the back of her neck. She listened, hearing the wind buffet the sides of the tent. And something else. A faint crunching sound between the gusts. Someone was walking around on the snow out there. She stared at the walls of the tent, waiting for a flash of light, but saw none. A full moon gave a diffused light, though heavy cloud cover, she guessed, prevented it from being too bright.

Snow had covered the tent, and with it nestled in a jumble of jagged ice, she knew it wouldn't be easy to spot in the darkness. But she didn't know if it was a polar bear out there or the poacher. She slid out of the sleeping bag. Casey stirred but didn't wake. Quietly she slipped her clothes on.

If it was the poacher, they were easy prey just waiting in the tent. Casey was in no condition to run or fight. She felt his clothes. They cracked under a layer of ice. He'd freeze if he had to put them on now.

If it was Old Sam, she had to lead him away.

Slowly she unzipped the tent, moving just a few centimeters at a time to keep as quiet as possible. She stuck her head out. Now she did see a muted, mobile light in the snowstorm. The fog was so dense that it lit up the mist like a glowing cloud.

That settled it. Poacher.

She crept out of the tent, grabbing the poacher's rifle as she went. It was empty, but he didn't know they had no additional ammo. Casey had been carrying a shotgun himself, after all, when they'd encountered the poacher. Bluffing might buy her some extra time if she came face-to-face with him.

She zipped the tent and slunk away from it, her boots crunching softly in the snow. Flurries collected on her eyelashes as she crept around a few towers of ice. Above her, the full moon illuminated a completely cloudy sky, but it still lent enough subdued light to the scene that she could see without a flashlight.

She rounded a mound of ice, coming up on the poacher from behind. He was walking in the opposite direction of the tent. Hope sprung up within her. If he kept going that way, maybe he wouldn't find the tent at all, and she wouldn't have to draw him away. He continued on, disappearing into the fog, so she moved closer to keep him in sight. He angled around several large pressure ridges, and then veered off in the direction of the tent. He kept going, heading straight for it. Alex held her breath, willing him to turn another way. But he didn't. He kept going, his light flashing through the fog. In minutes he'd be upon Casey lying prone in the tent.

She brought the rifle stock down hard on a piece of ice. The sound reverberated through the formations but was muffled by the fog. The man didn't turn. She struck the ice again, and the light swiveled in her direction. She didn't want to make it too obvious she was purposefully trying to get his attention, so she went silent.

He kept going for a few seconds in her direction, then swung the light back around toward the tent. She didn't think he'd spotted it yet.

She decided to take a risk and spoke aloud. "We only have a few more miles to walk until it gets light," she said, pretending she was talking to Casey and unaware of the poacher.

He snapped the light back in her direction and started approaching again.

"We have enough food to last a few more days in case Rescue doesn't come tomorrow," she added.

Soon his form became clearer, a white figure in the fog, obscured by the bright spot of his flashlight.

She crept farther away, then took refuge behind a pillar of ice.

If she could lure him this way, maybe she could surprise him and hit him with the rifle. There was a lead not too far away, covered with floating ice. In the blackness, she might be able to lure him to it, make him fall through.

Holding the rifle like a club, she pressed her back against the ice as he approached. She could hear the scrape of his boots, then heard his labored breathing in the dark. His flashlight went out. Now he was moving by only the muted glow of the full moon.

Her heart hammered as she gripped the rifle. She forced her breath to slow, her hands to steady. When she heard him crunch just to her left, she sprang out, swinging the rifle as hard as she could. It hit him square in the face and he cried out, staggering backward. Then he brought his rifle to bear.

Alex took off for the open lead.

TWENTY-TWO

Alex weaved between ridges and formations. A shot went off. She heard it ricochet off ice and kept going. He was following her now, and she continued to run in the opposite direction of the tent, toward the lead. He took another shot, which went wide, and she heard him cursing behind her. Snow drove into her face. Another crack rent the night, and she felt a tearing sensation on her upper thigh. Then it immediately went numb.

She could feel the wet stickiness of blood and willed her legs to keep going. She stared down at her pants, but it was too dark to see how bad it was.

Up ahead, she could see the broken ice of the lead coming up fast. It was the wide section where they'd had to skirt south to find a good place to cross. So much ice floated in it that it was nearly covered with white, certainly hard to make out in the gloom. Alex took a flying leap, clearing open water. She hoped the poacher would try the same and come up short.

She landed with a skid and glanced back. He was huddled over his rifle, the flashlight on again, struggling to reload it in the gale and darkness. He dropped the flashlight. Curse words came to her on the wind. She kept going. He looked up, slammed the bolt closed on the rifle, and continued forward.

Just as she'd hoped, he ran straight for her, his mind focused on her instead of the terrain. At the last minute, he looked down and saw the mostly ice-covered lead and she heard him gasp. He skittered to a halt, falling on his butt on the ice. One of his legs slid into the water.

He cursed, scooting backward. That would slow him down.

Alex stared around, trying to get her bearings. And then she saw it. The ice tower shaped like the back of an orca.

She raced for it, leaping over jagged chunks of ice and weaving between formations. Her thigh screamed in protest. The ice beneath her felt mushy in places, and she tried to skirt around the worst parts. She surprised a bearded seal, who had surfaced in a hole to breathe, and it ducked back down, swimming away.

The orca formation loomed closer. Behind her, she saw the bouncing light of the poacher in the thick fog. He had cut south to find a narrower place to cross the lead.

She reached the formation and fell to her knees, digging furiously in the snow. She got down to a layer of blood and kept going, exposing the narwhal tusk. "I'm sorry," she breathed as she gripped it tightly.

Then she ran on, making tracks in the snow toward another tower formation. Images of the labyrinth scene in *The Shining* suddenly flashed in her head. She stopped, then slowly walked in reverse in her own tracks, heading back to the narwhal burial site.

The going was slow and awkward and her heart pounded so painfully in her chest that she felt like it was about to burst.

And then she had made it and pressed her back against the shape of the orca fin, catching her breath, gripping the tusk. Following her tracks, the poacher drew closer. She forced herself to take long, slow, even breaths. In her mind she heard her Jeet Kune Do instructor's voice. *Don't let your feet turn to cement. Don't freeze in fear. Keep breathing.* She pictured her teacher disarming an opponent. She went over the moves in her mind, fighting off panic.

Then the poacher was almost on her, not slowing down, heading straight ahead. Her fake tracks had worked. Just as he raced past her, she sprang out and, with a powerful sweep of her foot, sent his legs flying out from beneath him. He went down hard on his face. Instantly she leapt on him, kneeling on his back. His rifle was pinned beneath him.

She raised the narwhal tusk above her head and then with all her strength drove it down into his neck. Blood spurted over the ice. He gurgled and she held him down, not letting up until he bled out moments later, his body slumping, lifeless.

She rocked back on her heels, staring down at him. Then she stood up over the body, making sure he was dead. His sightless eyes filmed over. The pulsing flow had stopped, blood congealing in the cold. She felt for a pulse and found none. No breath frosted in the air.

She wiped the narwhal tusk off on his jacket, then walked back to where it had been buried. She laid the tusk down and covered it again with snow.

Back at the body, she rolled him over and took his rifle, then searched through his pockets for extra ammunition. She also took his wallet, reading his ID. He was Sam Holbarth. Fifty-seven years old. The weathering on his face made him look twenty years older. She'd give the wallet to the RCMP when they got back and reported his death.

She went through the rest of his pockets hoping for his sat phone, but came up with only a flashlight, a pack of cigarettes, and a lighter with a skull on it. No key for the snowmobile. She wondered where he'd left it, where his boat was anchored. It might not be too far away. Because of the warming climate, there was an unusually large section of open water this year off the coast of Churchill, and she knew they weren't that far away from the town at this point.

She took the flashlight and lighter and started walking back toward the tent and then stopped. His clothes. They were dry except for the one leg of his pants where he'd slipped into the lead. She returned to the body and stripped him of his jacket, wool sweater, snow pants, and nylon pants beneath. He'd cleaned his shoulder wound and put on a fresh thermal shirt, so she took that as well. Under it all he wore a urine-stained white union suit and he smelled like bacon grease, stale sweat, and cigarettes. She left the union suit on him. No way was she touching that, and no way would Casey want to wear it, anyway. His shoes were way too small to fit Casey, so she left them.

Arms full of his clothes, with the two rifles slung over her shoulder, she started back to the tent. Then suddenly, when she was about halfway there, she started shaking uncontrollably. She wasn't cold and couldn't figure out why she was trembling so much. She felt strangely numb, like her mind was stuffed with cotton. Her hands shook as she tried to carry the clothes, and she dropped them. As she bent to pick them up a second time, bile rose up in her throat. She knelt over to vomit, but nothing came up. She couldn't catch her breath.

She fell, mind catching up. She'd killed a man. It was self-defense, she knew, but she still felt sick. All of the adrenaline flooded out of her body in a matter of seconds. The numb feeling that had allowed her to strip the man of his clothes, to methodically think of taking his wallet and searching his pockets, abandoned her, and she felt an unbearable tightness in her throat. All she wanted to do was get back to the tent and climb in the sleeping bag and squeeze her eyes shut.

She hurried back, dropping the clothes once more, the rifles banging together against her back when she had to stoop to pick up the garments. Her thigh ached where the bullet had grazed it.

She was so distraught that when she entered the maze of ice formations, suddenly nothing looked familiar. Where was the one shaped like the lounging bison? And the one that looked like a man pointing north?

She backtracked, trying to find where she'd come out of the tent, regain her former trail. But the rough ice all looked the same and she couldn't figure out which direction the tent lay in. Her compass was back in the tent, as was her GPS unit.

A panicked feeling suddenly seized her. She was lost.

TWENTY-THREE

The clothes began to feel heavier and heavier, and Alex's arms shook with the effort of carrying them. She knew she had muscle fatigue from dragging Casey so far. She dropped the clothes and forced the panic back down inside her. She wasn't lost. Couldn't be. She hadn't walked far enough to get lost. The tent had to be around here, somewhere close by. She switched on the poacher's flashlight and shone it around at the towers of ice, searching for any signs of her tracks.

Picking the clothes back up, she wound her way through the strange formations, moving into the heart of the maze. And then she saw some disturbed snow. Her heart picked up. But when she narrowed in on it, she saw that the trail wasn't hers. It was the poacher's tread she'd found.

She pictured where she'd been in relation to him and followed his tracks for a while. But then they stopped abruptly and turned around, moving off in a direction that definitely felt wrong.

She left them behind, stopping frequently to shine the flashlight around 360 degrees, hoping to see the tent. The maze of ice, the very thing that had kept the poacher from zeroing in on their location, was now preventing her from finding the tent. Her thigh throbbed with pain.

She forced her mind to still, to concentrate, and pressed on.

At last the beam fell on the snow-covered tent. Alex felt like letting out a whoop of joy. She hurried to it, shaking snow off the tent door before she unzipped it. Casey murmured in his sleep. She laid the poacher's dry clothes down on her side of the tent.

She took off her coat and snow pants, examining her thigh. As she suspected, the wound was a graze, and it had stopped bleeding. Her skin there was coated with sticky blood. She stuck her hand outside the tent, bringing back some snow, and cleaned off most of the dried blood. She dug the first aid kit out of the backpack and disinfected the wound, then bandaged it.

Shivering now, she crawled into the sleeping bag next to Casey, instantly feeling his warmth seep over her.

He stirred, barely conscious. "You're cold."

"I had to step outside."

He put his arms around her. "C'mere." She pressed into the warmth of his chest. "You're shivering."

"I can't seem to stop shaking." He rubbed his hands on her arms, shifting his legs next to hers. But even though she felt warm, the shaking wouldn't stop. She lay in the darkness, eyes wide and staring, watching the diffused glow of the moon on the tent.

Her shaking slowed, and Casey drifted back into sleep. But Alex lay awake, her mind playing over what she'd just done. Tomorrow she'd tell Casey. And then they'd finish walking toward Churchill.

ALEX WOKE TO DILUTED SUNLIGHT coming through the tent. Her thigh throbbed and burned. The wind still howled, and heavy snow had forced parts of the tent to bow. Condensation dripped from the walls. Beside her, Casey was awake.

He smiled. "How'd you sleep?"

"Dreamlessly." She felt like she'd crashed hard, at least for a few hours. "How are you feeling?"

"I'm naked," he said.

"Yeah, sorry about that. Your clothes were soaked."

"Yes. I don't think I'll ever forget the feeling of plunging into that freezing water. Let's hope we don't have another encounter with our friend."

She bit her lip, the images flashing back to her so powerfully she sucked in a breath. She closed her eyes for a moment, then opened them. "We don't have to worry about him anymore."

"What do you mean?"

"He came back again. Last night."

Casey's eyes went wide, and he struggled to sit up on one elbow. "What? Why didn't I hear anything?"

"I led him away. You were in no condition to fight. I wasn't even sure if you were going to make it through the night after I found you." She swallowed hard, then somehow found the words. "I killed him."

"Oh, Alex." He put his arms around her. "I'm so sorry."

Her body decided to start shaking again as she recounted the story, and the cold seeped into her core. "I took his clothes for you. They stink. But they'll be warmer than your frozen ones. I also took his wallet, so the RCMP can identify him when I report it."

"He was a nasty piece of work."

"I know," she said, "but . . ."

"It was him or us, Alex. Actually, it was him or us and who knows how many polar bears and other species."

"True." She remembered how it had felt to kneel on the man's back, driving the tusk down. She pushed the memory away. "I think we're getting closer to Churchill. If this weather clears, we might get picked up today or tomorrow."

Casey looked at his watch. "Hey, the barometer is holding. We might be in luck." He sat up, and now in the light, she could see a mass of scars crisscrossing his back.

Alex struggled to a sitting position, too, feeling so heavy she almost sank back down into the sleeping bag. But she forced herself to get up. Casey put on the poacher's clothes and stepped outside while she stuffed the sleeping bag into the backpack. She cleaned her bullet graze again and replaced the bandage. After strapping Casey's frozen clothes to the outside of the pack, she threw on her coat and snow pants.

Stepping outside, she was hit by a blast of wind. The fog had dissipated a little, but not nearly enough for a helicopter to find them. Together they took down the tent, and she rolled it up and stuffed it into the pack, too.

Then they each took a rifle, reloading them with the poacher's ammo. Alex strapped the set gun rifle to the pack.

She brought out her GPS unit. The RCMP would want to know where the poacher's body was. The tent location was close enough. She took a reading and saved it.

Alex double-checked that they'd packed everything, and they started heading west again.

After a few hours, the weather began to clear. Alex's thigh felt like it was on fire. Then a distant rhythmic sound broke the silence. She stopped. She reached out for Casey's arm and he drew up beside her. The sound grew louder. The unmistakable beating of a helicopter rotor.

TWENTY-FOUR

Alex and Casey looked at each other and grinned, then hugged each other. Alex couldn't help but jump up and down, then her injured thigh reminded her why that was a bad idea.

They pulled apart and she scanned the sky, trying to pinpoint the chopper's location. And then she saw it, coming in from the west, a sleek blue and red helicopter. She clocked its movement as it continued east, slightly banking to the north, away from them, and for a heart-stopping moment she thought it was going to miss them. But then the pilot changed course, heading straight for them. Casey grasped her gloved hand. Alex felt all the tension flow out of her aching, exhausted body.

The helicopter hovered over them but didn't land. The pilot swished the tail.

Casey stared up, confused, then blinked. He stared around at the rough ice. "They can't land here. We need to find a more stable place."

The helicopter then shifted to the northeast, moving close to the ground, and they watched as it set down about a half mile away.

"Guess our walk's not over," Casey said.

"I'm just glad they found us."

They walked toward the chopper, Alex's legs burning with every step. Her shoulders ached from shivering.

The pilot got out of the chopper as they approached. "Dr. Carter?"

"Yes," she said, relief washing over her.

He was a thickset man in his midforties, Alex guessed, with tousled brown hair and a clean-shaven tan face. "I thought there were three of you."

Alex's throat suddenly constricted.

"There were," Casey put in. "Her colleague didn't make it."

Alex didn't want to go into detail now, so she just nodded. They could explain it all to the RCMP.

"Well, I'm glad I found you. Three helos have been searching for you this morning. Found the wreckage of your bird. Why didn't you stay with it?"

"It's a long story," Alex told him.

"Well, climb in, and we'll get you back to safety."

"Thank you so much," she told him.

"I'm Roy, by the way."

"We appreciate the ride," Casey told him.

The pilot slid open the side door for them. The copilot seat was empty, so Casey offered to sit up front with him.

"Sure thing," Roy said.

Alex stepped into the back, sinking down into a velvety, padded seat. A built-in drinks cabinet stood to her left. The pilot and copilot seats held magazines in their seat backs. Blue strip lighting ran the length of the interior, giving a glow to the cabin. She realized this was a private helicopter, not typical search and rescue.

Roy returned to the left side of the chopper and climbed in. Donning the copilot headset, Casey turned back to her. "This is quite a posh ride."

Alex found her own headset on a hook behind the pilot's seat.

Roy pulled on his own and readied to lift off. "My boss volunteered the use of his personal chopper to aid in the search. News is all over Churchill about the missing scientists. When search and rescue got to your wreckage and didn't find you, they put out the call for more help."

"Who's your boss?" Casey asked.

"Paul White. Head of White Industries."

The name wasn't familiar to her. As the chopper lifted off, Alex stared out the window, watching details of the ice grow smaller and smaller. Then her eyes rested on the magazine in the back of the pilot's seat. It was sticking haphazardly out, the top half showing. The cover sported a smiling man in a suit with his arms crossed. Text across the top read, CEO PAUL WHITE TALKS ENERGY INVESTMENT FOR THE FUTURE.

"This him?" she asked, leaning forward to take the magazine.

Roy glanced backward. "Yep. He's made a mint all over the world. And not just in oil. He's got resorts all across Europe and the Middle East. He owns a fleet of luxury yachts across the globe. He splits his time between L.A. and Tokyo."

"What's he doing in tiny Churchill, Manitoba?" Casey asked.

"Oh, he's not here. He's in L.A. But his company's been doing a lot of surveying up here, so he had a house built and had this chopper brought out. He even has a luxury sailboat here for when he visits. He's got that big mansion out on Amundsen."

"I've seen it," Alex said, remembering spotting it during her drive out to the *Miss Piggy* Wreck.

She lifted up the magazine. Paul White stood in front of a large mahogany bookcase displaying not books but artifacts. He had Ancestral Puebloan pottery, an eighteenth-century clock, a Fabergé egg, and what looked like a gold Incan statue. He stood on an elaborate Persian rug that itself must have cost a fortune.

"Sounds like you've got a good setup," Casey said.

"It ain't too shabby," Roy told him. He turned to look at Alex. "So how is the polar bear study going?"

Alex almost laughed from disappointment and exhaustion. "Not too well. We've had a lot of problems."

"I can see that! Your helicopter going down. Did you lose your research in the crash?"

"No, thankfully."

"So how are polar bears doing out here?"

"Not too well," she told him. "They've been underweight. I saw one dangerously thin near Churchill. I tested the fat of a male polar bear and found it contained high levels of mercury and PCBs. And all of them have had elevated levels of a stress hormone."

"So you think they're doing bad? Why?" Roy asked.

Something about his tone bothered her. He was expressing curiosity but sounded almost confrontational. "Well, the biggest threat is climate change. The pack ice has been breaking up earlier each year and forming later. Polar bears rely on seals as the main staple of their diet. It's how they get fat enough to survive the summers when they can't hunt from the ice. So now they're fasting for longer stretches of time."

"So you're going to recommend stronger protections from the Canadian government." It almost sounded like a challenge.

"The data is certainly leaning that way."

"But you haven't yet?" he asked.

Alex shifted in her seat, feeling more and more uncomfortable with his line of questioning. "This is part of a multiyear study," she told him. "We're following up on bears that have been tagged in previous years, tagging new ones, taking measurements. After my study, I'll put all the data together and then make a recommendation."

"So you haven't yet, then," Roy said. He sounded smug now. Alex shifted in her seat. Something wasn't quite right. "That's good," he added, then reached under his seat. He brought out a pistol with a silencer. "Then there's still time to stop you."

TWENTY-FIVE

Casey's hand shot out, gripping Roy's wrist, driving the gun skyward as it went off. Alex heard it ping off metal above them. The pilot cursed and for a moment the chopper dipped to the right. Casey maintained his grip on Roy's wrist. Alex bent forward to help, but in the small confines of the chopper, Casey's back blocked her access to Roy. She watched the barrel of the pistol wave wildly around the cabin, ducking when it came back down in her direction. It went off again, piercing the window on her side. Casey banged Roy's gun hand against the cockpit controls.

The pilot punched Casey in the head with the butt of the gun, but Casey didn't let go of his arm. Alex reached forward, wrapping her arms around the pilot's neck, trying to immobilize him.

The gun waved in her direction again and she ducked her head as it went off for a third time. The helicopter went into a dive.

Alex's stomach pitched up into her throat as the helicopter spun out of control, plummeting so fast she thought she would vomit. Casey slammed Roy's hand against the cockpit controls again, and this time he let go of the gun. It clattered to the floor under Roy's feet.

Pressing her face tightly against the back of the pilot's seat, Alex kept her grip on the man's throat, trying to constrict his airflow so he'd pass out. Roy clawed at her arm, gasping for breath, coughing. But already she could feel him getting weaker. Finally he slumped down, limp.

"He's out," Casey said, his hands and feet flying to the copilot controls. He brought the helicopter level again.

"What the hell," she breathed. She reached forward and gripped Casey's shoulder, catching her breath. Then she slumped back into her own seat, worn out.

Casey gained altitude and headed for Churchill.

OVER THE RADIO, THE RCMP gave Casey directions to their helipad. He told them about the unconscious pilot. As he touched down on the pavement, an ambulance stood by. Two EMTs loaded the unconscious Roy into it and drove off toward the hospital. Two constables emerged from the police station beside the helipad. One of them was PC Bighetty, and the sight of his familiar face was comforting. Casey shut down the rotors and the police ushered them inside the warm station. Bighetty took her back to a private room where she exchanged her dirty, blood-spattered clothes for some clean ones provided by the RCMP. Casey was taken to a different room, and when she emerged, she didn't see him. Bighetty escorted her into an interrogation room and brought her a hot cup of coffee.

"The sergeant should be in in a few minutes," he told her, and closed the door.

She sipped gratefully on the hot coffee, glad to be in warm clothes. But the longer she sat there, the more nervous she got. She had killed someone, even if it had been in self-defense.

Finally the door clicked open and the sergeant walked in.

"I'm Detective Sergeant Moran," he said curtly and sat down opposite her.

She sipped at the coffee and shivered a little.

"I understand you've been through an ordeal," he said, eyeing her closely.

He switched on a tape recorder, introduced himself again, and had Alex state her name. He said the time and then asked her what had happened out on the ice.

She started with the helicopter going down and the snowmobilers who had arrived, the fight that ensued. She struggled through the second encounter and Neil's death, and had to take a minute to regain her voice. When the lump in her throat had eased up, she described the set guns, coming across the poacher, and the fight that led to his death and almost to Casey's. Then the trek across the ice and White's helicopter picking them up, the pilot turning on them in the helicopter, and the fight for their lives. When she finished, she took another sip of coffee and waited.

"You've really been through the wringer," he said. "Why do you think you were targeted three times by three different groups?"

Alex had been thinking about this on the helicopter ride on the way back, and during their long trek across the ice. "I'm not so sure it was three different groups."

"What do you mean?"

"Did PC Bighetty mention to you that our study had been tampered with?"

He thumbed through some paperwork on the desk. "I see that. Stolen samples and supplies."

"I surprised someone in the lab at the Centre who took only *my* research. The snowmobilers out on the ice were looking for something specific. Maybe it's all related. The helicopter pilot didn't want us to continue with the study, either. Both groups were willing to kill us."

"And the poacher?"

She bit her lip. "Maybe that *was* unrelated. We had dismantled his set guns, hidden the meat so he wouldn't have any bait."

"That was stupid. He could have killed you both."

"He almost did."

The sergeant was difficult to read. She couldn't tell if he believed her and was just being reserved due to his training, or if he really thought she and Casey were two roving killers who would murder anyone they came across, even poor Neil.

"How do you know Casey MacCrae?" he asked her.

"I met him when he applied to be our pilot for the field season."

"Sounds like he could hold his own out there."

"He could. He's had military training."

"And you?"

"My mom was in the U.S. Air Force. She taught me how to use guns. How to be resourceful."

"Huh." He went silent. She couldn't tell what was implied by his *huh,* so she just sat there, drinking more of her coffee.

"How much longer are you going to be in Churchill?" he asked.

"Well, if people would stop sabotaging our study, I was planning to stay until the ice completely breaks up, probably sometime in late June."

He went through the papers in the folder again, then shut it and stood up. "Hang tight."

He exited the room and Alex forced her shoulders to relax as she finished the last of the coffee.

They left her alone for a long time. An hour ticked by slowly. She wished she had a book. Or a pillow. PC Bighetty peeked in an hour and a half later and asked her if she wanted another cup. She said yes and he brought it in, then left. Still she waited.

She wondered how Casey was faring. She thought over what she'd told the sergeant. The person who broke into the lab, the missing supplies, the sabotaged helicopter. But the snowmobilers didn't take any of the samples, and the samples had certainly been there, out in the open for the taking. She still had them in her pack. No, they seemed to be connected with whatever had been going on with Steve.

She thought of Sonia's difficulties in getting the permits for the research in the first place and frowned. Someone definitely did want to ruin this study.

TWENTY-SIX

Alex's thoughts were interrupted by the sergeant, who came back through the door. "Okie dokie," he said. He sat down and slid a piece of paper across the table to her. "Here's your statement. Please make any corrections and sign it. Then you can go."

She read it over. It was transcribed from the digital recording of her statement, so she signed it, then slid it back.

"How is Casey?"

"He's just signing his statement, too. We'll hold on to your clothes for processing."

"Okay."

He set her GPS unit down on the table. "Got this out of your pack. Can you let me know the coordinates of the bodies?"

She reached over and took the unit. With shaky fingers she powered it on and scrolled through the waypoints. "Here they are." She slid the unit across to him.

"Thanks." He took down the numbers. "We'll hold on to your other belongings, too, process the ones touched by the snowmobilers. See if we can get anything useful."

"Okay. Thank you." She thought of the blood and tissue samples. "Can you preserve the samples, if possible? Keep them refrigerated?"

"I'll see what we can do."

"What about the pilot? Has he regained consciousness?"

Moran nodded. "Yes. He's given a statement at the hospital." Then, seeming satisfied, he added, "You're free to go. But don't leave town."

"I wasn't planning on it." She stood up and exited the room.

Out in the lobby, she saw Casey emerge from another interrogation room. He looked exhausted and haggard, but smiled when he saw her. "Just got grilled," he told her. "You?"

"The sergeant was nice. But he might think I'm a homicidal maniac."

"Ditto."

They were about to go out the front door when DS Moran appeared again. "Dr. Carter? Mr. MacCrae?"

They turned.

"Paul White would like to talk to you."

"He's here?" Casey asked.

"He's on Zoom."

He gestured for them to follow him, and they stepped into a briefing room. On a big screen mounted on the wall, a plump man in an expensive suit sat at a mahogany desk. Behind him, Alex recognized the shelving filled with artifacts. His beige face had a slightly unnatural orange tint to it, probably the result of spray tanning, and his white hair was perfectly styled. A look of concern creased his face.

"Dr. Carter. Mr. MacCrae," he said, his voice dripping with concern. "I'm Paul White. I employ the pilot who picked you up in the helicopter. I asked the sergeant here for a chance to speak with you and offer my apologies. I want to assure you that he acted independently, and you have my deepest regret about what you suffered."

Alex didn't know what to say, so she just let him continue.

"From what the police there have told me, he was afraid of losing his job if the polar bear study went forward. He was stationed out there to do some oil and gas surveying and I'm afraid he got used to the luxury of working for me and didn't want that jeopar-dized. If your study finds that oil and gas extraction are harming the polar bears in that region, his job would have evaporated, and it sounds like he acted out of desperation."

Alex and Casey remained silent, not immediately accepting his apology or saying anything in return at all. White's demeanor shifted slightly.

Alex could tell he was used to people jumping at any gesture he offered, be it an opportunity or an apology.

"What you gotta understand is that folks need jobs. If the gov-ernment decides to protect bears instead of providing jobs for de-cent, honest people, then folks get scared. They need to feed their families." His switch to folksy fell flat, like someone playing a part. She began to take a dislike to him, the same way she felt about slip-pery politicians who never directly answered questions and always seemed to have an agenda based on personal gain rather than the greater good.

She didn't believe for a second this guy actually cared about people's jobs. She got the feeling his own wealth was a hell of a lot more important, that he would sacrifice the livelihoods of his work-ers and even whole species in a second if it made him more cash.

Her face felt hot, and she noticed Casey's jaw was clenched.

White leaned forward, smiling in a way that probably charmed other people. "Listen, since your study is on hold now without a heli-copter, think about coming to work for me. Mr. MacCrae, I obviously need a good helicopter pilot, and Dr. Carter, your knowledge of the Arctic would be excellent for giving tours to my investors. You could continue to work together at a salary that's . . . let's just say well, *well* above anything you could earn in the scientific community."

Alex glared at him. She could hear Casey grinding his teeth. Neither said anything.

This seemed to make White edgy. "Is the sound on?" he asked, looking over at the sergeant.

"Oh yes, Mr. White. We can hear you."

Yes, Alex thought. *We can hear every word of your bullshit.*

He kept the fake grin on. "Any takers?"

Neither Casey nor Alex answered.

White started to look uncomfortable, shifting in his seat. He adjusted his tie. "Well, I guess that's all I wanted to say." He turned to DS Moran. "But say, how's my old friend the chief superintendent?"

DS Moran smiled. "Excellent, sir. Really enjoying his retirement."

"That's great to hear. He's a good man."

Subtle hint, Alex thought, disgusted. She turned away without acknowledging White and walked to the door. Casey followed.

"Okay, Mr. White. Thanks for your time," she heard the sergeant say as she opened the door.

As she left the room, she heard White murmur, "Did they hear what I had to say?"

"Yes, Mr. White."

And then the briefing room door swung closed behind her. She walked out to the front desk, where PC Bighetty was stacking up papers and putting them in folders.

"If you want to wait outside, I'll come out there momentarily and drop you both off at your lodgings," he offered.

"Thank you." She watched her own signed statement go into a folder.

He picked up another stack, patted the papers on the desk to straighten them, and then reached beneath the desk for a folder. She glanced down at the top paper. It was Casey's statement, with a few handwritten corrections in the margins. She froze. She recognized that tight, neat, block letter print. The postcards. All the unsigned creepy postcards. The note that had accompanied her stolen GPS unit she'd lost in New Mexico. The printing on the envelope that had contained the footage of the wetlands-ceremony shooting.

A strange, nervous, panicky feeling welled up inside her. Casey. He was the sender of the postcards. He was the man who had killed the shooter at the wetlands ceremony. He had tracked her movements, sent her GPS unit to her father's house. And now he was here, in Churchill, Manitoba, having arrived so conveniently after the last pilot quit. A frozen feeling crept into her stomach and rose up to her throat. She kept staring at the paper. PC Bighetty picked it up and stuffed it into a folder and she continued to stare at where it had been.

"Alex?" Casey said behind her, touching her elbow.

She pulled away from him, looking up into his eyes, as if truly seeing him for the first time. She'd felt bonded to him on that trek across the ice, their shared danger. And all along he'd known who she was, known for a long time, and had followed her out here. He wasn't just a nice pilot who showed up at the right time. He'd planned it.

She couldn't move. Couldn't think. Should she tell the cops? Should she even tell Casey she knew? Should she just pretend everything was normal and walk out of there? Or go back to DS Moran and tell him?

Casey seemed to have two identities as he stood before her: the capable pilot and fighter who'd had her back out on the ice, and this second, shadowy person who had been stalking her.

But even back then, when she still lived in Boston, he had saved her life at the wetlands ceremony.

Feeling numb, she walked out of the police station and stood on the other side of the doors.

Casey came after her, concern creasing his face. "What is it?"

"It's you."

"What's me?"

"You're the one who's been sending me those postcards. You shot the gunman in Boston."

He took a step back, clearly floored.

"Have you been following me?" she asked.

He opened his mouth but didn't say anything.

"Trying to insinuate yourself into my life?"

"It wasn't like that," he said finally. "I wasn't going to show up, but then I saw that your study would fall apart when your pilot quit."

"And if we hadn't needed a pilot, what? You would have continued to stalk me from the outskirts? Did you even have a father who taught you how to fly in Scotland?"

He looked hurt. "Yes, of course."

She turned away.

"Alex, I never lied to you. Everything I told you was true."

"Maybe," she said, turning to him. "But you certainly left out a lot, too."

He bent his head. "I know. I just didn't know how to bring it up."

"What, 'Hey, I've been sending you creepy postcards' wasn't good enough?"

He looked stung. "I didn't mean for them to be creepy."

They stood in silence for almost a minute, and then he added, "If I wanted to hurt you, Alex, don't you think I would have by now?"

She didn't know what to make of any of it. He'd saved her life more than once. She couldn't just turn him over to the cops. She was sure the Boston police were still looking for the shooter who killed the gunman in the wetlands that day.

"I need some time to think," she told him.

Just then PC Bighetty pulled around in his cruiser. Alex sat up front with him, while Casey took the back. They rode in tense silence. Bighetty dropped Casey off at his motel. Then he drove Alex on to the Centre, where her Jeep waited.

"I'm sorry you've been through such an ordeal," Bighetty said as he pulled up in the parking lot. "I can't even imagine."

"Thank you." She felt a pang of regret when she thought then of Casey, how vital he'd been out there. Then a darker thought crept into her mind as she remembered the pilot who had quit, Ilsa. Alex hadn't seen her since. Had she really quit? Or was she in some unmarked grave somewhere so Casey could take her place?

She paused before opening the car door. "Do you know Ilsa Angstrom?"

"The helicopter pilot?"

"Yes."

"Sure. I've known her for years."

"Have you seen her lately?"

He nodded. "Just last night. She was at Moe's having a beer. I heard that she quit. Got a better-paying offer. She's a good person. Really. She just couldn't pass up the money."

"It's okay. I don't hold it against her." *I'm just glad she's still alive.* "Thanks for the ride."

"No problem."

They parted and, thinking about the sabotage, Alex ducked inside the Centre and grabbed her backup drive and a portion of a hair sample to take back to her motel for safekeeping. Better to split up the locations of her data. Her body ached as she climbed into the Jeep, her legs sore from all the exertion and her thigh still throbbing from the bullet graze. She just wanted to shower and crawl into bed and sleep for a week. Her study was completely falling apart. Stolen samples, a wrecked helicopter, and now no pilot. Unless she kept working with Casey, but she couldn't imagine that. Not now.

TWENTY-SEVEN

Casey paced around his motel room. He'd blown it. He'd wanted to tell Alex who he was, but the time just never seemed right. He never should have offered to be the pilot on her project. From that moment on, revealing who he was seemed like a terrible idea, as if he'd come there under false pretenses, even though he genuinely wanted to help her project along. She had needed a pilot or the study would have been delayed even longer, and he didn't want her work to be interrupted.

He sat down on the edge of the bed. He hadn't lied to her. But she was right. He hadn't exactly told her everything, either. He was so drawn to her. He thought back to what had led him to encounter her the first time. Sometimes ugly things can lead to something beautiful.

It had been in New Mexico, and the ugliness had been white supremacists. When he was honorably discharged from the UN Peacekeeping Forces, Casey drifted around. A fellow soldier he had served with, Arturo Jacinto, had gone back home to New Mexico to take care of his grandmother. He'd invited Casey out anytime he'd wanted to visit. Casey had heard how beautiful the American Southwest was, but he'd never been. So after a stay in Thailand and then Hawaii, he took his friend up on the offer.

Arturo's grandmother lived on a homestead that had been in his family since the Enlarged Homestead Act of 1909. It was a beautiful stretch of land along a river, full of cacti, kit foxes, roaming javelinas, and myriad wildflowers, like firewheel and slender red-blooming ocotillo.

When Casey arrived, he found Arturo smiling and warm, just as he'd been in Darfur, a welcome light and pleasant company. His grandmother Pilar had made her living as a sculptor and painter, and her inviting adobe home was full of interesting pottery and painted landscapes of the dramatic mountains and desert of New Mexico.

More than a few times they spent pleasant evenings in a local cantina. Musicians gathered there, singing joyful and mournful songs in the fading light of day. Casey and Arturo shared *cervezas,* enjoying the company of the locals. Casey's Spanish was getting pretty good, too.

Other days, Casey lounged and watched Arturo's grandmother paint azure skies, and white-lined sphinx moths hover like hummingbirds in the purple blooms of trailing four-o'clock flowers.

It was the most peaceful place Casey had ever been, and the most welcoming. During the warm afternoons they kept to the shade, drinking pitchers of lemonade and watching the shadows dance across the mountain ranges as the sun arced across the sky.

At night, the fragrance of desert wildflowers carried on the wind. The moon rose, painting the desert silver. Javelinas snuffled around in the undergrowth, their little brown-and-white-striped babies skittering and prancing playfully among the adults. Coyotes serenaded them with their eerie yips and howls. Nectar-feeding bats came on silent wings, hovering over night-blooming cacti. And up above, the curve of the Milky Way spanned the heavens like a magical trail of campfires of ghosts long past.

But their peaceful heaven was shattered one night by gunfire. Casey heard shouts, then crying, out in the darkness. A man, a woman, a small child sobbing. From the porch, he saw the muzzle flashes of guns out in the expanse of darkness.

Arturo rushed to the door and they stood together on the porch, trying to pinpoint what was happening.

More shots rang out, and they heard a woman cry out in agony.

"Do you have any guns in the house?" Casey asked.

Arturo shook his head.

They heard angry shouts and yells of men, and a truck engine fire up. Headlights cut through the darkness, flipping a U-turn and speeding away in a cloud of dust.

"Get a flashlight!" Casey urged his friend.

Arturo came back with two, gesturing for his grandmother to stay put.

They followed a whimpering sound out into the desert, finding a family of five facedown in the dirt. One was a man in his forties, with a woman about the same age, two children, and an old woman. They'd all been shot in the back. One of the children was still alive, gasping in the dirt.

"Call an ambulance!" Casey shouted back to the house. He saw Arturo's grandmother duck inside to get to the phone.

But then the child sputtered and went still. The whole family was dead. With bloody swollen feet, their ochre skin dust-covered and sunburned, the family had obviously been walking for days or maybe even weeks.

Casey rocked back on his heels, finding Arturo's eyes in the dark. "Who did this?"

"Monsters," his friend responded, his mouth a tight slash.

The police arrived, took photographs and their statements, and carted the bodies away. The family had crossed into the U.S. in the darkness, trying to work their way north. The police said they had no idea who would have killed them.

When they left, Casey, Arturo, and his grandmother sat outside on the porch. "I think I know who did this," Pilar said, her voice barely audible.

Casey turned to her. "Who?"

"There's a group in town called the Sons of the White Star. They're white supremacists. Want to keep immigrants out, even though their own ancestors were immigrants from Ireland and Germany. Damn hypocrites. I'm sure they wouldn't give a rat's ass if a group of Norwegians wanted to come here. They've been stirring up trouble, inciting hatred. They've been having town meetings just north of here at the Church of the Blessed Cross. Gaining followers. I've heard their hateful talk. Saying they'll patrol the border themselves to keep people out."

"And you think they did this?" Arturo asked.

"I wouldn't be surprised."

They'd sat in silence for a long time after that, listening to the crickets sing. In the distant hills, the coyotes broke out in a chorus of song.

The next day, Casey and Arturo drove into town, seeking out the Sons of the White Star. They located the Church of the Blessed Cross and learned when the next meeting was.

Then they shared their suspicions with the police. The cops told them they'd had their eyes on the group, but that so far they'd been unable to prove anything. They'd tried to bust them on weapons charges, but the firearms they owned were all legal and registered.

The leader of the clan was Duane Rainer. Casey learned when Duane was going to speak next and attended the meeting. He could barely sit through the first five minutes of the hate-filled speech, a call to arms to make America white again. He seethed in his seat, a red mist swimming before his eyes. Duane riled up his followers, and they bought into all the ignorant lies he told them. His second-in-command, Wilbur Connell, was just as bad, a sycophantic yes-man who seconded every sick, heinous lie that Duane uttered.

But Casey swallowed his contempt and revulsion, wanting to infiltrate them. Get evidence. Turn them in to the cops.

He learned how they patrolled the border at night in pickups.

They talked about gunning down refugees they found crossing the border. They bragged about past killings. But when Casey went to the police, they told him it was all hearsay. They didn't have any solid proof. They might be bragging about something they didn't actually do.

Casey argued with the cops, challenging them, asking if another family had to die before the men were stopped. Casey could tell the sheriff was just as disgusted as he was, but he had no proof. Duane held power in the small community. Everyone feared him. Judges were reluctant to issue search warrants, and when they were served, Duane and his men were quick to produce licenses for all the guns they'd amassed.

Casey felt sick being among these people, infiltrating a hate group. At nights he came home, feeling ill and shaky. More than once he threw up after eating dinner. He could barely keep anything down and dropped twenty pounds.

Flashes of Darfur began flickering through Casey's mind as he relived that feeling of watching horrors unfold. He'd had to do something to stop the atrocities back then. And now he knew he'd have to take action once more. He'd reached the limit of his tolerance.

He knew the men broke off into groups when they went out "hunting," as they called it. Duane always took one group, and Wilbur another. They each drove their own trucks in order to cover more terrain every night.

Casey bought a high-powered rifle with a scope. He learned the route Duane would take one night. He waited on a rock outcropping, knowing that Duane would pass by that way on one of his nightly stops. As the moon rose over the desert floor, he spotted Duane as the man parked his truck on a high point and stared down onto the river with a pair of night vision goggles.

Casey held his breath and took the shot. The man's head exploded into a mist, and he slumped forward on the steering wheel.

Quickly Casey ran down from his position and dragged Duane's body from his truck. He buried him at the base of a rock outcropping in the loose soil. Then he drove the truck to a location several miles away, wiped off all the blood and prints, and dumped it.

He didn't want Duane's body to be found, or the followers to suspect he'd been killed. That would only create a martyr. They had to believe he'd left voluntarily. Casey knew the group had pooled a large sum of money together for night vision goggles, ammo, and guns. He knew where it was kept. He stole it that night, burying it out in the desert.

When Duane didn't turn up the next day and the money was gone, everyone believed he'd embezzled it and taken off. Casey hoped that would be the end of it. The death of the leader. His betrayal. But instead of disbanding, the group put their support behind Wilbur Connell wholeheartedly. The stockpile of money grew again.

Connell rose to power. He was even more abominable and intolerant than Duane had been, and now with the power of followers squarely behind him, he doubled down on his activities, and his loathsome rhetoric began attracting white supremacists from neighboring counties. The hunting parties grew larger.

Casey knew he had to do it again. He stalked Connell. Learned where he'd hidden the money, buried in his own backyard. Casey followed him on nights out, waiting for a clean shot when the man was alone in a desolate location. He didn't have to wait long. He blew a hole clean through Connell's skull on a night when the coyotes sang from the hills. As before, Casey cleaned the truck and hid the body.

Then he dug up the money where Connell had buried it and stashed it away. He waited.

With the second-in-command gone, all the money stolen again, the followers began to lose faith. The movement faltered, its fire dwindling. The group began to fragment and lose its drive. Men returned to their home counties. Eventually their group died out completely.

But Casey couldn't risk the bodies eventually being found, the followers learning that they'd been murdered rather than taking off with the money to start a new life somewhere else.

So one night he dug up the bodies, wrapped them in plastic tarps, and transported them hours away to the mountains. He buried them on a vast acreage of undeveloped land and donated all the money he'd stolen to several nonprofits that aided refugees.

A few years went by. Casey moved on to other places, other causes. But then he heard about the golf course development on the very piece of land where he'd buried the bodies. The development meant that foundations would be dug. Sand traps built. A clubhouse and restaurant, and fifty luxury condos. Depending on where they chose to dig, the bodies could be unearthed. He couldn't risk their discovery, and he couldn't be sure he hadn't made a mistake, left some telltale sign of himself. A hair. A fingerprint.

So he'd traveled back to the site to move the bodies somewhere else.

And that night he'd encountered Alex Carter, out there in the darkness, doing a spotted owl study. He learned she'd successfully found the threatened birds. The development had fallen through. A land trust was buying the property and it would be protected in perpetuity. The owls were safe. And his bodies were, too. Without knowing it, Alex had saved Casey. Saved him from identification. From prosecution. He resolved in that moment to always have her back whenever she needed him.

He'd traveled, checked out other places where she'd done studies, other places that were now protected because of the species she'd found there.

And he'd vowed to protect her just as she had those species.

And now he was closer to her than he'd ever imagined he would be.

TWENTY-EIGHT

After she'd showered and changed into her own clothes, Alex settled on the end of her motel bed and called Zoe.

"Alex! How's my favorite wildlife biologist?"

"Aren't I the only one you know?"

"That doesn't matter. You're still my favorite."

"How's the shoot going?"

Zoe exhaled. "Gross, gross, gross."

"That doesn't sound promising."

"It isn't. I had to kiss Nick Buchanan, you know, Mr. Prima Donna Actor with his own craft services table? There's this scene where I start to seduce him so I can drug him and get access to British troop movements. Major yuck."

"I take it he's no Casanova?"

"Far from it. I mean, does the guy ever brush his teeth? Has he heard of floss? And then, while we're shooting, I move in for the kiss and he embraces me in what I can only describe as a wrestling move. I mean, he practically puts me in a half nelson and bends me to this weird angle where I can't move. And then instead of kissing me like a normal human being, he just sort of drags his lips across mine like a slimy fish gasping for breath."

"Ewwww!"

"Tell me about it! I mean, the guy's fifty-four years old. How can you not know how to kiss yet when you're fifty-four years old?"

"Maybe his breath is so bad no one stuck around long enough to teach him," Alex suggested.

"I don't doubt that!" Zoe cried. "I can't get the smell of him out of my nose. I mean, this was the absolute worst kiss of my life, and I've had some doozies. And the worst part is that the director didn't like how the scene turned out, so we have to reshoot!"

"Can you slip some breath mints to him?"

"I'm sure he'd say there are too many calories or they aren't the right *kind* of imported breath mint from Luxembourg or Monaco, or wherever prima donnas demand their breath mints come from."

"Well, I hope you survive."

"I'm kind of gagging just thinking about it. But I'll do my best." She laughed. "So how is everything out there? Polar bears, ice, and blizzards. I think I'd rather be doing that than reshooting this scene."

"It's certainly been interesting." Alex regaled her with tales of their turmoil out on the ice.

Zoe was aghast. "That's horrible! Are you crazy? Why aren't you on the first plane out of there?"

"I can't give up now."

"You're insane. You should be at the airport terminal right now, bags packed, with a flight booked to L.A. You can stay at my place. Then when I get back, we'll just drink wine and chill. Out of mortal danger."

"That's really nice of you, Zoe, but I just can't abandon the study. Besides, the police are investigating now. They'll catch these guys."

"You don't know that for sure. You know how many murders go unsolved every year? What if you're one of them?"

"I will do my best not to be," Alex assured her friend.

"You're insane! There's no *way* you could get me to stay after all that. I don't like how dangerous this job has become."

"I don't, either, Zoe. But these species are endangered for a reason. If you're going to work around them, it comes at a risk. Think of the rangers who protect rhinos and elephants from poaching.

They get shot at and killed. Not to mention everything we just went through out on the ice."

"You're not making me feel any better. Are you sure you want a target on your back?"

"If that's what it takes to help."

"Well, I worry about you out there."

"I worry about me, too." Alex laughed.

"It isn't funny. We've been friends forever. What if I didn't have you to complain to about bad kissers and the lack of supergrains on the craft services tables?"

"That would truly be a loss."

"They expect us to survive on mini-cupcakes and flabby sandwiches that even a gas station wouldn't stock."

"I'll try to play it safe, just for you," Alex assured her.

"Thank you."

Alex thought of Casey. In spite of who he really was, she'd felt safe with him out there on the ice. Grateful for his presence, even. She debated telling Zoe about it, and then she heard the ringing of the set bell.

"That's me," her friend said. "I better go."

"Let me know how the kiss turns out."

"Don't forget the wrestling moves. And if you get shot, I'm going to kill you!"

"I'll do my best to avoid mortal danger."

"You better. I mean it."

"I know you do. Take care, Zoe."

"You too."

They hung up and Alex's stomach started rumbling. She hadn't eaten anything but MREs for the last few days, and the thought of the delicious, warm veggie food at Moe's sounded so appealing her mouth watered.

But first she wanted to touch base with her dad. She plugged her phone in to charge while they talked and dialed his number. At the sound of his kind voice, she immediately felt comforted.

"Pumpkin!"

"Hey, Dad. It's good to hear your voice."

"You sound tired. Is everything okay?"

"Just had a hell of a time out on the ice."

"What happened?"

She described what they'd been through, and he grew more concerned as she continued.

"This is turning out to be a dangerous job," he said.

"Don't I know it."

"I think you should leave. Come here and stay with me for a while."

"I'd love that, Dad, but I can't leave this study unfinished. We've got a rare opportunity here, the ear of the Minister of Environment and Climate Change."

"That may be, but your life is in danger," her father insisted.

"I know. But the police are on it. And I want to stay here for now."

He exhaled. "You're as stubborn as your mother. I know you believe in this work and that you're willing to take the risk, but..." His voice trailed off.

"I've got to stay."

"I don't like this at all." But then he relented. "A lot of people wouldn't be willing, I guess. Hell, a lot of people don't even think about the species going extinct, let alone try to do something about it."

The statement made Alex feel sad, though she knew he was right.

"I tell people what my daughter's doing and they always sound excited. There are people who care."

"That's true." It felt good to hear encouragement from her father. Zoe had been all fear, and that fear could be contagious.

"For what it's worth, I'm proud of you," her dad added. "What did the police say?"

"They're investigating."

"Well, you be careful out there, pumpkin. You want to come here for a visit when you're done?"

"I'd love to, Dad."

"Let's plan on that, then."

They talked for a while longer about what novels they were reading, and a performance he'd had with his barbershop quartet.

She decided to tell him about Casey. "You know that mystery package that arrived with my GPS unit?"

"Of course."

"I met the sender."

"What? Who was it?"

"He was the pilot I was stuck out on the ice with."

"So did he turn out to be a fellow biologist, then? Someone who found your GPS and returned it?"

"No. It's stranger than that, Dad. I think he's been following me. Keeping track of me." She debated telling him that he was the shooter who had saved her life in Boston.

"Did you meet him before Churchill?"

"No. That's the thing. But apparently he knew about me before then. I'm not sure how or when I got on his radar." Now she wished she'd asked him.

"I don't like this. Did you tell the cops?"

"Not yet. I don't think he means me any harm. If he'd wanted to do me in, he had ample opportunity out on the ice. In fact, he was a good ally out there."

"He could be mentally disturbed, Alex. If he's fixated on you . . ."

She knew her dad was right, but something in her gut didn't fear Casey. He'd saved her life, more than once. But he was definitely damaged somehow. Different. She wondered if she'd see him again, and under what circumstances.

"If you start feeling threatened, go to the police."

"I will, Dad."

"I love you, pumpkin."

"I love you, too."

They hung up, and Alex sat on the end of the bed, thinking about Casey and wondering where he was right then.

She jumped when someone knocked on her door. Half expecting it to be Casey, she looked through the peephole, seeing Detective Sergeant Moran. She removed the bolt and opened it.

"Can I come in?" he asked.

"Sure." She opened the door and ushered him in. There really wasn't anywhere for two people to sit, so she offered him the chair by the desk and she perched across from him on the foot of the bed. "What's up?"

"We have some more questions about the body you found on Cape Merry and Neil Trevors."

"Yes?"

He brought up a photo on his phone, showing a man with very light blond hair, blue eyes, and an average build. "Do you recognize this man?"

He looked a little like the man she'd found at Cape Merry, but his face had been so damaged she couldn't be sure. "Is that the man I found?"

Moran nodded. "His name was Rex Tildesen."

"So it was Sasha Talbot's dive partner."

"Yes. Forensics discovered that both Tildesen and Neil Trevors were killed with the same gun."

Alex's jaw fell open. "Are you serious?"

"All too. Is there something you're not telling us?"

"No," she said, feeling shocked.

"Are you sure you didn't know the victim found at Cape Merry?"

She shook her head. "I'd never seen him before."

"Yet your assistant was killed with the same gun, and you were around both bodies."

Alex grappled for an explanation. "I can't explain it. I have no idea how they're related."

The sergeant stood. Alex couldn't tell if he was satisfied with her answers or not. "That's all for now."

"Has Neil's family been notified?"

"Yes. They're flying in from Toronto tomorrow."

"I can't believe he's gone."

Moran walked to the door. "I'll leave you to rest up."

When he left, she bolted the door behind him. Her stomach rumbled again, and she threw on her coat, her mind a storm of thoughts. First she wanted to stop by Sasha's motel and give her condolences. Then she'd head off to Moe's. How could the two cases be connected? What were the snowmobilers after?

TWENTY-NINE

As Alex approached Sasha's motel room, she could hear the woman weeping inside. She quietly knocked, and moments later, Sasha opened the door. When she saw Alex standing there, her face twisted in grief and she reached out her arms. Though the two women had known each other only a short time, Alex liked Sasha immensely. She hugged her, and they stood in the doorway like that for several minutes, Sasha crying silently, her body shaking. Then she pulled away and invited Alex in.

"The police just came by," Sasha told her, plucking a tissue out of a box on the sink. She blew her nose. "I looked at Rex's body the other day. I was pretty sure it was him. I mean, he had the koi tattoo and everything. But his face was beaten so bad. It's terrible, but I hoped that it was someone else. But they just confirmed the ID through dental records."

"I'm so sorry."

"I still can't believe it was him. What the hell happened out there? Even the cops don't know."

"I have no idea."

Sasha threw the tissue away and took another one. "If you hadn't found him, I wonder how long he would have . . . I mean, he was out there, alone, his body just lying there . . ." Another sob wracked her and she went through several more tissues.

Alex moved to her, stroking her back. "I'm so sorry," she repeated.

Sasha wiped her nose. "I can't believe this. His parents are going to be crushed." She let out a long sob. "Hell, I'm crushed."

"I know. I can't even imagine. You two were partners for so long."

"I can't even picture my future without him. It's like looking down a dark, endless tunnel." She picked up her phone. "I guess I should call his parents now." Her hands trembled on the device.

"Do you want me to sit with you while you do?"

She sniffed, wiping at her nose. "No, it's going to be rough. You go on ahead with your evening. Afterward I think I'll need to be alone for a while, try to process this."

Alex stepped reluctantly toward the door. "Okay, if you're sure. I was going to get some food. Want me to bring some back?"

Sasha gripped her stomach. "There's no way I could eat. But thank you."

"Of course. Call me if you need anything."

"I will."

Alex quietly shut the door behind herself as Sasha began to dial. She felt so sorry for the woman. So much of Alex's own work was solo. She couldn't imagine finding a kindred spirit to do it with. And to find that kindred spirit as Sasha had and then lose him? She bit her lip, Sasha's tears infectious.

She climbed into her Jeep, her heart heavy.

At Moe's, the corner table by the dartboard was all abuzz about Neil's death. No one could believe it. Alex sat with them for a short time, and they lifted a glass to him. She decided not to mention his being paid to sabotage the study. He was gone. Let them think the best of him.

Wanting to be by herself then, she moved to the bar and ate in silence. She knew she should be exhausted, but her mind kept treading over what had happened on the ice.

Finally, feeling like she ate way too much, Alex walked over to the Centre. A couple researchers were milling around the lab, and

Alex joined them. She looked forward to getting the samples back from the police so she could run tests.

For now, she ran further cortisol tests on the fur and claw samples of the bear she'd tagged on her first day out with Casey.

As polar bear fur grew during the summer, the stress hormone cortisol was integrated into the hair. Examining the cortisol level gave her insight into the bear's condition and health at the time of the previous summer's ice breakup. She found the stress levels somewhat high in the bear, indicating that it had been a long ice-free period during which he didn't get a lot of nutrition.

Testing the fat sample, she found trace amounts of DDT, the dangerous pesticide that had been banned in the U.S. in 1972. It was still in use in other parts of the world, such as India, China, and North Korea, and it hung around for so long that its lingering residue caused problems even in areas where it had been outlawed.

She stretched, rubbing her neck. All of the adrenaline of the last few days had drained out of her body and she finally felt like she could sleep.

She climbed into her Jeep and drove back to her motel. Snow fell now, and the moon, obscured partially by clouds, illuminated the snowy terrain around her, making the scenery glow in an ethereal light. Fog filled the air, lending an aura of mystery. The drive did her good, as she gazed out over the silvery landscape. She pulled up at her motel and climbed out, still feeling stiff from the long walk across the ice.

When she reached the door, she froze. The lights were on. She was almost sure she'd left them off. She was habitual about never wasting energy. But she'd been so tired, it was possible she'd forgotten. She hesitated, thought of climbing back in her Jeep. But if someone was inside, they could be taking the hair sample she'd brought to the motel for safekeeping or stealing her laptop or backup drive with all her data.

Finally, she crept to the door and listened. She didn't hear anything. When she'd waited a couple minutes, still hearing nothing within, she decided she must have simply forgotten to turn off the light. She inserted the key and swung the door wide.

Inside, the room lay in shambles. Her suitcase had been overturned on the bed, all the contents spilled out. Her toiletries lay scattered all over the floor, the contents of the refrigerator strewn around. The wastebasket had been dumped upside down. She'd stepped inside only a foot when the door slammed shut behind her. A man in a balaclava stood behind the door and he leapt forward, grabbing her arm. "Where is it?" he demanded.

A woman in a black ski mask emerged from the bathroom. She had Alex's laptop tucked under her arm.

Alex swung around, wrenching free from the man's grip, and squared off against them. The woman flung her laptop down on the bed and pulled out a wicked-looking knife.

"You find it in there?" asked the man. He had a gruff voice, and she immediately recognized it. She didn't have to see him limp to know he was the leader of the snowmobilers who had attacked them.

"No," answered the woman.

"Tell us where it is," the leader said. He gestured for his comrade to approach her. "Or she'll cut your face so bad you'll never look the same again."

"I have no idea what you're talking about."

The woman narrowed in on her, her movements determined, the knife gripped tightly in her hand. Alex's eyes went down to the chair in front of the desk. In another second, the woman would be past it. She had to act now. She grabbed the back of it and swung it hard, slamming it into the knife-wielder's hand. Her weapon flew loose, arcing across the room and clattering against the wall above the bedside table. Alex continued swinging the chair, maintaining a tight grip on it, and advanced toward the leader like a lion tamer.

She ran at him, slamming the chair into him and driving him back against the wall.

Then she flung the door open, throwing the chair at the woman. It glanced off her shoulder and she cursed. Alex slammed the door hard into the leader, who was pinned behind it.

Then she was outside, running for her car. She fished the keys out of her jacket pocket.

A puff of snow flew up just to the right of her feet at the same instant she heard a muffled poof. She spun, the keys out in her hand. The leader stood in the open doorway, a pistol with a silencer aimed at her head.

"I said," he growled, "where is it?"

The woman joined him and they burst out of the motel room.

It was still early. Alex wondered if anyone else was in the motel at this hour, or if they'd be out at dinner or coming back from sightseeing. "Somebody call the cops!" she shouted. She didn't see anyone stir in their rooms.

"If she's dead, she won't be able to find it," the woman said.

"Yeah, but we don't know who she might have told."

She couldn't just stand there and get shot, but she didn't have time to swing the car door open, climb in, start it, and then drive off before he could fire a clean shot at her. He was less than twenty feet away.

Instead she dove down and rolled behind the car. Cold snow pressed into her face. Keeping the car between her and the two attackers, she crawled around to the far side of it. The parking lot had six other cars in it, and she rolled to the next one while their line of sight was still obstructed by her own car. Then she rolled to the next. Now she ran at a crouch, covering the distance to the next two cars.

She recognized the last car in the lot. It was the one that had pursued Steve out of Moe's parking lot the night she met him. It had to belong to the snowmobilers.

"Just tell us where it is!" the leader boomed.

Alex reached a small cluster of spruce trees at the edge of the parking lot and moved into them, snow shaking loose and cascading down the back of her coat. She shivered in the cold.

"Where'd she go?" the woman asked, sprinting down the line of cars.

Alex spotted another cluster of spruces across the street. She made a break for it, dashing across the open space.

"There!" the woman shouted. The leader took a shot and snow kicked up to Alex's left. She wondered if he was purposefully missing like before, out on the ice. Trying to scare her into standing still, giving up. He clearly needed some information from her, though she couldn't imagine what it was. But that wouldn't keep him from shooting her in the legs to slow her down.

The hair sample had been sitting out on the motel desk in plain view, undisturbed. But again, they hadn't been interested in taking samples.

She made it to the cluster of trees and squeezed between the branches. The street on this side was largely residential, and she raced between two houses, crossing through the backyard of the one on the left. But running in snow meant they could follow her tracks. She could hear them calling out to each other. They were trying to flank her. She had to get somewhere where she couldn't leave a trail.

A fence loomed up before her and she took a running leap at it, gripping the top. She hefted herself up and over, dropping down on the far side. A startled German shepherd, chained to the homeowner's porch, erupted in a fury of barking. She ran to the fence on the far side of the yard and vaulted over it, too.

She heard the gunning of an engine out on the street and wondered if they'd gone back to their car. She ran through more backyards. She heard the car stop and a door slam. She vaulted over a chain-link fence into someone else's yard, setting off another dog, a small one this time, who stood in the person's kitchen window and barked as furiously as its little Chihuahua body would allow.

She heard someone go over the fence one yard back and knew that at least one of them was following her on foot, probably calling back to the other one to cut her off at the next street.

She heard a car race by on the street ahead of her, and then screech to a halt. A car door slammed.

She jumped a railing into a new yard. This yard had no fence around the rest of the property, and she could see the headlights of a car glowing in the foggy, snow-filled night. A dog had been running around in this yard, creating a maze of tracks. She realized her own tracks could be obscured here, so she headed for a snow-covered tree and ducked down beneath its evergreen branches. She gasped, catching her breath, trying to quiet her breathing.

She heard someone scramble over the last fence she'd climbed. She inched back a little farther, covering her mouth to hide the frost as she exhaled.

Too late, she heard the crunching of boots on the snow directly behind her. A hand fell on her shoulder.

She whirled, coming face-to-face with Casey. He brought a gloved finger up to his lips and flicked out a collapsible combat baton. Just then the leader came scrambling over the fence into the yard, struggling with his injured leg. He stopped when he saw the maze of dog tracks confusing her trail. He took a few hesitant steps toward the tree, thought better of it, then turned back around, hunching over in the snow, trying to read the tracks. When he took a few more steps back toward the tree, Casey burst out with the ba-ton, bringing it down hard on the man's head. He crumpled, blood spattering on the snow, and went still, his breath frosting in the air. He was unconscious. Casey ripped the man's face mask off and took a photo with his phone.

Alex crept out and joined him, staring down at the familiar face. A scar ran across the bridge of his nose, and with his long black hair and goatee, Alex recognized him as being one of the men who'd chased Steve out of the bar that night.

The rumble of a car's engine sounded on the block next to them. Casey grabbed her hand and they ran to the next yard over. This property had a tall wooden fence. Alex leapt up and grabbed the top, climbing over. Casey landed next to her. The car drove slowly down the road, and they pressed into the fence, catching their breath. The vehicle motored onward. They crossed into another yard with a shed, the snow falling heavier now. The car's headlights pierced the foggy gloom but started to move away in the wrong direction.

"Hey!" she suddenly heard the leader's hoarse voice call in the distance. "Hey!" The car paused, and she heard a door slam. He'd recovered and rejoined his companion.

Alex pressed her back against the reassuring cold metal of the shed, Casey beside her. When the car's engine faded away into the distance, she turned to him. In a spur-of-the-moment reaction, she hugged him fiercely. "Thank you."

He held her, his familiar scent washing over her. He felt good in her arms. Reassuring. A part of her trusted him intrinsically, and yet another part of her didn't know what to make of him. She could feel the warmth of his neck against her cheek. She pulled away.

"I came by your motel to apologize," he said. "Saw them chasing you."

"I'm glad you were here."

They stood in silence, their bodies close together. She felt a little dizzy at his proximity. "We . . . we have to figure out what they're after."

His blue eyes stared down into hers. "To sabotage your study?"

"It's more than that. It doesn't add up. Why did the person steal my research from the lab, but the snowmobilers left it untouched out on the ice? And just now in my motel room, they asked again where 'it' was, but a hair sample was clearly visible on the motel desk, and they already had my laptop with the data on it. They were looking for something else."

He didn't answer, just looked down at her, concern creasing his brow. Their faces were only inches apart, his lips slightly parted.

"That man you hit just now," she went on. "He was with the man you killed on the ice. They were all in Moe's the other night, the ones who chased that nervous little guy, Steve, out of the restaurant."

"Do you know what they wanted from him?"

"No. But he was scared. Really scared. I wonder if they got to him."

They stood together in the silent neighborhood, snow cascading around them. It collected in Casey's tousled black hair, flakes melting as they landed on his handsome face. Suddenly the mystery of their attackers felt more distant than the mystery of Casey himself.

"Who are you?" she asked him. "Really?"

"I'm Casey MacCrae. I've never lied to you, Alex."

"Where do you know me from? Have we met?"

"No. Not until I came here."

"Then how?"

He went silent, staring down at her intently. She felt encapsulated with him there, in the shadowed darkness of the shed, the hush of the snowfall.

"In New Mexico. I was out in the mountains one night. I came across you out there. I learned that night that you'd found spotted owls on that land, and the sale to the golf course developers had fallen through. I'd been dreading that development. It . . . meant a lot to me that the land got protected, that it went to a land trust instead."

"You had a connection with that piece of land?"

He squeezed her hand. "Yes. After that, I followed your work." He looked down, biting his lip. "Forgive me. I was curious where else you'd worked. Got interested in your career. I confess I . . . borrowed your GPS unit."

"Borrowed it? Where did you find it?"

"I came across your pack. You'd set it down. I know I shouldn't have taken it . . . but I wanted to know where else you'd worked, places you might have aided with protections. Then I saw you were coming back, and I guess I sort of panicked. I took your GPS unit with me."

"Why not just talk to me? Why then mail it back to my dad?"

"I felt bad about taking it. Wanted you to have it back. I looked up your Garmin registration and mailed it to that address. I guess that was your dad's. I visited a lot of the places you'd worked to protect. I'd . . . been struggling since I got back from Darfur. Needed to get my head straight. It helped to be out in these amazing areas where wildlife was protected. Seeing the work you'd done was inspiring. It reminded me that not all people are evil. Some of them are working for good. I sent you postcards from those places to let you know how important I thought your work was, how beautiful those places were that you'd helped to protect." He met her gaze. "I really didn't mean the cards to be creepy. I guess I . . . just didn't know what to say. You didn't know me, after all. Somehow I thought it would be even weirder if I signed the cards."

"And Boston?" she asked.

"I was in New York when I heard you'd been instrumental in getting those wetlands protected. I wanted to come up and have a look for myself, see what you'd accomplished. I read about it online, and the more I dug into the history of that piece of land, the more worried I got."

"What do you mean?"

"I read about the luxury condos that were supposed to go up, and how the owner of the construction company lost his business after the deal fell through. His wife left him. He had all these hateful, ranting posts on environmentalist websites. He'd written angry letters to the *Boston Globe* about how the economy was going to be ruined if conservationists and other 'bleeding hearts' kept choosing animals instead of people's livelihoods. I began to worry he might do something drastic. I hacked into his email and learned that he'd bought a gun on the dark web. So I armed myself and went to the ceremony. I was worried he'd . . . well, do exactly what he did. And I was ready. I thought if I could get body cam footage of him if he brought a gun, I could call the police. But then everything just went insane."

She took a long deep breath, her brow so furrowed it began to hurt. She studied his worried face, his compassionate eyes. "You saved my life out there. And the lives of countless others."

"I couldn't let him hurt you."

"And Montana?"

"I'd done some digging around, wanted to know what kind of people you'd be dealing with when you got out there. Some of them were dangerous. I wanted to keep an eye on you."

"On the DVD you mailed me, you'd written that I had your back, and that now you had mine. How did I ever have your back? I didn't know you before now."

"I told you I've never lied to you . . ." He hesitated.

"Yes?"

"But I don't think I want to tell you that part. I'm not sure you'd . . . be okay with it."

"I want you to tell me, Casey."

"I'd like to. But maybe tonight isn't the right time. Maybe when we know each other better."

She felt the tiniest flutter of fear inside her. "And will we? Know each other better?"

"I'd like to."

Alex could sense something disturbed in him, something deep down. Maybe something broken. Or something deeply sad or lost. But she didn't feel danger from him, though she knew he was capable of killing. But now she knew that she was capable of killing, too, if it was in defense of herself or someone she cared about.

Casey's hair was wet now with snow, and water dripped off the ends of her own.

"We should get you somewhere warm," he said.

"And you?"

"I have something to do. I have to leave for a while."

"What are you going to do?"

"There's something I need to check out." He remained evasive. "But I think you should check into another motel tonight. I have a card we can use. Something untraceable. You'll be able to stay at a new place anonymously."

He put his hand just behind the small of her back as they walked out to the sidewalk. The streets were empty in the middle of the storm, and they walked undisturbed back to her motel room. She packed up her clothes. In the bathroom, her attackers had completely squeezed out her toothpaste into the sink, as if she could have hidden something inside the tube. Likewise her moisturizer and sunscreen. She'd have to get new ones.

Her laptop still waited on the bed where the woman had flung it. She grabbed the hair sample and took it with her.

The car rental place was open for another thirty minutes, and they traded out her Jeep for a Toyota 4Runner, using Casey's card. The name on it read DOUGLAS O'CONNOR, and Alex didn't ask.

Then they drove to the Caribou Motel across town and checked her in. When she was settled in her room, he walked to the door, readying to leave. He took out his phone. "I'm sending you the photo I took of that guy."

Her own phone beeped with a notification of the photo's receipt. Casey turned toward the door. She hesitated, part of her not wanting him to go, and the other part so full of questions and reservations she wasn't sure she was ready to know anything else about him.

"I'll be back," he told her. "I'm going to follow a possible lead in all this. Be careful." He took her hand again, pressed it between his own, and left.

She stood at the door, fingers resting on the handle. She heard his car start up and drive away. Only then did she slide the security bolt home.

She got her phone out and called DS Moran. When she told him about the break-in to her room, he grew concerned.

"I'll send out PC Bighetty to check it out. Maybe we can get some prints."

"I got a photo of one of them this time." She decided to leave Casey out of it. "I'll email it to you."

"That's a break."

"Please call me if PC Bighetty learns anything."

"I will."

They hung up and she sat down in the desk chair, staring at her laptop. She booted it up, half worried the hard drive would be wiped. But it wasn't. All her data was there. She breathed a sigh of relief.

But what had they been after? And why were they willing to kill for it?

THIRTY

It was only as she was getting ready for bed that she remembered about her toiletries being ruined. She looked at her watch. The local store was closed, as was the motel's office. Her teeth felt fuzzy, and she knew they'd only feel worse in the morning.

Then she remembered the backup toothbrush and toothpaste in her fleece jacket at the Centre. This new motel wasn't too far from there. Less than a mile. Besides, after what had happened tonight, she wanted to check on her samples from the young male bear in the lab, to make sure all was well.

She cautiously locked up her room and walked out to the new rental car, feeling paranoid. The streets were deserted, lights off in houses. She drove the empty streets, not passing a single car.

At the Centre, she found all the lights off. She let herself in. First she checked in the lab. Her biological samples were still in the fridge. Her data was still on the lab computer. The hair and claw samples were all accounted for.

Feeling better, she went to the gear room and retrieved her fleece jacket. She felt around in the pocket for her toothbrush and toothpaste and came away with a torn piece of napkin. She pulled it out.

It was a series of handwritten numbers, some single digits, some two, some three. She looked at the top line:

42 3 42 12 154 272 3 22 117 12

She brought it with her into the lab where the light was better. It wasn't her handwriting. She didn't remember anyone giving it to her. Was it lottery numbers or something?

She frowned. It actually looked like a cipher of some kind.

She'd been fascinated with codes and ciphers growing up. Her mother had even thought she might grow up to be a cryptographer, but Alex's passion had always been for wildlife. Still, she'd had fun writing coded letters and secret messages.

Mentally she went through the list of ciphers. Because the series was all numbers, it wasn't the ROT1, or "rotate one letter forward through the alphabet" cipher. Same went for transposition and the Caesar cipher, unless, and she hoped this wasn't the case, the answer itself was a complicated series of numbers. Nor could it be monoalphabetic substitution like the Pigpen cipher or something more complicated requiring a key word, like a Vigenère cipher. For that same reason, she ruled out a digraph substitution cipher like the Playfair.

She stared at the series of numbers. It reminded her of a cipher she'd looked at as a kid, but she couldn't quite place it. Memories of codes and ciphers that led to buried treasure filtered into her mind. Back then, she'd read all she could get her hands on about the Oak Island Mystery, a strange, booby-trapped pit on an island in Nova Scotia. Legend had it that Captain Kidd had buried his treasure there.

And then it hit her. This looked like the Beale cipher. In the 1820s, Thomas J. Beale had hidden a treasure of gold, silver, and jewels somewhere in Bedford County, Virginia. He and a group of friends had amassed the riches and wanted to keep them safe. As a backup, he gave an innkeeper a box containing three notes in cipher that told where to find the buried hoard. Beale intended to return one day to claim it. But he never did, and so the innkeeper held on to the notes. Never able to break the cipher, the innkeeper gave the notes to his friend before he died. For decades, the friend also tried unsuccessfully to decipher them.

The notes changed hands again, and finally one was deciphered. They turned out to be written in a document cipher. For each one, Beale had chosen a certain key document, and assigned numbers to its letters, then used those numbers to write out a new message. But no one knew what documents he'd used. Beale had revealed only that the three notes detailed respectively the location of the treasure, the content of the treasure, and the names of the treasure owners and their relatives. Only the second note had ever been deciphered. Cracked finally by using the Declaration of Independence as the key document, it revealed the contents to be gold, silver, and gems valued today at over $43,000,000.

But the treasure had never been found.

Alex eyed the cipher on the napkin. If it was a book or document cipher like Beale's, she'd have to figure out the key document.

But who had placed it in her pocket? The gear room at the Centre was crammed with coats and other equipment. It was possible someone had slipped it into her pocket by mistake.

Puzzling over it, she left the Centre and returned to her new motel room. As she absently brushed her teeth and put on her pj's, she wondered over the mysterious writing.

She tried to think of the last time she'd worn the jacket. The handwriting wasn't Casey's or Neil's. She'd seen how Casey wrote numbers on his postcards, and his fours were always closed. And Neil's field notes certainly didn't match these numbers, which slanted to the left. It might have been Ilsa's writing. And then she remembered—the last time she'd had the jacket with her was at Moe's, the night Steve sat down next to her. He could have slipped the piece of paper into her jacket.

But why had Steve placed it with her? He obviously didn't want it on him if that threesome caught up to him, Alex decided. She remembered now that he'd asked for a pen and had written something on a napkin. Then he'd taken what she thought had been a receipt out of his pocket, torn it up, and thrown it away. It was possible the real message had been written down on that slip of paper, and he'd transcribed it into a cipher on the napkin, disposing of the original.

Whatever the cipher was, perhaps it was too long to commit to memory. What was the book he'd been reading that night? He'd gotten it off the Take One, Leave One bookshelf. His choice had surprised her. What was it? Then she remembered. It was *Daisy Mouse and the Mystery of the Haunted Dollhouse.* That had to be the key document. He'd written the cipher while he was sitting right next to her. Her coat had hung by the little hook under the bar, and it would have been easy to slip it into her pocket.

The trio who followed him out must have caught up with him. Maybe tried to get him to reveal where he'd hidden the cipher or original document. Or maybe they hadn't caught up to him, and they'd seen him talking to her. Figured she might have it. Maybe they'd tortured him into confessing he'd given it to her. Then they'd killed him. She was a stranger here. It wouldn't have been hard for them to figure out who she was.

Where is it? the snowmobilers had kept asking. This had to be *it.* But what *was* it?

She called over at Moe's, but they'd closed for the night. She transcribed the numbers to her laptop just in case the cipher got lost or stolen.

Then she wrote it down on a piece of motel stationery. She took the ironing board out of the closet and pulled one rubber foot off a leg. She put the cipher inside the hollow tube and replaced the rubber foot. Then she made one last copy and gently slid it into the tissue box beneath all the tissues.

Tomorrow she'd go to Moe's and see if she could make sense of the cipher. She hoped no one had decided to take that book.

She finally lay down in bed, trying to sleep, her mind a tangle of thoughts. Casey swirled in and out of them. She wondered what he was checking out, where he'd gone. Her stomach tightened at the thought of seeing him again, anticipation with the slightest tinge of fear. But it was more of a fear of the unknown than a fear of danger. He was a mystery. Just like the cipher. Tomorrow, at least, she hoped to have the answer to one of them.

THIRTY-ONE

Paul White's mansion on Amundsen Road was dark as Casey broke into it. It stood alone on the outskirts of town, a sophisticated security system in place. But he was able to circumvent it. He knew the police were looking into the background of the man who'd picked them up in the helicopter, but Casey wanted to know if White had been in on it, or if the pilot really had acted independently. This wasn't the first corrupt CEO he'd investigated. He had no tolerance for powerful people who abused those less fortunate.

He moved silently through the house, on the lookout for additional motion detectors. He disarmed a secondary alert system. He found White's study and went through drawers, rifled papers. He hacked into White's desktop computer, finding nothing suspicious. Just tax statements, business contracts with exploratory geologists, and maintenance files on his helicopters, yachts, a private jet, and a fleet of limos for whatever city he happened to be in.

Other files included employee records. It looked like he employed about two thousand people worldwide, including fifteen here in Churchill. They included geologists, a helicopter pilot, a limousine driver, three oil rig workers, a geographic information systems specialist for mapping petroleum exploration. Looked like White was searching for local places to extract oil, places to frack, sources of natural gas.

But nothing looked suspicious. Casey stood up and felt around paintings that hung on the walls, looking for a safe. Then he checked under rugs. At the back of the house, an entertainment room opened into a steel corridor built out over the permafrost. It led to a large vault door with a wheel and an electronic locking mechanism. It was as big as a bank vault.

Casey had come prepared. He pulled out a descrambler and hooked it up to the electronic lock. While he waited for it to determine the correct combination, he walked through the rest of the house, looking in White's bedroom, under the bed, between the mattress and the box spring. He searched the CEO's medicine cabinet, finding prescriptions for high blood pressure. He pulled out drawers and felt their undersides. He went through the man's clothes, searching pockets for forgotten scraps of paper, anything that would point to nefarious intentions, but came up empty.

Finally he returned to the vault door. His descrambler had done its work and he entered the combination. The lock clicked open and he swung the vault door wide. Pulling out his penlight, he shone it into the dark recesses of the vault. It was completely empty. Maybe White had moved everything out of it. Or maybe he hadn't stored anything in here yet. The vault measured eight feet by ten feet. He'd have plenty of room for antiquities, money, gold bars, art, whatever he wanted to stash away. Casey remembered the photo from the magazine cover, showing all of the artifacts on the shelving behind him. Maybe White had yet to start a new collection here.

As he turned to leave the vault, something flashed on the floor in his penlight's beam. He knelt down, reaching a gloved hand out to the object. Tiny, it likely had skittered away out of sight, coming to rest beneath a slight overhanging lip on the metal wall. Casey picked it up, holding it between his thumb and forefinger.

A diamond, at least ten carats and beautifully cut.

Still kneeling, he shone his light around the perimeter of the vault, but the lone diamond was the only occupant. He left it where it was and stood. It seemed so out of place, if nothing had ever been stored here. More likely, the vault had once held valuables and upon a perhaps hasty removal of goods, this gem had fallen and escaped notice.

Casey shut the vault door, removed his descrambler, and took one last circuit through the house. Finally, satisfied nothing incriminating was there, Casey reset the alarm and left. But he couldn't fight the feeling that something just wasn't adding up. Who were the snowmobilers? And what were they after?

Now he took one last look at the exterior of Paul White's house. Something smelled rotten here, and Casey didn't like it.

As he climbed into his car, his mind drifted to Alex. He'd told her he was a UN peacekeeper, even told her about the warlord Darate in Darfur. He wondered if she'd understand if he told her everything, how he'd started on this path. He hadn't told her how that warlord had died. But what he'd said wasn't a lie. People *did* think that one of his own men killed him.

But that wasn't what happened. He put his head in his hands, trying to imagine how Alex would react if she knew the truth.

Darate had been a monster. He'd demanded tribute from villagers, everything from food to money to trade goods, all to keep his war machine going. If villagers couldn't pay, and usually they couldn't, he'd kill their families one by one, threaten to kill the rest if they didn't have tribute when he returned. But many families struggled just to support themselves, having nothing left over for marauders. Too many times Casey had witnessed gruesome acts of violence. The peacekeepers would enter a village after Darate had passed through, to find grieving parents weeping over their children, men strung up and left to die.

Pushed to the brink after seeing so much cruelty, Casey felt something inside him break. He couldn't let that monster continue to destroy whole villages of people.

As a kid he'd wanted to make the world a better place. His best friend growing up, Killian, didn't understand Casey's drive for change. While Casey attended rallies and protests for human rights, his friends stayed at home, playing video games or drinking at parties.

"One person can't make a difference," Killian told Casey over and over again. But Casey couldn't believe that. When Casey turned twenty, he saw the chance to right some of the wrongs, end some of the violence, and had been deployed with the UN Peacekeeping Forces as a combat medic.

And then he'd been sent to Darfur.

"We're already doing everything we can," his commanding officer said in response to the warlord's cruelty and ruthlessness. It hit home then that people who committed despicable acts had no rules to adhere to, whereas people who fought for justice had to play by legal restrictions that often let evildoers go unpunished. Things had to be done the "right" way, even if the right way wasn't effective.

In Darfur, Casey had stopped sleeping at night. He began stealing nearer and nearer to the warlord's camp, seeing how close he could get. A guard in camouflage always walked the perimeter, drinking coffee from a thermos throughout the night to stay awake.

A plan formed in Casey's mind. One night, after mixing together a powerful sedative from his med kit, Casey crept all the way to the perimeter. When the guard placed down his thermos to patrol the south side of the camp, Casey mixed the sedative into it. Then he withdrew and waited. He'd thought of strangling the man to unconsciousness, but that method wasn't as careful. It was difficult to know when the man would wake up again and sound an alert.

So Casey waited in the shadows. The man came back to his thermos, bent down, and retrieved it. He watched while the guard drank a cup, then replaced the thermos by an acacia tree. He recognized this guard. He'd watched him murder a young woman with a machete, then laugh as her father came out, crying in anguish. The guard had thrown down the old man and killed him with the blade, too, grinning the entire time.

Casey prowled parallel to the man, keeping his distance, out of sight. The guard walked more slowly, wiping his forehead, then slowed even more. He went down on one knee, then collapsed face-down into the dirt. Darting forward, Casey brought out his own thermos, dumped the remaining drugged coffee from the guard's, and replaced it with his own, untainted brew. He left the thermos where it was and returned to the sleeping guard. He hoisted him up over one shoulder and carried him to a dense growth of red ironwood. He stripped off the man's clothes, then undressed and donned them himself. He took the man's rifle.

His heart pounding in his chest, afraid of being discovered, Casey took the guard's place, patrolling casually along the perimeter, waiting for a bullet to tear through him at any moment, the fear of discovery so intense he could barely breathe. But it was too dark for anyone to see his face, to notice he was a stranger.

As he walked along the edge of camp, he drew closer and closer to where some men were talking around a fire. He was careful to keep his face in the shadows. He recognized the voice of the warlord and drew closer still. He was bragging to them about a man he'd burned alive, how the man had run around screaming like a pathetic chicken. Casey felt a surge of white-hot anger as he listened, but he forced himself to stroll by as if on his patrolling rounds.

The warlord continued to brag. Two of his men were playing cards off to the side of the fire.

Finally Darate stood up, announcing his intention to pee. This was it. Every muscle in Casey's body tightened. He became filled with a solitary purpose. Even if this cost him his own life, he was going to kill this evil man.

The warlord wandered away from the fire. The men went back to their card game, and the two by the fire talked among themselves. None paid much attention. They were, after all, safe in their compound.

Darate drew up next to a tamarisk tree and Casey flanked him, coming at him from behind. He didn't dare fire a shot from the rifle. That would rouse everyone in the camp.

He crept up behind Darate. At the last second, Casey's boot crunched on some gravel and the warlord began to turn, but Casey closed the distance, clamping a hand over the man's mouth. Casey drew out a knife and plunged it into the warlord's neck, severing his carotid.

Darate let out a terrified gurgle, but Casey's hand over his mouth muffled the sound. He kept his arm clenched tightly around the man's body as vital blood pumped out of his neck. The pulse grew weaker and weaker until it was just a dribble. The warlord slumped against Casey, and he let the despicable wretch slip to the ground. He stared down for a second at the sightless eyes, then hurried back to the perimeter. Staying to the deeper shadows, he walked casually back by the men playing cards, continuing on his rounds, just another person on patrol. No one looked up to notice the blood soaking one side of his shirt.

When he got past their line of sight he ran for the ironwood thicket.

Stripping out of the guard's clothes, he redressed the man in his uniform, the blood on it thick and coagulating. He placed the rifle beside him.

Then Casey donned his own clothes. He withdrew to the shadows as the guard began to stir. The man sat up, looked around in confusion, and clumsily stood up. He staggered back toward the perimeter just as a sharp cry rang out from the camp. The warlord's body had been discovered.

Casey ran back into the night, toward his own camp, his heart pounding, feeling exhilarated and free. He'd stopped evil, pure evil, and he hadn't lost his life.

As it turned out, one person could make a difference.

THIRTY-TWO

Alex woke the next day to stormy skies. Snow fell, lending a quiet hush over everything. Her phone rang as she was getting dressed. Seeing Sonia Bergstrom's name flash on the screen, she clicked the speaker button while she finished pulling on her outer layers.

"Sonia, hi. How are you?" She'd called Sonia when she returned from her ordeal on the ice, but it had gone to voicemail. Now she filled her in on the recent events, including Neil's death and his being paid off to delay the study with missing equipment.

"Unbelievable. I'm just shocked at everything that's happened. Poor Neil." She went silent for a few moments. "It's just been impossible to get this study off the ground. When I was there five years ago, it all went so much more smoothly. But since then, nothing has gone right. And now it's just one disaster after another."

"What do you think will happen with the study?"

"The permits are still good. If you're willing to tough it out, I'd like to find you another assistant. But I understand if you don't want to go out on the ice again."

Alex had to admit, at least to herself, that the thought of going back out there scared her. But that made her want to stay all the more. She wouldn't be frightened or intimidated. The study needed to be done. And if it could lead to stricter protections for polar bears, then it was vital she stick it out. "I want to stay," she told Sonia.

Her friend exhaled. "Oh good. I'm glad to hear it. How does Ilsa feel about it?"

"Ilsa?" For a moment, Alex was confused.

"Your pilot?"

"Didn't you know? She quit early on."

"Then who's been flying you around?"

"Casey MacCrae. He's a pilot who came out here for a job that fell through. I assumed Neil told you."

"No. I didn't even know Ilsa had quit. What happened?"

Alex sat down in the desk chair. "Apparently, she got a more lucrative job."

"I can't believe it. She's flown with my colleagues before. Came highly recommended. So what's this Casey guy like? Is he good?"

Alex had to admit the truth, even if she was conflicted about him. "Very."

"So he was who you were stuck out on the ice with?"

"Yes."

"Is he willing to continue with the study?"

Alex's stomach decided to do a few acrobatic exercises. "I'm not sure."

"Talk to him and let me know."

"I will."

"And, Alex? I'm really sorry about what you've been through. I still can't believe it about Neil. I have to call his parents. I'm sure they're devastated."

"I can't believe it, either."

"Hang tight for a few days and let me see what I can do to arrange things for you out there."

"Okay. Thanks, Sonia."

"You're the one who deserves thanks."

They hung up and Alex just stared down at her phone, not sure what to do. The study was on hold. Casey was gone.

At the Centre, she caught up on emails and double-checked that her samples and data were still safe there. She hoped to get back the samples confiscated by the police, once they finished processing their gear from their ordeal out on the ice.

Then, eager to get to Moe's and take a crack at solving the cipher, as soon as it opened for lunch, Alex gathered her coat and headed over there. Once inside the door, she immediately went to the Take One, Leave One bookshelf, happy to see that *Daisy Mouse and the Mystery of the Haunted Dollhouse* was still there. She pulled it down. Even if this was a book cipher, and even if Steve had used this book as the key, she still had to find the right pages. She brought it with her over to a booth where she could have some privacy. The server came over and Alex ordered a salad and a coffee.

When the server came back with her food, Alex brought the book out and started thumbing through the pages. She tried the first page, but what came out was nonsense:

N D N R O K D E Y R

To figure this out, she had to know not just which page Steve had started on, but if he counted each word and then used the first letter of that word.

If she had to, she could try each page. It wasn't a very long book. She tried the second and third pages, coming up with *W R W F L G R M U F* and *T S T A L F S P R A* respectively.

Then she flipped through the book, taking a bite of her salad, searching for something that might have caught his eye. A catchy chapter title maybe. She stopped at a slight ketchup stain on one of the pages. What had he been eating that night? Greasy french fries and ketchup. She started on that page, assigning a number to the first letter of each word, and skipping any duplicate letters.

She tried out the first few numbers in the cipher and got *F I F T Y E I G*. She kept going, resulting in *H T P O I N T S*. She paused. Words were forming. *Fifty-eight points.* This was it. She set her salad fork down, lunch forgotten, and finished out the cipher. When she was done, it read:

FIFTYEIGHTPOINTSEVENEIGHTTH
REEONEZEROTHREEDEGREESNORT
HNINETYFOURPOINTONEEIGHTTHR
EETWONINEFIVEDEGREESWEST

It was coordinates: 58.783103° N, 94.183295° W. It was definitely a long series of numbers to memorize. No wonder he'd written it down. She remembered him tearing up that other piece of paper and throwing it into the garbage. Maybe that had contained the undisguised numbers.

She finished her salad, wondering what could be at the coordinates. She pulled her GPS unit out of her pocket and entered them. Moving to the map screen, she zoomed out. Whatever it was lay on the northwestern part of the peninsula, on the narrow strip with the Hudson Bay to the north.

Her curiosity pulled at her to go to the location. If this was what the snowmobilers had been looking for, then there was a good chance they didn't know the coordinates. Otherwise they wouldn't be seeking them. Unless they *did* know the coordinates and just didn't want anyone else to find out about them. She decided to take her chances. She'd drive out to the location, stay in her car, just see what the area looked like.

She paid her bill and walked out to the 4Runner, careful of her surroundings. It had taken her a while to crack the code, and now the sun was low on the horizon. She didn't see anyone she recognized as she climbed into her car. She thought of calling the police, but then thought of White and his casual reference to being close to the retired chief of police. Until she learned more about what she was dealing with, she decided just to take a look at the location. If she found something dangerous, she could call the police then.

As she took La Vérendrye Avenue west, she found herself largely alone on the road. A few cars passed her headed in the other direction. No one was following her.

Her mind pulled inexorably toward Casey as she drove, wondering where he was. She couldn't possibly resume the study with him as the pilot, could she? But the study was more important to her than any personal feelings of discomfort about him. And right now her uncertainty about him was paired with a feeling of camaraderie for the ordeal they'd survived together.

She drove past the Town Centre Complex and continued west on La Vérendrye Avenue. She pulled off down a side dirt road, keeping an eye on her GPS screen. Her car bumped along the uneven terrain and then juddered as she hit a stretch of washboard. She could see the gray waters of Hudson Bay in the distance. The land here was snowy with long, flat, smooth stones. Clusters of spruce trees grew in patches along the road. Her GPS beeped with a proximity alert and she pulled off the road. Whatever it was, it lay three hundred feet to the west.

She stepped out of the 4Runner, switching to the compass screen of her GPS as she zeroed in on the location. Her boots crunched in snow. All around her stretched virgin white, untouched by any human footprints. In a few places, she saw the tracks of what was likely a raven.

When she reached the spot, she stood there, puzzled. It was just a flat section of land. She bent down, brushing snow off a long, flat gray stone. Her civilian GPS was Wide Area Augmentation System, or WAAS, enabled, which meant its accuracy was better than a smartphone and many other GPS units on the market.

She knelt down, brushing off snow all around her. All she found were rocks and some clumps of willows surviving beneath the snow. She rocked back on her heels, wondering. She looked all around her. Nothing but rocks and white.

Why would someone mark this spot?

She brushed snow away in a slightly wider circle. Maybe whoever had recorded the position didn't have a WAAS-enabled GPS
and therefore had at least a forty-five-foot inaccuracy working
against them, so the location they'd recorded had been off. She
stood, kicking around in the snow, dusting off objects beneath. But
they all turned out to be rocks. She returned to her initial location
and searched again, then stood staring out, turning in a full circle.

She just didn't get it. Maybe there had been something here, but
now it was gone. Maybe the snowmobilers *did* know the coordinates
all along and wanted to be sure no one else did. So when they'd been
unsuccessful in finding the cipher, they'd come out here and moved
whatever it had been, just in case someone else came looking.

It didn't look like anyone had been out here in days. Maybe the
snow had covered up the tracks.

The wind picked up, howling around her ears. She put up her
parka hood, staring out at the gray landscape. Finally she decided
that whatever had been here had been removed, and she started for
her 4Runner.

One of the large, flat rocks tipped up when she stepped on the
edge of it. She almost lost her balance. Stepping aside, she let the
rock slam back in place. She turned, staring at it. Then she got down
on her hands and knees and pressed on the end of the rock again.
The stone tipped upward. She dug her gloved fingers into the crack
where it had lifted. She slid it toward her, revealing a space in the
jumble of rocks. Clumps of dirt, grass, and snow filled the hole. She
started to dig it out, picking up handfuls of snow. Then she felt objects underneath. She worked her fingers around the edges of the
things and pulled them out.

The first was an ordinary flash drive double sealed in a clear
plastic bag. The second, also double sealed in a bag, looked like a
strange kind of GPS receiver with a small screen and antenna, but
she wasn't sure what it was. It had directional arrow buttons and
a power button. She turned it on, happy to find the batteries still

worked. A map flashed up on its screen, showing a pulsing red dot. She pressed the arrow buttons to move around on the map, zooming out.

Whatever was blinking lay off the northern coast of Churchill, out in Hudson Bay.

And Alex knew this was what everyone was after.

THIRTY-THREE

Alex picked up the receiver and flash drive and replaced the stone. Behind a thick bank of clouds, the sun had begun to set and twilight was approaching. She walked back to her car as the snowfall danced in the air. Flurries collected in her hair, the wind cold on her face. She reached her car as a dark blue SUV came rattling down the dirt road. It looked pristine, newly washed, fresh splatters of mud now covering its fenders. It passed her 4Runner, then drove on. She unlocked her car and got in as the SUV continued down the road. She didn't get a good look at the lone driver, just noticing he was male.

She climbed into her car, pulling her backpack off the passenger's seat. She moved a sketchbook and a scientific calculator out of the front pouch so she had room to place the receiver and flash drive in, along with her GPS unit. At the bottom of that pocket, in a zippered pouch she never used, she felt something strange.

When her groping fingers first felt the cold plastic, she thought it was a long-lost temperature logger she'd misplaced during an American pika study. But when she pulled it out, she puzzled over it. She didn't recognize it. In her hand was a 3D-printed plastic housing, and inside was a small circuit board. In the gloaming, she couldn't make out the details, so she pulled out her headlamp and switched it on. More light didn't reveal its function, nor trigger any memories as to what it was or how it had found its way into her backpack.

She frowned. What was it? A tracking device? She was just puzzling over what to do with it when the SUV came back, trundling along the dirt road. The guy was coming up fast. She'd seen people in trucks drive like mad on roads like this, and at first she chalked up his speed to impatience. But when he roared up right on her bumper, a thrill of fear quivered through her. She pulled out, her 4Runner jostling down the pitted road.

He accelerated, slamming into her bumper. She cried out in surprise and fear, almost dipping down into a gaping hole on the right side of the road. It would have given her a flat tire for sure.

She put on her high beams, weaving between pitted sections. The SUV roared up behind her again and smashed into her rear bumper, driving her forward. Her wheels slid in the slippery mixture of snow and mud and the tires briefly went off the road.

The track was barely wide enough for a single vehicle. Trying to swing in front of her, he drove off onto the tundra, kicking up clumps of dirt and snow behind him. She picked up speed, her eyes fixed on the holes in the road, her heart beating so fiercely that she felt like it would pound out of her chest. Her mouth went dry and her hands were slick on the steering wheel.

He jerked his car to the right and came up broadside to her. She slammed on the brakes, sliding to a halt in the mud. He stopped, pulling back onto the road in front of her, and started to back up. She jammed down on the gas pedal, swerving around him, and taking the dirt track at top speed. It was a dangerous proposition. She could hit one of the dips and get a flat. The car bumped and jostled and the seat belt cinched down painfully across her collarbone.

The SUV drove off the road again and pulled up alongside her. She looked over as he rolled down his window. A gun pointed straight at her. She ducked and stomped on the accelerator, her car fishtailing in the muddy roadbed.

She hit a stretch of washboard, and the car vibrated so violently she thought it was going to shake apart.

She heard the pistol fire and suddenly the car felt sluggish. The back end veered and lagged, sliding off to the side. He'd hit a tire. She was sure of it. Or one of the potholes had done its work.

But she kept driving. She couldn't remember how far ahead the paved road was, but if she could reach it, she could take the next road and the next, and then she'd be on the main thoroughfare through town. She doubted he'd continue firing at her then. Maybe she could make it to the RCMP station.

But her 4Runner was too sluggish with the flat tire. The SUV roared up behind her, then swerved up next to her and slammed into her car so hard she bounced off the road. She jostled over the tundra, her progress slowed exponentially. The SUV pursued, veering off the road. She saw the blinding flash of its headlights and then the SUV slammed into the driver's side of her 4Runner.

She struck her head on the driver's-side window and then felt her body toss up into the air, the seat belt tightening across her chest and lap. The SUV hit her again and she felt the whole car go up and over onto its side, rolling, tumbling violently across the rugged terrain. She grabbed the steering wheel, crying out as the white, blunt explosion of the airbags hit her in the face and chest. She held her breath as the 4Runner tumbled to a stop, upside down in the snow. The SUV's headlights still glared in through the window. She felt warm stickiness dripping off her forehead. She tasted the salty slick of blood. Holding her arms up, she pushed against the ceiling, all the blood rushing to her head.

Through the buzzing in her ears, she heard the SUV's door open. She fought against the airbag, punching it down, grappling with the seat belt. Her shaking fingers found the release and she unbuckled herself, slamming down onto the ceiling of the car. She scrambled for the passenger-side door, away from the SUV. The window there was shattered and she crawled through it, blood streaming down into her left eye. She wiped it away. She could hear him on the opposite side of the 4Runner. She grabbed her pack through the broken window. If she had to flee on foot, at least she'd have her phone, GPS unit, water, and a little food. She left the strange 3D-printed device in the 4Runner.

Twilight had now given way to night, and she pressed herself against the side of the 4Runner, trying to get her bearings. A cluster of spruce trees stood some hundred feet away. She didn't think she could make it there before he found her. Her head throbbed.

She could hear the man crunching around the side of the car, so she crawled on her hands and knees, trying to keep the 4Runner between them. Cold snow bit into her bare hands.

Headlights driving down the road drew her attention to the south. Another car was approaching. Hope swelled up within her. Maybe someone had called the cops after hearing the gunshot. But there were no lights and no siren. And whoever it was could be friends with her attacker.

She could hear him now, rounding the 4Runner. *Step. Drag. Step. Drag.* He had a limp. The leader of the snowmobilers.

He must have been following her, wondering if she had the coordinates. Her mind flew to the strange circuitry device she'd found in her backpack. Could it be a tracker? Her backpack had been on a chair in the motel room when the snowmobilers had broken in. It might have been a backup plan, track her movements. See how much she knew.

The fact that the receiver and flash drive had still been hidden at this location made her think they didn't know it was here. It *was* what they were after.

He rounded to the passenger side of the 4Runner. She could hear his breathing. She reached the rear bumper and kept going. He'd left his SUV running. If she could get to it, she could leap in and drive away.

The other car was almost on them now. The headlights cut through the gloom, illuminating all the moisture in the air. She saw now that it was a beat-up pickup truck.

"You folks need any help?" the driver called. His voice sounded familiar.

She rounded the rear bumper, coming again to the driver's side of the 4Runner, and instantly recognized the driver of the truck. He was Dave, the bartender from Moe's.

"This looks pretty bad," he said. "I can call a tow or an ambulance."

She bolted away from the 4Runner and sped for his truck. He had a gun rack in the back, a shotgun resting there.

She ducked down on the far side of his truck's engine block. The SUV driver came around the back of the ruined 4Runner. Now that Alex could clearly see his face in the SUV's headlights, she recognized him. With his long black hair, goatee, and scar across the bridge of his nose, he was definitely the leader of the snowmobilers.

She watched him neatly tuck his gun into the waistband of his jeans and wondered if the bartender had seen it.

"Oh hey, Jake, it's you," Dave said. "What are you doing way out here?"

"Just out for a drive. We're fine. We don't need help. Gal just took the road too fast. Tourists. You know how they can be. I just stopped to check on her. I'll call a tow for the lady. I just have to get something from her first."

He approached the truck, and Alex called out, "Don't trust him. He's got a gun! Let's get out of here!" She crouched low, moving toward the passenger-side door.

"What?" Dave's mouth fell open as he stared at the man. "Get in," he urged her, pulling the shotgun from its rack.

Jake advanced. "I said, I have to get something from her first."

"I'll take her back and call a tow," the bartender offered.

Jake pulled out his pistol.

Dave leveled the shotgun at him.

"I don't want to have to shoot you," Jake growled.

"That makes two of us."

"But I will."

"So will I."

Alex climbed into the passenger seat.

"We're just going to leave now," Dave said. He started to pull around in a circle.

"Stop!" shouted Jake. He fired, the bullet grazing Dave in the upper arm. The bartender cried out, then brought the shotgun up to bear. Jake dove to the side as the double-barreled weapon went off with a deafening boom.

Alex couldn't tell if Dave had hit him or not. The bartender finished the U-turn and came up alongside the SUV. He blew out two of the tires and then roared away.

They bounced down the road, Alex jostling violently as the truck's stiff shocks hit every bump and pothole. Her head pulsed with pain, and she wiped more blood out of her eye.

Dave winced, gripping his wound with his right arm. "Can you toss me that shirt behind you?"

Alex dug around in the extended cab and pulled out a T-shirt. "How bad is it?"

He clamped the T-shirt to the wound. "I've had worse."

"When?"

"Hunting with my drunk-ass cousins."

"We need to get you to a hospital."

"I won't argue with that."

She turned around in her seat, watching the headlights of the SUV fade into the distance. "Thank you for coming along when you did."

"My brother lives down this way. I was going out to see him when I saw your 4Runner go over. Actually, I just saw a pair of headlights going crazy, flying into the air and spinning. Looked like a bad wreck. I know there's no cell service out this way so I came to see if I could help."

"I'm so glad you did!"

He pulled the shirt away and looked at his arm. "I think it's just a flesh wound." He replaced the shirt and grimaced. "Stings like a motherfucker, though." His eyes met Alex's. "Why the hell was Jake after you?"

She shook her head. "I've been trying to figure that out for days."

"I always knew he was a little batshit crazy, but . . ."

They were only half a mile from the paved road when they came to a large car blocking the narrow road. Three men in suits stood around outside it, stomping their feet in the cold. But it didn't look like they were changing a tire or anything. As she and Dave drew closer, she saw the vehicle was an upscale Lincoln Town Car, the kind she saw wealthy businessmen chauffeured around in when she lived in Boston.

Dave pulled off the road behind the car. "Sit tight," he told her. "Looks like they broke down or something. Shouldn't have a car like that on this kind of road. I'm going to see if they need help."

As Dave approached, one of the men moved to the rear of the car and opened the back door. An older man with white hair got out. He exchanged words with Dave.

The bartender had left the headlights on, and as the older man turned to her, she recognized him. It was Paul White, the CEO of White Industries. He smiled at her and gave her a little wave, then began to mosey over to her side of the truck. She looked back at the three men, whom she now realized must be White's bodyguards. They were humongous, their suits fairly bursting at the seams. Who needed three bodyguards? What was this guy expecting, a hostile takeover of his corporation that involved a street fight in Churchill, Manitoba? They looked like a matching set: all blond and blue-eyed, all tan, all built like heavy machinery designed to crush things. She could see the bulge of gun holsters beneath their jackets.

She didn't like this. It was the middle of nowhere. And wasn't he supposed to be in L.A.?

"It's Dr. Carter, isn't it?" he asked when he reached her window.

She rolled it down. "That's right."

He reached a hand through. "Paul White." When she shook it, he had the kind of handshake that bothered her, when men just gripped her fingers instead of her hand, giving her a completely different kind of handshake than they'd give a man. It always said to her, *You're a woman, and I see you as someone different, someone I can condescend to.*

"Just wanted to extend my sincerest apologies about what happened with my pilot."

"Aren't you supposed to be in L.A.?" she asked.

"I was. Just flew out."

"And just happened to be here on this dirt road outside of town?"

He gave a small chuckle. "Well, now, I can see how that might seem a bit odd. We were just coming from the airport, when this little app on my phone sent out an aurora alert. I do love the auroras." He looked around. "Seemed like a dark place to pull off and watch for them. How are you? And your pilot friend? What was his name?"

Alex didn't answer.

White peered around in the cab. "He not with you tonight?"

Alex glanced at Dave talking to the bodyguards. He was starting back toward his truck. "If you're sure you don't need help," she heard him say, "we'll just drive around you, be on our way." The men just stared back at him, their mouths colorless slits.

A bad feeling crept over her like a chill.

And what of the gunman, Jake? Alex looked back the way they'd come. She didn't see headlights from the SUV coming out that way. Jake was likely still back there with two flat tires.

"Dave says y'all ran into trouble back there. You know what that fellow wanted?" White asked. "The one in the SUV?"

Now two of the bodyguards had come up behind White. The bigger one stood with his arms crossed, the other with his beefy arms at his sides. She could see his muscles pressing against the fabric of his jacket. The third remained next to Dave, watching the bartender with narrowed eyes, one hand looking ready to go for his holster.

"No idea," Alex said.

"Surely you must have some idea. Maybe he was looking for something?"

Alex glanced surreptitiously at the truck's ignition, hoping Dave had left the keys. He hadn't. Her backpack rested on the bench seat to her left.

"Look in her backpack," White said to the bodyguards, all civility suddenly gone. The biggest bodyguard uncoiled his arms and began to reach through the window. Alex grabbed her backpack and slid across the bench seat, opening the driver's-side door.

"Don't let her get out!" shouted White.

The two bodyguards rounded the side of the pickup just as Alex burst through the door.

THIRTY-FOUR

She fled the pool of light from the cars, plunging into utter darkness. She raced toward a stand of spruces. Behind her the bodyguards cursed.

"It's too damn dark!"

"Go back and get a flashlight!"

"Hey, stop!" she heard Dave yell. "What the hell do you think you're doing? What do you want with her?"

Entering the trees, she weaved between the branches, thrusting her arms out in front of her. She zigged and zagged, snow falling in clumps off the branches. She shook a few boughs, masking her tracks with cascading snow. Then she burst out of the stand on the other side and ran for a cluster of large rocks and willows. Here the wind had blown much of the snow off the bare rocks, and she sprinted across naked stone, leaving no trace. Pain shuddered through her leg where the poacher had grazed her, and her head pounded from smashing it against the car window.

She could see the two cars back on the road, their headlights silhouetting the men. She saw Dave struggling with one of the bodyguards, the one who'd gone back for the flashlight.

Up ahead, Alex could make out another dark patch of trees. She sprinted for it, reaching its shelter in a few seconds. Here again she weaved through the branches, shaking snow off the boughs to mask her tracks. This was a larger cluster and she raced through as fast as she could, hands stuck out before her. Branches scraped her hands and arms. One branch caught her hood and jerked her back. She freed her parka and pressed on. A branch scraped her scalp as she bent low under a dense cluster of limbs.

Then she burst from the stand of spruce and sprinted across another bare stretch of rock, the dark void of Hudson Bay beyond. The rock was icy and her feet slipped out from under her. She crashed down on her back, her tailbone slamming painfully onto a jagged piece of stone.

She lay stunned for a second, then got her wind back and scrambled to her feet. She glanced back but didn't see or hear anyone pursuing her. To her left, she saw another stand of spruce trees.

If she could start making her way back toward town, she could get help. She ran in that direction, keeping low. She pulled out her phone, only to discover she had no cell reception out here.

She could still see the headlights from the two cars. One of them was moving now, driving northwest down the dirt road, right in her direction. There was a chance she could cut them off, cross the road before they got there.

She decided to risk it. She sped to another cluster of trees, then sprinted across an open stretch. Now she moved perpendicular to the dirt track. But when she crossed where she thought the road was, she found no track there. She took shelter in the next stand of spruce, glancing back toward the approaching car. Then it abruptly stopped, and she saw the silhouetted shape of a gate across the road. The track ended there.

Despite the freezing cold, she had started to sweat inside her polypropylene shirt. All those layers were trapping in her body heat as she ran.

Now she watched as the Lincoln Town Car sped around the gate, driving onto the tundra, bouncing across the snowy ground straight toward her. Soon Alex would be within reach of its headlights. The terrain opened up to the east, toward town. She'd have to sprint across completely open terrain and would be spotted easily.

So she ran back the way she'd come. She had to choose a different direction. There was civilization to the south, she knew—the boatyard. She reached a section of dense willows, similar to the ones the polar bear had napped in. She hunkered down among the branches, trying to catch her breath.

She saw the lights from Dave's truck hurrying back toward town. Maybe he would get the cops.

The Town Car stopped, a spotlight shining over the terrain. She lay down flat. Then slowly the car turned, driving back toward town, the bright light still searching. Whoever drove it had predicted she'd do exactly what she'd originally wanted to do—head toward the town center. So she remained still. When it was some distance away, she listened for any signs of the bodyguards. Had they given up their foot chase?

At a crouch she shifted to another grouping of willows, then another and another, moving along bare rock when she was able. The snow cascaded down, and she hoped it was covering her tracks.

Up ahead something moved in the darkness, a living mound of snow, prowling and sniffing around the willows. She froze, bending down behind a clump of willows. The shape shuffled, and she could hear its massive paws digging in the snow and dirt. Polar bear. With her eyes now adjusted to the dim light, she could see that it was gaunt, starving. It looked like the same polar bear she'd seen rooting around where the body had been.

With a slight shudder Alex realized she had to be very near that spot. The polar bear had likely returned to see if it could devour more of the corpse.

But the police had removed the body, and now the polar bear sniffed where it had lain, smelling the traces of flesh. It rooted around, then moved away from her, nose to the ground, following a scent. With relief she realized she was downwind of the bear. She kept very still. The bear moved steadily northward, digging a little as it went, then putting its nose back to the ground and continuing in the same direction.

Then it stopped, pawing at the ground with renewed vigor. It pulled something up from the willows, something about the size of its head. Alex couldn't make out what it was. It tore and pawed at the object, then discarded it, continuing its trek north.

When the bear had moved off into the distance, Alex stirred from her spot. She crept forward, following the places in the snow where the bear had dug down to earth. At last she came upon the object. She knelt beside it, taking out her headlamp to see what it was.

The beam fell on netting and corroded objects. It was a dive bag, she realized, full of artifacts. A patch with a name was sewn into it: *Tildesen*. It belonged to Sasha's partner. She saw that the bear had torn large holes in the bag, spilling out the objects. She picked one up, turning it over in her hand. It was heavy and severely corroded, but it looked like some sort of ax-head. With it was a long, thin object that could be a badly damaged sword tip. Smaller objects lay scattered about, some circular in shape.

She picked up each piece, turning it over in her hands, wondering if the objects had to do with the man's death. She replaced all the pieces and brought the bag with her.

She came upon a dense cluster of spruce around a small rise of rocks. If she sheltered on the far side, she would be hidden in tightly packed cover. And if she heard someone approach, she could circle the rocks, stay out of sight.

She slid in next to the stones, pressing her back against them, and slumped down in the snow. She was grateful for her waterproof Marmot pants and coat. She could sit in the snow without getting wet. She let herself catch her breath and tried to figure out her next move.

The trees offered a little break from the wind, and she was grateful. She wanted to give those men some time to give up their search for her. They'd expect her to head toward town, not hang out by the water.

She wondered how it was all related: the snowmobilers who'd gone through her things but left the samples alone; the thief in the lab who'd stolen the samples; Sasha's partner, his murdered body left in the willows; the helicopter pilot and the CEO. Then there was the cipher and the flash drive. The receiver and whatever was out in the water.

She hugged her knees to her chest, rocking back and forth, trying to stay warm. But being still meant that cold started seeping in. Her teeth began to chatter. She thought of the nights out on the ice with Casey. Wondered where he was now.

Her head stung. She tenderly felt the wound there. It was sticky with blood that had trickled down one side of her face.

She pulled out the receiver, studying its blinking light out in the bay. She had no doubt that whatever waited there was what all of this trouble had been about. But she had no idea why.

She had to figure out her next move. She could go back to town, but they might be waiting for her. With no signal, she had no way to call the police. But she wasn't far from the boatyard, and she knew there was a phone there. She could call the RCMP, get them to send out a cruiser to pick her up. She still worried about White's possible connection with Moran, but there was no doubt White had crossed the line now. He couldn't claim he had nothing to do with it, like he had with the helicopter pilot. Maybe PC Bighetty could help.

She had to get moving anyway. If she sat here like this, she could freeze. Already her body felt heavy and tired from the cold, and she felt the urge to doze off.

She rose, stretching her legs. Then she moved through the spruce trees to the edge of the cluster. She didn't see any lights. The only sound she heard was the wind, sighing through the branches.

A dim glow on the horizon to the southeast was likely the boatyard, she reasoned. Keeping a watchful eye for the gaunt polar bear, she headed in that direction.

THIRTY-FIVE

Alex reached the boatyard, moving cautiously. If she saw any sign of White or his men, she'd withdraw into the darkness. A couple dusk-to-dawn lights burned over the tallest building. A few boats bobbed up and down on the current, but most of the deep-sea berths were empty. It wasn't exactly shipping weather out there with most of Hudson Bay still frozen over.

She crept cautiously to the building where she'd used the phone before, but found the door locked and the lights off.

She scanned the few boats in the slips, wondering if anyone was still awake, or even on their boats at all. Lights glowed in the cabin windows of one boat, a thirty-six-foot Chris-Craft trawler. She read the ship's name: *Uruk*. Keeping out of the light pools from the dusk-to-dawn lights, she moved to the boat. She watched a lone woman checking over the deck. Alex recognized her and couldn't believe her luck. It was Sasha Talbot.

Alex hurried over to the boat. "Sasha!"

The woman startled, then saw Alex down below on the pier. "Alex? What are you doing out here?"

"I'm in trouble. You don't happen to have a radio or sat phone, do you? I need to call the Mounties."

"Come aboard."

"Thank you!"

As Alex stepped onto the boat, Sasha's gaze went down to the dive bag Alex held in her left hand. The woman bent over to get a better look. "It's Rex's. I can't believe it. I'd just come aboard to see if I could find a clue as to what happened to him out there. Where did you find it?"

Alex stared down at the bag. "I found it to the north of here." She gestured toward the way she'd come. "Near where I found his body."

Alex handed it over. Sasha turned the name tag toward the light and ran her hand over the label. She reached inside the bag and examined some of the artifacts. "He was excited that he'd found something." She held the bag tightly, then noticed Alex's head wound. "That looks bad. What happened?"

Alex touched it with tentative fingers. "I think it's stopped bleeding now. So much has happened that I haven't told you yet. Our helicopter was sabotaged. We were stranded out on the ice. And gunmen showed up. My assistant was killed."

Sasha gripped Alex's arm with concern. "Oh, Alex . . ."

"My pilot and I managed to escape. But just now, one of those same gunmen ran me off the road." She thought of the Lincoln Town Car blocking the road. "Do you know Paul White?"

"The oil exec?" Sasha shook her head. "Only by reputation."

"I think he has something to do with all this. He just had his bodyguards chase me out there."

Sasha grimaced. "Do you think this has something to do with Rex's murder?"

"It's got to all be connected."

"Let me get my sat phone." Sasha disappeared below, then emerged with a yellow satellite phone and handed it to Alex. Alex dialed 911 and was put through to Detective Sergeant Moran.

"Dr. Carter?" the sergeant asked. "Are you all right?"

"No. I've been attacked."

"We know all about it."

"You do?"

"Yes. Paul White came in here and explained everything."

Alex was floored. "He did?"

"Yes. Told us how that drunk driver ran you off the road and how shaken up you were."

"That guy was no drunk—" Alex started, but he interrupted her.

"Mr. White explained how he tried to help you, but you were so shaken you ran off. He even sent his bodyguards after you to make sure you wouldn't get lost and succumb to exposure."

"That's not what happened, Sergeant."

"You don't have to worry, Dr. Carter. You can come in. Mr. White is not going to press charges."

Alex almost shouted. "Press charges! For what?"

"The assault."

"Excuse me?"

"He said you attacked his men, but you were confused from the nasty bump on your head."

"This is ridiculous. I did not assault anyone. *I* was assaulted."

"We've been really worried with you out in the cold with that head injury. Let me know where you are, and I'll come pick you up."

Alex felt a flush of fear go through her. This was not right. Not at all. She'd already gotten the impression that White wielded a lot of power locally. He played the good ole boy in public, with his smiling face and folksy charm, but underneath he was a dangerous, conniving man.

"Listen, Sergeant. I was purposefully run off the road by the same man whose photo I gave you last night. It was no drunk driver. And Paul White ordered his men to chase me down."

"We understand how it could seem that way when you'd had such a shock. But he swears he was only trying to help you."

Moran sounded so calm and reassured that she didn't think there was any chance he'd believe her, short of a video showing White siccing his henchmen on her.

White-hot anger shot through Alex like lightning. White had

twisted the whole thing around. Part of her wanted to ask to speak to PC Bighetty, but she wondered if he'd be able to go over his boss's head.

"Tell us where you are, and we'll come get you. Besides, there are some additional questions we need to ask you."

"What additional questions?"

"Another victim has surfaced, shot with the same gun. That's three victims now, including Neil Trevors."

"Who was the other victim?"

"A Steve Gunderson. Are you familiar with him?"

"Did he have a tattoo of a blackjack hand on his arm?"

"He did."

"If he's the guy I'm thinking of, I sat next to him once at a bar. Those same people who attacked us out on the ice were after him." Alex brought a hand to her aching head. She decided not to mention the cipher.

"We'd like you to come in for questioning. PC Bighetty keeps insisting this is all one big misunderstanding. I'm sure we can get it straightened out if you come in. I assure you White doesn't want to press charges."

Cold crept up onto Alex. She didn't answer him. She just hung up.

"What happened?" Sasha asked.

"The same person seems to have killed my grad student and your friend Rex. And now a third man—that guy who wanted to rent your boat. I know Paul White is wrapped up in this, but I'm not sure how. He holds a lot of sway. I'm not sure how much weight they're going to give my side of the story." She handed back Sasha's phone. "How were they when they informed you of Rex's death?"

"Kind. But they didn't have a lot of information. Or at least they couldn't share it with me."

"I can't go back to town. I have a terrible feeling."

"What do you want to do?"

Alex wanted to get to the truth behind all of this. None of it made sense. She thought of the cipher and the receiver. "The guy who wanted to rent your boat approached me at Moe's one night, too. He slipped a scrap of paper into my jacket pocket. It was a cipher."

Sasha raised her brow in surprise. "What?"

"I managed to figure it out. It was coordinates. I followed them out here to a location where I found a flash drive and this." She dug into her backpack and pulled out the receiver. "Do you know what this is?"

Sasha took the receiver from Alex, turning it over in her hands. "Looks like it's from a beacon. I've seen divers use these. Treasure hunters. When they make an interesting find, they sometimes deploy these. They operate sort of like a private EPIRB."

"An EPIRB?"

"An emergency position indicating radio beacon."

"How do those work?"

"In the case of an EPIRB, a beacon is set off, usually when a ship is in distress. The signal goes to a satellite, and from the satellite to a receiving facility, and then rescuers are dispatched. But these are a little different. They're meant for personal use, not rescues. The beacon out in the water still transmits to a satellite, but only the person with the receiver can read it. Each beacon has its own unique code that is transmitted to the receiver. No rescue crews are involved. It's just a nonemergency locator device."

"So this could be a ship?"

"It could be just about anything out in the water. A ship, an interesting dive site. A person in the water."

"Someone has been sabotaging my polar bear study. I think it's tied in to Paul White, but I don't know why they were after the cipher. Why they wanted this receiver so much. I think your friend was killed over this."

"He had been logging wrecks that day. Maybe he stumbled across whatever is out there," Sasha suggested.

"Or maybe they thought he *might* stumble across it and they killed him before he could."

Sasha bit her lip. "Question is, what is it, and why do they want it so bad?"

"And what does it have to do with your friend, if anything?"

"If they *did* kill Rex for this, I want to know what it is." Sasha gripped the dive bag, her fingers laced through the mesh. "You care to go for a boat ride?"

"You'll take me out there?"

"Hell, yes, I will. Especially if it can nail these guys for Rex."

"I wonder if all this trouble is because they're trying to find the location of what's out there, or if they already know and are trying to keep others from finding it."

"There's one way to find out," Sasha said, moving to untie the boat. "Let's go."

THIRTY-SIX

Once they were under way on the *Uruk*, Alex spotted Sasha's laptop in the cabin. She fished the flash drive out of her backpack. "Can I use your computer?"

Sasha stood at the helm, checking their bearing against the receiver. "Sure. Go ahead."

Alex sat down at a table and opened the laptop. "I found this with the receiver, and I want to know what's on it." Alex inserted the flash drive and clicked on its contents. It held folders, but all of them were encrypted. "Damn. It's all protected. I'd need a password to access them."

"Can you hack into it?" Sasha asked.

"I wouldn't know where to begin." Alex frowned, examining the folders. At the bottom of the contents, she found a text file. "Wait . . ." Alex leaned in closer to the laptop's screen and opened the file. The text scrolled on and on, jumbled words and numbers. Some formed coherent messages. "I think there's a keylogger file on here."

"What's that?"

"Basically, a form of spyware. Someone wanted to record every key pressed on a computer. They could have been hoping to record correspondence someone typed to people and later deleted. Or maybe they wanted passwords for email accounts and encrypted files."

Alex scanned through the document, looking for words or number series that recurred out of context. These could be passwords. She found a few instances of repeated words and tried those as a password to decrypt the files. Her fourth attempt revealed the files in the encrypted folders.

She scrolled through the first folder. It seemed to be a collection of documents: invoices, spreadsheets, correspondence, all from Paul White's company. She clicked on one of the spreadsheets and found a list of income and expenses. The sums were huge, in the hundreds of thousands. Some were purchases, including a fleet of luxury yachts, all with White's name in them: *White Knight, Great White, White Tiger.*

Other documents seemed to be payouts, but the recipients were designated only with initials. She closed the spreadsheet and highlighted the file, then examined its properties. The creator was Paul White. She clicked on several more. All of them had been created by Paul White.

She opened one of the documents in the invoices folder. It was a receipt for equipment received, but the prices didn't add up. One was a forklift for $432,000, which seemed exorbitantly expensive. Another was a forty-foot shipping container for $323,500. One of her college friends had bought one for a tiny house, and Alex was sure he hadn't paid more than $6,000 for it. Still another payment was for a twenty-foot shipping container totaling $156,000. All of them were way too expensive. She examined the names of the companies: ADK Storage. Bayside Equipment Rentals. PD & Co. Sales. The addresses were in Churchill, Port Nelson, and Gillam, Manitoba.

"Does your computer have access to the web?"

The woman nodded. "I've got maritime satellite internet."

Alex opened a browser and searched for Bayside Equipment Rentals in Port Nelson. There was no such company. She tried PD & Co. Sales. Again, no such organization. She looked at the name on the invoice of Bayside Equipment Rentals. Gregor Renchant. G.R. She flashed back to the spreadsheet and filtered it by recipient.

The initials G.R. were recorded as receiving several generous pay-ments, ranging from $50,000 up to $72,000.

She checked the other invoices and matched initials to the spreadsheets. She found match after match.

So Paul White had been making payments to bogus companies. Payoffs?

She opened another folder, taking a few swallows from her water bottle.

"Find anything interesting?" Sasha asked her.

"I think I did."

This folder seemed to include memos and letters. The first was a note from Paul White to himself: *$272K to GR for permit papers.*

Another read: *$126K to NR for environmental impact report.*

Still another read: *$372K to PF for hydrogen sulfide level report.*

The list read on and on, all payouts for documents. In another decrypted folder, she found the documents he referenced, reports giving the all-clear for a number of projects spanning oil and gas extraction to mining. All of the reports gave White's companies glowing reviews, with pollution levels well under the permissible levels. Environmental impact studies for proposed sites of oil and gas extraction reported zero to minimal risk to the environment. If one went by these reports alone, one would think White's compa-nies were operating within the strictest environmental parameters. A report for a formerly polluted coal ash site in West Virginia stated that the coal ash ponds had been completely cleaned up and all tox-ins removed.

Alex opened another decrypted folder. This included reports for the same sites she'd just read about. Only the scientists on these reports didn't have the same initials as the ones in the first file. She compared a few of the reports, finding them for the same sites in the same range of dates. The coal ash site that had been reported as being completely cleaned up had been reviewed by a scientist with the EPA. It had been found to still contain deadly chemicals such as mercury, cadmium, and arsenic. The site had not been cleaned up whatsoever.

Another report matched the location and date of the environmental impact study for one of White's fracking locations. The operation proved of considerable risk to humans and wildlife, including exposure to benzene, hydrogen sulfide, and toluene. Proper safety precautions had not been taken to limit the seeping of chemicals from drill sites.

Another report from an offshore oil well near New Orleans determined that it had not been properly maintained and that spills had been disastrous for wildlife and plant life all along the coast. The inspector had recommended that further extraction not be allowed to take place under any circumstances until repairs and updates were made.

Even more projects, now in the development stage, had been given the green light, despite White's disastrous history. She found approval documents for White's various polluting projects to continue, based on falsified reports that he had paid for. She also found evidence of bribes to city officials, from the Canadian Arctic and Alaska to the Eastern Seaboard of the United States and the Gulf of Mexico. His corruption was sweeping and deep.

She opened another folder, finding plans for offshore and near-shore oil drilling platforms scattered all across the Arctic. Accompanying them were reports of diminishing sea ice, with projections of when the Arctic would be completely ice-free. White was planning to build a network of offshore oil platforms in areas that had been historically impossible due to sea ice. But now, as the earth warmed, arctic areas were opening up for oil exploration and shipping. She clicked through the rest of the contents of that folder, finding evidence of bribes to push through permits. He was already planning several platforms off the coast of Alaska and Canada, including some in Western Hudson Bay.

Right now, his permits were being held up due to environmental review because they were in sensitive polar bear habitat. Before plans for the platforms could move forward, more data needed to be collected on the status of the Western Hudson Bay polar bear population, which was one of the populations known to be in decline.

Alex leaned back in her seat. She knew that in 2008, the polar bear had been listed under the Endangered Species Act in the U.S. But ironically, though climate change was the biggest threat to their survival, the fossil fuel industry was exempted from any responsibility, and was not required to change its practices to curb emissions. Though you couldn't hunt polar bears in some parts of Canada, they had no protection against climate change and the fossil fuel industry. If the polar bears' listing was strengthened and this time the industry *was* held accountable, it would have profound effects on White's empire. CO_2 emissions would have to be cut. Not only would his empire be held back from further expansion, but the energy concerns he already held, from his coal-fired plants to his fracking and oil extraction operations, would be impacted as well.

White knew that gathered data on polar bears wouldn't do anything but hurt his cause. He wanted to push his projects through before more studies could be submitted.

Alex knew from experience that he could well be successful.

She continued to read through the records on the flash drive. White had bribed officials to block Sonia's repeated requests to undertake polar bear research there. He'd also blocked other researchers' proposals to study not just polar bears, but sea ice extent and narwhal and beluga population studies.

Alex suspected that if the Canadian Minister of Environment and Climate Change hadn't taken a personal interest in polar bears, Sonia's permits still wouldn't have gone through this season.

White must be fuming that Alex was out here. And he'd done so much to obstruct her efforts at every turn. She didn't doubt he was behind the sabotage of the helicopter. But once again she wondered why the snowmobilers hadn't taken the samples. Was it possible they weren't connected? That the snowmobilers were only after the cipher?

Alex leaned back, exhaling in disbelief at the contents of the flash drive. Whatever waited for her and Sasha at the coordinates could be even more evidence of Paul White's corruption. And it was something she knew he would kill to hide.

She logged on to her iCloud account and uploaded the entire contents of the flash drive, then emailed them to Zoe and her dad.

Sasha slowed the motor. "There's a pretty intense storm coming. Visibility's going to be shot. I think we need to drop anchor for a while. Let it pass. Besides, I don't want to come upon whatever this is in the dark. We don't know what we're looking for. I say we catch a few hours of sleep and check the weather again at first light."

Alex agreed. Her eyes burned with exhaustion. As much as she wanted to find out what was out there, she knew it was smarter to wait.

Sasha dropped anchor. Even in the dark, Alex could see the glowing white sheet of ice a few hundred yards to the northeast of where they bobbed on the water. Most of the bay was still covered in ice as expected, but sections of open water now ran along the coast. Ice had been shrinking year after year.

Sasha offered her the second bunk in the cabin and they retired. Now Alex lay down in the darkness, the swell of the waves gently rocking the boat. She felt her head, finding a large knot now where she'd hit the window. She closed her burning eyes and tried to still her mind.

But it was a tangle of thoughts. Paul White, Neil's murder, Casey's strange confession. She lay awake, listening to the even breathing of Sasha, worried she'd never be able to get to sleep. But finally, lulled by the motion of the boat, she dropped off and drifted into a fitful slumber.

THIRTY-SEVEN

Alex awoke to a faint glow spilling in through the cabin. Cracks of light glowed around the edges of the curtain. She looked at her watch: 10:30 A.M. She'd slept longer and deeper than she'd expected.

Stretching, she glanced over at the other bunk, finding it empty. From the tranquil rocking of the boat, she suspected they were still anchored. She crawled down from the berth and climbed up the stairs to the deck. Her head swam with the movement. She gingerly felt where she'd slammed into the 4Runner's window, finding the lump there even bigger now.

A gray day had dawned, the world misty and mysterious beyond the boat. The fog was so thick that it curled around the bow and stern of the *Uruk,* lending a soft aura of mystery to the scene.

Sasha stood at the helm and smiled over her shoulder as Alex appeared at the top of the stairs. "Needless to say, we're still in the same spot," she said to Alex. "I made some coffee."

Alex moved to the tiny kitchen and poured a cup. It was so strong that when she added cream, the coffee barely changed color. She took a sip and sat down at the table. The warm liquid felt comforting going down her throat, even if it was bitter.

Beyond the window, the gray waters of the bay lapped against the side of the boat. Flurries cascaded down, dusting the boat's deck and rails.

"We're stuck here for a while." Sasha joined her at the table and they fell into conversation. With a deep sadness, Sasha regaled her with tales of dives she and Rex had done together.

"I can't believe he's gone. We've been dive partners for over thirty years. Discovered wrecks in the Mediterranean, the Indian Ocean. The Pacific. We even have a few great pieces in the British Museum, including an intact Greek statue of Artemis."

"What were you searching for out here?"

Sasha smiled ruefully. "Believe it or not, Viking longships."

Alex was taken aback. "What?"

"Rex believed they sailed into Hudson Bay. It's not that crazy when you think about it. From Greenland to Newfoundland was only a few days' sail for them. Vikings had explored all over Europe and the Atlantic, as far south as Morocco. It actually makes more sense that they explored more of North America than we think. It's not like their adventurous spirit would have suddenly stopped when they reached Newfoundland. Especially when you consider the latest scientific thinking. They now believe that the Newfoundland site at L'Anse aux Meadows was occupied for as long as a century."

Sasha wiped away another tear. "Anyway, I think Rex was right. I think they probably did come down this way. Check this out." She moved to one of the drawers. She slid it open, revealing rolled-up charts, a compass, and a wide, rusted piece of metal. She pulled it out. It was a badly corroded ax-head. "Rex bought this off a fisherman. It's fourteenth century. Guess where he found it?"

"Greenland?"

"Minnesota."

"What?"

"Yep. Rex was home visiting family and he met a fisherman who said he found it on a riverbank there. It really captured Rex's imagination that the Vikings might have made it that far west. Maybe the ax-head had been placed there in recent times. Maybe it was a hoax. But maybe not. Rex became obsessed after that. Thought if he could prove it, he'd go down in history along with the Ingstads,

who discovered L'Anse aux Meadows. So we started looking here."
She smiled, a bittersweet expression, and placed the ax gently back
into the drawer. Then she turned to Alex. "Just before I lost contact
with him, he'd radioed to me onshore. He'd found a wreck, one that
matched the dimensions of a Viking longship. He was too excited
to wait for me to come out. He dove alone. It was the last I heard
from him."

"I'm so sorry."

They lapsed into silence, finishing the last of the coffee.

Finally the fog began to lift and the snow stopped. A wind
picked up, carrying away the rest of the mist. The sun peeked out
above a bank of clouds, adding a golden light to the world around
them. Alex could see now that they were anchored not too far offshore, floating in a narrow strip of water between wild, untamed
land and a world of ice.

"I think we can get going." She pulled up the anchor and fired
up the motor. They headed south now, moving parallel to the ice.

Alex looked at the boat's GPS. "To the south of here is Wapusk
National Park. That's where the female polar bears go to have cubs in
peat dens. They're the only polar bears in the world to den on land."

"Really?"

"Yes. They dig into the earth. Even males use the dens during
the summer, when the biting insects get so bad they need some
relief. The bears just keep digging them, making them deeper and
deeper. Some dens go back a considerable distance and are hundreds of years old."

"Wow!"

"I'd love to be here in the summer to see that."

"Do you think you'll stay?"

"I think so."

They motored on, lapsing into silence. Alex watched the sonar
display showing their depth and objects on the bay's floor. "Is this
how you search for wrecks?"

"Yes. It's one of the ways. Usually we search through historic records and try to narrow down a location." She laughed. "But Rex had this bee in his bonnet about Vikings in North America, and there aren't a lot of historical records of that. We've been here since last summer. So we took to trolling around, eyes glued to the sonar. We were saving up for an ROV—a submersible remotely operated vehicle we could program to go down and check out wrecks in deeper water." Sasha wiped quickly at her eyes and looked away out the window. Her chin quivered.

"Are you okay?"

She sniffed. "I just want to get these bastards." She returned her gaze to the helm and checked the receiver. "We're almost there."

Alex peered over her shoulder, seeing how close they'd drawn to the blinking light. Shielding her eyes against the bright sky, she searched the horizon. She'd expected to see a ship or some kind of floating cargo, but only open water met her gaze, and the white expanse of ice to their left.

Sasha slowed the boat, moving along at a slow clip as they closed the distance. According to the receiver, they were almost on top of it. Alex scanned the water, finding no vessel or wreckage or anything but water.

Then she spotted it, something small tossing on the waves. She pointed it out. "There!"

Sasha cut the motor and they glided the last few feet. Bobbing on the surface was the beacon. It was a small device, two feet or so in diameter, with a blinking light. Alex reached over the railing and managed to grab it. But when she pulled, she found that it was attached to a long thin cable that descended into the depths.

Sasha joined her at the railing, examining the beacon.

"It's attached to something below. Cargo?" Alex suggested.

Sasha cocked an eyebrow. "Could be. Smugglers sometimes dump contraband at sea, marking it with a beacon like this for later recovery."

Alex tugged on the cable, hoping that whatever it was could be hefted up. The cable wouldn't budge. "It's heavy. How deep are we here?"

Sasha moved to her depth gauge. "Seventy-two feet. Let me check the sonar." Alex joined Sasha beneath the sonar monitor. The red and yellow display showed a shelf that fell off sharply into deeper water. A boatlike shape lay near the edge, close to the drop-off.

Sasha studied the display. "It's a vessel of some kind. Looks about forty feet long." A slender shape suddenly appeared on the display, moving under the boat. Sasha pointed it out. "Seal." Another shape swam by. "A couple of them." A bigger mass moved through the display. "School of fish. The seals are hunting." The three shapes moved off the screen and didn't come back.

Alex studied the vessel's shape as it rested on the shelf. "Any idea what it is?"

Sasha shook her head. "Rex and I mapped the location of about six wrecks. But this wasn't one of them. It's too bad we never got that ROV." She bit her lip and went quiet.

Alex placed a comforting hand on her back. She looked up at the sonar display. "Do you think maybe this is the wreck that he found that last day?"

Sasha shook her head. "The coordinates are different. And this is too small to be a Viking longship. This is something else."

Alex squinted at the sonar display. If the vessel down below was valuable, someone might kill to keep the discovery to themselves. But White was already wealthy beyond anything someone could spend in a lifetime. She thought back to the photo on the magazine cover, showing all of the artifacts on the shelf behind him. He was a collector of antiquities. And Rex's dive bag had indeed contained corroded artifacts that, when cleaned, could well be Viking in origin. Whether they'd been planted there recently or were actually part of an ancient Viking expedition would remain to be proven.

"We'll have to dive," Alex said.

Sasha pursed her lips and regarded Alex dubiously.

"What's wrong?"

"You know how I mentioned that bout with the bends?"

"Yes."

Sasha peered out at the water. "It was really bad. I . . . I don't think I can go out there again. It was the latest in a long line of mishaps."

"What do you mean?"

She sighed, leaning a hip against the helm. "I got hung up on a wreck a couple years ago. I actually drowned. Rex got me to the surface, managed to resuscitate me. And this last time? Had the bends something terrible. I had to spend hours in a decompression chamber. And I'm claustrophobic. I panicked in there." She shook her head, dispelling the memory. "I lost my nerve after that. Haven't been down since."

Alex had dived a few times, short dives off Kauai when she was on vacation during graduate school, and several times off the coast of Svalbard. Nothing extensive. But these were unusual circumstances. "Do you have scuba equipment on board?"

"Yes. I've still got all my gear. Do you dive?"

"I've done cold-water dives a few times." She remembered the incredibly thick, bulky dry suit she had to wear in Svalbard. Nothing like the lightweight wet suits she'd donned in Hawaii.

"We're about the same size and weight. I think my dry suit and weights should be pretty good for you." Sasha stared down into the depths. "I'll run things from up here. I guess if you get into trouble, I could go down there. I've got some spare gear." She met Alex's eyes. "But don't get into trouble. You hear?"

"Aye, aye, Captain." She stared over the edge of the boat. "Let's do it. If White shows up or any of his goons, I'd feel better with someone topside anyway." The thought of being down in the cold and dark when those men showed up sent a zing of fear skittering down her back.

Suddenly *she* felt claustrophobic.

"Don't stay down for too long," Sasha warned her. "My dry suit is pretty good for water this cold, but don't take any chances."

They went to work suiting Alex up. Sasha outfitted her with a dry suit, a tank, fins, a mask, a dive knife and bag, a strong flashlight with a pistol grip and wrist strap, and a dive computer.

Twenty minutes later, Alex sat on the edge of the boat, ready to go into the water. She took one last opportunity to scan the horizon for any sign of White or his men. No other boats were out. The white expanse of ice in the distance was unmarred by moving vehicles. All she could hear was the wind and the lapping of waves against the hull of the boat.

Alex swung her legs over the side of the boat and gently lowered herself into the frigid water.

THIRTY-EIGHT

Alex felt cold water press in around her as she descended into the bay, the diving light's beam piercing the darkness below. As she kicked, her leg pulsed with pain where the poacher had shot her.

Checking her depth gauge, she swam downward, following the thin cable that was attached to the beacon above. A mottled ringed seal dashed by her, curious. She paused in the water, watching it trek by, stopping to stare at her. Then she continued on her way.

Soon the floor of the bay came into view. She spotted something shining in the silt at the bottom and swam for it. She was taken aback to see that it was a gleaming mask. It looked Incan in design. Apparently made of gold, no corrosion covered it, and she couldn't tell how long it had been down there. Another shiny object caught her eye, and she swam over to it. A sack of Spanish doubloons flashed in the sediment, spilling out onto the seafloor. She reached for them, sifting through the coins. There were at least twenty of them. Then she came upon a metal box that had opened from wave action. Even more Spanish doubloons were inside. But the box looked steel and modern.

A huge dark shape loomed nearby, and she swam toward it, following a trail of treasure. She spotted a number of bags and opened them, finding cut diamonds, emeralds, sapphires. Other gold artifacts lay haphazardly about, some Egyptian, others Mesopotamian with inlaid lapis lazuli.

The looming shape took form in the gloom—a yacht, and one that looked brand-new. An explosion had torn through its portside, leaving a gaping hole. Treasure spilled out through the hole: gold statues of Egyptian and Mayan design, intricate jade carvings. She swam to the boat, sifting through the treasure as she went. She swam around to the starboard side, finding it undamaged. Here the yacht balanced precariously on the edge of the steep drop-off. Alex felt a little disconcerted staring down into those dark depths.

As much as she logically knew no sinister creature prowled the depths of Hudson Bay, she'd always had a bit of an irrational fear of deep, murky water. When she'd dived off the coast of Kauai, it hadn't been sharks she was afraid of but undiscovered sea monsters. She'd swum over those reefs, occasionally coming upon dark cracks that made her realize just how deep the water was that she was swimming over. Cracks in the reef where tentacles could snake out and grab her.

She brushed those thoughts away, knowing it wasn't helping her frame of mind as she hovered over the blackness. As she came around the rear of the boat, she confirmed a suspicion she'd had since they first saw the shape on the sonar screen. It was one of Paul White's yachts: *White Knight*.

So someone had loaded all of this treasure onto the yacht, and then what, had an accident? Or maybe scuttled the boat? Why? Either way, they'd recorded the location and hidden the receiver that could lead to it.

When she'd encountered White last night, he didn't seem to know if she had the receiver or not. Was he trying to prevent anyone from finding this trove? Or did he not know where it was himself? And then there was the flash drive. Obviously, with the secret keylogger file, White himself hadn't made the flash drive. But he was nervous; he could know of its existence and it would obviously be in his best interest to recover it.

Had someone stolen all of this treasure? Were the three who'd attacked them out on the ice the thieves or the people working for White? Was Steve, the nervous little man at Moe's, one of the thieves? He'd written the coordinates down in code and hidden them on her for safekeeping. And the other three had been gunning for him, eventually catching up with him and killing him.

But she hadn't seen those three directly in White's employ. The woman snowmobiler was the only one whose face she hadn't seen, so Alex didn't know if she was the same one from Moe's who had pursued Steve. And none of White's bodyguards had been a woman.

Maybe Steve was one of the thieves and had double-crossed the others, scuttling the boat without their knowledge and hiding the coordinates from them.

She swam back around to the side of the yacht with the yawning hole. Given the direction of the wood splintering, the hole had been blasted from the inside, from a section that was nowhere near the fuel tanks or engine. So it hadn't been some kind of devastating engine malfunction. A bomb? Whoever had done this had sunk the boat on purpose.

THIRTY-NINE

Sasha Talbot leaned over the edge of the *Uruk,* watching Alex descend into darkness. Water sloshed against the side of the boat. To the east, ice chunks floated at the edge of a vast white expanse.

She thought of Rex diving alone, being killed while out there by himself. She should have gone with him that day. Sure, she'd been laid up, feeling too sick after acquiring the bends, but after thirty-four years of partnership, she knew how stubborn he was. Sick or not, she should have gone with him and been surface support. Maybe the day would have gone differently. Maybe she could have helped him and now he'd still be alive. She grimaced. Or maybe she'd be dead, too.

She studied the murky depths. The thought of going down there sent a cold wave of fear trembling through her. But if Alex got into trouble, what good would she be up here? She watched Alex's bubbles ripple to the surface and pop.

This was ridiculous. She had to pull herself together. She was going down there. Resolved, she went inside the relative warmth of the cabin and pulled on her backup gear. She slid into a dry suit. From a cabinet, she grabbed an air tank and regulator, weight belt, light, and dive bag. She couldn't find her dive knife at first and dug around at the back of the cabinet. Her fingers closed around a small plastic disk, and she pulled it out.

With a clear plastic casing, it held a small circuitry board. She turned it over in her hand, puzzled. She had no idea what it was. But the plastic casing was clean and unscratched, looking brand-new. Whatever it was, it had been placed there recently, or it would have been scuffed up under all her equipment.

She was just finishing her safety check when the drone of a boat's engine cut through the silence. She stepped out of the cabin, scanning the waters where the rumbling came from. A huge white sailing yacht was bearing down on her location. It ran on its engine alone, the sail still stowed on the boom. She took in the polished railings, the gleaming wooden details. She recognized it. The *Great White*. She'd seen it tied up at its own private dock back in Churchill.

It pulled up alongside her boat. A red-faced man with white hair, wearing an expensive tailored gray suit, stood at the bow. It could only be Paul White.

"Miss Talbot?" he called.

She sensed a sneer behind the greeting. "Yes?" She lifted her hand above her eyes to shield them from the glare of the setting sun.

"Are you with Dr. Carter?"

She didn't like his demanding, entitled tone. "Who wants to know?"

"We're just concerned for her safety. Is she aboard?"

Behind him stood a blond, burly fellow wearing a black suit and sunglasses. He held a gun to two people who sat out on the deck, a portly man with a goatee and a woman with long brown hair, their hands bound in front of them.

Two other men nearly identical to the man with the gun were slipping into scuba gear near the railing.

"I see you're in a diving suit," the white-haired man said. "What are you diving for?"

Sasha's stomach turned over like a sour flapjack. "How did you even find us out here?"

"I've been tracking your boat. I'm looking for some stolen goods."

Sasha went silent.

"And a flash drive. Or maybe a portable hard drive? Seen anything like that?"

Sasha shook her head. "What do you want?"

"Just to know where Dr. Carter is. Is she already in the water? What is she diving for?"

"Seals," Sasha said. "She is a biologist, you know."

"And a marine archaeologist is helping with a biology project? Why do I find that hard to believe?"

His voice was cool, calm, almost deadpan. How did he know she was an archaeologist? His eyes were piggy, his expression cocky. His boat alone must have cost a million easily. He turned to the edifice of muscle in the black business suit and gave an almost imperceptible nod. Still pointing the gun at the two prisoners, the man flipped up a storage bench and bent to retrieve something.

"It's no matter whether you want to tell me or not," White droned on arrogantly. "I know those files must be on your boat. I'm afraid I'm going to have to take drastic measures."

The suit straightened, and Sasha blinked in disbelief. He was holding a massive gun. She'd seen them before only in movies. It held rocket-propelled grenades.

Sasha held up her hand in a placating gesture. "This is crazy! It's no good killing me. We uploaded that info to the cloud. You kill us, and the Mounties will know exactly who did it."

"I'm not going to kill you," White said, his voice suddenly sweet. "You're going to have a terrible accident. You really should have kept your boat in better condition. Fires can break out when engines aren't tuned properly."

Before she could even open her mouth again, the bodyguard fired off a quick succession of grenades. They came screaming toward the deck of her boat and Sasha turned and fled for the railing. She vaulted over the side into the icy waters beyond.

She hit the surface hard, and for a second her whole body was so jarred she couldn't move her limbs. Her head went under, the water so cold it sucked the air right out of her chest. She fought back to the surface and bobbed on the water, blinking, trying to process what had just happened. Her ears rang and her vision tunneled. Her head went under again and she struggled back to the air. Splintered wood filled the water around her. She hadn't had time to grab her scuba tank.

As she watched her boat burning, she spotted her partner's dive bag bobbing along, snagged on a piece of the hull. She swam over and grabbed it.

Sucking in a deep breath, she swam down, down, into the dark depths. She peered up to see flames spreading across the surface of the water, bright white and gold against the gray.

With powerful kicks, she swam underwater, heading for the patches of ice. If she didn't have the dry suit on, already her muscles would be locking up from the cold. As it was, she could still feel the cold press of the water against the suit and knew she couldn't stay in the water for very long. With her lungs bursting for a breath, she reached the floating chunks of ice and slowly emerged between several large pieces.

She clung to one, watching as flames consumed her boat. She'd had it for twenty years. Saved up with Rex to buy it. And now it was just a chunk of burning debris and fire. The flash drive was gone, her laptop. Her expensive sonar equipment, her underwater cameras, the rest of her dive gear. Everything they'd built together.

Above the crackling sound of fire and the lapping of the water, she heard White shout. "Carter's got to be diving under the boat. Find her!"

Sasha looked on in horror as the two divers jumped off the stern of the sailing yacht and descended, armed with harpoon guns, on the hunt for Alex.

FORTY

Alex was just about to enter the yacht to find more clues as to what had happened when a thunderous boom thrummed in the water around her. A concussive wave hit her hard, slamming her against the portside of the yacht. The boat groaned as the blast wave hit it, and it rolled up on the starboard side, creeping ever closer to the drop-off.

Alex stared up at the silhouette of Sasha's boat above her. Fire surrounded it, glowing gold against the gray of the surface. The shadowed underbelly of another boat had drawn up beside the *Uruk*. She saw no lifeboats in the water.

Alex was about to begin her ascent when splashes from the new boat marked the entry of two divers.

She knew then that White had found them. The two divers descended, bubbles from their regulators spilling out as they made a beeline for the sunken yacht. Alex had only minutes before they'd reach her, and she knew they wouldn't let her live.

The divers kicked downward and Alex withdrew to the far side of the yacht. Now unstable from the explosion, it shifted incrementally toward the edge of the shelf. Silt clouded around the base with each shift toward the drop-off. She had to make two safety stops on her way up, at least six minutes' worth. She checked her dive computer. She'd been down for fourteen minutes and had eighteen minutes of air left. Plenty of time if she could avoid the notice of the divers.

But it would be hard to escape their beams as they pierced the gloom. Bubbles spiraled out over her head with each breath she took. She decided to swim out over the ledge, moving parallel to the surface, gain enough distance that the murkiness of the water would hide her breathing.

She pushed off from the hull of the yacht and swam outward. She glanced back, checking their progress, and almost stopped breathing. They'd split up. One was gathering the treasure that had collected on the seafloor. But the other one was swimming straight for her, a harpoon gun aimed at her head.

Alex kicked out as powerfully as she could, trying to get some distance, but seconds later something impacted her back with such force that she was thrown forward in the water, gulping into her regulator. A sharp stinging had hit her neck just above the dry suit, and she watched a harpoon whiz away into the darkness. She clapped a hand to her neck, watching a bloom of red swirl in the water around her.

A fury of bubbles erupted from her tank, and when she tried to kick away again, water seeped into her air line. Coughing, she tasted the salty tang of the bay. She struggled with her air hose, but it completely filled with water and she spat it out, reaching desperately for her backup regulator. She grasped it in the dark water, bringing it to her mouth, then again choked and spat out salt water when she tried to breathe through it.

Holding her breath, she stripped off her tank, seeing her attacker swimming closer, and looked at it. The harpoon had struck the housing where both of her air lines fed into the tank, causing the oxygen to escape. She let the tank fall to the edge of the drop-off.

She turned to face the diver. He came at her, his one harpoon spent. As she struggled to hold her breath, fear exploded in her head, sheer panic. He collided with her, grabbing her around the throat, forcing her down to the seafloor. His hands closed so tightly around her neck that the blood pressure inside her skull shot up. Her vision started to tunnel.

He started reaching down to his side for something as she struggled to break his hold around her throat. But in the water her Jeet Kune Do felt like she was working in slow motion. All moves lost their force.

She glanced down, her vision going black and white, and spotted the dive knife he was reaching for on his belt. But with the effort of holding her down, he was slower, and Alex got there first. She pulled it free and drove it into his rib cage, twisting it with an upward thrust. Instantly he released her, a scream of bubbles erupting around him.

Alex's vision tunneled to a fine point of light. She was one second away from involuntarily gulping in water.

She grabbed for the man's backup regulator and clamped it to her mouth, taking several long, glorious breaths. He whipped around, trying to face her. The slack from the harpoon cord floated around in the water. She grabbed it and wrapped it around the man's neck, moving behind him. She pulled the cord tight, cinching it around his throat, but he managed to get the fingers of one hand between the rope and his skin. He struggled as she tightened it, still breathing from his regulator. She chanced a look behind, seeing the other diver. He was watching them but was still greedily cramming everything he could into dive bags.

The man reached around with his free hand, trying to pull the regulator out of her mouth. He bucked against her, attempting to throw her off, but she wrapped her legs around his midriff and clung on. With a swipe of her hand, she knocked the regulator from his mouth.

He bent forward, desperately flailing to find it, and she tightened the rope around his neck, pulling with everything in her. A violent tremor passed through him. He found the regulator and put it back in, but the rope was too tight now. His whole body spasmed, shuddering, and sagged to the seafloor.

Alex ripped off his tank. She was just throwing it on, the bubbles chaotic in the water around her, when the other diver swam toward her, harpoon gun ready to fire.

Alex pushed off the seafloor as the man aimed. She didn't have time to fasten the straps around her chest, so she held on to them and kicked with her flippers while she attached the straps mid-swim. At any moment another harpoon could hit her. Alex hurried toward the ruined yacht, driving the last buckle home. If she could get something solid between herself and the harpoon, she could buy some time.

She swam through one of the shattered windows of the yacht, her tank bumping on the hull as she passed through. Moments later the man followed her, leading with the harpoon gun.

Alex pulled herself through what had been a lavish sitting room with plush couches and a glass liquor cabinet, still locked up and full of bottles. She turned, seeing her pursuer pull himself into the room, his massive bulk barely squeezing through the window. Beyond lay a long hallway with sleeping quarters.

Just then a second explosion from above hit the yacht with concussive force. The whole boat shifted, groaning, rolling over on its side. Alex's world turned upside down as the yacht rolled toward the edge of the drop-off. She tumbled in the water, her tank colliding with the wall and then the ceiling. Several doors swung open, floating objects emerging: sheets, clothing, an empty can of beer.

Thrusting her legs against the corridor wall, she shoved off as the boat continued to roll. She grabbed one of the bedroom doors and threw it open. She swam through, well aware she'd just cornered herself. An unbroken window led to the outside. Debris floated in the water: bits of sodden wood, stuffing from pillows, silt churned up from the tumbling yacht.

She cast around desperately for something to break the window with. She found a fire extinguisher mounted on the wall. Seizing it, she tried to slam it against the window, but the impediment of the water slowed her so much that she felt like she was struggling in slow motion in a nightmare.

And then it was too late. The diver appeared in the doorway, bringing the harpoon gun to bear. Alex stood in front of the window. She threw the extinguisher at the man, who moved easily to one side as the force of the throw slacked off in the water. He fired the harpoon and Alex pushed off the floor, springing to the right. The harpoon hit the glass and shattered it.

Not wasting a moment, Alex grabbed the window frame and pulled herself through, her tank banging against it.

She felt an iron grip as the man's hand closed around her ankle and she kicked backward, hitting him in the face and knocking out his regulator. He paused to grapple for it, and then Alex was swimming away into the gloom.

The yacht kept rolling, tumbling with more momentum toward the drop-off.

The diver pulled himself out through the window but didn't clear the boat before the outer deck became a ceiling, striking his head. The deck railing hit the seafloor with considerable force, crumpling, and when the yacht rolled around again, she saw him pinned there beneath the railing, which had flattened around him like a cage. His grasping hands reached out toward Alex, and then the whole boat went over the edge, plunging down into the deep.

Alex stared after him until the murkiness swallowed the boat.

She checked her dive computer. She was at seventy-two feet. It would take her six minutes to surface, making stops along the way.

She stared up, seeing the bright pool of fire covering the water's surface, emanating from the *Uruk*. Debris floated all around the vessel, and its shadow leaned precariously. The other boat still looked intact.

She rose to forty feet. Darkness now filled the water around her. The sun had likely gone below the horizon and only the diffused light of dusk was left. But she didn't dare turn on her dive light and give away her position.

She rose another twenty feet, and the three minutes she had to stop there felt like an eternity.

FORTY-ONE

As Alex approached the surface, she swam parallel to it, wanting to get some distance between her and the burning *Uruk*. She headed toward the ice that floated nearby. As she drew close to it, she saw two legs hanging down. The person was in a dry suit but wore no flippers.

Alex surfaced a few feet away, finding Sasha clinging with one hand on a chunk of ice and the other on a large piece of splintered wood. The woman startled violently as Alex came up, and raised the piece of wood like a weapon.

Alex brought up an arm to fend off the blow, then flipped up her face mask and whispered, "It's me."

Sasha lowered the wood, bringing a hand to her chest. "Thank god."

"What happened?" Alex whispered.

In hushed tones, Sasha related the events. "He's holding two people at gunpoint, too. I don't know who they are."

Sudden shouts from the *Great White* drew their attention. The yacht bobbed on the water about a hundred feet away in the growing darkness, and Alex had no problem hearing them. "Where the fuck are they?" White yelled, pacing angrily on deck. He gripped the railing and peered down into the darkening water. "I want to know if it's down there!"

Alex craned to get a better look at the two prisoners and froze as she recognized them. One was her old friend Jake, the one Neil had shot, who had run her off the road. A tall brown-haired woman sat next to him. Without a balaclava masking her identity, Alex immediately recognized her as the woman who had pursued Steve out of Moe's. Their hands were bound in front of them.

"You sure this is the spot?" White roared at Jake.

"It's got to be," Jake answered. "That's why we put the tracker on her boat. We knew her partner was hiding something." His usual gruff tone was quieter. He stared down the barrel of the bodyguard's gun.

"It better be down there," White growled. "Where the fuck are the divers?"

From what Alex could see, only one bodyguard had remained on the yacht with White. The man was huge, his muscular frame silhouetted against the purple sky. Alex recognized him from the night before. He looked at his watch. "They have twelve minutes of air left, sir. They should be surfacing shortly."

"Did they get her?" White fumed, pacing once more.

"I'm sure they did, sir."

"Fuck!" White shouted, pounding the rail with his fist. Then he stormed inside the cabin. "We don't have forever to waste out here. We still have to find the other damn woman." He made a sweeping gesture at the water around them.

"She can't go far, sir. She wasn't even wearing flippers. She'll probably drown or die of exposure."

"I don't give a shit if she was wearing flippers or not, Garrett!" he shouted at the man. "I give a shit about the contents of my vault!"

"I know, sir." The bodyguard's cool, patient tone belied what Alex suspected was a history of dealing with the spoiled and entitled White.

When they both disappeared inside the cabin, Sasha turned to Alex. The woman's eyes creased with worry. "It won't take them long to catch up with us," Sasha whispered. "What happened with those divers?"

Alex swallowed, still shivering from the encounter in the depths. "They're both dead."

Sasha's mouth fell open.

The current swirled around Alex. "As soon as White realizes his divers are gone, he's going to come after us. We'll be dead within minutes." Clinging to a piece of ice, Alex stared around her. The *Uruk* continued to burn on the water. Their only choice was to somehow take over White's boat. But given the armed bodyguard, Garrett, still on board, she didn't like their chances.

The clock ticked away. The divers didn't surface.

White stormed out of the cabin, straight over to the prisoners. "I don't think this *is* the spot. I think you're stalling. I could be wasting my time here. For all I know they *were* out here looking at damn seals."

White towered over Jake, fists balled at his sides. With a grunt of fury, he lifted one leg and kicked him in the chest, sending him sprawling back onto the railing. He almost plunged into the sea, but grabbed at the woman and steadied himself.

"Wait, wait, wait!" Jake yelled. "We're here to help you."

"You must have a death wish!" White shouted. "You and your crew should have holed up in Mexico. You must be even stupider than I thought. I trusted your company to install that vault. I could have chosen a hundred other ones, but I chose yours. And you repay me by robbing me blind? Making a copy of my private files?"

"We weren't the ones who robbed your vault. It was Steve Gunderson," Jake said.

White snorted. "Steve? He couldn't think his way out of a tic-tac-toe game."

"It's true," the woman chimed in. "He was the one who transported everything to the boat and then scuttled it. We've been trying to figure out where he sank it ever since. We wanted to help you get everything back."

"And where is Steve?" White roared.

Jake spoke up. "We took care of him for you." He looked pleadingly at White. "Let us go down there. We could salvage-dive it for you."

White sneered. "It's so nice of you to have my best interests at heart."

"We do," the woman insisted. Fear tinged her voice.

White blanched, bright red spots flecking his face. "Do you think I'm a fucking idiot?" he roared. He grabbed Garrett by the shoulder. "Shoot them!"

Jake stood up suddenly, kicking the guard's gun hand. Garrett's pistol went flying and the woman leapt up, grabbing it as it skittered across the deck. Garrett immediately retrieved a gun from his ankle holster. Jake flipped up the storage bench and pulled out a pistol from the weapon stash there. He and the woman raced for cover on the far side of the cabin, exchanging gunfire with Garrett. White ran inside the cabin.

Beside Alex, Sasha hung on to her piece of ice, her teeth chattering. They didn't have much time. Alex had to somehow get control of White's boat. It was the only way they were going to live.

FORTY-TWO

Alex still had a few minutes of air left. She used it to dive down beneath the surface and close the distance to the *Great White*. She emerged quietly just off the side.

The bodyguard had braced himself against the far end of the cabin, on the opposite side of the two escaped prisoners, waiting for them to pop out.

"Kill them, Garrett!" White shouted from the safety of the cabin.

Alex ducked below the surface, out of sight. Then she dared a peek from the side of the boat. As Garrett circled the cabin, the two thieves rounded it, too, obstructing Garrett's line of sight.

White peered out nervously from one of the cabin's windows. For all his bravado, she could tell he was scared to be in an actual physical confrontation. He was used to being surrounded by bodyguards, and now he was down to only one.

The thieves ducked down behind the exterior of the cabin, and then suddenly the woman sprang out, feet planted in front of her, the gun braced in her bound hands. She leveled it at the window, right at White's head. Garrett leapt out, and the crack of his handgun split the air. A single hole appeared in her skull. She slipped, going backward off the railing.

Alex closed the remaining few feet to the side of the boat, ducking underwater as the woman's body hit the surface. The thief's hands opened and Alex dove down, grabbing the pistol before it could sink into the darkness. The woman's body floated facedown on the water, sightless eyes staring, red blooming out from the wound in her head.

Cautiously Alex swam flush with the sailing yacht. The way its deck flared out meant that they'd have to lean way over to spot her in the water, and with Jake as a distraction, she thought she might just be able to reach the rear of the boat and climb aboard.

She slid onto the boat and hid behind the transom.

Jake dove out from behind the cabin and fired, hitting Garrett in the leg. The bodyguard cursed, slapping his hand over the wound. He brought up his gun and fired point-blank into Jake's chest three times. The thief stared down in disbelief, blinking, and crumpled to the deck.

"We gotta go back," Garrett said to White. Red seeped through his fingers as the bodyguard tried to stanch the bleeding.

"Now listen here, you piece of shit!" White shouted, emerging from the cabin. "You pull yourself together and find Carter and that damned treasure hunter and finish them off. Then we can go."

The bodyguard looked out into the gloaming. Alex knew where Sasha floated, but in the dim light, finding her would be a challenge.

"They can't still be alive. They must have frozen by now," Garrett said. "Please, Mr. White. I'm hit bad."

"I don't care if he hit you right in the goddamn brainpan. You're going to do the job I hired you for."

Alex didn't know how many bullets were left in the woman's gun and didn't want to make noise by checking. She just prayed there were two. From her perch behind the transom, she studied the deck of the sailboat. The only cover beyond the transom was the raised cabin.

Keeping out of their line of sight, she slunk around the stern of the ship. She detached the jibe preventer, the mechanism that kept the boom from dangerously sweeping across the deck. Then she untied the mainsheet, the rope that held the boom in place, leaving it just loosely draped in the cleat.

A slight wind blew, moving the boom a little, but not too no-
ticeably. She hoped it would stay that way. Then she crept to the
opposite side of the boom, ducking under it as she went. Now across
from where White and Garrett stood, she straightened. They instantly spotted her.

"The front of the boat!" White yelled.

Garrett hurried toward her, blood soaking his pants leg. She
took off, ducking again under the boom. He trained his gun on her,
but she rounded the other side before he could get off a shot, grabbing the mainsheet as she went. He pursued, bending under the
boom, his gun fully extended. As soon as he was on the other side,
she wrenched the rope as hard as she could.

The mainsheet pulled tight, yanking on the boom and sending
it careening toward Garrett. It struck his head with a sickening crack
and he went over the railing, landing with a splash in the freezing
water below.

She ran to the edge of the boat, her own gun pointing down into
the waves. Garrett splashed there. "Help!" he cried.

"Drop your gun!" she commanded.

He tried to swim around to the stern in order to climb onto the
boat, and she fired a warning shot into the water next to him. He
stared up, eyes wide. "I said drop it!" she shouted again.

This time he did, his teeth chattering. His head slipped under
and emerged seconds later. He spat out water. "Okay, okay. Just
let me get aboard." He held up his hands to show they were empty.
"My muscles are freezing up!"

Farther down the railing, White rushed to the edge. "You damn
fool!" he cursed at Garrett.

"Freeze!" she yelled at White. He spun, but he was a second
too slow. He saw that she had the drop on him.

"Wait! Wait!" White pleaded. "I'm unarmed! Don't shoot!"

Beyond him Garrett climbed up onto the boat and slumped on
the deck.

Alex breathed deeply, stilling her rage. "Get over there!" she shouted, pointing to one of the benches along the rail. "Don't make any sudden moves! Sit down!" She pointed the gun at Garrett. "You too!"

They did as she asked, Garrett limping.

"Do something!" White barked at him, but Garrett just wobbled, about to pass out.

Keeping the gun trained on them, Alex moved to the boat's controls and lifted the anchor. She motored the short distance over to where Sasha floated in the water.

"You still with me?" Alex called down to her.

"Barely," came the weak reply.

Still staring at White, Alex waited while Sasha climbed aboard. Alex handed her the gun. "Don't let them move."

Inside the cabin, Alex found fresh dry clothes. She gave a set to Garrett, along with a blanket.

She checked them both for weapons and came up empty. Then using the rope from the life preserver, Alex bound the men's hands and feet to the railing.

"You're cutting off my circulation," White whined.

Alex tightened the rough nylon rope even more.

Then she and Sasha changed out of their dry suits. Alex found the thermostat and turned up the heat in the cabin.

After securing the boom again, Alex turned the *Great White* toward Churchill.

As they began to warm up, Sasha took over the helm.

"I don't know what the salvage laws are here," Alex told her, "but there are a lot of valuables down there for the taking."

Sasha raised her eyebrows. "Like what?"

"Some of it's even archaeological treasures. A golden Incan figurine, for one. Some jade carvings that look old. I'm sure museums would be grateful to have them. Plus a lot of things you could cash in on yourself: gems—"

White, listening in, curled his lip in fury. His face flushed beet red. "That is *my* property! Do you really think I'd let some fucking bitch take it?"

Alex just ignored him, which made White's jowls quiver in anger.

She continued talking to Sasha as if he weren't there. "It's not like he's going to need money where he's going."

But even as she said it, doubt gnawed at her gut. White himself hadn't pulled the trigger. He was loaded with money and could hire the slipperiest lawyers. He could potentially make the case that he hadn't given any orders at all for the killings. It would be their word against his that he tried to murder them out on the water.

Considering the long list of crimes she'd found on that flash drive, he'd obviously been getting away with illegal activities for years. She thought of the files she'd backed up to the cloud. They were damning for certain, but they also related a history of bribery and corruption, not capital crimes like murder. He could plea-bargain down. Maybe not serve any time at all.

As they continued to ignore him, he shouted at Alex. "You are going to pay for this! I will ruin you! Your career is over! Your *life* is over! I'll destroy everything you know, everything you love. Don't think I haven't had my men gather information on you, Carter. I know where your father lives. I even know what markets he goes to, and where his cute little barbershop quartet practices. He'd be easy to get to. If you turn that evidence over to the police, you'll find out just *how* easy he is to get to. I promise you that!" Spittle formed white foam around his lips as he threatened her.

Alex went quiet, her determination faltering. This scum meant it. She knew he did.

"And you, Little Miss Treasure Diver," White spat at Sasha. "You think I can't get your salvage license revoked? You think I can't bankrupt you and make sure you never get another boat as long as you live? You think I can't cast doubt on the authentication of every marine excavation you've ever done? You're finished! Both of you!

No fucking bitches are going to take me down. This is a joke! A fucking joke!" He turned his fiery gaze back to Alex. "You're nothing to me. I won't even remember you a week from now, and you'll be crying over your father's grave, honey. I promise you that!"

Alex glanced over at the gun where she'd laid it. Rage welled up within her, shaking her very core. She could just take the gun. Blow him away. Or better yet, just kick him off the boat into the icy water.

"Let's gag him," Sasha said. "What's the most disgusting rag we can find on this tub?" She disappeared into the cabin, and for a full minute Alex was alone with White. Her fists balled at her sides.

Then suddenly Sasha was next to her again. "Check out this one," Sasha said, holding up a greasy rag that looked like someone had blown their nose on it. "This is perfect."

White turned to Garrett. "You worthless piece of shit! Why don't you do something? What the hell did I hire you for, you idiot?"

Garrett fixed him with an icy stare. "Okay. I'll do something. I quit."

Sasha tied the gag around White's neck. "Don't you dare put that filthy—" But the rest of his sentence was garbled as she cinched the gag tight across his mouth. Garrett just watched quietly.

Sasha burst into laughter, and Alex thought White's eyes were going to bulge right out of their sockets. His face went so red that he looked like he might pop a blood vessel. And she realized that laughter was the best way to get to White. To completely dismiss him.

Sasha returned to the helm and Alex eyed the radio. "We should contact the Mounties. Let them know we're bringing White in."

"Let's hope this time they'll listen."

"This time I'm not going to give them a choice."

Alex picked up the handset and sent a message to shore, asking for a police cruiser to meet them as they docked. She explained that White and his men had murdered two people out on the water and attempted to kill Sasha and Alex.

The dispatcher listened attentively and said a cruiser would be waiting for them.

Night had set in now, and they motored back toward the diffuse glow of the town. A cold wind picked up, but overhead the sky was clear. The arc of the Milky Way gleamed from horizon to horizon. Soon the moon would be up, but for now, it was a twinkling wonderland of thousands of lights.

Then in the north, a green curtain descended, streaming down in the darkness. It flashed and danced, ribboning down to red in the lower elevations.

"Will you look at that?" Alex breathed.

They stared up, watching the magical play of the aurora weaving bands of light across the black sky.

"Beautiful," whispered Sasha.

As they motored up to Churchill in the dark, the flashing lights of a police cruiser painted the docked boats in reds and blues. Alex pulled up to one of the slips and bumped the sailboat gently against the wood. Out in the parking lot, dark shapes passed in front of the cruiser's headlights, and she knew the Mounties were walking out to take custody of White and his bodyguard.

She thought of jerking White up, marching him down the dock, but decided she didn't want to touch him. Let the RCMP handle it.

She hopped off the boat and grabbed the stern line, tying it off on a dockside cleat. She was moving toward the bowline when a shadow on a neighboring boat came to life.

A figure stepped off that boat and sprinted over to her.

"Casey!" she said, startled. Immediately she saw the flash of a gun in his hand. "What are you doing?"

"What has to be done." He pushed past her and boarded the *Great White*.

Alex followed him. "Casey, no, wait! He'll be brought into custody." Already she could see the closer forms of the officers, silhouetted against the flashing lights, drawing near to the water's edge. Soon they'd step onto the dock. "They've got it handled. We have evidence. He's going to jail."

Casey looked back over his shoulder at her. "He won't go to jail, Alex. He's corrupt. He's paid off people in the past. He'll do it again. I've spent the last two days going through his finances, his correspondence. He'll never stop until he's gotten to you. To others. I have to do this."

"No, you don't!" she pleaded, following him back to where White was bound.

Casey strode purposefully toward him. White struggled against his bonds, trying to stand. He managed to wriggle out of the gag, and spat onto the deck.

"You think I'm scared of you, you pissant? You're dead. Just as much as those two bitches are."

The RCMP were almost at the dock.

Alex rushed toward Casey as he leveled the gun at White's head.

Garrett turned away in fear and squeezed his eyes shut.

White snorted, a smug, sneering expression crawling over his face. "You expect me to believe you'll really pull that trigger when the cops are—"

Casey fired the gun just as Alex reached him.

The bullet pierced White's skull, a surprised expression stealing over the CEO's face. Then Casey shot him once more in the heart.

"Hey!" she heard the police yell. Now they were running onto the dock. "You there! Stop!"

Casey vaulted over the boat's railing, landing on the dock. He raced off in the opposite direction. He took a running leap onto a parallel dock, then another leap to the next one. In the dark, she couldn't see him anymore.

The Mounties approached the *Great White,* guns drawn.

But when they reached the sailboat, only Alex and Sasha stood there, with White's limp form slumped on the bench, only the rope keeping him upright.

Casey had vanished into the darkness.

EPILOGUE

The next few weeks were so busy Alex barely got a break. Sonia Bergstrom arranged for a new helicopter pilot and grad assistant, and Alex returned to the field. She didn't discover any more set guns. Now that the Mounties had recovered the body of Old Sam the poacher, along with all the evidence in his field tent, including the polar bear pelts, Manitoba Conservation closed his poaching case.

Dave, the bartender from Moe's, provided valuable information to the RCMP. He was close friends with Steve Gunderson. Steve's boss Jake had been hired to install a vault in the mansion White had built on Amundsen Road, and employed Steve and two other workers to help. White liked to spread his wealth around the globe, not keeping all his valuables in the same place. Jake decided to pull off a heist. Dave had tried to talk his friend out of participating, but Steve wouldn't hear it. They robbed the vault while White was away, loading the valuables onto White's yacht, the *White Knight,* to transport it down to the States.

Because Jake knew of White's less-than-legal dealings, he'd installed a keystroke recorder on White's computer, in the hopes of recording the CEO's passwords and finding dirt on him. Then Jake had copied the contents of the CEO's laptop and phone onto a flash drive. If White came after them, they had leverage. He'd have to let them go with the valuables or be exposed for the criminal he was.

But Steve had double-crossed them.

From what he had told Dave, Steve had planted a fake bomb on the yacht, a device designed to give a loud bang and put out a lot of smoke. They'd all fled to the lifeboat, but Steve had remained on board a few minutes longer, saying he was going to activate the locator beacon so they could find the sunken yacht later.

But as the others waited in the frigid water, Steve hadn't activated the beacon. He'd fired up the yacht's engines and raced away from the lifeboat, leaving his comrades behind. Then when he was miles away, he'd jumped into the second lifeboat and remotely detonated a real bomb, sinking the yacht. He'd written down the coordinates, then hid the receiver and flash drive, and planned to return to the sunken yacht much later to retrieve the valuables.

But in the meantime, he had to flee, get some distance between himself and his cohorts. On the run, he blew through his entire supply of cash finding places to stay. When he heard later that Jake and the others had left Manitoba to seek him out, he returned to Churchill, broke but anxious to get out to the site. But he had no more cash to pay a boatman to take him out there. So he'd tried begging, to no avail, saying he'd pay later, but no one would go for it. And then the trio had returned to Churchill. They'd caught up to him and killed him.

But they didn't know where Steve had scuttled the yacht. They figured he'd either kept the location to himself or passed the information on to someone else.

The RCMP pieced together the rest. They figured the thieves overheard Rex talking about the wrecks he'd found and tortured him for that information before killing him. But none of those wrecks had turned out to be the yacht. Remembering that Steve had made contact with Alex, they became convinced he'd passed on the location to her, probably without her knowledge.

But their attempts to retrieve the location from her had failed, and now the other thieves were just as dead as Steve.

The RCMP searched for Casey, but he had vanished from Churchill. And though border crossings and airports were on the lookout for him, searches turned up nothing.

White's bodyguard Garrett filled in some other missing pieces. Wanting to gloat over stopping Alex's study, White had arranged to buy a polar bear pelt off Old Sam to install as a rug in his home in L.A. Garrett was supposed to meet the poacher to purchase it, but White kept lowering the price he was willing to pay.

In exchange for reduced sentences, some of White's other employees admitted to thwarting scientific studies, cutting corners in coal ash cleanup, fracking, and oil drilling sites. White's corporation was fined an exorbitant sum for environmental cleanup. The *New York Times* and the *Washington Post* received anonymous information about the illegal dealings of White's company and ran exposés. Disgraced, it was forced to shut down.

Sasha left town, vowing to come back when she got a new boat and finish the dive that Rex had been so excited about. "Maybe Vikings did make it this far west," she'd told Alex as they parted. "The artifacts he found certainly *look* Viking. But they need cleaning and more analysis. I'll find out. For Rex."

Now Alex stood out on the ice, blinking in the bright sunlight, fastening a Burr on Fur to a female polar bear. Her two cubs climbed on their mother's back, tumbling with each other playfully. One landed with a plume of snow next to Alex and stood up on its hind legs, making another lunge at its sibling. Soon the ice would break up, and the seal hunting season would be over. Then she'd submit her findings to the Minister of Environment and Climate Change.

As she stood out on the ice, taking in the vast, white terrain around her, thinking of everything she'd risked to stay out here, she felt hopeful that finally substantive steps would be taken to save this majestic animal while it still roamed this magnificent icy landscape.

AFTERWORD

The Canadian Arctic is a beautiful, enchanting place. I've happily spent months there, watching the tundra shift from the greens of summer to the reds and golds of fall to the white dusting of winter. I've thrilled to the sight of snow geese paddling about small lakes, and black-phase red foxes bounding on the colorful terrain. I've dipped my hands into the frigid gray waters of the Arctic Ocean and watched long-tailed jaegers wheeling on the gusting winds above the waves.

The Arctic is a magical, unique place with a variety of amazing ecosystems. And we need to protect it. Musk ox, caribou, walrus, beluga, and narwhal all need our help. Narwhal and beluga are susceptible to a number of human-caused threats, including seismic-exploration noise generated by the oil and gas industries and military sonar. Because cetaceans use sound to communicate and navigate, noise on this level reduces their ability to survive.

If steps aren't taken to protect these whales, they could go the way of other cetaceans like the vaquita porpoise, only ten individuals of which are left on the planet, at the mercy of poachers who use gill nets.

And yes, the polar bears need our help, too.

The latest research estimates that all nineteen subpopulations of polar bears will be gone by 2080.

A number of factors contribute to their decline.

Environmental pollutants are a real problem, including persistent organic pollutants containing chlorine, fluorine, and bromine, the latter of which works its way into the environment due to the human use of brominated flame retardants.

Then there are industrial compounds like polychlorinated biphenyls, or PCBs. Though the U.S. banned production of PCBs in 1979, they still contaminate much of the globe, working their way into the soil, air, and water. They compromise a body's ability to produce antibodies, making humans and wildlife more susceptible to infection.

In addition, heavy metals such as lead, mercury, selenium, and cadmium are released into the environment through a variety of human activities, from fossil fuel burning to the production of cement to the process of metal smelting. Burning oil, wood, and coal releases mercury into the environment. Emissions from coal-fired power plants are the biggest culprit. Mercury particles become airborne and settle into the water, working their way through the food chain.

The potency of toxins increases as one moves up the food chain. Called biomagnification, it happens like this: Toxins such as mercury seep into the food chain and are consumed by small organisms such as plankton. Then crustaceans eat the plankton, and a fish eats the crustacean. When a seal eats that fish, the mercury concentration is higher. And when a bear eats the seal, the concentration is even more magnified and dangerous. These toxins not only build up in their bodies as bears grow older, but they are passed on to cubs from their mother's milk.

But the biggest threat to polar bears is human-caused climate change. Warming temperatures mean not only less sea ice, as well as a lower quality of sea ice that is thin and rotten, but a far shorter season of ice. Polar bears rely on sea ice for hunting platforms from which to catch seals, their main food source for bulking up. Being able to fatten up means a far better chance to survive the long summer months of fasting. But with polar bears able to catch fewer and fewer seals, they starve for longer. Mothers cannot feed their cubs and cub mortality increases. As polar bears give birth an average of only every three years, this mortality doesn't take long to seriously deplete a subpopulation of bears.

When the polar bear was finally listed as threatened in the U.S. under the Endangered Species Act in 2008, the oil and gas industries were exempted from being held accountable. So the listing does nothing to protect polar bears from their biggest existential threat—the alarming reduction of yearly sea ice due to global warming.

The vanishing of the polar bear is a dire prediction, and something we can avert if we make our voices heard. Write and call your representatives. Support the restoration and strengthening of the Endangered Species Act, which has been weakened in recent years. Encourage your representatives to pass the PAW and FIN Conservation Act and to enact green-minded legislation that will bolster renewable energy.

Anthropogenic climate change is a dire threat to species that are struggling to survive under its pall, including not just the polar bear, but the wolverine, the American pika, and so many other species that will vanish if we do nothing. But if we speak out, if we make it known that we want things to change, to improve, that we want clean air, clean water, and clean power, we can save these iconic species that we share the earth with, and in turn save ourselves.

TO LEARN MORE ABOUT POLAR BEARS

Books About Polar Bears

Derocher, Andrew E. *Polar Bears: A Complete Guide to Their Biology and Behavior*. Baltimore, MD: Johns Hopkins University Press, 2012.

Stirling, Ian. *Polar Bears: The Natural History of a Threatened Species*, rev. ed. Brighton, MA: Fitzhenry & Whiteside, 2011.

Viola, Jason. *Polar Bears: Survival on the Ice* (Science Comics Series). Illustrated by Zack Giallongo. New York: First Second, 2019.

Articles on Polar Bears

Fountain, Henry. "Global Warming Is Driving Polar Bears Toward Extinction, Researchers Say." *New York Times*, July 20, 2020.

Molnár, P. K., C. M. Bitz, M. M. Holland, et al. "Fasting Season Length Sets Temporal Limits for Global Polar Bear Persistence." *Nature Climate Change* 10 (2020): 732–38. https://doi.org/10.1038/s41558-020-0818-9.

Polar Bear Cams

Polar Bears International offers Tundra Connections, a program with interesting talks: https://polarbearsinternational.org/tundra -connections.

The YouTube channel for Polar Bears International has a wealth of fascinating bear footage: https://www.youtube.com /c/PolarbearsinternationalOrg/videos.

To Learn More About the Movement of the Hudson Bay Bear Population

Polar Bears International offers a polar bear tracker, where you can watch how individual bears have moved across the frozen expanse of Hudson Bay over time: https://polarbearsinternational.org/polar-bears/tracking.

Organizations That Aid and Contribute to Polar Bear Research and Conservation

Polar Bears International: https://polarbearsinternational.org.

World Wildlife Fund: https://www.worldwildlife.org/species/polar-bear.

Volunteer Opportunities

1. The Whiskerprint Project is looking for volunteers to submit facial profile photographs of polar bears (taken with big telephoto lenses, of course). Each bear has its own unique whisker pattern, and this pattern can be used to identify individuals and track their movements and behavior in a noninvasive way: https://churchillwild.com/polar-bear-id-whiskerprint-analysis.

2. Earthwatch offers a trip where you can contribute to our knowledge of climate change in the Arctic. It's located in Churchill, Manitoba, where you can take part in vital research on global warming by accessing snowpack and taking water and snow samples. Program name: Climate Change at the Arctic's Edge. https://earthwatch.org/expeditions/climate-change-at-the-arctics-edge.

3. Polar Bears International has a fantastic resource page for how you can get involved with helping polar bears: https://polarbearsinternational.org/get-involved.

4. Write letters to your representatives urging them to strengthen the Endangered Species Act, which has been weakened in recent years. In addition, encourage them to pass the PAW and FIN Conservation Act, which would greatly benefit wildlife. Many nonprofit organizations, including those listed below, make sending such letters quick and easy:

   Center for Biological Diversity: https://www.biologicaldiversity.org.

   Natural Resources Defense Council: https://www.nrdc.org.

Wonderful References for Excellent, Hopeful Solutions to Combat Climate Change

Hawken, Paul, ed. *Drawdown: The Most Comprehensive Plan Ever Proposed to Reverse Global Warming.* New York: Penguin Books, 2017.

Stoknes, Per Espen. *What We Think About When We Try Not to Think About Global Warming: Toward a New Psychology of Climate Action.* White River Junction, VA: Chelsea Green Publishing, 2015.

ACKNOWLEDGMENTS

Many thanks to my amazing agent, Alexander Slater, who has been a steadfast champion of this series. I am grateful to my fantastic editor, Lyssa Keusch, for her invaluable feedback and being such a delight to work with. Our shared love of wildlife has only made this book stronger. Once again, Elsie Lyons has created an absolutely stunning cover, and I am very thankful to her and her depictions of Alex Carter out in the wilds. Many thanks to Nancy Singer for her wonderful interior design and to production editor Jeanie Lee for all her hard work.

Fellow writers Angela Sanders, Steve Hockensmith, Terry Shames, and James Ziskin have provided wonderful camaraderie. A huge thank-you to them as well as Nevada Barr, James Rollins, Craig Johnson, Douglas Preston, Owl Goingback, Lisa Morton, and Michael Laurence for their glowing reviews.

Polar bear researchers Thea Bechshoft and Andrew Derocher proved absolutely invaluable in the writing of this book, and I'm so grateful for their answering my questions down to the minutiae of the polar bear tagging process.

I hope those familiar with Churchill can forgive the few small changes I made to the area for the sake of plot.

As always, I am very grateful to my readers, so thank you to Tina, Dawn, Jon, Sarah, Mary, and so many others.

My lifelong friend Becky continues to be a source of support and encouragement, and I am very grateful for her.

And finally, many, many thanks to the incomparable Jason, champion of my writing, always ready with an encouraging talk, my fellow wildlife researcher and activist, my best friend. You are amazing.

ABOUT THE AUTHOR

In addition to being a writer, Alice Henderson is a wildlife sanctuary monitor, geographic information systems specialist, and bioacoustician. She documents wildlife on specialized recording equipment, checks remote cameras, creates maps, and undertakes surveys to determine what species are present on preserves, while ensuring there are no signs of poaching. She's surveyed for the presence of grizzlies, wolves, wolverines, jaguars, endangered bats, and more. These experiences in remote corners of wilderness inspired her to create the Alex Carter mystery series. Please visit her at AliceHenderson.com, where you can also sign up for her author newsletter.